Charles Dickens, Wilkie Collins

The Lazy Tour of Two Idle Apprentices: No throughfare

The perils of certain English prisoners

Charles Dickens, Wilkie Collins

The Lazy Tour of Two Idle Apprentices: No throughfare
The perils of certain English prisoners

ISBN/EAN: 9783744743402

Printed in Europe, USA, Canada, Australia, Japan

Cover: Foto ©Andreas Hilbeck / pixelio.de

More available books at **www.hansebooks.com**

THE LAZY TOUR OF TWO IDLE APPRENTICES.

NO THOROUGHFARE.

THE PERILS OF CERTAIN ENGLISH PRISONERS.

NOTE.

These Stories, which originally appeared in "Household Words," are now reprinted in a complete form.

THE LAZY TOUR
OF TWO IDLE APPRENTICES.

NO THOROUGHFARE.

THE PERILS OF CERTAIN ENGLISH PRISONERS.

BY

CHARLES DICKENS AND WILKIE COLLINS.

WITH ILLUSTRATIONS.

LONDON: CHAPMAN AND HALL,
LIMITED.
1895.

F. M. EVANS AND CO., LIMITED, PRINTERS,
CRYSTAL PALACE, S.E.

F. M. EVANS AND CO., LIMITED, PRINTERS,
CRYSTAL PALACE, S.E.

CONTENTS.

THE LAZY TOUR OF TWO IDLE APPRENTICES.

NO THOROUGHFARE.

NO THOROUGHFARE—*continued*.

THE PERILS OF CERTAIN ENGLISH PRISONERS.

LIST OF ILLUSTRATIONS.

THE LAZY TOUR OF TWO IDLE APPRENTICES.

THE LAZY TOUR OF TWO IDLE APPRENTICES.

THE LAZY TOUR OF
TWO IDLE APPRENTICES.

CHAPTER I.

In the autumn month of September, eighteen hundred and fifty-seven, wherein these presents bear date, two idle apprentices, exhausted by the long, hot summer, and the long, hot work it had brought with it, ran away from their employer. They were bound to a highly meritorious lady (named Literature), of fair credit and repute, though, it must be acknowledged, not quite so highly esteemed in the City as she might be. This is the more remarkable, as there is nothing against the respectable lady in that quarter, but quite the contrary ; her family having rendered eminent service to many famous citizens of London. It may be sufficient to name Sir William Walworth, Lord Mayor under King Richard II., at the time of Wat Tyler's insurrection, and Sir Richard Whittington : which latter distinguished man and magistrate was doubtless indebted to the lady's family for the gift of his celebrated cat. There is also strong reason to suppose that they rang the Highgate bells for him with their own hands.

The misguided young men who thus shirked their duty to the mistress from whom they had received many favours, were actuated by the low idea of making a perfectly idle trip, in any direction. They had no intention of going anywhere in particular; they wanted to see nothing, they wanted to know nothing, they wanted to learn nothing, they wanted to do nothing. They wanted only to be idle. They took to themselves (after HOGARTH), the names of Mr. Thomas Idle and Mr. Francis Goodchild ; but there was not a moral pin to choose between them, and they were both idle in the last degree.

Between Francis and Thomas, however, there was this difference of character : Goodchild was laboriously idle, and would take upon himself any amount of pains and labour to assure himself that he was idle ; in short, had no better idea of idleness than that it was useless industry.   Thomas Idle, on the other hand, was an idler of the unmixed Irish or Neapolitan type ; a passive idler, a born-and-bred idler, a consistent idler, who practised what he would have preached if he had not been too idle to preach ; a one entire and perfect chrysolite of idleness.

The two idle apprentices found themselves, within a few hours of their escape, walking down into the North of England, that is to say, Thomas was lying in a meadow, looking at the railway trains as they passed over a distant viaduct—which was *his* idea of walking down into the North ; while Francis was walking a mile due South against time—which was *his* idea of walking down into the North. In the meantime the day waned, and the milestones remained unconquered.

"Tom," said Goodchild, "the sun is getting low. Up, and let us go forward !"

"Nay," quoth Thomas Idle, "I have not done with Annie Laurie yet." And he proceeded with that idle but popular ballad, to the effect that for the bonnie young person of that name he would "lay him doon and dee"—equivalent, in prose, to lay him down and die.

"What an ass that fellow was !" cried Goodchild, with the bitter emphasis of contempt.

"Which fellow ?" asked Thomas Idle.

"The fellow in your song. Lay him doon and dee ! Finely he'd show off before the girl by doing *that*. A sniveller ! Why couldn't he get up, and punch somebody's head !"

"Whose ?" asked Thomas Idle.

"Anybody's. Everybody's would be better than nobody's ! If I fell into that state of mind about a girl, do you think I'd lay me doon and dee ? No, sir," proceeded Goodchild, with a disparaging assumption of the Scottish accent, "I'd get me oop and peetch into somebody. Wouldn't you ?"

"I wouldn't have anything to do with her," yawned Thomas Idle. "Why should I take the trouble?"

"It's no trouble, Tom, to fall in love," said Goodchild, shaking his head.

"It's trouble enough to fall out of it, once you're in it," retorted Tom. "So I keep out of it altogether. It would be better for you, if you did the same."

Mr. Goodchild, who is always in love with somebody, and not unfrequently with several objects at once, made no reply. He heaved a sigh of the kind which is termed by the lower orders "a bellowser," and then, heaving Mr. Idle on his feet (who was not half so heavy as the sigh), urged him northward.

These two had sent their personal baggage on by train: only retaining each a knapsack. Idle now applied himself to constantly regretting the train, to tracking it through the intricacies of Bradshaw's Guide, and finding out where it is now—and where now—and where now—and to asking what was the use of walking, when you could ride at such a pace as that. Was it to see the country? If that was the object, look at it out of the carriage-windows. There was a great deal more of it to be seen there than here. Besides, who wanted to see the country? Nobody. And again, whoever did walk? Nobody. Fellows set off to walk, but they never did it. They came back and said they did, but they didn't. Then why should he walk? He wouldn't walk. He swore it by this milestone!

It was the fifth from London, so far had they penetrated into the North. Submitting to the powerful chain of argument, Goodchild proposed a return to the Metropolis, and a falling back upon Euston Square Terminus. Thomas assented with alacrity, and so they walked down into the North by the next morning's express, and carried their knapsacks in the luggage-van.

It was like all other expresses, as every express is and must be. It bore through the harvest country a smell like a large washing-day, and a sharp issue of steam as from a huge brazen tea-urn. The greatest power in nature and art combined, it yet glided over dangerous heights in the sight of people looking up from fields and roads, as smoothly and unreally as a light miniature plaything. Now, the engine shrieked in hysterics of such intensity, that it seemed desirable that the men who had her in charge should hold her feet, slap her hands, and bring her to ; now, burrowed into tunnels with a stubborn and undemonstrative energy so confusing that the train seemed to be flying back into leagues of darkness. Here, were station after station, swallowed up by the express without stopping ; here, stations where it fired itself in like a volley of cannon-balls, swooped away four country-people with nosegays, and three men of business with portmanteaus, and fired itself off again, bang, bang, bang ! At long intervals were uncomfortable refreshment-rooms, made more uncomfortable by the scorn of Beauty towards Beast, the public (but to whom she never re-lented, as Beauty did in the story, towards the other Beast), and where sensitive stomachs were fed, with a contemptuous sharp-ness occasioning indigestion. Here, again, were stations with nothing going but a bell, and wonderful wooden razors set aloft on great posts, shaving the air. In these fields, the horses, sheep, and cattle were well used to the thundering meteor, and didn't mind ; in those, they were all set scampering together, and a herd of pigs scoured after them. The pastoral country darkened, became coaly, became smoky, became infernal, got better, got worse, improved again, grew rugged, turned romantic ; was a wood, a stream, a chain of hills, a gorge, a moor, a cathedral town, a fortified place, a waste. Now, miserable black dwell-ings, a black canal, and sick black towers of chimneys ; now, a trim garden, where the flowers were bright and fair ; now, a wilderness of hideous altars all a-blaze ; now, the water meadows with their fairy rings ; now, the mangy patch of unlet building ground outside the stagnant town, with the larger ring where the Circus was last week. The temperature changed, the dialect changed, the people changed, faces got sharper, manner got shorter, eyes got shrewder and harder ; yet all so quickly, that the spruce guard in the London uniform and silver lace, had not yet rumpled his shirt-collar, delivered half the dispatches in his shiny little pouch, or read his newspaper.

Carlisle ! Idle and Goodchild had got to Carlisle. It looked congenially and delightfully idle. Something in the way of public amusement had happened last month, and some-thing else was going to happen before Chrismas ; and, in the meantime there was a lecture on India for those who liked it—which Idle and Goodchild did not. Likewise, by those who liked them, there were impressions to be bought of all the vapid prints, going and gone, and of nearly all the vapid books.　For those who wanted to put anything in missionary boxes, here were the boxes.　For those who wanted the Reverend Mr. Podgers (artist's proofs, thirty shillings), here was Mr. Podgers to any amount.　Not less gracious and abundant, Mr. Codgers also of the vineyard, but opposed to Mr. Podgers, brotherly tooth and nail.　Here, were guide-books to the neighbouring antiquities, and eke the Lake country, in several dry and husky sorts; here, many physically and morally impossible heads of both sexes, for young ladies to copy, in the exercise of the art of drawing; here, further, a large impression of Mr. SPURGEON, solid as to the flesh, not to say even something gross.　The working young men of Carlisle were drawn up, with their hands in their pockets, across the pavements, four and six abreast, and appeared (much to the satisfaction of Mr. Idle) to have nothing else to do.　The working and growing young women of Carlisle, from the age of twelve upwards, promenaded the streets in the cool of the evening, and rallied the said young men.　Sometimes the young men rallied the young women, as in the case of a group gathered round an accordion-player, from among whom a young man advanced behind a young woman for whom he appeared to have a tenderness, and hinted to her that he was there and playful, by giving her (he wore clogs) a kick.

On market morning, Carlisle woke up amazingly, and became (to the two Idle Apprentices) disagreeably and reproachfully busy. There were its cattle market, its sheep market, and its pig market down by the river, with raw-boned and shock-headed Rob Roys hiding their Lowland dresses beneath heavy plaids, prowling in and out among the animals, and flavouring the air with fumes of whiskey.　There was its corn market down the main street, with hum of chaffering over open sacks.　There was its general market in the street too, with heather brooms on which the purple flower still flourished, and heather baskets primitive and fresh to behold.　With women trying on clogs and caps at open stalls, and "Bible stalls" adjoining.　With "Doctor Mantle's Dispensary for the cure of all Human Maladies and no charge for advice," and with Doctor Mantle's "Laboratory of Medical, Chemical, and Botanical Science"—both healing institutions established on one pair of trestles, one board, and one sun-blind. With the renowned phrenologist from London, begging to be favoured (at sixpence each) with the company of clients of both sexes, to whom, on examination of their heads, he would make revelations " enabling him or her to know themselves." Through all these bargains and blessings, the recruiting-serjeant watchfully elbowed his way, a thread of War in the peaceful skein. Likewise on the walls were printed hints that the Oxford Blues might not be indisposed to hear of a few fine active young men; and that whereas the standard of that distinguished corps is full six feet, "growing lads of five feet eleven" need not absolutely despair of being accepted.

Scenting the morning air more pleasantly than the buried majesty of Denmark did, Messrs. Idle and Goodchild rode away from Carlisle at eight o'clock one forenoon, bound for the village of Heske, Newmarket, some fourteen miles distant.   Goodchild (who had already begun to doubt whether he was idle : as his way always is when he has nothing to do), had read of a certain black old Cumberland hill or mountain, called Carrock, or Carrock Fell ; and had arrived at the conclusion that it would be the culminating triumph of Idleness to ascend the same. Thomas Idle, dwelling on the pains inseparable from that achievement, had expressed the strongest doubts of the expediency, and even of the sanity, of the enterprise ; but Goodchild had carried his point, and they rode away.

Up hill and down hill, and twisting to the right, and twisting to the left, and with old Skiddaw (who has vaunted himself a great deal more than his merits deserve ; but that is rather the way of the Lake country), dodging the apprentices in a picturesque and pleasant manner. Good, weather-proof, warm, pleasant houses, well white-limed, scantily dotting the road. Clean children coming out to look, carrying other clean children as big as themselves. Harvest still lying out and much rained upon ; here and there, harvest still unreaped. Well cultivated gardens attached to the cottages, with plenty of produce forced out of their hard soil. Lonely nooks, and wild ; but people can be born, and married, and buried in such nooks, and can live and love, and be loved, there as elsewhere, thank God ! (Mr. Goodchild's remark.) By-and-by, the village. Black, coarse-stoned, rough - windowed houses ; some with outer staircases, like Swiss houses; a sinuous and stony gutter winding up hill and round the corner, by way of street. All the children running out directly. Women pausing in washing, to peep from doorways and very little windows. Such were the observations of Messrs. Idle and Goodchild, as their conveyance stopped at the village shoemaker's. Old Carrock gloomed down upon it all in a very ill-tempered state; and rain was beginning.

The village shoemaker declined to have anything to do with Carrock. No visitors went up Carrock. No visitors came there at all. Aa' the world ganged awa' yon. The driver appealed to the Innkeeper. The Innkeeper, had two men working in the fields, and one of them should be called in, to go up Carrock as guide. Messrs. Idle and Goodchild, highly approving, entered the Innkeeper's house, to drink whiskey and eat oatcake.

The Innkeeper was not idle enough—was not idle at all, which was a great fault in him—but was a fine specimen of a north-country man, or any kind of man. He had a ruddy cheek, a bright eye, a well-knit frame, an immense hand, a cheery outspeaking voice, and a straight, bright, broad look. He had a drawing-room, too, upstairs, which was worth a visit to the Cumberland Fells. (This was Mr. Francis Goodchild's opinion, in which Mr. Thomas Idle did not concur.)

The ceiling of this drawing-room was so crossed and recrossed by beams of unequal lengths, radiating from a centre, in a corner, that it looked like a broken star-fish. The room was comfortably and solidly furnished with good mahogany and horsehair. It had a snug fire-side, and a couple of well-curtained windows, looking out upon the wild country behind the house. What it most developed was, an unexpected taste for little ornaments and nick-nacks, of which it contained a most surprising number. They were not very various, consisting in great part of waxen babies with their limbs more or less mutilated, appealing on one leg to the parental affections from under little cupping glasses; but, Uncle Tom was there, in crockery, receiving theological instructions from Miss Eva, who grew out of his side like a wen, in an exceedingly rough state of profile propagandism. Engravings of Mr. Hunt's country boy, before and after his pie, were on the wall, divided by a highly-coloured nautical piece, the subject of which had all her colours (and more) flying, and was making great way through a sea of a regular pattern, like a lady's collar. A benevolent, elderly gentleman of the last century, with a powdered head, kept guard, in oil and varnish, over a most perplexing piece of furniture on a table ; in appearance between a driving seat and an angular knife-box, but, when opened, a musical instrument of tinkling wires, exactly like David's harp packed for travelling. Everything became a nick-nack in this curious room. The copper tea-kettle, burnished up to the highest point of glory, took his station on a stand of his own at the greatest possible distance from the fire-place, and said : " By your leave, not a kittle, but a bijou." The Staffordshire-ware butter-dish with the cover on, got upon a little round occasional table in a window, with a worked top, and announced itself to the two chairs accidentally placed there, as an aid to polite conversation, a graceful trifle in china to be chatted over by callers, as they airily trifled away the visiting moments of a butterfly existence, in that rugged old village on the Cumberland Fells. The very footstool could not keep the floor, but got upon a sofa, and therefrom proclaimed itself, in high relief of white and liver-coloured wool, a favourite spaniel coiled up for repose. Though, truly, in spite of its bright glass eyes, the spaniel was the least successful assumption in the collection : being perfectly flat, and dismally suggestive of a recent mistake in sitting down on the part of some corpulent member of the family.

There were books, too, in this room ; books on the table, books on the chimney-piece, books in an open press in the corner. Fielding was there, and Smollett was there, and Steele and Addison were there, in dispersed volumes ; and there were tales of those who go down to the sea in ships, for windy nights ; and there was really a choice of good books for rainy days or fine. It was so very pleasant to see these things in such a lonesome by-place — so very agreeable to find these evidences of a taste, however homely, that went beyond the beautiful cleanliness and trimness of the house—so fanciful to imagine what a wonder a room must be to the little children born in the gloomy village—what grand impressions of it those of them who became wanderers over the earth would carry away ; and how, at distant ends of the world, some old voyagers would die, cherishing the belief that the finest apartment known to men was once in the Hesket-Newmarket Inn, in rare old Cumberland—it was such a charmingly lazy pursuit to entertain these rambling thoughts over the choice oatcake and the genial whiskey, that Mr. Idle and Mr. Goodchild never asked themselves how it came to pass that the men in the fields were never heard of more, how the stalwart landlord replaced them without explanation, how his dog-cart came to be waiting at the door, and how everything was arranged without the least arrangement for climbing to old Carrock's shoulders, and standing on his head.

Without a word of inquiry, therefore, the Two Idle Apprentices drifted out resignedly into a fine, soft, close, drowsy, penetrating rain ; got into the landlord's light dog-cart, and rattled off through the village for the foot of Carrock. The journey at the outset was not remarkable. The Cumberland road went up and down like all other roads ; the Cumberland curs burst out from backs of cottages and barked like other curs, and the Cumberland peasantry stared after the dog-cart amazedly, as long as it was in sight, like the rest of their race. The approach to the foot of the mountain resembled the approaches to the feet of most other mountains all over the world. The cultivation gradually ceased, the trees grew gradually rare, the road became gradually rougher, and the sides of the mountain looked gradually more and more lofty, and more and more difficult to get up. The dog-cart was left at a lonely farm-house. The landlord borrowed a large umbrella, and, assuming in an instant the character of the most cheerful and adventurous of guides, led the way to the ascent. Mr. Goodchild looked eagerly at the top of the mountain, and, feeling apparently that he was now going to be very lazy indeed, shone all over wonderfully to the eye, under the influence of the contentment within and the moisture without. Only in the bosom of Mr. Thomas Idle did Despondency now hold her gloomy state. He kept it a secret ; but he would have given a very handsome sum, when the ascent began, to have been back again at the inn. The sides of Carrock looked fearfully steep, and the top of Carrock was hidden in mist. The rain was falling faster and faster. The knees of Mr. Idle—always weak on walking excursions—shivered and shook with fear and damp. The wet was already penetrating through the young man's outer coat to a brand-new shooting-jacket, for which he had reluctantly paid the large sum of two guineas on leaving town; he had no stimulating refreshment about him but a small packet of clammy gingerbread nuts; he had nobody to give him an arm, nobody to push him gently behind, nobody to pull him up tenderly in front, nobody to speak to who really felt the difficulties of the ascent, the dampness of the rain, the denseness of the mist, and the unutterable folly of climbing, undriven, up any steep place in the world, when there is level ground within reach to walk on instead.   Was it for this that Thomas had left London?   London, where there are nice short walks in level public gardens, with benches of repose set up at convenient distances for weary travellers— London, where rugged stone is humanely pounded into little lumps for the road, and intelligently shaped into smooth slabs for the pavement!   No! it was not for the laborious ascent of the crags of Carrock that Idle had left his native city, and travelled to Cumberland.   Never did he feel more disastrously convinced that he had committed a very grave error in judgment than when he found himself standing in the rain at the bottom of a steep mountain, and knew that the responsibility rested on his weak shoulders of actually getting to the top of it.

The honest landlord went first, the beaming Goodchild followed, the mournful Idle brought up the rear.   From time to time, the two foremost members of the expedition changed places in the order of march; but the rearguard never altered his position.   Up the mountain or down the mountain, in the water or out of it, over the rocks, through the bogs, skirting the heather, Mr. Thomas Idle was always the last, and was always the man who had to be looked after and waited for.   At first the ascent was delusively easy, the sides of the mountain sloped gradually, and the material of which they were composed was a soft spongy turf, very tender and pleasant to walk upon.   After a hundred yards or so, however, the verdant scene and the easy slope disappeared, and the rocks began.   Not noble, massive rocks, standing upright, keeping a certain regularity in their positions, and possessing, now and then, flat tops to sit upon, but little irritating, comfortless, rocks, littered about anyhow by Nature; treacherous, disheartening rocks of all sorts of small shapes and small sizes, bruisers of tender toes and trippers-up of wavering feet. When these impediments were passed, heather and slough followed. Here the steepness of the ascent was slightly mitigated; and here the exploring party of three turned round to look at the view below them. The scene of the moorland and the fields was like a feeble water-colour drawing half sponged out. The mist was darkening, the rain was thickening, the trees were dotted about like spots of faint shadow, the division-lines which mapped out the fields were all getting blurred together, and the lonely farm-house where the dog-cart had been left, loomed spectral in the grey light like the last human dwelling at the end of the habitable world. Was this a sight worth climbing to see? Surely—surely not!

Up again—for the top of Carrock is not reached yet. The landlord, just as good-tempered and obliging as he was at the bottom of the mountain. Mr. Goodchild brighter in the eyes and rosier in the face than ever; full of cheerful remarks and apt quotations; and walking with a springiness of step wonderful to behold. Mr. Idle, farther and farther in the rear, with the water squeaking in the toes of his boots, with his two-guinea shooting-jacket clinging damply to his aching sides, with his overcoat so full of rain, and standing out so pyramidically stiff, in consequence, from his shoulders downwards, that he felt as if he was walking in a gigantic extinguisher—the despairing spirit within him representing but too aptly the candle that had just been put out. Up and up and up again, till a ridge is reached and the outer edge of the mist on the summit of Carrock is darkly and drizzingly near. Is this the top? No, nothing like the top. It is an aggravating peculiarity of all mountains, that, although they have only one top when they are seen (as they ought always to be seen) from below, they turn out to have a perfect eruption of false tops whenever the traveller is sufficiently ill-advised to go out of his way for the purpose of ascending them. Carrock is but a trumpery little mountain of fifteen hundred feet, and it presumes to have false tops, and even precipices, as if it were Mont Blanc. No matter; Goodchild enjoys it, and will go on; and Idle, who is afraid of being left behind by himself, must follow. On entering the edge of the mist, the landlord stops, and says he hopes that it will not get any thicker. It is twenty years since he last ascended Carrock, and it is barely possible, if the mist increases, that the party may be lost on the mountain. Goodchild hears this dreadful intimation, and is not in the least impressed by it. He marches for the top that is never to be found, as if he was the Wandering Jew, bound to go on for ever, in defiance of everything. The landlord faithfully accompanies him. The two, to the dim eye of Idle, far below, look in the exaggerative mist, like a pair of friendly giants, mounting the steps of some invisible castle together. Up and up, and then down a little, and then up, and then along a strip of level ground, and then up again. The wind, a wind unknown in the happy valley, blows keen and strong; the rain-mist gets impenetrable; a dreary little cairn of stones appears. The landlord adds one to the heap, first walking all round the cairn as if he were about to perform an incantation, then dropping the stone on to the top of the heap with the gesture of a magician adding an ingredient to a cauldron in full bubble. Goodchild sits down by the cairn as if it was his study-table at home; Idle, drenched and panting, stands up with his back to the wind, ascertains distinctly that this is the top at last, looks round with all the little curiosity that is left in him, and gets, in return, a magnificent view of—Nothing !

The effect of this sublime spectacle on the minds of the exploring party is a little injured by the nature of the direct conclusion to which the sight of it points—the said conclusion being that the mountain mist has actually gathered round them, as the landlord feared it would. It now becomes imperatively necessary to settle the exact situation of the farm-house in the valley at which the dog-cart has been left, before the travellers attempt to descend. While the landlord is endeavouring to make this discovery in his own way, Mr. Goodchild plunges his hand under his wet coat, draws out a little red morocco-case, opens it, and displays to the view of his companions a neat pocket-compass. The north is found, the point at which the farm-house is situated is settled, and the descent begins. After a little downward walking, Idle (behind as usual) sees his fellow-travellers turn aside sharply—tries to follow them—loses them in the mist—is shouted after, waited for, recovered—and then finds that a halt has been ordered, partly on his account, partly for the purpose of again consulting the compass.

The point in debate is settled as before between Goodchild and the landlord, and the expedition moves on, not down the mountain, but marching straight forward round the slope of it.

The difficulty of following this new route is acutely felt by Thomas Idle.   He finds the hardship of walking at all greatly increased by the fatigue of moving his feet straight forward along the side of a slope, when their natural tendency, at every step, is to turn off at a right angle, and go straight down the declivity. Let the reader imagine himself to be walking along the roof of a barn, instead of up or down it, and he will have an exact idea of the pedestrian difficulty in which the travellers had now involved themselves.   In ten minutes more Idle was lost in the distance again, was shouted for, waited for, recovered as before ; found Goodchild repeating his observation of the compass, and remonstrated warmly against the sideway route that his companions persisted in following.   It appeared to the uninstructed mind of Thomas that when three men want to get to the bottom of a mountain, their business is to walk down it ; and he put this view of the case, not only with emphasis, but even with some irritability.   He was answered from the scientific eminence of the compass on which his companions were mounted, that there was a frightful chasm somewhere near the foot of Carrock, called The Black Arches, into which the travellers were sure to march in the mist, if they risked continuing the descent from the place where they had now halted. Idle received this answer with the silent respect which was due to the commanders of the expedition, and followed along the roof of the barn, or rather the side of the mountain, reflecting upon the assurance which he received on starting again, that the object of the party was only to gain "a certain point," and, this haven attained, to continue the descent afterwards until the foot of Carrock was reached.   Though quite unexceptionable as an abstract form of expression, the phrase "a certain point" has the disadvantage of sounding rather vaguely when it is pronounced on unknown ground, under a canopy of mist much thicker than a London fog.   Nevertheless, after the compass, this phrase was all the clue the party had to hold by, and Idle clung to the extreme end of it as hopefully as he could.

More sideway walking, thicker and thicker mist, all sorts of points reached except the " certain point ; " third loss of Idle, third shouts for him, third recovery of him, third consultation of compass.   Mr. Goodchild draws it tenderly from his pocket, and prepares to adjust it on a stone.   Something falls on the turf—it is the glass. Something else drops immediately after —it is the needle.   The compass is broken, and the exploring party is lost !

It is the practice of the English portion of the human race to receive all great disasters in dead silence.   Mr. Goodchild restored the useless compass to his pocket without saying a word, Mr. Idle looked at the landlord, and the landlord looked at Mr. Idle.   There was nothing for it now but to go on blindfold, and trust to the chapter of chances.   Accordingly, the lost travellers moved forward, still walking round the slope of the mountain, still desperately resolved to avoid the Black Arches, and to succeed in reaching the "certain point."

A quarter of an hour brought them to the brink of a ravine, at the bottom of which there flowed a muddy little stream. Here another halt was called, and another consultation took place.   The landlord, still clinging pertinaciously to the idea of reaching the " point," voted for crossing the ravine, and going on round the slope of the mountain.   Mr. Goodchild, to the great relief of his fellow-traveller, took another view of the case, and backed Mr. Idle's proposal to descend Carrock at once, at any hazard—the rather as the running stream was a sure guide to follow from the mountain to the valley.   Accordingly, the party descended to the rugged and stony banks of the stream ; and here again Thomas lost ground sadly, and fell far behind his travelling companions.   Not much more than six weeks had elapsed since he had sprained one of his ankles, and he began to feel this same ankle getting rather weak when he found himself among the stones that were strewn about the running water.   Goodchild and the landlord were getting farther and farther ahead of him. He saw them cross the stream and disappear round a projection on its banks. He heard them shout the moment after as a signal that they had halted and were waiting for him.   Answering the shout, he mended his pace, crossed the stream where they had crossed it, and was within one step of the opposite bank, when his foot slipped on a wet stone, his weak ankle gave a twist outwards, a hot, rending, tearing pain ran through it at the same moment, and down fell the idlest of the Two Idle Apprentices, crippled in an instant.

The situation was now, in plain terms, one of absolute

danger.   There lay Mr. Idle writhing with pain, there was the mist as thick as ever, there was the landlord as completely lost as the strangers whom he was conducting, and there was the compass broken in Goodchild's pocket.   To leave the wretched Thomas on unknown ground was plainly impossible ; and to get him to walk with a badly sprained ankle seemed equally out of the question.   However, Goodchild (brought back by his cry for help) bandaged the ankle with a pocket-handkerchief, and assisted by the landlord, raised the crippled Apprentice to his legs, offered him a shoulder to lean on, and exhorted him for the sake of the whole party to try if he could walk.   Thomas, assisted by the shoulder on one side, and a stick on the other, did try, with what pain and difficulty those only can imagine who have sprained an ankle and have had to tread on it afterwards.   At a pace adapted to the feeble hobbling of a newly-lamed man, the lost party moved on, perfectly ignorant whether they were on the right side of the mountain or the wrong, and equally uncertain how long Idle would be able to contend with the pain in his ankle, before he gave in altogether and fell down again, unable to stir another step.

Slowly and more slowly, as the clog of crippled Thomas weighed heavily and more heavily on the march of the expedition, the lost travellers followed the windings of the stream, till they came to a faintly-marked cart-track, branching off nearly at right angles, to the left.   After a little consultation it was resolved to follow this dim vestage of a road in the hope that it might lead to some farm or cottage, at which Idle could be left in safety.   It was now getting on towards the afternoon, and it was fast becoming more than doubtful whether the party, delayed in their progress as they now were, might not be overtaken by the darkness before the right route was found, and be condemned to pass the night on the mountain, without bit or drop to comfort them, in their wet clothes.

The cart-track grew fainter and fainter, until it was washed out altogether by another little stream, dark, turbulent, and rapid.   The landlord suggested, judging by the colour of the water, that it must be flowing from one of the lead mines in the neighbourhood of Carrock ; and the travellers accordingly kept by the stream for a little while, in the hope of possibly wandering towards help in that way.   After walking forward about two hundred yards, they came upon a mine indeed, but a mine, exhausted and abandoned; a dismal, ruinous place, with nothing but the wreck of its works and buildings left to speak for it. Here, there were a few sheep feeding. The landlord looked at them earnestly, thought he recognised the marks on them—then thought he did not—finally gave up the sheep in despair—and walked on just as ignorant of the whereabouts of the party as ever.

The march in the dark, literally as well as metaphorically in the dark, had now been continued for three-quarters of an hour from the time when the crippled Apprentice had met with his accident. Mr. Idle, with all the will to conquer the pain in his ankle, and to hobble on, found the power rapidly failing him, and felt that another ten minutes at most would find him at the end of his last physical resources. He had just made up his mind on this point, and was about to communicate the dismal result of his reflections to his companions, when the mist suddenly brightened, and begun to lift straight ahead. In another minute, the landlord, who was in advance, proclaimed that he saw a tree. Before long, other trees appeared—then a cottage—then a house beyond the cottage, and a familiar line of road rising behind it. Last of all, Carrock itself loomed darkly into view, far away to the right hand. The party had not only got down the mountain without knowing how, but had wandered away from it in the mist, without knowing why—away, far down on the very moor by which they had approached the base of Carrock that morning.

The happy lifting of the mist, and the still happier discovery that the travellers had groped their way, though by a very roundabout direction, to within a mile or so of the part of the valley in which the farm-house was situated, restored Mr. Idle's sinking spirits and reanimated his failing strength. While the landlord ran off to get the dog-cart, Thomas was assisted by Goodchild to the cottage which had been the first building seen when the darkness brightened, and was propped up against the garden wall, like an artist's lay figure waiting to be forwarded, until the dog-cart should arrive from the farm-house below. In due time—and a very long time it seemed to Mr. Idle—the rattle of wheels was heard, and the crippled Apprentice was lifted into the seat. As the dog-cart was driven back to the inn,

the landlord related an anecdote which he had just heard at the
farm-house, of an unhappy man who had been lost, like his two
guests and himself, on Carrock; who had passed the night
there alone; who had been found the next morning, "scared
and starved;" and who never went out afterwards, except on
his way to the grave. Mr. Idle heard this sad story, and
derived at least one useful impression from it. Bad as the pain
in his ankle was, he contrived to bear it patiently, for he felt
grateful that a worse accident had not befallen him in the wilds
of Carrock.

CHAPTER II.

The dog-cart, with Mr. Thomas Idle and his ankle on the hanging seat behind, Mr. Francis Goodchild and the Innkeeper in front, and the rain in spouts and splashes everywhere, made the best of its way back to the little inn ; the broken moor country looking like miles upon miles of Pre-Adamite sop, or the ruins of some enormous jorum of antediluvian toast-and-water.   The trees dripped ; the eaves of the scattered cottages dripped ; the barren stone walls dividing the land, dripped ; the yelping dogs dripped ; carts and waggons under ill-roofed penthouses, dripped ; melancholy cocks and hens perching on their shafts, or seeking shelter underneath them, dripped ; Mr. Goodchild dripped ; Francis Idle dripped ; the Innkeeper dripped ; the mare dripped ; the vast curtains of mist and cloud passed before the shadowy forms of the hills, streamed water as they were drawn across the landscape.   Down such steep pitches that the mare seemed to be trotting on her head, and up such steep pitches that she seemed to have a supplementary leg in her tail, the dog-cart jolted and tilted back to the village.   It was too wet for the women to look out, it was too wet even for the children to look out ; all the doors and windows were closed, and the only sign of life or motion was in the rain-punctured puddles.

Whiskey and oil to Thomas Idle's ankle, and whiskey without oil to Francis Goodchild's stomach, produced an agreeable change in the systems of both ; soothing Mr. Idle's pain, which was sharp before, and sweetening Mr. Goodchild's temper, which was sweet before.   Portmanteaus being then opened and clothes

changed, Mr. Goodchild, through having no change of outer garments but broadcloth and velvet, suddenly became a magnificent
portent in the Innkeeper's house, a shining frontispiece to the
fashions for the month, and a frightful anomaly in the Cumberland village.

Greatly ashamed of his splendid appearance, the conscious
Goodchild quenched it as much as possible, in the shadow of
Thomas Idle's ankle, and in a corner of the little covered
carriage that started with them for Wigton—a most desirable
carriage for any country, except for its having a flat roof and
no sides; which caused the plumps of rain accumulating on the
roof to play vigorous games of bagatelle into the interior all the
way, and to score immensely. It was comfortable to see how
the people coming back in open carts from Wigton market made
no more of the rain than if it were sunshine; how the Wigton
policeman taking a country walk of half-a-dozen miles (apparently for pleasure), in resplendent uniform, accepted satura-
tion as his normal state; how clerks and schoolmasters in black,
loitered along the road without umbrellas, getting varnished at
every step; how the Cumberland girls, coming out to look after
the Cumberland cows, shook the rain from their eyelashes and
laughed it away; and how the rain continued to fall upon all, as
it only does fall in hill countries.

Wigton market was over, and its bare booths were smoking
with rain all down the street. Mr. Thomas Idle, melo-
dramatically carried to the inn's first floor, and laid upon three
chairs (he should have had the sofa, if there had been one), Mr.
Goodchild went to the window to take an observation of Wigton,
and report what he saw to his disabled companion.

"Brother Francis, brother Francis," cried Thomas Idle.
"What do you see from the turret?"

"I see," said Brother Francis, "what I hope and believe to
be one of the most dismal places ever seen by eyes. I see the
houses with their roofs of dull black, their stained fronts, and
their dark-rimmed windows, looking as if they were all in
mourning. As every little puff of wind comes down the street,
I see a perfect train of rain let off along the wooden stalls in the
market-place and exploded against me. I see a very big gas
lamp in the centre which I know, by a secret instinct, will not
be lighted to-night. I see a pump, with a trivet underneath its

spout whereon to stand the vessels that are brought to be filled with water. I see a man come to pump, and he pumps very hard, but no water follows, and he strolls empty away."

"Brother Francis, brother Francis," cried Thomas Idle, "what more do you see from the turret, besides the man and the pump, and the trivet and the houses all in mourning and the rain ?"

"I see," said Brother Francis, "one, two, three, four, five, linen-drapers' shops in front of me. I see a linen-draper's shop next door to the right—and there are five more linen-drapers' shops down the corner to the left. Eleven homicidal linen-drapers' shops within a short stone's throw, each with its hands at the throats of all the rest ! Over the small first-floor of one of these linen-drapers' shops appears the wonderful inscription, BANK."

"Brother Francis, brother Francis," cried Thomas Idle, "what more do you see from the turret, besides the eleven homicidal linen-drapers' shops, and the wonderful inscription, 'Bank' on the small first-floor, and the man and the pump and the trivet and the houses all in mourning and the rain ?"

"I see," said Brother Francis, "the depository for Christian Knowledge, and through the dark vapour I think I again make out Mr. Spurgeon looming heavily. Her Majesty the Queen, God bless her, printed in colours, I am sure I see. I see the *Illustrated London News* of several years ago, and I see a sweet-meat shop—which the proprietor calls a 'Salt Warehouse'—with one small female child in a cotton bonnet looking in on tip-toe, oblivious of rain. And I see a watchmaker's with only three great pale watches of a dull metal hanging in his window, each in a separate pane."

"Brother Francis, brother Francis," cried Thomas Idle, "what more do you see of Wigton, besides these objects, and the man and the pump and the trivet and the houses all in mourning and the rain ?"

"I see nothing more," said Brother Francis, "and there is nothing more to see, except the curlpaper bill of the theatre, which was opened and shut last week (the manager's family played all the parts), and the short, square, chinky omnibus that goes to the railway, and leads too rattling a life over the stones to hold together long. O yes ! Now, I see two men with their hands in their pockets and their backs towards me."

"Brother Francis, brother Francis," cried Thomas Idle, "what do you make out from the turret, of the expression of the two men with their hands in their pockets and their backs towards you?"

"They are mysterious men," said Brother Francis, "with inscrutable backs. They keep their backs towards me with persistency. If one turns an inch in any direction, the other turns an inch in the same direction, and no more. They turn very stiffly, on a very little pivot, in the middle of the market-place. Their appearance is partly of a mining, partly of a ploughing, partly of a stable, character. They are looking at nothing—very hard. Their backs are slouched, and their legs are curved with much standing about. Their pockets are loose and dog's-eared, on account of their hands being always in them. They stand to be rained upon, without any movement of impatience or dissatisfaction, and they keep so close together that an elbow of each jostles an elbow of the other, but they never speak. They spit at times, but speak not. I see it growing darker and darker, and still I see them, sole visible population of the place, standing to be rained upon with their backs towards me, and looking at nothing very hard."

"Brother Francis, brother Francis," cried Thomas Idle, "before you draw down the blind of the turret and come in to have your head scorched by the hot gas, see if you can, and impart to me, something of the expression of those two amazing men."

"The murky shadows," said Francis Goodchild, "are gathering fast; and the wings of evening, and the wings of coal, are folding over Wigton. Still, they look at nothing very hard, with their backs towards me. Ah! Now, they turn, and I see——"

"Brother Francis, brother Francis," cried Thomas Idle, "tell me quickly what you see of the two men of Wigton!"

"I see," said Francis Goodchild, "that they have no expression at all. And now the town goes to sleep, undazzled by the large unlighted lamp in the market-place; and let no man wake it."

At the close of the next day's journey, Mr. Thomas Idle's ankle became much swollen and inflamed.   There are reasons which will presently explain themselves for not publicly indicating the exact direction in which that journey lay, or the place in which it ended.   It was a long day's shaking of Thomas Idle over the rough roads, and a long day's getting out and going on before the horses, and fagging up hills, and scouring down hills, on the part of Mr. Goodchild, who in the fatigues of such labours congratulated himself on attaining a high point of idleness.   It was at a little town, still in Cumberland, that they halted for the night—a very little town, with the purple and brown moor close upon its one street; a curious little ancient market-cross set up in the midst of it ; and the town itself looking much as if it were a collection of great stones piled on end by the Druids long ago, which a few recluse people had since hollowed out for habitations.

"Is there a doctor here?" asked Mr. Goodchild, on his knee, of the motherly landlady of the little Inn : stopping in his examination of Mr. Idle's ankle, with the aid of a candle.

"Ey, my word !" said the landlady, glancing doubtfully at the ankle for herself ; "there's Doctor Speddie."

"Is he a good Doctor?"

"Ey !" said the landlady, "I ca' him so. A' cooms efther nae doctor that I ken. Mair nor which, a's just THE doctor heer."

"Do you think he is at home ?"

Her reply was, "Gang awa', Jock, and bring him."

Jock, a white-headed boy, who, under pretence of stirring up some bay salt in a basin of water for the laving of this unfortunate ankle, had greatly enjoyed himself for the last ten minutes in splashing the carpet, set off promptly. A very few minutes had elapsed when he showed the Doctor in, by tumbling against the door before him and bursting it open with his head.

"Gently, Jock, gently," said the Doctor as he advanced with a quiet step. "Gentlemen, a good evening. I am sorry that my presence is required here. A slight accident, I hope? A slip and a fall? Yes, yes, yes. Carrock, indeed? Hah! Does that pain you, sir? No doubt, it does. It is the great connecting ligament here, you see, that has been badly strained. Time and rest, sir ! They are often the recipe in greater cases," with a slight sigh, "and often the recipe in small. I can send a lotion to relieve you, but we must leave the cure to time and rest."

This he said, holding Idle's foot on his knee between his two hands, as he sat over against him. He had touched it tenderly and skilfully in explanation of what he said, and, when his careful examination was completed, softy returned it to its former horizontal position on a chair.

He spoke with a little irresolution whenever he began, but afterwards fluently. He was a tall, thin, large-boned, old gentleman, with an appearance at first sight of being hard-featured; but, at a second glance, the mild expression of his face and some particular touches of sweetness and patience about his mouth, corrected this impression and assigned his long professional rides, by day and night, in the bleak hill-weather, as the true cause of that appearance. He stooped very little, though past seventy and very grey. His dress was more like that of a clergyman than a country doctor, being a plain black suit, and a plain white neck-kerchief tied behind like a band. His black was the worse for wear, and there were darns in his coat, and his linen was a little frayed at the hems and edges, He might have been poor—it was likely enough in that out-of-the-way spot—or he might have been a little self-forgetful and eccentric. Any one could have seen directly, that he had neither wife nor child at home. He had a scholarly air with him, and that kind of considerate humanity towards others which claimed a gentle consideration for himself. Mr. Goodchild made this study of him while he was examining the limb, and as he laid it down. Mr. Goodchild wishes to add that he considers it a very good likeness.

It came out in the course of a little conversation, that Doctor Speddie was acquainted with some friends of Thomas Idle's, and had, when a young man, passed some years in Thomas Idle's birthplace on the other side of England. Certain idle labours, the fruit of Mr. Goodchild's apprenticeship, also happened to be well known to him. The lazy travellers were thus placed on a more intimate footing with the Doctor than the casual circumstances of the meeting would of themselves have established; and when Doctor Speddie rose to go home, remarking that he would send his assistant with the lotion, Francis

Goodchild said that was unnecessary, for, by the Doctor's leave, he would accompany him, and bring it back. (Having done nothing to fatigue himself for a full quarter of an hour, Francis began to fear that he was not in a state of idleness.)

Doctor Speddie politely assented to the proposition of Francis Goodchild, " as it would give him the pleasure of enjoying a few more minutes of Mr. Goodchild's society than he could otherwise have hoped for," and they went out together into the village street. The rain had nearly ceased, the clouds had broken before a cool wind from the north-east, and stars were shining from the peaceful heights beyond them.

Doctor Speddie's house was the last house in the place. Beyond it, lay the moor, all dark and lonesome. The wind moaned in a low, dull, shivering manner round the little garden, like a houseless creature that knew the winter was coming. It was exceedingly wild and solitary. " Roses," said the Doctor, when Goodchild touched some wet leaves overhanging the stone porch ; " but they get cut to pieces."

The Doctor opened the door with a key he carried, and led the way into a low but pretty ample hall with rooms on either side. The door of one of these stood open, and the Doctor entered it, with a word of welcome to his guest. It, too, was a low room, half surgery and half parlour, with shelves of books and bottles against the walls, which were of a very dark hue. There was a fire in the grate, the night being damp and chill. Leaning against the chimney-piece looking down into it, stood the Doctor's Assistant.

A man of a most remarkable appearance. Much older than Mr. Goodchild had expected, for he was at least two-and-fifty ; but, that was nothing. What was startling in him was his remarkable paleness. His large black eyes, his sunken cheeks, his long and heavy iron-grey hair, his wasted hands, and even the attenuation of his figure, were at first forgotten in his extraordinary pallor. There was no vestige of colour in the man. When he turned his face, Francis Goodchild started as if a stone figure had looked round at him.

" Mr. Lorn," said the Doctor. " Mr. Goodchild."

The Assistant, in a distraught way—as if he had forgotten something—as if he had forgotten everything, even to his own name and himself—acknowledged the visitor's presence, and stepped further back into the shadow of the wall behind him. But, he was so pale that his face stood out in relief against the dark wall, and really could not be hidden so.

" Mr. Goodchild's friend has met with an accident, Lorn," said Doctor Speddie.   " We want the lotion for a bad sprain."

A pause.

" My dear fellow, you are more than usually absent to-night. The lotion for a bad sprain."

" Ah ! yes ! Directly."

He was evidently relieved to turn away, and to take his white face and his wild eyes to a table in a recess among the bottles. But, though he stood there, compounding the lotion with his back towards them, Goodchild could not, for many moments, withdraw his gaze from the man. When he at length did so, he found the Doctor observing him, with some trouble in his face. " He is absent," explained the Doctor, in a low voice. " Always absent. Very absent."

" Is he ill ?"

" No, not ill."

" Unhappy ?"

" I have my suspicions that he was," assented the Doctor, " once."

Francis Goodchild could not but observe that the Doctor accompanied these words with a benignant and protecting glance at their subject, in which there was much of the expression with which an attached father might have looked at a heavily afflicted son.   Yet, that they were not father and son must have been plain to most eyes.   The Assistant, on the other hand, turning presently to ask the Doctor some question, looked at him with a wan smile as if he were his whole reliance and sustainment in life.

It was in vain for the Doctor in his easy-chair, to try to lead the mind of Mr. Goodchild in the opposite easy-chair, away from what was before him.   Let Mr. Goodchild do what he would to follow the Doctor, his eyes and thoughts reverted to the Assistant.   The Doctor soon perceived it, and, after falling silent, and musing in a little perplexity, said:

" Lorn !"

" My dear Doctor."

" Would you go to the Inn, and apply that lotion ?   You

will show the best way of applying it, far better than Mr. Goodchild can."

" With pleasure."

The Assistant took his hat, and passed like a shadow to the door.

" Lorn !" said the Doctor, calling after him.

He returned.

" Mr. Goodchild will keep me company till you come home. Don't hurry.   Excuse my calling you back."

" It is not," said the Assistant, with his former smile, " the first time you have called me back, dear Doctor."   With those words he went away.

" Mr. Goodchild," said Doctor Speddie, in a low voice, and with his former troubled expression of face, " I have seen that your attention has been concentrated on my friend."

" He fascinates me.   I must apologise to you, but he has quite bewildered and mastered me."

" I find that a lonely existence and a long secret," said the Doctor, drawing his chair a little nearer to Mr. Goodchild's, " become in the course of time very heavy.   I will tell you something.   You may make what use you will of it, under fictitious names.   I know I may trust you.   I am the more inclined to confidence to-night, through having been unexpectedly led back, by the current of our conversation at the Inn, to scenes in my early life.   Will you please to draw a little nearer ?"

Mr. Goodchild drew a little nearer, and the Doctor went on thus : speaking, for the most part, in so cautious a voice, that the wind, though it was far from high, occasionally got the better of him.

When this present nineteenth century was younger by a good many years than it is now, a certain friend of mine, named Arthur Holliday, happened to arrive in the town of Doncaster, exactly in the middle of a race-week, or, in other words, in the middle of the month of September.   He was one of those reckless, rattle-pated, open-hearted, and open-mouthed young gentlemen, who possess the gift of familiarity in its highest perfection, and who scramble carelessly along the journey of life making friends, as the phrase is, wherever they go.   His father was a

rich manufacturer, and had brought landed property enough in
one of the midland counties to make all the born squires in his
neighbourhood thoroughly envious of him.   Arthur was his
only son, possessor in prospect of the great estate and the great
business after his father's death; well supplied with money,
and not too rigidly looked after, during his father's lifetime.
Report, or scandal, whichever you please, said that the old
gentleman had been rather wild in his youthful days, and that,
unlike most parents, he was not disposed to be violently indignant when he found that his son took after him.   This may
be true or not.   I myself only knew the elder Mr. Holliday
when he was getting on in years ; and then he was as quiet and
as respectable a gentleman as ever I met with.

Well, one September, as I told you, young Arthur comes to
Doncaster, having decided all of a sudden, in his hare-brained
way, that he would go to the races.   He did not reach the
town till towards the close of the evening, and he went at once
to see about his dinner and bed at the principal hotel.   Dinner
they were ready enough to give him; but as for a bed, they
laughed when he mentioned it.   In the race-week at Doncaster,
it is no uncommon thing for visitors who have not bespoken
apartments, to pass the night in their carriages at the inn doors.
As for the lower sort of strangers, I myself have often seen
them, at that full time, sleeping out on the doorsteps for want
of a covered place to creep under.   Rich as he was, Arthur's
chance of getting a night's lodging (seeing that he had not
written beforehand to secure one) was more than doubtful.   He
tried the second hotel, and the third hotel, and two of the
inferior inns after that ; and was met everywhere by the same
form of answer.   No accommodation for the night of any sort
was left.   All the bright golden sovereigns in his pocket would
not buy him a bed at Doncaster in the race-week.

To a young fellow of Arthur's temperament, the novelty
of being turned away into the street, like a penniless vagabond,
at every house where he asked for a lodging, presented
itself in the light of a new and highly amusing piece of
experience.   He went on, with his carpet-bag in his hand,
applying for a bed at every place of entertainment for travellers
that he could find in Doncaster, until he wandered into the
outskirts of the town.   By this time, the last glimmer of

twilight had faded out, the moon was rising dimly in a mist, the wind was getting cold, the clouds were gathering heavily, and there was every prospect that it was soon going to rain.

The look of the night had rather a lowering effect on young Holliday's good spirits. He began to contemplate the houseless situation in which he was placed, from the serious rather than the humorous point of view; and he looked about him, for another public-house to inquire at, with something very like downright anxiety in his mind on the subject of a lodging for the night. The suburban part of the town towards which he had now strayed was hardly lighted at all, and he could see nothing of the houses as he passed them, except that they got progressively smaller and dirtier, the farther he went. Down the winding road before him shone the dull gleam of an oil lamp, the one faint, lonely light that struggled ineffectually with the foggy darkness all round him. He resolved to go on as far as this lamp, and then, if it showed him nothing in the shape of an Inn, to return to the central part of the town and to try if he could not at least secure a chair to sit down on, through the night, at one of the principal Hotels.

As he got near the lamp, he heard voices; and, walking close under it, found that it lighted the entrance to a narrow court, on the wall of which was painted a long hand in faded flesh-colour, pointing with a lean fore-finger, to this inscription :—

THE TWO ROBINS.

Arthur turned into the court without hesitation, to see what The Two Robins could do for him. Four or five men were standing together round the door of the house which was at the bottom of the court, facing the entrance from the street. The men were all listening to one other man, better dressed than the rest, who was telling his audience something, in a low voice, in which they were apparently very much interested.

On entering the passage, Arthur was passed by a stranger with a knapsack in his hand, who was evidently leaving the house.

"No," said the traveller with the knapsack, turning round and addressing himself cheerfully to a fat, sly-looking, bald-headed man, with a dirty white apron on, who had followed him down the passage.   "No, Mr. Landlord, I am not easily scared by trifles; but, I don't mind confessing that I can't quite stand *that*."

It occurred to young Holliday, the moment he heard these words, that the stranger had been asked an exorbitant price for a bed at The Two Robins; and that he was unable or unwilling to pay it. The moment his back was turned, Arthur, comfortably conscious of his own well-filled pockets, addressed himself in a great hurry, for fear any other benighted traveller should slip in and forestall him, to the sly-looking landlord with the dirty apron and the bald head.

"If you have got a bed to let," he said, "and if that gentleman who has just gone out won't pay your price for it, I will."

The sly landlord looked hard at Arthur.

"Will you, sir?" he asked, in a meditative, doubtful way.

"Name your price," said young Holliday, thinking that the landlord's hesitation sprang from some boorish distrust of him. "Name your price, and I'll give you the money at once if you like?"

"Are you game for five shillings?" enquired the landlord, rubbing his stubbly double chin, and looking up thoughtfully at the ceiling above him.

Arthur nearly laughed in the man's face; but thinking it prudent to control himself, offered the five shillings as seriously as he could. The sly landlord held out his hand, then suddenly drew it back again.

"You're acting all fair and above-board by me," he said: "and, before I take your money, I'll do the same by you. Look here, this is how it stands. You can have a bed all to yourself for five shillings; but you can't have more than a half-share of the room it stands in. Do you see what I mean, young gentleman?"

"Of course I do," returned Arthur, a little irritably. "You mean that it is a double-bedded room, and that one of the beds is occupied?"

The landlord nodded his head, and rubbed his double chin harder than ever. Arthur hesitated, and mechanically moved back a step or two towards the door. The idea of sleeping in the same room with a total stranger, did not present an attractive prospect to him. He felt more than half-inclined to drop his five shillings into his pocket, and to go out into the street once more.

"Is it yes, or no?" asked the landlord. "Settle it as quick as you can, because there's lots of people wanting a bed at Doncaster to-night, besides you."

Arthur looked towards the court, and heard the rain falling heavily in the street outside. He thought he would ask a question or two before he rashly decided on leaving the shelter of The Two Robins.

"What sort of a man is it who has got the other bed?" he inquiried. "Is he a gentleman?   I mean, is he a quiet, well-behaved person?"

"The quietest man I ever came across," said the landlord, rubbing his fat hands stealthily one over the other. "As sober as a judge, and as regular as clock-work in his habits. It hasn't struck nine, not ten minutes ago, and he's in his bed already.   I don't know whether that comes up to your notion of a quiet man : it goes a long way ahead of mine, I can tell you."

"Is he asleep, do you think?" asked Arthur.

"I know he's asleep," returned the landlord.   "And what's more, he's gone off so fast, that I'll warrant you don't wake him. This way, sir," said the landlord, speaking over young Holliday's shoulder, as if he was addressing some new guest who was approaching the house.

"Here you are," said Arthur, determined to be before-hand with the stranger, whoever he might be. "I'll take the bed.' And he handed the five shillings to the landlord, who nodded, dropped the money carelessly into his waistcoat-pocket, and lighted the candle.

"Come up and see the room," said the host of The Two Robins, leading the way to the staircase quite briskly, considering how fat he was.

They mounted to the second-floor of the house.   The landlord half opened a door, fronting the landing, then stopped, and turned round to Arthur.

"It's a fair bargain, mind, on my side as well as on yours," he said. "You give me five shillings, I give you in return a

OUTSIDE THE DEAD MAN'S ROOM.

clean, comfortable bed ; and I warrant, beforehand, that you won't be interfered with, or annoyed in any way, by the man who sleeps in the same room as you."   Saying those words, he looked hard, for a moment, in young Holliday's face, and then lead the way into the room.

It was larger and cleaner than Arthur had expected it would be.   The two beds stood parallel with each other—a space of about six feet intervening between them.   They were both of the same medium size, and both had the same plain white curtains, made to draw, if necessary, all round them.   The occupied bed was the bed nearest the window.   The curtains were all drawn round this, except the half curtain at the bottom, on the side of the bed farthest from the window. Arthur saw the feet of the sleeping man raising the scanty clothes into a sharp little eminence, as if he was lying flat on his back.   He took the candle, and advanced softly to draw the curtain—stopped half way, and listened for a moment—then turned to the landlord.

" He's a very quiet sleeper," said Arthur.

" Yes," said the landlord, " very quiet."

Young Holliday advanced with the candle, and looked in at the man cautiously.

" How pale he is ! " said Arthur.

" Yes," returned the landlord, "pale enough, isn't he ? "

Arthur looked closer at the man.   The bed-clothes were drawn up to his chin, and they lay perfectly still over the region of his chest.   Surprised and vaguely startled, as he noticed this, Arthur stooped down closer over the stranger ; looked at his ashy, parted lips ; listened breathlessly for an instant ; looked again at the strangely still face, and the motionless lips and chest ; and turned round suddenly on the landlord, with his own cheeks as pale for the moment as the hollow cheeks of the man on the bed.

" Come here," he whispered, under his breath.   " Come here, for God's sake !   The man's not asleep—he is dead ! "

" You have found that out sooner than I thought you would," said the landlord composedly.   " Yes, he's dead, sure enough.   He died at five o'clock to-day."

" How did he die ?   Who is he ? " asked Arthur, staggered, for a moment, by the audacious coolness of the answer.

"As to who is he," rejoined the landlord, " I know no more about him than you do. There are his books and letters and things, all sealed up in that brown paper parcel, for the Coroner's inquest to open to-morrow or next day. He's been here a week, paying his way fairly enough, and stopping in-doors, for the most part, as if he was ailing. My girl brought him up his tea at five to-day ; and as he was pouring of it out, he fell down in a faint, or a fit, or a compound of both, for anything I know. We could not bring him to—and I said he was dead. And the doctor couldn't bring him to—and the doctor said he was dead. And there he is. And the Coroner's inquest's coming as soon as it can. And that's as much as I know about it."

Arthur held the candle close to the man's lips. The flame still burnt straight up, as steadily as before. There was a moment of silence ; and the rain pattered drearily through it against the panes of the window.

" If you haven't got nothing more to say to me," continued the landlord, " I suppose I may go. You don't expect your five shillings back, do you ? There's the bed I promised you, clean and comfortable. There's the man I warranted not to disturb you, quiet in this world for ever. If you're frightened to stop alone with him, that's not my look out. I've kept my part of the bargain, and I mean to keep the money. I'm not Yorkshire, myself, young gentleman ; but I've lived long enough in these parts to have my wits sharpened ; and I shouldn't wonder if you found out the way to brighten up yours, next time you come amongst us." With these words, the landlord turned towards the door, and laughed to himself softly, in high satisfaction at his own sharpness.

Startled and shocked as he was, Arthur had by this time sufficiently recovered himself to feel indignant at the trick that had been played on him, and at the insolent manner in which the landlord exulted in it.

"Don't laugh," he said sharply, " till you are quite sure you have got the laugh against me. You shan't have the five shillings for nothing, my man. I'll keep the bed."

" Will you ?" said the landlord. " Then I wish you a good night's rest." With that brief farewell, he went out, and shut the door after him.

A good night's rest ! The words had hardly been spoken, the

door had hardly been closed, before Arthur half-repented the hasty words that had just escaped him.   Though not naturally over-sensitive, and not wanting in courage of the moral as well as the physical sort, the presence of the dead man had an instantaneously chilling effect on his mind when he found himself alone in the room—alone, and bound by his own rash words to stay there till the next morning.   An older man would have thought nothing of those words, and would have acted, without reference to them, as his calmer sense suggested.   But Arthur was too young to treat the ridicule, even of his inferiors, with contempt—too young not to fear the momentary humiliation of falsifying his own foolish boast, more than he feared the trial of watching out the long night in the same chamber with the dead.

"It is but a few hours," he thought to himself, "and I can get away the first thing in the morning."

He was looking towards the occupied bed as that idea passed through his mind, and the sharp angular eminence made in the clothes by the dead man's upturned feet again caught his eye. He advanced and drew the curtains, purposely abstaining, as he did so, from looking at the face of the corpse, lest he might unnerve himself at the outset by fastening some ghastly impression of it on his mind.   He drew the curtain very gently, and sighed involuntarily as he closed it.   "Poor fellow," he said, almost as sadly as if he had known the man.   "Ah, poor fellow!"

He went next to the window.   The night was black, and he could see nothing from it.   The rain still pattered heavily against the glass.   He inferred, from hearing it, that the window was at the back of the house; remembering that the front was sheltered from the weather by the court and the buildings over it.

While he was still standing at the window—for even the dreary rain was a relief, because of the sound it made; a relief, also, because it moved, and had some faint suggestion, in consequence, of life and companionship in it—while he was standing at the window, and looking vacantly into the black darkness outside, he heard a distant church-clock strike ten.   Only ten! How was he to pass the time till the house was astir the next morning?

Under any other circumstances, he would have gone down to the public-house parlour, would have called for his grog, and would have laughed and talked with the company assembled as familiarly as if he had known them all his life.   But the very thought of whiling away the time in this manner was distasteful to him.   The new situation in which he was placed seemed to have altered him to himself already.   Thus far, his life had been the common, trifling, prosaic, surface-life of a prosperous young man, with no troubles to conquer, and no trials to face. He had lost no relation whom he loved, no friend whom he treasured.   Till this night, what share he had of the immortal inheritance that is divided amongst us all, had laid dormant within him.   Till this night, Death and he had not once met, even in thought.

He took a few turns up and down the room—then stopped. The noise made by his boots on the poorly carpeted floor, jarred on his ear.   He hesitated a little, and ended by taking the boots off, and walking backwards and forwards noiselessly.   All desire to sleep or to rest had left him.   The bare thought of lying down on the unoccupied bed instantly drew the picture on his mind of a dreadful mimicry of the position of the dead man.   Who was he ?   What was the story of his past life ?   Poor he must have been, or he would not have stopped at such a place as The Two Robins Inn—and weakened, probably, by long illness, or he could hardly have died in the manner in which the landlord had described.   Poor, ill, lonely,—dead in a strange place ; dead, with nobody but a stranger to pity him.   A sad story : truly, on the mere face of it, a very sad story.

While these thoughts were passing through his mind, he had stopped insensibly at the window, close to which stood the foot of the bed with the closed curtains.   At first he looked at it absently ; then he became conscious that his eyes were fixed on it ; and then, a perverse desire took possession of him to do the very thing which he had resolved not to do, up to this time— to look at the dead man.

He stretched out his hand towards the curtains ; but checked himself in the very act of undrawing them, turned his back sharply on the bed, and walked towards the chimney-piece, to see what things were placed on it, and to try if he could keep the dead man out of his mind in that way.

There was a pewter inkstand on the chimney-piece, with some mildewed remains of ink in the bottle.   There were two coarse china ornaments of the commonest kind ; and there was a square of embossed card, dirty and fly-blown, with a collection of wretched riddles printed on it, in all sorts of zig-zag directions, and in variously coloured inks.   He took the card, and went away, to read it, to the table on which the candle was placed ; sitting down, with his back resolutely turned to the curtained bed.

He read the first riddle, the second, the third, all in one corner of the card—then turned it round impatiently to look at another.   Before he could begin reading the riddles printed here, the sound of the church-clock stopped him.   Eleven.   He had got through an hour of the time, in the room with the dead man.

Once more he looked at the card.   It was not easy to make out the letters printed on it, in consequence of the dimness of the light which the landlord had left him—a common tallow candle, furnished with a pair of heavy old-fashioned steel snuffers.   Up to this time, his mind had been too much occupied to think of the light.   He had left the wick of the candle unsnuffed, till it had risen higher than the flame, and had burnt into an odd pent-house shape at the top, from which morsels of the charred cotton fell off, from time to time, in little flakes.   He took up the snuffers now, and trimmed the wick.   The light brightened directly, and the room became less dismal.

Again he turned to the riddles ; reading them doggedly and resolutely, now in one corner of the card, now in another.   All his efforts, however, could not fix his attention on them.   He pursued his occupation mechanically, deriving no sort of impression from what he was reading.   It was as if a shadow from the curtained bed had got between his mind and the gaily printed letters—a shadow that nothing could dispel.   At last, he gave up the struggle, and threw the card from him impatiently, and took to walking softly up and down the room again.

The dead man, the dead man, the *hidden* dead man on the bed ! There was the one persistent idea still haunting him.   Hidden ? Was it only the body being there, or was it the body being there, concealed, that was preying on his mind ?   He stopped at the window, with that doubt in him ; once more listening to the pattering rain, once more looking out into the black darkness.

Still the dead man !   The darkness forced his mind back upon itself, and set his memory at work, reviving, with a painfully-vivid distinctness the momentary impression it had received from the first sight of the corpse. Before long the face seemed to be hovering out in the middle of the darkness, confronting him through the window, with the paleness whiter, with the dreadful dull line of light between the imperfectly-closed eyelids broader than he had seen it—with the parted lips slowly dropping farther and farther away from each other—with the features growing larger and moving closer, till they seemed to fill the window and to silence the rain, and to shut out the night.

The sound of a voice, shouting below stairs, woke him suddenly from the dream of his own distempered fancy. He recognised it as the voice of the landlord. "Shut up at twelve, Ben," he heard it say. "I'm off to bed."

He wiped away the damp that had gathered on his forehead, reasoned with himself for a little while, and resolved to shake his mind free of the ghastly counterfeit which still clung to it, by forcing himself to confront, if it was only for a moment, the solemn reality.   Without allowing himself an instant to hesitate, he parted the curtains at the foot of the bed, and looked through.

There was a sad, peaceful, white face, with the awful mystery of stillness on it, laid back upon the pillow. No stir, no change there !   He only looked at it for a moment before he closed the curtains again—but that moment steadied him, calmed him, restored him—mind and body—to himself.

He returned to his old occupation of walking up and down the room ; persevering in it, this time, till the clock struck again. Twelve.

As the sound of the clock-bell died away, it was succeeded by the confused noise, downstairs, of the drinkers in the taproom leaving the house. The next sound, after an interval of silence, was caused by the barring of the door, and the closing of the shutters, at the back of the Inn. Then the silence followed again, and was disturbed no more.

He was alone now—absolutely, utterly, alone with the dead man, till the next morning.

The wick of the candle wanted trimming again.   He took up the snuffers—but paused suddenly on the very point of using them, and looked attentively at the candle—then back, over his shoulder, at the curtained bed—then again at the candle.   It had been lighted, for the first time, to show him the way upstairs, and three parts of it, at least, were already consumed.   In another hour it would be burnt out.   In another hour—unless he called at once to the man who had shut up the Inn, for a fresh candle—he would be left in the dark.

Strongly as his mind had been affected since he had entered the room, his unreasonable dread of encountering ridicule, and of exposing his courage to suspicion, had not altogether lost its influence over him, even yet.   He lingered irresolutely by the table, waiting till he could prevail on himself to open the door, and call, from the landing, to the man who had shut up the Inn. In his present hesitating frame of mind, it was a kind of relief to gain a few moments only by engaging in the trifling occupation of snuffing the candle.   His hand trembled a little, and the snuffers were heavy and awkward to use.   When he closed them on the wick, he closed them a hair's breath too low.   In an instant the candle was out, and the room was plunged in pitch darkness.

The one impression which the absence of light immediately produced on his mind, was distrust of the curtained bed—distrust which shaped itself into no distinct idea, but which was powerful enough, in its very vagueness, to bind him down to his chair, to make his heart beat fast, and to set him listening intently.   No sound stirred in the room but the familiar sound of the rain against the window, louder and sharper now than he had heard it yet.

Still the vague distrust, the inexpressible dread possessed him, and kept him to his chair.   He had put his carpet bag on the table, when he first entered the room ; and he now took the key from his pocket, reached out his hand softly, opened the bag, and groped in it for his travelling writing-case, in which he knew that there was a small store of matches.   When he had got one of the matches, he waited before he struck it on the coarse wooden table, and listened intently again, without knowing why.   Still there was no sound in the room but the steady, ceaseless, rattling sound of the rain.

He lighted the candle again, without another moment of delay; and, on the instant of its burning up, the first object in the room that his eyes sought for was the curtained bed.

Just before the light had been put out, he had looked in that direction, and had seen no change, no disarrangement of any sort, in the folds of the closely-drawn curtains.

When he looked at the bed, now, he saw, hanging over the side of it, a long white hand.

It lay perfectly motionless, midway on the side of the bed, where the curtain at the head and the curtain at the foot met. Nothing more was visible.   The clinging curtains hid everything but the long white hand.

He stood looking at it unable to stir, unable to call out; feeling nothing, knowing nothing, every faculty he possessed gathered up and lost in the one seeing faculty.   How long that first panic held him he never could tell afterwards.   It might have been only for a moment; it might have been for many minutes together.   How he got to the bed—whether he ran to it headlong, or whether he approached it slowly—how he wrought himself up to unclose the curtains and look in, he never his remembered, and never will remember to his dying day. It is enough that he did go to the bed, and that he did look inside the curtains.

The man had moved.   One of his arms was outside the clothes; his face was turned a little on the pillow; his eyelids were wide open.   Changed as to position, and as to one of the features, the face was, otherwise, fearfully and wonderfully unaltered.   The dead paleness and the dead quiet were on it still.

One glance showed Arthur this—one glance, before he flew breathlessly to the door, and alarmed the house.

The man whom the landlord called " Ben," was the first to appear on the stairs.   In three words, Arthur told him what had happened, and sent him for the nearest doctor.

I, who tell you this story, was then staying with a medical friend of mine, in practice at Doncaster, taking care of his patients for him, during his absence in London; and I, for the time being, was the nearest doctor.   They had sent for me from the Inn, when the stranger was taken ill in the afternoon; but I was not at home, and medical assistance was sought for elsewhere.   When the man from The Two Robins rang the nightbell, I was just thinking of going to bed.   Naturally enough, I did not believe a word of his story about "a dead man who had come to life again."   However, I put on my hat, armed myself with one or two bottles of restorative medicine, and ran to the Inn, expecting to find nothing more remarkable, when I got there, than a patient in a fit.

My surprise at finding that the man had spoken the literal truth was almost, if not quite, equalled by my astonishment at finding myself face to face with Arthur Holliday as soon as I entered the bedroom.   It was no time then for giving or seeking explanations.   We just shook hands amazedly; and then I ordered everybody but Arthur out of the room, and hurried to the man on the bed.

The kitchen fire had not been long out.   There was plenty of hot water in the boiler, and plenty of flannel to be had. With these, with my medicines, and with such help as Arthur could render under my direction, I dragged the man, literally, out of the jaws of death.   In less than an hour from the time when I had been called in, he was alive and talking in the bed on which he had been laid out to wait for the Coroner's inquest.

You will naturally ask me, what had been the matter with him; and I might treat you, in reply, to a long theory, plentifully sprinkled with, what the children call, hard words.   I prefer telling you that, in this case, cause and effect could not be satisfactorily joined together by any theory whatever. There are mysteries in life, and the condition of it, which human science has not fathomed yet; and I candidly confess to you, that, in bringing that man back to existence, I was, morally speaking, groping hap-hazard in the dark.   I know (from the testimony of the doctor who attended him in the afternoon) that the vital machinery, so far as its action is appreciable by our senses, had, in this case, unquestionably stopped; and I am equally certain (seeing that I recovered him) that the vital principle was not extinct.   When I add, that he had suffered from a long and complicated illness, and that his whole nervous system was utterly deranged, I have told you all I really know of the physical condition of my dead-alive patient at The Two Robins Inn.

When he "came to," as the phrase goes, he was a startling object to look at, with his colourless face, his sunken cheeks, his wild black eyes, and his long black hair. The first question he asked me about himself, when he could speak, made me suspect that I had been called in to a man in my own profession. I mentioned to him my surmise; and he told me that I was right.

He said he had come last from Paris, where he had been attached to a hospital. That he had lately returned to England, on his way to Edinburgh, to continue his studies; that he had been taken ill on the journey; and that he had stopped to rest and recover himself at Doncaster. He did not add a word about his name, or who he was: and, of course, I did not question him on the subject. All I inquired, when he ceased speaking, was what branch of the profession he intended to follow.

"Any branch," he said, bitterly, "which will put bread into the mouth of a poor man."

At this, Arthur, who had been hitherto watching him in silent curiosity, burst out impetuously in his usual good-humoured way:—

"My dear fellow!" (everybody was "my dear fellow" with Arthur) "now you have come to life again, don't begin by being downhearted about your prospects. I'll answer for it, I can help you to some capital thing in the medical line—or, if I can't, I know my father can."

The medical student looked at him steadily.

"Thank you," he said, coldly. Then added, "May I ask who your father is?"

"He's well enough known all about this part of the country," replied Arthur. "He is a great manufacturer, and his name is Holliday"

My hand was on the man's wrist during this brief conversation. The instant the name of Holliday was pronounced I felt the pulse under my fingers flutter, stop, go on suddenly with a bound, and beat afterwards, for a minute or two, at the fever rate.

"How did you come here?" asked the stranger, quickly, excitably, passionately almost.

Arthur related briefly what had happened from the time of his first taking the bed at the inn.

"I am indebted to Mr. Holliday's son then for the help that has saved my life," said the medical student, speaking to himself, with a singular sarcasm in his voice.   "Come here!"

He held out, as he spoke, his long, white, bony, right hand.

"With all my heart," said Arthur, taking the hand cordially. "I may confess it now," he continued, laughing. "Upon my honour, you almost frightened me out of my wits."

The stranger did not seem to listen. His wild black eyes were fixed with a look of eager interest on Arthur's face, and his long bony fingers kept tight hold of Arthur's hand. Young Holliday, on his side, returned the gaze, amazed and puzzled by the medical student's odd language and manners. The two faces were close together; I looked at them; and, to my amazement, I was suddenly impressed by the sense of a likeness between them—not in features, or complexion, but solely in expression. It must have been a strong likeness, or I should certainly not have found it out, for I am naturally slow at detecting resemblances between faces.

"You have saved my life," said the strange man, still looking hard in Arthur's face, still holding tightly by his hand. "If you had been my own brother, you could not have done more for me than that."

He laid a singularly strong emphasis on those three words "my own brother," and a change passed over his face as he pronounced them,—a change that no language of mine is competent to describe.

"I hope I have not done being of service to you yet," said Arthur. "I'll speak to my father, as soon as I get home."

"You seem to be fond and proud of your father," said the medical student. "I suppose, in return, he is fond and proud of you?"

"Of course, he is!" answered Arthur, laughing. "Is there anything wonderful in that? Isn't *your* father fond——"

The stranger suddenly dropped young Holliday's hand, and turned his face away.

"I beg your pardon," said Arthur. "I hope I have not unintentionally pained you. I hope you have not lost your father."

"I can't well lose what I have never had," retorted the medical student, with a harsh, mocking laugh.

"What you have never had!"

The strange man suddenly caught Arthur's hand again, suddenly looked once more hard in his face.

"Yes," he said, with a repetition of the bitter laugh. "You have brought a poor devil back into the world, who has no business there. Do I astonish you? Well! I have a fancy of my own for telling you what men in my situation generally keep a secret. I have no name and no father. The merciful law of Society tells me I am Nobody's Son! Ask your father if he will be my father too, and help me on in life with the family name."

Arthur looked at me, more puzzled than ever. I signed to him to say nothing, and then laid my fingers again on the man's wrist. No! In spite of the extraordinary speech that he had just made, he was not, as I had been disposed to suspect, beginning to get light-headed. His pulse, by this time, had fallen back to a quiet, slow beat, and his skin was moist and cool. Not a symptom of fever or agitation about him.

Finding that neither of us answered him, he turned to me, and began talking of the extraordinary nature of his case, and asking my advice about the future course of medical treatment to which he ought to subject himself. I said the matter required careful thinking over, and suggested that I should submit certain prescriptions to him the next morning. He told me to write them at once, as he would, most likely, be leaving Doncaster, in the morning, before I was up. It was quite useless to represent to him the folly and danger of such a proceeding as this. He heard me politely and patiently, but held to his resolution, without offering any reasons or any explanations, and repeated to me, that if I wished to give him a chance of seeing my prescription, I must write it at once. Hearing this, Arthur volunteered the loan of a travelling writing-case, which, he said, he had with him; and, bringing it to the bed, shook the note-paper out of the pocket of the case forthwith in his usual careless way. With the paper, there fell out on the counterpane of the bed a small packet of sticking-plaster, and a little water-colour drawing of a landscape.

The medical student took up the drawing and looked at it.

His eye fell on some initials neatly written, in cypher, in one corner. He started and trembled ; his pale face grew whiter than ever ; his wild black eyes turned on Arthur, and looked through and through him.

"A pretty drawing," he said in a remarkably quiet tone of voice.

"Ah ! and done by such a pretty girl," said Arthur. "Oh, such a pretty girl ! I wish it was not a landscape—I wish it was a portrait of her !"

"You admire her very much ?"

Arthur half in jest, half in earnest, kissed his hand for answer.

"Love at first sight !" he said, putting the drawing away again. "But the course of it doesn't run smooth. It's the old story. She's monopolised as usual. Trammelled by a rash engagement to some poor man who is never likely to get money enough to marry her. It was lucky I heard of it in time, or I should certainly have risked a declaration when she gave me that drawing. Here, doctor ! Here is pen, ink, and paper all ready for you."

"When she gave you that drawing ? Gave it. Gave it." He repeated the words slowly to himself, and suddenly closed his eyes. A momentary distortion passed across his face, and I saw one of his hands clutch up the bedclothes and squeeze them hard. I thought he was going to be ill again, and begged that there might be no more talking. He opened his eyes when I spoke, fixed them once more searchingly on Arthur, and said, slowly and distinctly, "You like her, and she likes you. The poor man may die out of your way. Who can tell that she may not give you herself as well as her drawing, after all ?"

Before young Holliday could answer, he turned to me, and said in a whisper, "Now for the prescription." From that time, though he spoke to Arthur again, he never looked at him more.

When I had written the prescription, he examined it, approved of it, and then astonished us both by abruptly wishing us good night. I offered to sit up with him, and he shook his head. Arthur offered to sit up with him, and he said, shortly, with his face turned away, "No." I insisted on having somebody left to watch him. He gave way when he found I was determined, and said he would accept the services of the waiter at the inn.

"Thank you, both," he said, as we rose to go. "I have one last favour to ask—not of you, doctor, for I leave you to exercise your professional discretion—but of Mr. Holliday." His eyes, while he spoke, still rested steadily on me, and never once turned towards Arthur. "I beg that Mr. Holliday will not mention to any one—least of all to his father—the events that have occurred, and the words that have passed, in this room. I entreat him to bury me in his memory, as, but for him, I might have been buried in my grave. I cannot give my reasons for making this strange request. I can only implore him to grant it."

His voice faltered for the first time, and he hid his face on the pillow. Arthur, completely bewildered, gave the required pledge. I took young Holliday away with me, immediately afterwards, to the house of my friend ; determining to go back to the inn, and to see the medical student again before he had left in the morning.

I returned to the inn at eight o'clock, purposely abstaining from waking Arthur, who was sleeping off the past night's excitement on one of my friend's sofas. A suspicion had occurred to me as soon as I was alone in my bedroom, which made me resolve that Holliday and the stranger whose life he had saved should not meet again, if I could prevent it. I have already alluded to certain reports, or scandals, which I knew of, relating to the early life of Arthur's father. While I was thinking, in my bed, of what had passed at the Inn—of the change in the student's pulse when he heard the name of Holliday ; of the resemblance of expression that I had discovered between his face and Arthur's ; of the emphasis he had laid on those three words, "my own brother;" and of his incomprehensible acknowledgment of his own illegitimacy— while I was thinking of these things, the reports I have mentioned suddenly flew into my mind, and linked themselves fast to the chain of my previous reflections. Something within me whispered, "It is best that those two young men should not meet again." I felt it before I slept ; I felt it when I woke ; and I went, as I told you, alone to the Inn the next morning.

I had missed my only opportunity of seeing my nameless

patient again. He had been gone nearly an hour when I inquired for him.

I have now told you everything that I know for certain, in relation to the man whom I brought back to life in the double-bedded room of the Inn at Doncaster.   What I have next to add is matter for inference and surmise, and is not, strictly speaking, matter of fact.

I have to tell you, first, that the medical student turned out to be strangely and unaccountably right in assuming it as more than probable that Arthur Holliday would marry the young lady who had given him the water-colour drawing of the landscape. That marriage took place a little more than a year after the events occurred which I have just been relating.   The young couple came to live in the neighbourhood in which I was then established in practice.   I was present at the wedding, and was rather surprised to find that Arthur was singularly reserved with me, both before and after his marriage, on the subject of the young lady's prior engagement.   He only referred to it once, when we were alone, merely telling me, on that occasion, that his wife had done all that honour and duty required of her in the matter, and that the engagement had been broken off with the full approval of her parents.   I never heard more from him than this.   For three years he and his wife lived together happily.   At the expiration of that time, the symptoms of a serious illness first declared themselves in Mrs. Arthur Holliday.   It turned out to be a long, lingering, hopeless malady.   I attended her throughout.   We had been great friends when she was well, and we became more attached to each other than ever when she was ill.   I had many long and interesting conversations with her in the intervals when she suffered least.   The result of one of these conversations I may briefly relate, leaving you to draw any inferences from it that you please.

The interview to which I refer, occurred shortly before her death. I called one evening, as usual, and found her alone, with a look in her eyes which told me that she had been crying.   She only informed me at first, that she had been depressed in spirits ; but, by little and little, she became more communicative, and confessed to me that she had been looking over some old letters, which had been addressed to her, before she had seen Arthur, by a man to whom she had been engaged to be married. I asked her how the engagement came to be broken off. She replied that it had not been broken off, but that it had died out in a very mysterious way. The person to whom she was engaged — her first love, she called him—was very poor, and there was no immediate prospect of their being married. He followed my profession, and went abroad to study. They had corresponded regularly, until the time when, as she believed, he had returned to England. From that period she heard no more of him. He was of a fretful, sensitive temperament; and she feared that she might have inadvertently done or said something that offended him. However that might be, he had never written to her again; and, after waiting a year, she had married Arthur. I asked when the first estrangement had begun, and found that the time at which she ceased to hear anything of her first lover exactly corresponded with the time at which I had been called in to my mysterious patient at The Two Robins Inn.

A fortnight after that conversation, she died. In course of time, Arthur married again. Of late years, he has lived principally in London, and I have seen little or nothing of him.

I have many years to pass over before I can approach to anything like a conclusion of this fragmentary narrative. And even when that later period is reached, the little that I have to say will not occupy your attention for more than a few minutes. Between six and seven years ago, the gentleman to whom I introduced you in this room, came to me, with good professional recommendations, to fill the position of my assistant. We met, not like strangers, but like friends—the only difference between us being, that I was very much surprised to see him, and that he did not appear to be at all surprised to see me. If he was my son, or my brother I believe he could not be fonder of me than he is; but he has never volunteered any confidences since he has been here, on the subject of his past life. I saw something that was familiar to me in his face when we first met; and yet it was also something that suggested the idea of change. I had a notion once that my patient at the Inn might be a natural son of Mr. Holliday's; I had another idea that he might also have been the man who was engaged to Arthur's first wife; and I have a third idea, still clinging to me, that Mr. Lorn is the only man in England who could really enlighten me, if he chose, on both those doubtful points. His hair is not black, now, and his eyes are dimmer than the piercing eyes that I remember, but, for all that, he is very like the nameless medical student of my young days—very like him. And, sometimes, when I come home late at night, and find him asleep, and wake him, he looks, in coming to, wonderfully like the stranger at Doncaster, as he raised himself in the bed on that memorable night!

The doctor paused. Mr. Goodchild who had been following every word that fell from his lips, up to this time, leaned forward eagerly to ask a question. Before he could say a word, the latch of the door was raised, without any warning sound of footsteps in the passage outside. A long, white, bony hand appeared through the opening, gently pushing the door, which was prevented from working freely on its hinges by a fold in the carpet under it.

"That hand! Look at that hand, Doctor!" said Mr. Goodchild, touching him.

At the same moment, the doctor looked at Mr. Goodchild, and whispered to him, significantly:

"Hush! he has come back."

CHAPTER III.

The Cumberland Doctor's mention of Doncaster Races, inspired Mr. Francis Goodchild with the idea of going down to Don caster to see the races. Doncaster being a good way off, and quite out of the way of the Idle Apprentices (if anything could be out of their way, who had no way), it necessarily followed that Francis perceived Doncaster in the race-week to be, of all possible idlenesses, the particular idleness that would completely satisfy him.

Thomas, with an enforced idleness grafted on the natural and voluntary power of his disposition, was not of this mind; objecting that a man compelled to lie on his back on a floor, a sofa, a table, a line of chairs, or anything he could get to lie upon, was not in racing condition, and that he desired nothing better than to lie where he was, enjoying himself in looking at the flies on the ceiling. But, Francis Goodchild, who had been walking round his companion in a circuit of twelve miles for two days, and had begun to doubt whether it was reserved for him ever to be idle in his life, not only overpowered this objection, but even converted Thomas Idle to a scheme he formed (another idle inspiration), of conveying the said Thomas to the sea-coast, and putting his injured leg under a stream of salt-water.

Plunging into this happy conception headforemost, Mr. Goodchild immediately referred to the county-map, and ardently discovered that the most delicious piece of sea-coast to be found within the limits of England, Ireland, Scotland, Wales, the Isle of Man, and the Channel Islands, all summed up together, was Allonby on the coast of Cumberland. There was the coast of Scotland opposite to Allonby, said Mr. Goodchild with enthusiasm ; there was a fine Scottish mountain on that Scottish coast ; there were Scottish lights to be seen shining across the glorious Channel, and at Allonby itself there was every idle luxury (no doubt), that a watering-place could offer to the heart of idle man.   Moreover, said Mr. Goodchild, with his finger on the map, this exquisite retreat was approached by a coach-road, from a railway-station called Aspatria —a name, in a manner, suggestive of the departed glories of Greece, associated with one of the most engaging and most famous of Greek women.   On this point, Mr. Goodchild continued at intervals to breathe a vein of classic fancy and eloquence exceedingly irksome to Mr. Idle, until it appeared that the honest English pronunciation of that Cumberland country shortened Aspatria into " Spatter."   After this supplementary discovery, Mr. Goodchild said no more about it.

By way of Spatter, the crippled Idle was carried, hoisted, pushed, poked, and packed, into and out of carriages, into and out of beds, into and out of tavern resting-places, until he was brought at length within sniff of the sea. And now, behold the apprentices gallantly riding into Allonby in a one-horse fly, bent upon staying in that peaceful marine valley until the turbulent Doncaster time shall come round upon the wheel, in its turn among what are in sporting registers called the "Fixtures " for the month.

"Do you see Allonby !" asked Thomas Idle.

"I don't see it yet," said Francis looking out of window.

"It must be there," said Thomas Idle.

"I don't see it," returned Francis.

"It must be there," repeated Thomas Idle, fretfully.

"Lord bless me !" exclaimed Francis, drawing in his head, "I suppose this is it !"

"A watering-place," retorted Thomas Idle, with the pardonable sharpness of an invalid, " can't be five gentlemen in strawhats, on a form on one side of a door, and four ladies in hats and falls, on a form on another side of a door, and three geese in a dirty little brook before them, and a boy's legs hanging over a bridge (with a boy's body I suppose on the other side of the parapet), and a donkey running away. What are you talking about ?"

"Allonby, gentlemen," said the most comfortable of land-ladies, as she opened one door of the carriage; "Allonby, gentlemen," said the most attentive of landlords, as he opened the other.

Thomas Idle yielded his arm to the ready Goodchild, and descended from the vehicle. Thomas, now just able to grope his way along, in a doubled-up condition, with the aid of two thick sticks, was no bad embodiment of Commodore Trunnion, or of one of those many gallant Admirals of the stage, who have all ample fortunes, gout, thick-sticks, tempers, wards, and nephews. With this distinguished naval appearance upon him, Thomas made a crab-like progress up a clean little bulk-headed staircase, into a clean little bulk-headed room, where he slowly deposited himself on a sofa, with a stick on either hand of him, looking exceedingly grim.

"Francis," said Thomas Idle, "what do you think of this place?"

"I think," returned Mr. Goodchild, in a glowing way, "it is everything we expected."

"Hah!" said Thomas Idle.

"There is the sea," cried Mr. Goodchild, pointing out of window; "and here," pointing to the lunch on the table, "are shrimps. Let us——" here Mr. Goodchild looked out of window, as if in search of something, and looked in again,—"let us eat 'em."

The shrimps eaten and the dinner ordered, Mr. Goodchild went out to survey the watering-place. As Chorus of the Drama, without whom Thomas could make nothing of the scenery, he by-and-bye returned, to have the following report screwed out of him.

In brief, it was the most delightful place ever seen.

"But," Thomas Idle asked, "where is it?"

"It's what you may call generally up and down the beach, here and there," said Mr. Goodchild, with a twist of his hand.

"Proceed," said Thomas Idle.

It was, Mr. Goodchild went on to say, in cross-examination, what you might call a primitive place. Large? No, it was not large. Who ever expected it would be large? Shape? What a question to ask! No shape. What sort of a street? Why, no street. Shops? Yes, of course (quite indignant). How many? Who ever went into a place to count the shops? Ever so many. Six? Perhaps. A library? Why, of course (indignant again). Good collection of books? Most likely—couldn't say—had seen nothing in it but a pair of scales. Any reading-room? Of course, there was a reading-room. Where? Where! why, over there. Where was over there? Why, *there!* Let Mr. Idle carry his eye to that bit of waste-ground above high water-mark, where the rank grass and loose stones were most in a litter; and he would see a sort of a long ruinous brick loft, next door to a ruinous brick outhouse, which loft had a ladder outside, to get up by. That was the reading-room, and if Mr. Idle didn't like the idea of a weaver's shuttle throbbing under a reading-room, that was his look out. *He* was not to dictate, Mr. Goodchild supposed (indignant again), to the company.

"By-the-bye," Thomas Idle observed; "the company?"

Well! (Mr. Goodchild went on to report) very nice company. Where were they? Why, there they were. Mr. Idle could see the tops of their hats, he supposed. What? Those nine straw hats again, five gentlemen's and four ladies'? Yes, to be sure. Mr. Goodchild hoped the company were not to be expected to wear helmets, to please Mr. Idle.

Beginning to recover his temper at about this point, Mr. Goodchild voluntarily reported that if you wanted to be primitive, you could be primitive here, and that if you wanted to be idle, you could be idle here. In the course of some days, he added, that there were three fishing-boats, but no rigging, and that there were plenty of fishermen who never fished. That they got their living entirely by looking at the ocean. What nourishment they looked out of it to support their strength, he couldn't say; but, he supposed it was some sort of Iodine. The place was full of their children, who were always upside down on the public buildings (two small bridges over the brook), and always hurting themselves or one another, so that their wailings made more continual noise in the air than could have been got in a busy place. The houses people lodged in, were nowhere in particular, and were in capital accordance with the beach; being all more or less cracked and damaged as its shells were, and all empty—as its shells were. Among them, was an edifice of destitute appearance, with a number of wall-eyed windows in it, looking desperately out to Scotland as if for help, which said it was a Bazaar (and it ought to know), and where you might buy anything you wanted—supposing what you wanted, was a little camp-stool or a child's wheelbarrow. The brook crawled or stopped between the houses and the sea, and the donkey was always running away, and when he got into the brook he was pelted out with stones, which never hit him, and which always hit some of the children who were upside down on the public buildings, and made their lamentations louder. This donkey was the public excitement of Allonby, and was probably supported at the public expense.

The foregoing descriptions, delivered in separate items, on separate days of adventurous discovery, Mr. Goodchild severally wound up, by looking out of window, looking in again, and saying, " But there is the sea, and here are the shrimps—let us eat 'em."

There were fine sunsets at Allonby when the low flat beach, with its pools of water and its dry patches, changed into long bars of silver and gold in various states of burnishing, and there were fine views—on fine days—of the Scottish coast. But, when it rained at Allonby, Allonby thrown back upon its ragged self, became a kind of place which the donkey seemed to have found out, and to have his highly sagacious reasons for wishing to bolt from. Thomas Idle observed, too, that Mr. Goodchild, with a noble show of disinterestedness, became every day more ready to walk to Maryport and back, for letters ; and suspicions began to harbour in the mind of Thomas, that his friend deceived him, and that Maryport was a preferable place.

Therefore, Thomas said to Francis on a day when they had looked at the sea and eaten the shrimps, " My mind misgives me, Goodchild, that you go to Maryport, like the boy in the story-book, to ask *it* to be idle with you."

" Judge, then," returned Francis, adopting the style of the story-book, " with what success. I go to a region which is a bit of water-side Bristol, with a slice of Wapping, a seasoning of Wolverhampton, and a garnish of Portsmouth, and I say, 'Will *you* come and be idle with me ?' And it answers, 'No ; for I am a great deal too vaporous, and a great deal too rusty, and a great deal too muddy, and a great deal too dirty altogether; and

I have ships to load, and pitch and tar to boil, and iron to hammer, and steam to get up, and smoke to make, and stone to quarry, and fifty other disagreeable things to do, and I can't be idle with you.' Then I go into jagged up-hill and down-hill streets, where I am in the pastrycook's shop at one moment, and next moment in savage fastnesses of moor and morass, beyond the confines of civilisation, and I say to those murky and black-dusky streets, 'Will *you* come and be idle with me?' To which they reply, ' No, we can't, indeed, for we haven't the spirits, and we are startled by the echo of your feet on the sharp pavement, and we have so many goods in our shop-windows which nobody wants, and we have so much to do for a limited public which never comes to us to be done for, that we are altogether out of sorts and can't enjoy ourselves with any one.' So I go to the Post-office, and knock at the shutter, and I say to the Post-master, ' Will *you* come and be idle with me ?' To which he rejoins, ' No, I really can't, for I live, as you may see, in such a very little Post-office, and pass my life behind such a very little shutter, that my hand, when I put it out, is as the hand of a giant crammed through the window of a dwarf's house at a fair, and I am a mere Post-office anchorite in a cell much too small for him, and I can't get out, and I can't get in, and I have no space to be idle in, even if I would.' So, the boy," said Mr. Goodchild, concluding the tale, " comes back with the letters after all, and lives happy never afterwards."

But it may, not unreasonably, be asked—while Francis Goodchild was wandering hither and thither, storing his mind with perpetual observation of men and things, and sincerely believing himself to be the laziest creature in existence all the time—how did Thomas Idle, crippled and confined to the house, contrive to get through the hours of the day?

Prone on the sofa, Thomas made no attempt to get through the hours, but passively allowed the hours to get through *him.* Where other men in his situation would have read books and improved their minds, Thomas slept and rested his body. Where other men would have pondered anxiously over their future prospects, Thomas dreamed lazily of his past life. The one solitary thing he did, which most other people would have done in his place, was to resolve on making certain alterations and improvements in his mode of existence, as soon as the effects of the misfortune that had overtaken him had all passed away Remembering that the current of his life had hitherto oozed along in one smooth stream of laziness, occasionally troubled on the surface by a slight passing ripple of industry, his present ideas on the subject of self-reform, inclined him—not as the reader may be disposed to imagine, to project schemes for a new existence of enterprise and exertion—but, on the contrary, to resolve that he would never, if he could possibly help it, be active or industrious again, throughout the whole of his future career.

It is due to Mr. Idle to relate that his mind sauntered towards this peculiar conclusion on distinct and logically-producible grounds. After reviewing, quite at his ease, and with many needful intervals of repose, the generally-placid spectacle of his past existence, he arrived at the discovery that all the great disasters which had tried his patience and equanimity in early life, had been caused by his having allowed himself to be deluded into imitating some pernicious example of activity and industry that had been set him by others. The trials to which he here alludes were three in number, and may be thus reckoned up : First, the disaster of being an unpopular and a thrashed boy at school ; secondly, the disaster of falling seriously ill ; thirdly, the disaster of becoming acquainted with a great bore.

The first disaster occurred after Thomas had been an idle and a popular boy at school, for some happy years. One Christmas-time, he was stimulated by the evil example of a companion, whom he had always trusted and liked, to be untrue to himself, and to try for a prize at the ensuing half-yearly examination. He did try, and he got a prize—how, he did not distinctly know at the moment, and cannot remember now. No sooner, however, had the book—Moral Hints to the Young on the Value of Time — been placed in his hands, than the first troubles of his life began. The idle boys deserted him, as a traitor to their cause. The industrous boys avoided him, as a dangerous interloper ; one of their number, who had always won the prize on previous occasions, expressing just resentment at the invasion of his privileges by calling Thomas into the play-ground, and then and there administering to him the first sound and genuine thrashing that he had ever received in his life. Unpopular from that moment, as a beaten boy, who belonged to no side and was rejected by all parties, young Idle soon lost caste with his masters, as he had previously lost caste with his school-fellows.   He had forfeited the comfortable reputation of being the one lazy member of the youthful community whom it was quite hopeless to punish.   Never again did he hear the head-master say reproachfully to an industrious boy who had committed a fault, "I might have expected this in Thomas Idle, but it is inexcusable, sir, in you, who know better."   Never more, after winning that fatal prize, did he escape the retributive imposition, or the avenging birch.   From that time, the masters made him work, and the boys would not let him play.   From that time his social position steadily declined, and his life at school became a perpetual burden to him.

So, again, with the second disaster.   While Thomas was lazy, he was a model of health.   His first attempt at active exertion and his first suffering from severe illness are connected together by the intimate relations of cause and effect. Shortly after leaving school, he accompanied a party of friends to a cricket-field, in his natural and appropriate character of spectator only.   On the ground it was discovered that the players fell short of the required number, and facile Thomas was persuaded to assist in making up the complement.   At a certain appointed time, he was roused from peaceful slumber in a dry ditch, and placed before three wickets with a bat in his hand.   Opposite to him, behind three more wickets, stood one of his bosom friends, filling the situation (as he was informed) of bowler.   No words can describe Mr. Idle's horror and amazement, when he saw this young man — on ordinary occasions, the meekest and mildest of human beings—suddenly contract his eyebrows, compress his lips, assume the aspect of an infuriated savage, run back a few steps, then run forward, and, without the slightest previous provocation, hurl a detestably hard ball with all his might straight at Thomas's legs.   Stimulated to preternatural activity of body and sharpness of eye by the instinct of self-preservation, Mr. Idle contrived, by jumping deftly aside at the right moment, and by using his bat (ridiculously narrow as it was for the purpose) as a shield, to preserve his life and limbs from the dastardly attack that had been made on both, to leave the full force of the deadly missile to strike his wicket instead of his leg; and to end the innings, so far as his side was concerned, by being immediately bowled out.   Grateful for his escape he was about to return to the dry ditch, when he was peremptorily stopped, and told that the other side was "going in," and that he was expected to "field."   His conception of the whole art and mystery of "fielding," may be summed up in the three words of serious advice which he privately administered to himself on that trying occasion —avoid the ball.   Fortified by this sound and salutary principle, he took his own course, impervious alike to ridicule and abuse.   Whenever the ball came near him, he thought of his shins, and got out of the way immediately.   "Catch it !" "Stop it !"   "Pitch it up !" were cries that passed by him like the idle wind that he regarded not.   He ducked under it, he jumped over it, he whisked himself away from it on either side.   Never once, through the whole innings did he and the ball come together on anything approaching to intimate terms. The unnatural activity of body which was necessarily called forth for the accomplishment of this result threw Thomas Idle, for the first time in his life, into a perspiration.   The perspiration, in consequence of his want of practice in the management of that particular result of bodily activity, was suddenly checked ; the inevitable chill succeeded ; and that, in its turn, was followed by a fever.   For the first time since his birth, Mr. Idle found himself confined to his bed for many weeks together, wasted and worn by a long illness, of which his own disastrous muscular exertion had been the sole first cause.

The third occasion on which Thomas found reason to reproach himself bitterly for the mistake of having attempted to be industrious, was connected with his choice of a calling in life.   Having no interest in the Church, he appropriately selected the next best profession for a lazy man in England— the Bar.   Although the Benchers of the Inns of Court have lately abandoned their good old principles, and oblige their students to make some show of studying, in Mr. Idle's time no such innovation as this existed.   Young men who aspired to the honourable title of barrister were, very properly, not asked to learn anything of the law, but were merely required to eat a certain number of dinners at the table of their Hall, and to pay a certain sum of money ; and were called to the Bar as soon as they could prove that they had sufficiently complied with these extremely sensible regulations.   Never did Thomas move more harmoniously in concert with his elders and betters than when he was qualifying himself for admission among the barristers of his native country.   Never did he feel more deeply what real laziness was in all the serene majesty of its nature, than on the memorable day when he was called to the bar, after having carefully abstained from opening his law-books during his period of probation, except to fall asleep over them.   How he could ever again have become industrious, even for the shortest period, after that great reward conferred upon his idleness, quite passes his comprehension.   The kind benchers did everything they could to show him the folly of exerting himself.   They wrote out his probationary exercise for him, and never expected him even to take the trouble of reading it through when it was written.   They invited him, with seven other choice spirits as lazy as himself, to come and be called to the bar, while they were sitting over their wine and fruit after dinner.   They put his oaths of allegiance, and his dreadful official denunciations of the Pope and the Pretender so gently into his mouth, that he hardly knew how the words got there.   They wheeled all their chairs softly round from the table, and sat surveying the young barristers with their backs to their bottles, rather than stand up, or adjourn to hear the exercises read.   And when Mr. Idle and the seven unlabouring neophytes, ranged in order, as a class, with their backs considerately placed against a screen, had begun, in rotation, to read the exercises which they had not written, even then, each Bencher, true to the great lazy principle of the whole proceeding, stopped each neophyte before he had stammered through his first line, and bowed to him, and told him politely that he was a barrister from that moment.   This was all the ceremony.   It was followed by a social supper, and by the presentation, in accordance with ancient custom, of a pound of sweetmeats and a bottle of Madeira, offered in the way of needful refreshment, by each grateful neophyte to each beneficent Bencher.   It may seem inconceivable that Thomas should ever have forgotten the great do-nothing principle instilled by such a ceremony as this; but it is, nevertheless, true, that certain designing students of industrious habits found him out, took advantage of his easy humour, persuaded him that it was discreditable to be a barrister and to know nothing whatever about the law, and lured him, by the force of their own

evil example, into a conveyancer's chambers, to make up for
lost time, and to qualify himself for practice at the Bar.   After
a fortnight of self-delusion, the curtain fell from his eyes ; he
resumed his natural character, and shut up his books.   But the
retribution which had hitherto always followed his little casual
errors of industry followed them still.   He could get away from
the conveyancer's chambers, but he could not get away from
one of the pupils, who had taken a fancy to him,—a tall, serious,
raw-boned, hard-working, disputatious pupil, with ideas of his
own about reforming the Law of Real Property, who has been
the scourge of Mr. Idle's existence ever since the fatal day when
he fell into the mistake of attempting to study the law.   Before
that time his friends were all sociable idlers like himself.   Since
that time the burden of bearing with a hard-working young man
has become part of his lot in life.   Go where he will now, he can
never feel certain that the raw-boned pupil is not affectionately
waiting for him round a corner, to tell him a little more
about the Law of Real Property.   Suffer as he may under the
infliction, he can never complain, for he must always remember,
with unavailing regret, that he has his own thoughtless industry
to thank for first exposing him to the great social calamity of
knowing a bore.

These events of his past life, with the significant results
that they brought about, pass drowsily through Thomas Idle's
memory, while he lies alone on the sofa at Allonby and elsewhere, dreaming away the time which his fellow-apprentice gets
through so actively out of doors.   Remembering the lesson of
laziness which his past disasters teach, and bearing in mind
also the fact that he is crippled in one leg because he exerted
himself to go up a mountain, when he ought to have known
that his proper course of conduct was to stop at the bottom of
it, he holds now, and will for the future firmly continue to hold,
by his new resolution never to be industrious again, on any
pretence whatever, for the rest of his life.   The physical results
of his accident have been related in a previous chapter.   The
moral results now stand on record ; and, with the enumeration
of these, that part of the present narrative which is occupied by
the Episode of The Sprained Ankle may now perhaps be considered, in all its aspects, as finished and complete.

"How do you propose that we get through this present

afternoon and evening?" demanded Thomas Idle, after two or three hours of the foregoing reflections at Allonby.

Mr. Goodchild faultered, looked out of window, looked in again, and said, as he had so often said before, "There is the sea, and here are the shrimps;—let us eat 'em!"

But, the wise donkey was at that moment in the act of bolting : not with the irresolution of his previous efforts which had been wanting in sustained force of character, but with real vigor of purpose : shaking the dust off his mane and hind-feet at Allonby, and tearing away from it, as if he had nobly made up his mind that he never would be taken alive. At sight of this inspiring spectacle, which was visible from his sofa, Thomas Idle stretched his neck and dwelt upon it rapturously.

"Francis Goodchild," he then said, turning to his companion with a solemn air, "this is a delightful little Inn, excellently kept by the most comfortable of landladies and the most attentive of landlords, but——the donkey's right!"

The words, "There is the sea, and here are the——," again trembled on the lips of Goodchild, unaccompanied however by any sound.

"Let us instantly pack the portmanteaus," said Thomas Idle, "pay the bill, and order a fly out, with instructions to the driver to follow the donkey!"

Mr. Goodchild, who had only wanted encouragement to disclose the real state of his feelings, and who had been pining beneath his weary secret, now burst into tears, and confessed that he thought another day in the place would be the death of him.

So, the two idle apprentices followed the donkey until the night was far advanced. Whether he was recaptured by the town-council, or is bolting at this hour through the United Kingdom, they know not. They hope he may be still bolting; if so, their best wishes are with him.

It entered Mr. Idle's head, on the borders of Cumberland, that there could be no idler place to stay at, except by snatches of a few minutes each, than a railway station. "An intermediate station on a line—a junction—anything of that sort," Thomas suggested. Mr. Goodchild approved of the idea as eccentric, and they journeyed on and on, until they came to such a station where there was an Inn.

"Here," said Thomas, "we may be luxuriously lazy; other people will travel for us, as it were, and we shall laugh at their folly."

It was a Junction-Station, where the wooden razors before mentioned shaved the air very often, and where the sharp electric-telegraph bell was in a very restless condition. All manner of cross-lines of rails came zig-zaging into it, like a Congress of iron vipers; and, a little way out of it, a pointsman in an elevated signal-box was constantly going through the motions of drawing immense quantities of beer at a public-house bar. In one direction, confused perspectives of embankments and arches were to be seen from the platform; in the other, the rails soon disentangled themselves into two tracks, and shot away under a bridge, and curved round a corner. Sidings were there, in which empty luggage-vans and cattle-boxes often butted against each other as if they couldn't agree; and warehouses were there, in which great quantities of goods seemed to have taken the veil (of the consistency of tarpaulin), and to have retired from the world without any hope of getting back to it. Refreshment-rooms were there; one, for the hungry and thirsty Iron Locomotives where their coke and water were ready, and of good quality, for they were dangerous to play tricks with; the other, for the hungry and thirsty human Locomotives, who might take what they could get, and whose chief consolation was provided in the form of three terrific urns or vases of white metal, containing nothing, each forming a breast-work for a defiant and apparently much-injured woman.

Established at this Station, Mr. Thomas Idle and Mr. Francis Goodchild resolved to enjoy it. But, its contrasts were very violent, and there was also an infection in it.

First, as to its contrasts. They were only two, but they were Lethargy and Madness. The Station was either totally unconscious, or wildly raving. By day, in its unconscious state, it looked as if no life could come to it,—as if it were all rust, dust, and ashes—as if the last train for ever, had gone without issuing any Return-Tickets—as if the last Engine had uttered its last shriek and burst. One awkward shave of the air from the wooden razor, and everything changed. Tight office-doors flew open, panels yielded, books, newspapers, travelling-caps and wrappers broke out of brick walls, money chinked, conveyances oppressed by nightmares of luggage came careering into the yard, porters started up from secret places, ditto the much-injured women, the shining bell, whe lived in a little tray on stilts by himself, flew into a man's hand and clamoured violently.   The pointsman aloft in the signal-box made the motions of drawing, with some difficulty, hogs-heads of beer.   Down Train !   More beer.   Up Train !   More beer.   Cross Junction Train !   More beer.   Cattle Train ! More beer.   Goods Train !   Simmering, whistling, trembling, rumbling, thundering.   Trains on the whole confusion of inter-secting rails, crossing one another, bumping one another, hissing one another, backing to go forward, tearing into dis-tance to come close.   People frantic.   Exiles seeking restora-tion to their native carriages, and banished to remoter climes. More beer and more bell.   Then, in a minute, the Station re-lapsed into stupor as the stoker of the Cattle Train, the last to depart, went gliding out of it, wiping the long nose of his oil-can with a dirty pocket-handkerchief.

By night, in its unconscious state, the station was not so much as visible.   Something in the air, like an enterprising chemist's established in business on one of the boughs of Jack's beanstalk, was all that could be discerned of it under the stars. In a moment it would break out, a constellation of gas.   In another moment, twenty rival chemists, on twenty rival beanstalks, came into existence.   Then, the Furies would be seen, waving their lurid torches up and down the confused perspectives of embank-ments and arches—would be heard, too, wailing and shrieking. Then, the Station would be full of palpitating trains, as in the day; with the heightening difference that they were not so clearly seen as in the day, whereas the station walls, starting forward under the gas, like a hippopotamus's eyes, dazzled the human loco-motives with the sauce-bottle, the cheap music, the bedstead, the distorted range of buildings where the patent safes are made, the gentleman in the rain with the registered umbrella, the lady returning from the ball with the registered respirator, and all their other embellishments.   And now, the human locomotives, creased as to their countenances and purblind as to their eyes, would swarm forth in a heap, addressing themselves to the mysterious urns and the much-injured women; while the iron loco-motives, dripping fire and water, shed their steam about plentifully, making the dull oxen in their cages, with heads depressed, and foam hanging from their mouths as their red looks glanced fearfully at the surrounding terrors, seem as though they had been drinking at half-frozen waters and were hung with icicles. Through the same steam would be caught glimpses of their fellow-travellers, the sheep, getting their white kid faces together, away from the bars, and stuffing the interstices with trembling wool. Also, down among the wheels, of the man with the sledge-hammer, ringing the axles of the fast night-train ; against whom the oxen have a misgiving that he is the man with the pole-axe who is to come by-and-bye, and so the nearest of them try to get back, and get a purchase for a thrust at him through the bars. Suddenly, the bell would ring, the steam would stop with one hiss and a yell, the chemists on the beanstalks would be busy, the avenging Furies would bestir themselves, the fast night-train would melt from eye and ear, the other trains going their ways more slowly would be heard faintly rattling in the distance like old-fashioned watches running down, the sauce-bottle and cheap music retired from view, even the bedstead went to bed, and there was no such visible thing as the Station to vex the cool wind in its blowing, or perhaps the autumn lightning, as it found out the iron rails.

The infection of the Station was this :—When it was in its raving state, the Apprentices found it impossible to be there, without labouring under the delusion that they were in a hurry. To Mr. Goodchild, whose ideas of idleness were so imperfect, this was no unpleasant hallucination, and accordingly that gentleman went through great exertions in yielding to it, and running up and down the platform, jostling everybody, under the impression that he had a highly important mission somewhere, and had not a moment to lose. But, to Thomas Idle, this contagion was so very unacceptable an incident of the situation, that he struck on the fourth day, and requested to be moved.

" This place fills me with a dreadful sensation," said Thomas, "of having something to do. Remove me, Francis."

" Where would you like to go next ?" was the question of the ever-engaging Goodchild.

"I have heard there is a good old Inn at Lancaster, established in a fine old house: an Inn where they give you Bride-cake every day after dinner," said Thomas Idle. "Let us eat Bride-cake without the trouble of being married, **or of knowing** anybody in that ridiculous dilemma."

Mr. Goodchild, with a lover's sigh, assented. They departed from the Station in a violent hurry (for which, it is unnecessary to observe, there was not the least occasion), and were delivered at the fine old house at Lancaster, on the same night.

It is Mr. Goodchild's opinion, that if a visitor on his arrival at Lancaster could be accommodated with a pole which would push the opposite side of the street some yards farther off, it would be better for all parties. Protesting against being required to live in a trench, and obliged to speculate all day upon what the people can possibly be doing within a mysterious opposite window, which is a shop-window to look at, but not a shop-window in respect of its offering nothing for sale and declining to give any account whatever of itself, Mr. Goodchild concedes Lancaster to be a pleasant place. A place dropped in the midst of a charming landscape, a place with a fine ancient fragment of castle, a place of lovely walks, a place possessing staid old houses richly fitted with old Honduras mahogany, which has grown so dark with time that it seems to have got something of a retrospective mirror-quality into itself, and to show the visitor, in the depth of its grain, through all its polish, the hue of the wretched slaves who groaned long ago under old Lancaster merchants. And Mr. Goodchild adds that the stones of Lancaster do sometimes whisper, even yet, of rich men passed away—upon whose great prosperity some of these old doorways frowned sullen in the brightest weather—that their slave-gain turned to curses, as the Arabian Wizard's money turned to leaves, and that no good ever came of it, even unto the third and fourth generations, until it was wasted and gone.

It was a gallant sight to behold, the Sunday procession of the Lancaster elders to Church—all in black, and looking fearfully like a funeral without the Body—under the escort of Three Beadles.

"Think," said Francis, as he stood at the Inn window, admiring, "of being taken to the sacred edifice by three Beadles! I have, in my early time, been taken out of it by one Beadle; but, to be taken into it by three, O Thomas, is a distinction I shall never enjoy!"

CHAPTER IV.

WHEN Mr. Goodchild had looked out of the Lancaster Inn-window for two hours on end, with great perseverance, he began to entertain a misgiving that he was growing industrious. He therefore set himself next, to explore the country from the tops of all the steep hills in the neighbourhood.

He came back at dinner-time, red and glowing, to tell Thomas Idle what he had see. Thomas, on his back reading, listened with great composure, and asked him whether he really had gone up those hills, and bothered himself with those views, and walked all those miles?

"Because I want to know," added Thomas, "what you would say of it, if you were obliged to do it?"

"It would be different, then," said Francis. "It would be work, then; now, it's play."

"Play!" replied Thomas Idle, utterly repudiating the reply. "Play! Here is a man goes systematically tearing himself to pieces, and putting himself through an incessant course of training, as if he were always under articles to fight a match for the champion's belt, and he calls it Play! Play!" exclaimed Thomas Idle, scornfully contemplating his one boot in the air. "You *can't* play. You don't know what it is. You make work of everything."

The bright Goodchild amiably smiled.

"So you do," said Thomas. "I mean it. To me you are an absolutely terrible fellow. You do nothing like another man. Where another fellow would fall into a footbath of action or emotion, you fall into a mine. Where any other fellow would be a painted butterfly, you are a fiery dragon. Where another man would stake a sixpence, you stake your existence. If you were to go up in a balloon, you would make for Heaven ; and if you were to dive into the depths of the earth, nothing short of the other place would content you. What a fellow you are, Francis !"

The cheerful Goodchild laughed.

"It's all very well to laugh, but I wonder you don't feel it to be serious," said Idle.   "A man who can do nothing by halves appears to me to be a fearful man."

"Tom, Tom," returned Goodchild, "if I can do nothing by halves, and be nothing by halves, it's pretty clear that you must take me as a whole, and make the best of me."

With this philosophical rejoinder, the airy Goodchild clapped Mr. Idle on the shoulder in a final manner, and they sat down to dinner.

" By the bye," said Goodchild, " I have been over a lunatic asylum too, since I have been out."

" He has been," exclaimed Thomas Idle, casting up his eyes, "over a lunatic asylum ! Not content with being as great an Ass as Captain Barclay in the pedestrian way, he makes a Lunacy Commissioner of himself—for nothing !"

"An immense place," said Goodchild, "admirable offices, very good arrangements, very good attendants; altogether a remarkable place."

"And what did you see there ?" asked Mr. Idle, adapting Hamlet's advice to the occasion, and assuming the virtue of interest, though he had it not.

"The usual thing," said Francis Goodchild, with a sigh. "Long groves of blighted men-and-women-trees ; interminable avenues of hopeless faces ; numbers, without the slightest power of really combining for any earthly purpose; a society of human creatures who have nothing in common but that they have all lost the power of being humanly social with one another."

"Take a glass of wine with me," said Thomas Idle, "and let *us* be social."

"In one gallery, Tom," pursued Francis Goodchild, "which looked to me about the length of the Long Walk at Windsor, more or less——"

" Probably less," observed Thomas Idle.

"In one gallery, which was otherwise clear of patients (for they were all out), there was a poor little dark-chinned, meagre man, with a perplexed brow and a pensive face, stooping low over the matting on the floor, and picking out with his thumb and forefinger the course of its fibres. The afternoon sun was slanting in at the large end-window, and there were cross patches of light and shade all down the vista, made by the unseen windows and the open doors of the little sleeping cells on either side. In about the centre of the perspective, under an arch, regardless of the pleasant weather, regardless of the solitude, regardless of approaching footsteps was the poor little dark-chinned, meagre man, poring over the matting. ' What are you doing there ?' said my conductor, when we came to him. He looked up, and pointed to the matting. ' I wouldn't do that, I think,' said my conductor, kindly; ' if I were you, I would go and read, or I would lie down if I felt tired ; but I wouldn't do that.' The patient considered a moment, and vacantly answered, ' No, sir, I won't; I'll—I'll go and read,' and so he lamely shuffled away into one of the little rooms. I turned my head before we had gone many paces. He had already come out again, and was again poring over the matting, and tracking out its fibres with his thumb and forefinger. I stopped to look at him, and it came into my mind, that probably the course of those fibres as they plaited in and out, over and under, was the only course of things in the whole wide world that it was left to him to understand — that his darkening intellect had narrowed down to the small cleft of light which showed him, ' This piece was twisted this way, went in here, passed under, came out there, was carried on away here to the right where I now put my finger on it, and in this progress of events, the thing was made and came to be here.' Then, I wondered whether he looked into the matting, next, to see if it could show him anything of the process through which *he* came to be there, so strangely poring over it. Then, I thought how all of us, GOD help us ! in our different ways are poring over our bits of matting, blindly enough, and what confusions and mysteries we make in the pattern. I had a sadder fellow-feeling with the little dark-chinned, meagre man, by that time, and I came away."

Mr. Idle diverting the conversation to grouse, custards, and

THE MADMAN.

bride-cake, Mr. Goodchild followed in the same direction. The bride-cake was as bilious and indigestible as if a real Bride had cut it, and the dinner it completed was an admirable performance.

The house was a genuine old house of a very quaint description, teeming with old carvings, and beams, and panels, and having an excellent old staircase, with a gallery or upper staircase, cut off from it by a curious fence-work of old oak, or of the old Honduras Mahogany wood. It was, and is, and will be, for many a long year to come, a remarkably picturesque house; and a certain grave mystery lurking in the depth of the old mahogany panels, as if they were so many deep pools of dark water—such, indeed, as they had been much among when they were trees—gave it a very mysterious character after nightfall.

When Mr. Goodchild and Mr. Idle had first alighted at the door, and stepped into the sombre handsome old hall, they had been received by half-a-dozen noiseless old men in black, all dressed exactly alike, who glided up the stairs with the obliging landlord and waiter—but without appearing to get into their way, or to mind whether they did or no—and who had filed off to the right and left on the old staircase, as the guests entered their sitting-room. It was then broad, bright day. But, Mr. Goodchild had said, when their door was shut, "Who on earth are those old men?" And afterwards, both on going out and coming in, he had noticed that there were no old men to be seen.

Neither, had the old men, or any one of the old men, re-appeared since. The two friends had passed a night in the house, but had seen nothing more of the old men. Mr. Goodchild, in rambling about it, had looked along passages, and glanced in at doorways, but had encountered no old men; neither did it appear that any old men were, by any member of the establishment, missed or expected.

Another odd circumstance impressed itself on their attention. It was, that the door of their sitting-room was never left untouched for a quarter of an hour. It was opened with hesitation, opened with confidence, opened a little way, opened a good way,—always clapped-to again without a word of explanation. They were reading, they were writing, they were eating, they were drinking, they were talking, they were dozing; the door was always opened at an unexpected moment, and they looked towards it, and it was clapped-to again, and nobody was to be seen. When this had happened fifty times or so, Mr. Goodchild had said to his companion, jestingly: "I begin to think, Tom, there was something wrong with those six old men."

Night had come again, and they had been writing for two or three hours : writing, in short, a portion of the lazy notes from which these lazy sheets are taken. They had left off writing, and glasses were on the table between them. The house was closed and quiet. Around the head of Thomas Idle, as he lay upon his sofa, hovered light wreaths of fragrant smoke. The temples of Francis Goodchild, as he leaned back in his chair, with his two hands clasped behind his head, and his legs crossed, were similarly decorated.

They had been discussing several idle subjects of speculation, not omitting the strange old men, and were still so occupied, when Mr. Goodchild abruptly changed his attitude to wind up his watch. They were just becoming drowsy enough to be stopped in their talk by any such slight check. Thomas Idle, who was speaking at the moment, paused and said, "How goes it?"

"One," said Goodchild.

As if he had ordered One old man, and the order were promptly executed (truly, all orders were so, in that excellent hotel), the door opened, and One old man stood there.

He did not come in, but stood with the door in his hand.

"One of the six, Tom, at last!" said Mr. Goodchild, in a surprised whisper.—"Sir, your pleasure?"

"Sir, *your* pleasure?" said the One old man

"I didn't ring."

"The bell did," said the One old man.

He said BELL, in a deep strong way, that would have expressed the church Bell.

"I had the pleasure, I believe, of seeing you, yesterday?" said Goodchild.

"I cannot undertake to say for certain," was the grim reply of the One old man.

"I think you saw me? Did you not?"

"Saw *you?*" said the old man. "O yes, I saw *you.* But, I see many who never see me."

A chilled, slow, earthy, fixed old man. A cadaverous old man of measured speech. An old man who seemed as unable to wink, as if his eyelids had been nailed to his forehead. An old man whose eyes—two spots of fire—had no more motion than if they had been connected with the back of his skull by screws driven through it, and rivetted and bolted outside, among his grey hair.

The night had turned so cold, to Mr. Goodchild's sensations, that he shivered. He remarked lightly, and half apologetically, " I think somebody is walking over my grave."

" No," said the weird old man, " there is no one there."

Mr. Goodchild looked at Idle, but Idle lay with his head enwreathed in smoke.

" No one there ? " said Goodchild.

" There is no one at your grave, I assure you," said the old man.

He had come in and shut the door, and he now sat down. He did not bend himself to sit, as other people do, but seemed to sink bolt upright, as if in water, until the chair stopped him.

" My friend, Mr. Idle," said Goodchild, extremely anxious to introduce a third person into the conversation.

" I am," said the old man, without looking at him, " at Mr. Idle's service."

" If you are an old inhabitant of this place," Francis Goodchild resumed :

" Yes."

" Perhaps you can decide a point my friend and I were in doubt upon, this morning. They hang condemned criminals at the Castle, I believe ? "

" *I* believe so," said the old man.

" Are their faces turned towards that noble prospect ? "

" Your face is turned," replied the old man, " to the Castle wall. When you are tied up, you see its stones expanding and contracting violently, and a similar expansion and contraction seem to take place in your own head and breast. Then, there is a rush of fire and an earthquake, and the Castle springs into the air, and you tumble down a precipice."

His cravat appeared to trouble him. He put his hand to

his throat, and moved his neck from side to side. He was an old man of a swollen character of face, and his nose was immoveably hitched up on one side, as if by a little hook inserted in that nostriL Mr. Goodchild felt exceedingly uncomfortable, and began to think the night was hot, and not cold.

"A strong description, sir," he observed.

"A strong sensation," the old man rejoined.

Again, Mr. Goodchild looked to Mr. Thomas Idle ; but Thomas lay on his back with his face attentively turned towards the One old man, and made no sign. At this time Mr. Goodchild believed that he saw threads of fire stretch from the old man's eyes to his own, and there attach themselves. (Mr. Goodchild writes the present account of his experience, and, with the utmost solemnity, protests that he had the strongest sensation upon him of being forced to look at the old man along those two fiery films, from that moment.)

"I must tell it to you," said the old man, with a ghastly and a stony stare.

"What?" asked Francis Goodchild.

"You know where it took place. Yonder!"

Whether he pointed to the room above, or to the room below, or to any room in that old house, or to a room in some other old house in that old town, Mr. Goodchild was not, nor is, nor ever can be, sure. He was confused by the circumstance that the right forefinger of the One old man seemed to dip itself in one of the threads of fire, light itself, and make a fiery start in the air, as it pointed somewhere. Having pointed somewhere, it went out.

"You know she was a Bride," said the old man.

"I know they still send up Bride-cake," Mr. Goodchild faltered. "This is a very oppressive air."

"She was a Bride," said the old man. "She was a fair, flaxen-haired, large-eyed girl, who had no character, no purpose. A weak, credulous, incapable, helpless nothing. Not like her mother. No, no. It was her father whose character she reflected.

"Her mother had taken care to secure everything to herself, for her own life, when the father of this girl (a child at that time) died—of sheer helplessness ; no other disorder—and then He renewed the acquaintance that had once subsisted between

THE GHOST'S NARRATIVE

the mother and Him.   He had been put aside for the flaxen-haired, large-eyed man (or nonentity) with Money.   He could overlook that for Money.   He wanted compensation in Money.

"So, he returned to the side of that woman the mother, made love to her again, danced attendance on her, and sub-mitted himself to her whims.   She wreaked upon him every whim she had, or could invent.   He bore it.   And the more he bore, the more he wanted compensation in Money, and the more he was resolved to have it.

"But, lo !   Before he got it, she cheated him.   In one of her imperious states, she froze, and never thawed again.   She put her hands to her head one night, uttered a cry, stiffened, lay in that attitude certain hours, and died.   And he had got no com-pensation from her in Money, yet.   Blight and Murrain on her ! Not a penny.

"He had hated her throughout that second pursuit, and had longed for retaliation on her.   He now counterfeited her signa-ture to an instrument, leaving all she had to leave, to her daughter—ten years old then—to whom the property passed absolutely, and appointing himself the daughter's Guardian. When He slid it under the pillow of the bed on which she lay, He bent down in the deaf ear of Death, and whispered : ' Mis-tress Pride, I have determined a long time that, dead or alive, you must make me compensation in Money.'

"So, now there were only two left.   Which two were, He, and the fair flaxen-haired, large-eyed foolish daughter, who afterwards became the Bride.

"He put her to school.   In a secret, dark, oppressive, ancient house, he put her to school with a watchful and un-scrupulous woman.   ' My worthy lady,' he said, ' here is a mind to be formed ; will you help me to form it ? '   She accepted the trust.   For which she, too, wanted compensation in Money, and had it.

"The girl was formed in the fear of him, and in the con-viction, that there was no escape from him.   She was taught, from the first, to regard him as her future husband—the man who must marry her—the destiny that overshadowed her—the appointed certainty that could never be evaded.   The poor fool was soft white wax in their hands, and took the impression that they put upon her.   It hardened with time.   It became a part of herself.   Inseparable from herself, and only to be torn away from her, by tearing life away from her.

"Eleven years she had lived in the dark house and its gloomy garden.   He was jealous of the very light and air getting to her, and they kept her close.   He stopped the wide chimneys, shaded the little windows, left the strong-stemmed ivy to wander where it would over the house-front, the moss to accumulate on the untrimmed fruit-trees in the red-walled garden, the weeds to over-run its green and yellow walks.   He surrounded her with images of sorrow and desolation.   He caused her to be filled with fears of the place and of the stories that were told of it, and then on pretext of correcting them, to be left in it in solitude, or made to shrink about it in the dark. When her mind was most depressed and fullest of terrors, then, he would come out of one of the hiding-places from which he overlooked her, and present himself as her sole resource.

"Thus, by being from her childhood the one embodiment her life presented to her of power to coërce and power to relieve, power to bind and power to loose, the ascendency over her weakness was secured.   She was twenty-one years and twenty-one days old, when he brought her home to the gloomy house, his half-witted, frightened, and submissive Bride of three weeks.

"He had dismissed the governess by that time—what he had left to do, he could best do alone—and they came back, upon a rainy night, to the scene of her long preparation.   She turned to him upon the threshold, as the rain was dripping from the porch, and said :

"'O sir, it is the Death-watch ticking for me !'

"'Well !' he answered.   'And if it were ?'

"'O sir !' she returned to him, 'look kindly on me, and be merciful to me !   I beg your pardon.   I will do anything you wish, if you will only forgive me !'

"That had become the poor fool's constant song : 'I beg your pardon,' and 'Forgive me !'

'She was not worth hating ; he felt nothing but contempt for her.   But, she had long been in the way, and he had long been weary, and the work was near its end, and had to be worked out.

"'You fool,' he said.   'Go up the stairs !'

" She obeyed very quickly, murmuring, ' I will do anything you wish!'   When he came into the Bride's Chamber, having been a little retarded by the heavy fastenings of the great door (for they were alone in the house, and he had arranged that the people who attended on them should come and go in the day), he found her withdrawn to the furthest corner, and there standing pressed against the paneling as if she would have shrunk through it : her flaxen hair all wild about her face, and her large eyes staring at him in vague terror.

" ' What are you afraid of ?   Come and sit down by me.'

" ' I will do anything you wish.   I beg your pardon, sir. Forgive me!'   Her monotonous tune as usual.

" ' Ellen, here is a writing that you must write out to-morrow, in your own hand.   You may as well be seen by others, busily engaged upon it.   When you have written it all fairly, and corrected all mistakes, call in any two people there may be about the house, and sign your name to it before them. Then, put it in your bosom to keep it safe, and when I sit here again to-morrow night, give it to me.'

" ' I will do it all, with the greatest care.   I will do anything you wish.'

" ' Don't shake and tremble, then.'

" ' I will try my utmost not to do it—if you will only forgive me!'

" Next day, she sat down at her desk, and did as she had been told.   He often passed in and out of the room, to observe her, and always saw her slowly and laboriously writing : repeating to herself the words she copied, in appearance quite mechanically, and without caring or endeavouring to comprehend them, so that she did her task. He saw her follow the directions she had received, in all particulars ; and at night, when they were alone again in the same Bride's Chamber, and he drew his chair to the hearth, she timidly approached him from her distant seat, took the paper from her bosom, and gave it into his hand.

" It secured all her possessions to him, in the event of her death.   He put her before him, face to face, that he might look at her steadily ; and he asked her, in so many plain words, neither fewer nor more, did she know that ?

" There were spots of ink upon the bosom of her white dress, and they made her face look whiter and her eyes look larger as she nodded her head. There were spots of ink upon the hand with which she stood before him, nervously plaiting and folding her white skirts.

"He took her by the arm, and looked her, yet more closely and steadily, in the face. 'Now, die! I have done with you.'

"She shrunk, and uttered a low, suppressed cry.

"'I am not going to kill you. I will not endanger my life for yours. Die!'

"He sat before her in the gloomy Bride's Chamber, day after day, night after night, looking the word at her when he did not utter it. As often as her large unmeaning eyes were raised from the hands in which she rocked her head, to the stern figure, sitting with crossed arms and knitted forehead, in the chair, they read in it, 'Die!' When she dropped asleep in exhaustion, she was called back to shuddering consciousness, by the whisper, 'Die!' When she fell upon her old entreaty to be pardoned, she was answered, 'Die!' When she had out-watched and out-suffered the long night, and the rising sun flamed into the sombre room, she heard it hailed with, 'Another day and not dead?—Die!'

"Shut up in the deserted mansion, aloof from all mankind, and engaged alone in such a struggle without any respite, it came to this—that either he must die, or she. He knew it very well, and concentrated his strength against her feebleness. Hours upon hours he held her by the arm when her arm was black where he held it, and bade her Die!

"It was done, upon a windy morning, before sunrise. He computed the time to be half-past four; but, his forgotten watch had run down, and he could not be sure. She had broken away from him in the night, with loud and sudden cries—the first of that kind to which she had given vent—and he had had to put his hands over her mouth. Since then, she had been quiet in the corner of the paneling where she had sunk down; and he had left her, and had gone back with his folded arms and his knitted forehead to his chair.

' Paler in the pale light, more colourless than ever in the leaden dawn, he saw her coming, trailing herself along the floor towards him—a white wreck of hair, and dress, and wild eyes, pushing itself on by an irresolute and bending hand.

" 'O, forgive me ! I will do anything. O, sir, pray tell me I may live !'

" ' Die !'

" ' Are you so resolved ? Is there no hope for me ?'

" ' Die !'

" Her large eyes strained themselves with wonder and fear; wonder and fear changed to reproach; reproach to blank nothing. It was done. He was not at first so sure it was done, but that the morning sun was hanging jewels in her hair—he saw the diamond, emerald, and ruby, glittering among it in little points, as he stood looking down at her—when he lifted her and laid her on her bed.

" She was soon laid in the ground. And now they were all gone, and he had compensated himself well.

" He had a mind to travel. Not that he meant to waste his Money, for he was a pinching man and liked his Money dearly (liked nothing else, indeed), but, that he had grown tired of the desolate house and wished to turn his back upon it and have done with it. But, the house was worth Money, and Money must not be thrown away. He determined to sell it before he went. That it might look the less wretched and bring a better price, he hired some labourers to work in the overgrown garden ; to cut out the dead wood, trim the ivy that drooped in heavy masses over the windows and gables, and clear the walks in which the weeds were growing mid-leg high.

" He worked, himself, along with them. He worked later than they did, and, one evening at dusk, was left working alone, with his bill-hook in his hand. One autumn evening, when the Bride was five weeks dead.

" ' It grows too dark to work longer,' he said to himself, 'I must give over for the night.'

" He detested the house, and was loath to enter it. He looked at the dark porch waiting for him like a tomb, and felt that it was an accursed house. Near to the porch, and near to where he stood, was a tree whose branches waved before the old bay-window of the Bride's Chamber, where it had been done. The tree swung suddenly, and made him start. It swung again, although the night was still. Looking up into it, he saw a figure among the branches.

" It was the figure of a young man. The face looked down,

as his looked up ; the branches cracked and swayed ; the figure rapidly descended, and slid upon its feet before him. A slender youth of about her age, with long light brown hair.

" ' What thief are you ?' he said, seizing the youth by the collar.

" The young man, in shaking himself free, swung him a blow with his arm across the face and throat. They closed, but the young man got from him and stepped back, crying, with great eagerness and horror, 'Don't touch me ! I would as lieve be touched by the Devil ! '

" He stood still, with his bill-hook in his hand, looking at the young man. For, the young man's look was the counter-part of her last look, and he had not expected ever to see that again.

" ' I am no thief. Even if I were, I would not have a coin of your wealth, if it would buy me the Indies. You murderer !'

" ' What ! '

" ' I climbed it,' said the young man, pointing up into the tree, 'for the first time, nigh four years ago. I climbed it, to look at her. I saw her. I spoke to her. I have climbed it, many a time, to watch and listen for her. I was a boy, hidden among its leaves, when from that bay-window she gave me this ! '

" He showed a tress of flaxen hair, tied with a mourning ribbon.

" ' Her life,' said the young man, ' was a life of mourning. She gave me this, as a token of it, and a sign that she was dead to every one but you. If I had been older, if I had seen her sooner, I might have saved her from you. But, she was fast in the web when I first climbed the tree, and what could I do then to break it ! '

" In saying those words, he burst into a fit of sobbing and crying : weakly at first, then passionately.

" ' Murderer ! I climbed the tree on the night when you brought her back. I heard her, from the tree, speak of the Death-watch at the door. I was three times in the tree while you were shut up with her, slowly killing her. I saw her, from the tree, lie dead upon her bed. I have watched you, from the tree, for proofs and traces of your guilt. The manner of it, is a mystery to me yet, but I will pursue you until you have rendered up your life to the hangman.　You shall never, until then, be rid of me.　I loved her!　I can know no relenting towards you.　Murderer, I loved her!'

"The youth was bare-headed, his hat having fluttered away in his descent from the tree.　He moved towards the gate.　He had to pass—Him—to get to it.　There was breadth for two old-fashioned carriages abreast; and the youth's abhorrence, openly expressed in every feature of his face and limb of his body, and very hard to bear, had verge enough to keep itself at a distance in.　He (by which I mean the other) had not stirred hand or foot, since he had stood still to look at the boy. He faced round, now, to follow him with his eyes.　As the back of the bare light-brown head was turned to him, he saw a red curve stretch from his hand to it.　He knew, before he threw the bill-hook, where it had alighted—I say, had alighted, and not, would alight; for, to his clear perception the thing was done before he did it.　It cleft the head, and it remained there, and the boy lay on his face.

"He buried the body in the night, at the foot of the tree. As soon as it was light in the morning, he worked at turning up all the ground near the tree, and hacking and hewing at the neighbouring bushes and undergrowth.　When the labourers came, there was nothing suspicious, and nothing suspected.

"But, he had, in a moment, defeated all his precautions, and destroyed the triumph of the scheme he had so long concerted, and so successfully worked out.　He had got rid of the Bride, and had acquired her fortune without endangering his life; but now, for a death by which he had gained nothing, he had evermore to live with a rope around his neck.

"Beyond this, he was chained to the house of gloom and horror, which he could not endure.　Being afraid to sell it or to quit it, lest discovery should be made, he was forced to live in it.　He hired two old people, man and wife, for his servants; and dwelt in it, and dreaded it.　His great difficulty, for a long time, was the garden.　Whether he should keep it trim, whether he should suffer it to fall into its former state of neglect, what would be the least likely way of attracting attention to it?

"He took the middle course of gardening, himself, in his evening leisure, and of then calling the old serving-man to help him ; but, of never letting him work there alone. And he made himself an arbour over against the tree, where he could sit and see that it was safe.

" As the seasons changed, and the tree changed, his mind perceived dangers that were always changing. In the leafy time, he perceived that the upper boughs were growing into the form of the young man—that they made the shape of him exactly, sitting in a forked branch swinging in the wind. In the time of the falling leaves, he perceived that they came down from the tree, forming tell-tale letters on the path, or that they had a tendency to heap themselves into a church-yard-mound above the grave. In the winter, when the tree was bare, he perceived that the boughs swung at him the ghost of the blow the young man had given, and that they threatened him openly. In the spring, when the sap was mounting in the trunk, he asked himself, were the dried-up particles of blood mounting with it : to make out more ob-viously this year than last, the leaf-screened figure of the young man, swinging in the wind ?

" However, he turned his Money over and over, and still over. He was in the dark trade, the gold-dust trade, and most secret trades that yielded great returns. In ten years, he had turned his Money over, so many times, that the traders and shippers who had dealings with him, absolutely did not lie— for once—when they delared that he had increased his fortune, Twelve Hundred Per Cent.

" He possessed his riches one hundred years ago, when people could be lost easily. He had heard who the youth was, from hearing of the search that was made after him ; but, it died away, and the youth was forgotten.

" The annual round of changes in the tree had been re-peated ten times since the night of the burial at its foot, when there was a great thunder-storm over this place. It broke at midnight, and raged until morning. The first intelligence he heard from his old serving-man that morning, was, that the tree had been struck by Lightning.

" It had been riven down the stem, in a very surprising manner, and the stem lay in two blighted shafts : one resting against the house, and one against a portion of the old red garden-wall in which its fall had made a gap. The fissure went

down the tree to a little above the earth, and there stopped.
There was great curiosity to see the tree, and, with most of his
former fears revived, he sat in his arbour—grown quite an old
man—watching the people who came to see it.

"They quickly began to come, in such dangerous numbers,
that he closed his garden-gate and refused to admit any more.
But, there were certain men of science who travelled from a
distance to examine the tree, and, in an evil hour, he let them
in—Blight and Murrain on them, let them in!

"They wanted to dig up the ruin by the roots, and closely
examine it, and the earth about it.   Never, while he lived!
They offered money for it.   They!   Men of science, whom he
could have bought by the gross, with a scratch of his pen!   He
showed them the garden-gate again, and locked and barred it.

"But they were bent on doing what they wanted to do, and
they bribed the old serving-man—a thankless wretch who
regularly complained when he received his wages, of being
underpaid—and they stole into the garden by night with their
lanterns, picks, and shovels, and fell to at the tree.   He was
lying in a turret-room on the other side of the house (the
Bride's Chamber had been unoccupied ever since), but he soon
dreamed of picks and shovels, and got up.

"He came to an upper window on that side, whence he
could see their lanterns, and them, and the loose earth in a
heap which he had himself disturbed and put back, when it
was last turned to the air.   It was found!   They had that minute
lighted on it.   They were all bending over it.   One of them
said, 'The skull is fractured;' and another, 'See here the
bones;' and another, 'See here the clothes;' and then the first
struck in again, and said, 'A rusty bill-hook!'

"He became sensible, next day, that he was already put
under a strict watch, and that he could go nowhere without
being followed.   Before a week was out, he was taken and laid
in hold.   The circumstances were gradually pieced together
against him, with a desperate malignity, and an appalling ingenuity.   But, see the justice of men, and how it was extended
to him!   He was further accused of having poisoned that
girl in the Bride's Chamber.   He, who had carefully and expressly avoided imperilling a hair of his head for her, and
who had seen her die of her own incapacity!

"There was doubt for which of the two murders he should be first tried; but, the real one was chosen, and he was found Guilty, and cast for Death. Bloodthirsty wretches! They would have made him Guilty of anything, so set they were upon having his life.

"His money could do nothing to save him, and he was hanged. *I* am He, and I was hanged at Lancaster Castle with my face to the wall, a hundred years ago!"

At this terrific announcement, Mr. Goodchild tried to rise and cry out. But, the two fiery lines extending from the old man's eyes to his own, kept him down, and he could not utter a sound. His sense of hearing, however, was acute, and he could hear the clock strike Two. No sooner had he heard the clock strike Two, than he saw before him Two old men!

Two.

The eyes of each, connected with his eyes by two films of fire: each, exactly like the other: each, addressing him at precisely one and the same instant: each, gnashing the same teeth in the same head, with the same twitched nostril above them, and the same suffused expression around it. Two old men. Differing in nothing, equally distinct to the sight, the copy no fainter than the original, the second as real as the first.

"At what time," said the Two old men, "did you arrive at the door below?"

"At Six."

"And there were Six old men upon the stairs!"

Mr. Goodchild having wiped the perspiration from his brow, or tried to do it, the Two old men proceeded in one voice, and in the singular number:

"I had been anatomised, but had not yet had my skeleton put together and re-hung on an iron hook, when it began to be whispered that the Bride's Chamber was haunted. It *was* haunted, and I was there.

"*We* were there. She and I were there. I, in the chair upon the hearth; she, a white wreck again, trailing itself towards me on the floor. But, I was the speaker no more, and the one word that she said to me from midnight until dawn was, 'Live!'

"The youth was there, likewise. In the tree outside the window. Coming and going in the moonlight, as the tree bent and gave. He has, ever since, been there, peeping in at me in my torment; revealing to me by snatches, in the pale lights and slatey shadows where he comes and goes, bare-headed—a bill-hook, standing edgewise in his hair.

"In the Bride's Chamber, every night from midnight until dawn—one month in the year excepted, as I am going to tell you—he hides in the tree, and she comes towards me on the floor; always approaching; never coming nearer; always visible as if by moonlight, whether the moon shines or no; always saying, from midnight until dawn, her one word, 'Live!'

"But, in the month wherein I was forced out of this life— this present month of thirty days—the Bride's Chamber is empty and quiet. Not so my old dungeon. Not so the rooms where I was restless and afraid, ten years. Both are fitfully haunted then. At One in the morning, I am what you saw me when the clock struck that hour—One old man. At Two in the morning, I am Two old men. At Three, I am Three. By Twelve at noon, I am Twelve old men, One for every hundred per cent. of old gain. Every one of the Twelve, with Twelve times my old power of suffering and agony. From that hour until Twelve at night, I, Twelve old men in anguish and fearful foreboding, wait for the coming of the executioner. At Twelve at night, I, Twelve old men turned off, swing invisible outside Lancaster Castle, with Twelve faces to the wall!

"When the Bride's Chamber was first haunted, it was known to me that this punishment would never cease, until I could make its nature, and my story, known to two living men together. I waited for the coming of two living men together into the Bride's Chamber, years upon years. It was infused into my knowledge (of the means I am ignorant) that if two living men, with their eyes open, could be in the Bride's Chamber at One in the morning, they would see me sitting in my chair.

"At length, the whispers that the room was spiritually troubled, brought two men to try the adventure. I was scarcely struck upon the hearth at midnight (I come there as if the Lightning blasted me into being), when I heard them ascending the stairs. Next, I saw them enter. One of them was a bold, gay, active man, in the prime of life, some five and forty years of age ; the other, a dozen years younger. They brought provisions with them in a basket, and bottles. A young woman accompanied them, with wood and coals for the lighting of the fire. When she had lighted it, the bold, gay, active man accompanied her along the gallery outside the room, to see her safely down the staircase, and came back laughing.

"He locked the door, examined the chamber, put out the contents of the basket on the table before the fire—little recking of me, in my appointed station on the hearth, close to him —and filled the glasses, and ate and drank. His companion did the same, and was as cheerful and confident as he : though he was the leader. When they had supped, they laid pistols on the table, turned to the fire, and began to smoke their pipes of foreign make.

"They had travelled together, and had been much together, and had an abundance of subjects in common. In the midst of their talking and laughing, the younger man made a reference to the leader's being always ready for any adventure ; that one, or any other. He replied in these words :

"'Not quite so, Dick ; if I am afraid of nothing else, I am afraid of myself.'

"His companion seeming to grow a little dull, asked him, in what sense ? How ?

"'Why, thus,' he returned. 'Here is a Ghost to be disproved. Well ! I cannot answer for what my fancy might do if I were alone here, or what tricks my senses might play with me if they had me to themselves. But, in company with another man, and especially with you, Dick, I would consent to outface all the Ghosts that were ever told of in the universe.'

"'I had not the vanity to suppose that I was of so much importance to-night,' said the other.

"'Of so much,' rejoined the leader, more seriously than he had spoken yet, 'that I would, for the reason I have given, on no account have undertaken to pass the night here alone.'

"It was within a few minutes of One. The head of the younger man had drooped when he made his last remark, and it drooped lower now.

" ' Keep awake, Dick ! ' said the leader, gaily.   ' The small hours are the worst.'

" He tried, but his head drooped again.

" ' Dick ! ' urged the leader.   ' Keep awake ! '

" ' I can't,' he indistinctly muttered.   ' I don't know what strange influence is stealing over me.   I can't.'

" His companion looked at him with a sudden horror, and I, in my different way, felt a new horror also ; for, it was on the stroke of One, and I felt that the second watcher was yielding to me, and that the curse was upon me that I must send him to sleep.

" Get up and walk, Dick ! ' cried the leader.   ' Try ! '

" It was in vain to go behind the slumberer's chair and shake him.   One o'clock sounded, and I was present to the elder man, and he stood transfixed before me.

" To him alone, I was obliged to relate my story, without hope of benefit.   To him alone, I was an awful phantom making a quite useless confession.   I foresee it will ever be the same.   The two living men together will never come to release me.   When I appear, the senses of one of the two will be locked in sleep ; he will neither see nor hear me ; my communication will ever be made to a solitary listener, and will ever be unserviceable.   Woe !   Woe !   Woe ! "

As the Two old men, with these words, wrung their hands, it shot into Mr. Goodchild's mind that he was in the terrible situation of being virtually alone with the spectre, and that Mr. Idle's immoveability was explained by his having been charmed asleep at One o'clock.   In the terror of this sudden discovery which produced an indescribable dread, he struggled so hard to get free from the four fiery threads, that he snapped them, after he had pulled them out to a great width.   Being then out of bonds, he caught up Mr. Idle from the sofa and rushed down stairs with him.

" What are you about, Francis ? " demanded Mr. Idle. " My bedroom is not down here.   What the deuce are you carrying me at all for ?   I can walk with a stick now.   I don't want to be carried.   Put me down."

Mr. Goodchild put him down in the old hall, and looked about him wildly.

"What are you doing?   Idiotically plunging at your own sex, and rescuing them or perishing in the attempt?" asked Mr. Idle, in a highly petulant state.

"The One old man!" cried Mr. Goodchild, distractedly,— "and the Two old men!"

Mr. Idle deigned no other reply than "The One old woman, I think you mean," as he began hobbling his way back up the staircase, with the assistance of its broad balustrade.

"I assure you, Tom," began Mr. Goodchild, attending at his side, "that since you fell asleep——"

"Come, I like that!" said Thomas Idle, "I haven't closed an eye!"

With the peculiar sensitiveness on the subject of the disgraceful action of going to sleep out of bed, which is the lot of all mankind, Mr. Idle persisted in this declaration. The same peculiar sensitiveness impelled Mr. Goodchild, on being taxed with the same crime, to repudiate it with honourable resentment. The settlement of the question of The One old man and The Two old men was thus presently complicated, and soon made quite impracticable. Mr. Idle said it was all Bride-cake, and fragments, newly arranged, of things seen and thought about in the day. Mr. Goodchild said how could that be, when he hadn't been asleep, and what right could Mr. Idle have to say so, who had been asleep? Mr. Idle said he had never been asleep, and never did go to sleep, and that Mr. Goodchild, as a general rule, was always asleep. They consequently parted for the rest of the night, at their bedroom doors, a little ruffled. Mr. Goodchild's last words were, that he had had, in that real and tangible old sitting-room of that real and tangible old Inn (he supposed Mr. Idle denied its existence?), every sensation and experience, the present record of which is now within a line or two of completion; and that he would write it out and print it every word. Mr. Idle returned that he might if he liked—and he did like, and has now done it.

CHAPTER V.

Two of the many passengers by a certain late Sunday evening train, Mr. Thomas Idle and Mr. Francis Goodchild, yielded up their tickets at a little rotten platform (converted into artificial touch-wood by smoke and ashes), deep in the manufacturing bosom of Yorkshire. A mysterious bosom it appeared, upon a damp, dark, Sunday night, dashed through in the train to the music of the whirling wheels, the panting of the engine, and the part-singing of hundreds of third-class excursionists, whose vocal efforts "bobbed arayound" from sacred to profane, from hymns, to our transatlantic sisters the Yankee Gal and Mairy Anne, in a remarkable way. There seemed to have been some large vocal gathering near to every lonely station on the line. No town was visible, no village was visible, no light was visible ; but, a multitude got out singing, and a multitude got in singing, and the second multitude took up the hymns, and adopted our transatlantic sisters, and sang of their own egregious wickedness, and of their bobbing arayound, and of how the ship it was ready and the wind it was fair, and they were bayound for the sea, Mairy Anne, until they in their turn became a getting-out multitude, and were replaced by another getting-in multitude, who did the same. And at every station, the getting-in multitude, with an artistic reference to the completeness of their chorus, incessantly cried, as with one voice while scuffling into the carriages, " We mun aa' gang toogither !"

The singing and the multitudes had trailed off as the lonely places were left and the great towns were neared, and the way had lain as silently as a train's way ever can, over the vague black streets of the great gulfs of towns, and among their branchless woods of vague black chimneys. These towns looked, in the cinderous wet, as though they had one and all been on fire and were just put out—a dreary and quenched panorama, many miles long.

Thus, Thomas and Francis got to Leeds; of which enterprising and important commercial centre it may be observed with delicacy, that you must either like it very much or not at all. Next day, the first of the Race-Week, they took train to Doncaster.

And instantly the character, both of travellers and of luggage, entirely changed, and no other business than race-business any longer existed on the face of the earth. The talk was all of horses and "John Scott." Guards whispered behind their hands to station-masters, of horses and John Scott. Men in cut-away coats and speckled cravats fastened with peculiar pins, and with the large bones of their legs developed under tight trousers, so that they should look as much as possible like horses' legs, paced up and down by twos at junction-stations, speaking low and moodily of horses and John Scott. The young clergyman in the black strait-waistcoat, who occupied the middle seat of the carriage, expounded in his peculiar pulpit-accent to the young and lovely Reverend Mrs. Crinoline, who occupied the opposite middle-seat, a few passages of rumour relative to "Oartheth, my love, and Mithter John Eth-corr." A bandy vagabond, with a head like a Dutch cheese, in a fustian stable-suit, attending on a horse-box and going about the platforms with a halter hanging round his neck like a Calais burgher of the ancient period much degenerated, was courted by the best society, by reason of what he had to hint, when not engaged in eating straw, concerning "t'harses and Joon Scott." The engine-driver himself, as he applied one eye to his large stationary double-eye-glass on the engine, seemed to keep the other open, sideways, upon horses and John Scott.

Breaks and barriers at Doncaster station to keep the crowd off; temporary wooden avenues of ingress and egress, to help the crowd on. Forty extra porters sent down for this present blessed Race-Week, and all of them making up their betting-books in the lamp-room or somewhere else, and none of them to come and touch the luggage. Travellers disgorged into an open space, a howling wilderness of idle men.   All work but race-work at a stand-still; all men at a stand-still. "Ey my word! Deant ask noon o' us to help wi' t' luggage. Bock your opinion loike a mon. Coom! Dang it, coom, t'harses and Joon Scott!" In the midst of the idle men, all the fly horses and omnibus horses of Doncaster and parts adjacent, rampant, rearing, backing, plunging, shying—apparently the result of their hearing of nothing but their own order and John Scott.

Grand Dramatic Company from London for the Race-Week. Poses Plastiques in the Grand Assembly Room up the Stable-Yard at seven and nine each evening, for the Race-Week. Grand Alliance Circus in the field beyond the bridge, for the Race-Week.   Grand Exhibition of Aztec Lilliputians, important to all who want to be horrified cheap, for the Race-Week.   Lodgings, grand and not grand, but at all grand prices, ranging from ten pounds to twenty, for the Grand Race-Week!

Rendered giddy enough by these things, Messieurs Idle and Goodchild repaired to the quarters they had secured beforehand, and Mr. Goodchild looked down from the window into the surging street.

"By heaven, Tom!" cried he, after contemplating it, "I am in the Lunatic Asylum again, and these are all mad people under the charge of a body of designing keepers!"

All through the Race-Week, Mr. Goodchild never divested himself of this idea.   Every day he looked out of window, with something of the dread of Lemuel Gulliver looking down at men after he returned home from the horse-country ; and every day he saw the Lunatics, horse-mad, betting-mad, drunken-mad, vice-mad, and the designing Keepers always after them.   The idea pervaded, like the second colour in shot-silk, the whole of Mr. Goodchild's impressions.   They were much as follows :

Monday, mid-day.   Races not to begin until to-morrow, but all the mob-Lunatics out, crowding the pavements of the one main street of pretty and pleasant Doncaster, crowding the road, particularly crowding the outside of the Betting Rooms, whooping and shouting loudly after all passing vehicles. Frightened lunatic horses occasionally running away, with infinite clatter.   All degrees of men, from peers to paupers, betting incessantly.   Keepers very watchful, and taking all good chances.   An awful family likeness among the Keepers, to Mr. Palmer and Mr. Thurtell. With some knowledge of expression and some acquaintance with heads (thus writes Mr. Goodchild), I never have seen anywhere, so many repetitions of one class of countenance and one character of head (both evil) as in this street at this time. Cunning, covetousness, secresy, cold calculation, hard callousness and dire insensibility, are the uniform Keeper characteristics. Mr. Palmer passes me five times in five minutes, and, as I go down the street, the back of Mr. Thurtell's skull is always going on before me.

Monday evening.   Town lighted up; more Lunatics out than ever; a complete choke and stoppage of the thoroughfare outside the Betting Rooms. Keepers, having dined, pervade the Betting Rooms, and sharply snap at the moneyed Lunatics. Some Keepers flushed with drink, and some not, but all close and calculating. A vague echoing roar of "t'harses" and "t'races" always rising in the air, until midnight, at about which period it dies away in occasional drunken songs and straggling yells.   But, all night, some unmannerly drinking-house in the neighbourhood opens its mouth at intervals and spits out a man too drunk to be retained: who thereupon makes what uproarious protest may be left in him, and either falls asleep where he tumbles, or is carried off in custody.

Tuesday morning, at daybreak.   A sudden rising, as it were out of the earth, of all the obscene creatures, who sell "correct cards of the races." They may have been coiled in corners, or sleeping on door-steps, and, having all passed the night under the same set of circumstances, may all want to circulate their blood at the same time; but, however that may be, they spring into existence all at once and together, as though a new Cadmus had sown a race-horse's teeth. There is nobody up, to buy the cards; but, the cards are madly cried. There is no patronage to quarrel for; but, they madly quarrel and fight. Conspicuous among these hyænas, as breakfast-time discloses, is a fearful creature in the general semblance of a man : shaken off his next-to-no legs by drink and devilry, bare-headed and bare-footed, with a great shock of hair like a horrible broom, and nothing on him but a ragged pair of trousers and a pink glazed-calico coat—made on him—so very tight that it is as evident that he could never take it off, as that he never does.   This hideous apparition, inconceivably drunk, has a terrible power of making a gong-like imitation of the braying of an ass : which feat requires that he should lay his right jaw in his begrimed right paw, double himself up, and shake his bray out of himself, with much staggering on his next-to-no legs, and much twirling of his horrible broom, as if it were a mop.   From the present minute, when he comes in sight holding up his cards to the windows, and hoarsely proposing purchase to My Lord, Your Excellency, Colonel, the Noble Captain, and Your Honorable Worship—from the present minute until the Grand Race-Week is finished, at all hours of the morning, evening, day, and night, shall the town reverberate, at capricious intervals, to the brays of this frightful animal the Gong-Donkey.

No very great racing to-day, so no very great amount of vehicles : though there is a good sprinkling, too : from farmers' carts and gigs, to carriages with post-horses and to fours-in-hand, mostly coming by the road from York, and passing on straight through the main street to the Course.   A walk in the wrong direction may be a better thing for Mr. Goodchild to-day than the Course, so he walks in the wrong direction.   Everybody gone to the races.   Only children in the street.   Grand Alliance Circus deserted ; not one Star-Rider left ; omnibus which forms the Pay-Place, having on separate panels Pay here for the Boxes, Pay here for the Pit, Pay here for the Gallery, hove down in a corner and locked up ; nobody near the tent but the man on his knees on the grass, who is making the paper balloons for the Star young gentlemen to jump through to-night.   A pleasant road, pleasantly wooded.   No labourers working in the fields ; all gone "t'races."   The few late wenders of their way "t'races," who are yet left driving on the road, stare in amazement at the recluse who is not going "t'races."   Roadside innkeeper has gone "t'races."   Turnpike-man has gone "t'races."   His thrifty wife, washing clothes at the toll-house door, is going "t'races" to-morrow.   Perhaps there may be no one left to take the toll to-morrow ; who knows ?   Though assuredly that would be neither turnpike-like, nor Yorkshire-like.   The very wind and dust seem to be hurrying "t'races," as they briskly pass the only wayfarer on the road.   In the distance, the Railway Engine, waiting at the town-end, shrieks despairingly.   Nothing but the difficulty of getting off the Line, restrains that Engine from going "t'races," too, it is very clear.

At night, more Lunatics out than last night—and more Keepers. The latter very active at the Betting Rooms, the street in front of which is now impassable. Mr. Palmer as before. Mr. Thurtell as before. Roar and uproar as before. Gradual subsidence as before. Unmannerly drinking house expectorates as before. Drunken negro-melodists, Gong-donkey, and correct cards, in the night.

On Wednesday morning, the morning of the great St. Leger, it becomes apparent that there has been a great influx since yesterday, both of Lunatics and Keepers. The families of the tradesmen over the way are no longer within human ken; their places know them no more; ten, fifteen, and twenty guinea-lodgers fill them. At the pastry-cook's second-floor window, a Keeper is brushing Mr. Thurtell's hair—thinking it his own. In the wax-chandler's attic, another Keeper is putting on Mr. Palmer's braces. In the gunsmith's nursery, a Lunatic is shaving himself. In the serious stationer's best sitting-room, three Lunatics are taking a combination-breakfast, praising the (cook's) devil, and drinking neat brandy in an atmosphere of last midnight's cigars. No family sanctuary is free from our Angelic messengers—we put up at the Angel—who in the guise of extra waiters for the grand Race-Week, rattle in and out of the most secret chambers of everybody's house, with dishes and tin covers, decanters, soda-water bottles, and glasses. An hour later. Down the street and up the street, as far as eyes can see and a good deal farther, there is a dense crowd; outside the Betting Rooms it is like a great struggle at a theatre door—in the days of theatres; or at the vestibule of the Spurgeon temple —in the days of Spurgeon. An hour later. Fusing into this crowd, and somehow getting through it, are all kinds of conveyances, and all kinds of foot-passengers; carts, with brick-makers and brick-makeresses jolting up and down on planks; drags, with the needful grooms behind, sitting cross-armed in the needful manner, and slanting themselves backward from the soles of their boots at the needful angle; postboys, in the shining hats and smart jackets of the olden time, when stokers were not; beautiful Yorkshire horses, gallantly driven by their own breeders and masters. Under every pole, and every shaft, and every horse, and every wheel as it would seem, the Gong-donkey—metallically braying, when not struggling for life, or whipped out of the way.

By one o'clock, all this stir has gone out of the streets, and there is no one left in them but Francis Goodchild. Francis Goodchild will not be left in them long; for, he too is on his way " t'races."

A most beautiful sight, Francis Goodchild finds " t'races" to be, when he has left fair Doncaster behind him, and comes out on the free course, with its agreeable prospect, its quaint Red House oddly changing and turning as Francis turns, its green grass, and fresh heath. A free course and an easy one, where Francis can roll smoothly where he will, and can choose between the start, or the coming-in, or the turn behind the brow of the hill, or any out-of-the-way point where he lists to see the throbbing horses straining every nerve, and making the sympathetic earth throb as they come by. Francis much delights to be, not in the Grand Stand, but where he can see it, rising against the sky with its vast tiers of little white dots of faces, and its last high rows and corners of people, looking like pins stuck into an enormous pin-cushion—not quite so symmetrically as his orderly eye could wish, when people change or go away. When the race is nearly run out, it is as good as the race to him to see the flutter among the pins, and the change in them from dark to light, as hats are taken off and waved. Not less full of interest, the loud anticipation of the winner's name, the swelling, and the final, roar; then, the quick dropping of all the pins out of their places, the revelation of the shape of the bare pin-cushion, and the closing-in of the whole host of Lunatics and Keepers, in the rear of the three horses with bright-coloured riders, who have not yet quite subdued their gallop though the contest is over.

Mr. Goodchild would appear to have been by no means free from lunacy himself at " t'races," though not of the prevalent kind. He is suspected by Mr. Idle to have fallen into a dreadful state concerning a pair of little lilac gloves and a little bonnet that he saw there. Mr. Idle asserts, that he did afterwards repeat at the Angel, with an appearance of being lunatically seized, some rhapsody to the following effect: "O little lilac gloves! And O winning little bonnet, making in conjunction with her golden hair quite a Glory in the sunlight round the pretty head, why anything in the world but you and me! Why may not this day's running—of horses, to all the rest: of precious sands of life to me—be prolonged through an everlasting autumn-sunshine, without a sunset! Slave of the Lamp, or Ring, strike me yonder gallant equestrian Clerk of the Course, in the scarlet coat, motionless on the green grass for ages! Friendly Devil on Two Sticks, for ten times ten thousand years, keep Blink-Bonny jibbing at the post, and let us have no start! Arab drums, powerful of old to summon Genii in the desert, sound of yourselves and raise a troop for me in the desert of my heart, which shall so enchant this dusty barouche (with a conspicuous excise-plate, resembling the Collector's door-plate at a turnpike), that I, within it, loving the little lilac gloves, the winning little bonnet, and the dear unknown-wearer with the golden hair, may wait by her side for ever, to see a Great St. Leger that shall never be run!"

Thursday morning. After a tremendous night of crowding, shouting, drinking-house expectoration, Gong-donkey, and correct cards. Symptoms of yesterday's gains in the way of drink, and of yesterday's losses in the way of money, abundant. Money-losses very great. As usual, nobody seems to have won; but, large losses and many losers are unquestionable facts. Both Lunatics and Keepers, in general very low. Several of both kinds look in at the chemist's while Mr. Goodchild is making a purchase there, to be "picked up." One red-eyed Lunatic, flushed, faded, and disordered, enters hurriedly and cries savagely, "Hond us a gloss of sal volatile in wather, or soom dommed thing o' thot sart!" Faces at the Betting-Rooms very long, and a tendency to bite nails observable. Keepers likewise given this morning to standing about solitary, with their hands in their pockets, looking down at their boots as they fit them into cracks of the pavement, and then looking up whistling and walking away. Grand Alliance Circus out, in procession; buxom lady-member of Grand Alliance, in crimson riding-habit, fresher to look at, even in her paint under the day sky, than the cheeks of Lunatics or Keepers. Spanish Cavalier appears to have lost yesterday, and jingles his bossed bridle with disgust, as if he were paying. Re-action also apparent at the Guildhall opposite, whence certain pickpockets come out handcuffed together, with that peculiar walk which is never seen under any other circumstances—a walk expressive of going to jail, game, but still of jails being in bad taste and arbitrary, and how would *you* like it if it was you instead of me, as it ought to be!   Mid-day.   Town filled as yesterday, but not so full; and emptied as yesterday, but not so empty. In the evening, Angel ordinary where every Lunatic and Keeper has his modest daily meal of turtle, venison, and wine, not so crowded as yesterday, and not so noisy.   At night, the theatre.   More abstracted faces in it, than one ever sees at public assemblies; such faces wearing an expression which strongly reminds Mr. Goodchild of the boys at school who were "going up next," with their arithmetic or mathematics.   These boys are, no doubt, going up to-morrow with *their* sums and figures.   Mr. Palmer and Mr. Thurtell in the boxes O. P.   Mr. Thurtell and Mr. Palmer in the boxes P. S.   The firm of Thurtell, Palmer, and Thurtell, in the boxes Centre.   A most odious tendency observable in these distinguished gentlemen to put vile constructions on sufficiently innocent phrases in the play, and then to applaud them in a Satyr-like manner. Behind Mr. Goodchild, with a party of other Lunatics and one Keeper, the express incarnation of the thing called a "gent." A gentleman born; a gent manufactured.   A something with a scarf round its neck, and a slipshod speech issuing from behind the scarf; more depraved, more foolish, more ignorant, more unable to believe in any noble or good thing of any kind, than the stupidest Bosjesman.   The thing is but a boy in years, and is addled with drink.   To do its company justice, even its company is ashamed of it, as it drawls its slang criticisms on the representation, and inflames Mr. Goodchild with a burning ardour to fling it into the pit.   Its remarks are so horrible, that Mr. Goodchild, for the moment, even doubts whether that *is* a wholesome Art, which sets women apart on a high floor before such a thing as this, though as good as its own sisters, or its own mother—whom Heaven forgive for bringing it into the world! But, the consideration that a low nature must make a low world of its own to live in, whatever the real materials, or it could no more exist than any of us could without the sense of touch, brings Mr. Goodchild to reason: the rather, because the thing soon drops its downy chin upon its scarf, and slobbers itself asleep.

Friday Morning. Early fights. Gong-donkey, and correct cards. Again, a great set towards the races, though not so great a set as on Wednesday. Much packing going on too, up-stairs at the gunsmith's, the wax-chandler's, and the serious stationer's; for there will be a heavy drift of Lunatics and Keepers to London by the afternoon train. The course as pretty as ever; the great pincushion as like a pincushion, but not nearly so full of pins; whole rows of pins wanting. On the great event of the day, both Lunatics and Keepers become inspired with rage; and there is a violent scuffling, and a rushing at the losing jockey, and an emergence of the said jockey from a swaying and menacing crowd, protected by friends, and looking the worse for wear; which is a rough proceeding, though animating to see from a pleasant distance. After the great event, rills begin to flow from the pincushion towards the railroad; the rills swell into rivers; the rivers soon unite into a lake. The lake floats Mr. Goodchild into Doncaster, past the Itinerant personage in black, by the way-side telling him from the vantage ground of a legibly printed placard on a pole that for all these things the Lord will bring him to judgment. No turtle and venison ordinary this evening; that is all over. No Betting at the rooms; nothing there but the plants in pots, which have, all the week, been stood about the entry to give it an innocent appearance, and which have sorely sickened by this time.

Saturday. Mr. Idle wishes to know at breakfast, what were those dreadful groanings in his bedroom doorway in the night? Mr. Goodchild answers, Nightmare. Mr. Idle repels the calumny, and calls the waiter. The Angel is very sorry—had intended to explain; but you see, gentlemen, there was a gentleman dined down stairs with two more, and he had lost a deal of money, and he would drink a deal of wine, and in the night he "took the horrors," and got up; and as his friends could do nothing with him he laid himself down and groaned at Mr. Idle's door. "And he DID groan there," Mr. Idle says; "and you will please to imagine me inside, 'taking the horrors' too!"

So far, the picture of Doncaster on the occasion of its great sporting anniversary, offers probably a general representation of the social condition of the town, in the past as well as in the present time.   The sole local phenomenon of the current year, which may be considered as entirely unprecedented in its way, and which certainly claims, on that account, some slight share of notice, consists in the actual existence of one remarkable individual, who is sojourning in Doncaster, and who, neither directly nor indirectly, has anything at all to do, in any capacity whatever, with the racing amusements of the week.   Ranging throughout the entire crowd that fills the town, and including the inhabitants as well as the visitors, nobody is to be found altogether disconnected with the business of the day, excepting this one unparalleled man.   He does not bet on the races, like the sporting men.   He does not assist the races, like the jockeys, starters, judges, and grooms.   He does not look on at the races, like Mr. Goodchild and his fellow-spectators.   He does not profit by the races, like the hotel-keepers and the trades-people.   He does not minister to the necessities of the races, like the booth-keepers, the postilions, the waiters, and the hawkers of Lists.   He does not assist the attractions of the races, like the actors at the theatre, the riders at the circus, or the posturers at the Poses Plastiques.   Absolutely and literally, he is the only individual in Doncaster who stands by the brink of the full-flowing race-stream, and is not swept away by it in common with all the rest of his species.   Who is this modern hermit, this recluse of the St. Leger-week, this inscrutably ungregarious being, who lives apart from the amusements and activities of his fellow-creatures?   Surely, there is little difficulty in guessing that clearest and easiest of all riddles.   Who could he be, but Mr. Thomas Idle?

Thomas had suffered himself to be taken to Doncaster, just as he would have suffered himself to be taken to any other place in the habitable globe which would guarantee him the temporary possession of a comfortable sofa to rest his ankle on.   Once established at the hotel, with his leg on one cushion and his back against another, he formally declined taking the slightest interest in any circumstance whatever connected with the races, or with the people who were assembled to see them.   Francis Goodchild, anxious that the hours should pass by his crippled travelling-companion as lightly as possible, suggested that his sofa should be moved to the window, and that he should amuse himself by looking out at the moving panorama of humanity, which the view from it of the principal street presented. Thomas, however, steadily declined profiting by the suggestion.

"The farther I am from the window," he said, "the better, Brother Francis, I shall be pleased. I have nothing in common with the one prevalent idea of all those people who are passing in the street. Why should I care to look at them?"

"I hope I have nothing in common with the prevalent idea of a great many of them, either," answered Goodchild, thinking of the sporting gentlemen whom he had met in the course of his wanderings about Doncaster. "But, surely, among all the people who are walking by the house, at this very moment, you may find——"

"Not one living creature," interposed Thomas, "who is not, in one way or another, interested in horses, and who is not, in a greater or less degree, an admirer of them. Now, I hold opinions in reference to these particular members of the quadruped creation, which may lay claim (as I believe) to the disastrous distinction of being unpartaken by any other human being, civilised or savage, over the whole surface of the earth. Taking the horse as an animal in the abstract, Francis, I cordially despise him from every point of view."

"Thomas," said Goodchild, "confinement to the house has begun to affect your biliary secretions. I shall go to the chemist's and get you some physic."

"I object," continued Thomas, quietly possessing himself of his friend's hat, which stood on a table near him, — "I object, first, to the personal appearance of the horse. I protest against the conventional idea of beauty, as attached to that animal. I think his nose too long, his forehead too low, and his legs (except in the case of the cart-horse) ridiculously thin by comparison with the size of his body. Again, considering how big an animal he is, I object to the contemptible delicacy of his constitution. Is he not the sickliest creature in creation? Does any child catch cold as easily as a horse? Does he not sprain his fetlock, for all his appearance of superior strength, as easily as I sprained my ankle! Furthermore, to take him from another point of view, what a helpless wretch he is! No fine lady requires more constant waiting-on than a horse. Other animals can make their own toilette: he must have a groom.

You will tell me that this is because we want to make his coat
artificially glossy. Glossy! Come home with me, and see my
cat,—my clever cat, who can groom herself! Look at your
own dog! see how the intelligent creature curry-combs himself
with his own honest teeth! Then, again, what a fool the
horse is, what a poor, nervous fool!   He will start at a piece
of white paper in the road as if it was a lion.   His one idea,
when he hears a noise that he is not accustomed to, is to run
away from it.   What do you say to those two common instances
of the sense and courage of this absurdly overpraised animal?
I might multiply them to two hundred, if I chose to exert my
mind and waste my breath, which I never do.   I prefer coming
at once to my last charge against the horse, which is the most
serious of all, because it affects his moral character.   I accuse
him boldly, in his capacity of servant to man, of slyness and
treachery.   I brand him publicly, no matter how mild he may
look about the eyes, or how sleek he may be about the coat, as
a systematic betrayer, whenever he can get the chance, of the
confidence reposed in him.   What do you mean by laughing
and shaking your head at me?"

"Oh, Thomas, Thomas!" said Goodchild.   "You had
better give me my hat; you had better let me get you that
physic."

"I will let you get anything you like, including a composing
draught for yourself," said Thomas, irritably alluding to his
fellow-apprentice's inexhaustible activity, "if you will only sit
quiet for five minutes longer, and hear me out.   I say again
the horse is a betrayer of the confidence reposed in him ; and
that opinion, let me add, is drawn from my own personal
experience, and is not based on any fanciful theory whatever.
You shall have two instances, two overwhelming instances.   Let
me start the first of these by asking, what is the distinguishing
quality which the Shetland Pony has arrogated to himself, and
is still perpetually trumpeting through the world by means of
popular report and books on Natural History? I see the
answer in your face: it is the quality of being Sure-Footed.
He professes to have other virtues, such as hardiness and
strength, which you may discover on trial ; but the one thing
which he insists on your believing, when you get on his back,
is that he may be safely depended on not to tumble down with

you. Very good. Some years ago, I was in Shetland with a party of friends. They insisted on taking me with them to the top of a precipice that overhung the sea. It was a great distance off, but they all determined to walk to it except me. I was wiser then than I was with you at Carrock, and I determined to be carried to the precipice. There was no carriage road in the island, and nobody offered (in consequence, as I suppose, of the imperfectly-civilised state of the country) to bring me a sedan-chair, which is naturally what I should have liked best. A Shetland pony was produced instead. I remembered my Natural History, I recalled popular report, and I got on the little beast's back, as any other man would have done in my position, placing implicit confidence in the sureness of his feet. And how did he repay that confidence? Brother Francis, carry your mind on from morning to noon. Picture to yourself a howling wilderness of grass and bog, bounded by low stony hills. Pick out one particular spot in that imaginary scene, and sketch me in it, with outstretched arms, curved back, and heels in the air, plunging headforemost into a black patch of water and mud. Place just behind me the legs, the body, and the head of a sure-footed Shetland pony, all stretched flat on the ground, and you will have produced an accurate representation of a very lamentable fact. And the moral device, Francis, of this picture will be to testify that when gentlemen put confidence in the legs of Shetland ponies, they will find to their cost that they are leaning on nothing but broken reeds. There is my first instance—and what have you got to say to that?"

"Nothing, but that I want my hat," answered Goodchild, starting up and walking restlessly about the room.

"You shall have it in a minute," rejoined Thomas. "My second instance "—(Goodchild groaned, and sat down again)—" My second instance is more appropriate to the present time and place, for it refers to a race-horse. Two years ago an excellent friend of mine, who was desirous of prevailing on me to take regular exercise, and who was well enough acquainted with the weakness of my legs to expect no very active compliance with his wishes on their part, offered to make me a present of one of his horses. Hearing that the animal in question had started in life on the turf, I declined accepting the gift with many thanks; adding, by way of explanation, that I looked on a race-horse as a kind of embodied hurricane, upon which no sane man of my character and habits could be expected to seat himself. My friend replied that, however appropriate my metaphor might be as applied to race-horses in general, it was singularly unsuitable as applied to the particular horse which he proposed to give me. From a foal upwards this remarkable animal had been the idlest and most sluggish of his race. Whatever capacities for speed he might possess he had kept so strictly to himself, that no amount of training had ever brought them out. He had been found hopelessly slow as a racer, and hopelessly lazy as a hunter, and was fit for nothing but a quiet, easy life of it with an old gentleman or an invalid. When I heard this account of the horse, I don't mind confessing that my heart warmed to him. Visions of Thomas Idle ambling serenely on the back of a steed as lazy as himself, presenting to a restless world the soothing and composite spectacle of a kind of sluggardly Centaur, too peaceable in his habits to alarm anybody, swam attractively before my eyes. I went to look at the horse in the stable. Nice fellow ! he was fast asleep with a kitten on his back. I saw him taken out for an airing by the groom. If he had had trousers on his legs I should not have known them from my own, so deliberately were they lifted up, so gently were they put down, so slowly did they get over the ground. From that moment I gratefully accepted my friend's offer. I went home ; the horse followed me—by a slow train. Oh, Francis, how devoutly I believed in that horse ! how carefully I looked after all his little comforts ! I had never gone the length of hiring a man-servant to wait on myself ; but I went to the expense of hiring one to wait upon him. If I thought a little of myself when I bought the softest saddle that could be had for money, I thought also of my horse. When the man at the shop afterwards offered me spurs and a whip, I turned from him with horror. When I sallied out for my first ride, I went purposely unarmed with the means of hurrying my steed. He proceeded at his own pace every step of the way ; and when he stopped, at last, and blew out both his sides with a heavy sigh, and turned his sleepy head and looked behind him, I took him home again, as I might take home an artless child who said to me, 'If you please, sir, I am tired.' For a week this complete harmony between me and my horse lasted undisturbed. At the end of that time, when he had made quite sure of my friendly confidence in his laziness, when he had thoroughly acquainted himself with all the little weaknesses of my seat (and their name is Legion), the smouldering treachery and ingratitude of the equine nature blazed out in an instant. Without the slightest provocation from me, with nothing passing him at the time but a pony-chaise driven by an old lady, he started in one instant from a state of sluggish depression to a state of frantic high spirits. He kicked, he plunged, he shied, he pranced, he capered fearfully. I sat on him as long as I could, and when I could sit no longer, I fell off. No, Francis! this is not a circumstance to be laughed at, but to be wept over. What would be said of a Man who had requited my kindness in that way? Range over all the rest of the animal creation, and where will you find me an instance of treachery so black as this? The cow that kicks down the milking-pail may have some reason for it; she may think herself taxed too heavily to contribute to the dilution of human tea and the greasing of human bread. The tiger who springs out on me unawares has the excuse of being hungry at the time, to say nothing of the further justification of being a total stranger to me. The very flea who surprises me in my sleep may defend his act of assassination on the ground that I, in my turn, am always ready to murder him when I am awake. I defy the whole body of Natural Historians to move me, logically, off the ground that I have taken in regard to the horse. Receive back your hat, Brother Francis, and go to the chemist's, if you please; for I have now done. Ask me to take anything you like, except an interest in the Doncaster races. Ask me to look at anything you like, except an assemblage of people all animated by feelings of a friendly and admiring nature towards the horse. You are a remarkably well-informed man, and you have heard of hermits. Look upon me as a member of that ancient fraternity, and you will sensibly add to the many obligations which Thomas Idle is proud to owe to Francis Goodchild."

Here, fatigued by the effort of excessive talking, disputatious Thomas waved one hand languidly, laid his head back on the sofa-pillow, and calmly closed his eyes.

At a later period, Mr. Goodchild assailed his travelling companion boldly from the impregnable fortress of common sense.

But Thomas, though tamed in body by drastic discipline, was still as mentally unapproachable as ever on the subject of his favourite delusion.

The view from the window after Saturday's breakfast is altogether changed. The tradesmen's families have all come back again. The serious stationer's young woman of all work is shaking a duster out of the window of the combination breakfast-room; a child is playing with a doll, where Mr. Thurtell's hair was brushed; a sanitary scrubbing is in progress on the spot where Mr. Palmer's braces were put on. No signs of the Races are in the streets, but the tramps and the tumble-down carts and trucks laden with drinking-forms and tables and remnants of booths, that are making their way out of the town as fast as they can. The Angel, which has been cleared for action all the week, already begins restoring every neat and comfortable article of furniture to its own neat and comfortable place. The Angel's daughters (pleasanter angels Mr. Idle and Mr. Goodchild never saw, nor more quietly expert in their business, nor more superior to the common vice of being above it), have a little time to rest, and to air their cheerful faces among the flowers in the yard. It is market-day. The market looks unusually natural, comfortable, and wholesome; the market-people too. The town seems quite restored, when, hark ! a metallic bray—The Gong-donkey !

The wretched animal has not cleared off with the rest, but is here, under the window. How much more inconceivably drunk now, how much more begrimed of paw, how much more tight of calico hide, how much more stained and daubed and dirty and dunghilly, from his horrible broom to his tender toes, who shall say ! He cannot even shake the bray out of himself now, without laying his cheek so near to the mud of the street, that he pitches over after delivering it. Now, prone in the mud, and now backing himself up against shop-windows, the owners of which come out in terror to remove him ; now, in the drinking-shop, and now in the tobacconist's, where he goes to buy tobacco, and makes his way into the parlor, and where he gets a cigar, which in half-a-minute he forgets to smoke ; now dancing, now dozing, now cursing, and now complimenting My Lord, the Colonel, the Noble Captain, and Your Honoiable

Worship, the Gong-donkey kicks up his heels, occasionally braying, until suddenly, he beholds the dearest friend he has in the world coming down the street.

The dearest friend the Gong-donkey has in the world, is a sort of Jackall, in a dull mangy black hide, of such small pieces that it looks as if it were made of blacking bottles turned inside out and cobbled together. The dearest friend in the world (inconceivably drunk too) advances at the Gong-donkey, with a hand on each thigh, in a series of humorous springs and stops, wagging his head as he comes. The Gong-donkey regarding him with attention and with the warmest affection, suddenly perceives that he is the greatest enemy he has in the world, and hits him hard in the countenance. The astonished Jackall closes with the Donkey, and they roll over and over in the mud, pummelling one another. A Police Inspector, supernaturally endowed with patience, who has long been looking on from the Guildhall-steps, says, to a myrmidon, "Lock 'em up! Bring 'em in!"

Appropriate finish to the Grand Race Week. The Gong-donkey, captive and last trace of it, conveyed into limbo, where they cannot do better than keep him until next Race Week. The Jackall is wanted too, and is much looked for, over the way and up and down. But, having had the good-fortune to be undermost at the time of the capture, he has vanished into air.

On Saturday afternoon, Mr. Goodchild walks out and looks at the Course. It is quite deserted; heaps of broken crockery and bottles are raised to its memory; and correct cards and other fragments of paper are blowing about it, as the regulation little paper-books, carried by the French soldiers in their breasts, were seen, soon after the battle was fought, blowing idly about the plains of Waterloo.

Where will these present idle leaves be blown by the idle winds, and where will the last of them be one day lost and forgotten? An idle question, and an idle thought; and with it Mr. Idle fitly makes his bow, and Mr. Goodchild his, and thus ends the Lazy Tour of Two Idle Apprentices.

NO THOROUGHFARE.

NO THOROUGHFARE.

THE OVERTURE.

Day of the month and year, November the thirtieth, one thousand eight hundred and thirty-five. London Time by the great clock of Saint Paul's, ten at night. All the lesser London churches strain their metallic throats. Some, flippantly begin before the heavy bell of the great cathedal ; some, tardily begin three, four, half a dozen, strokes behind it; all are in sufficiently near accord, to leave a resonance in the air, as if the winged father who devours his children, had made a sounding sweep with his gigantic scythe in flying over the city.

What is this clock lower than most of the rest, and nearer to the ear, that lags so far behind to-night as to strike into the vibration alone? This is the clock of the Hospital for Foundling Children. Time was, when the Foundlings were received without question in a cradle at the gate. Time is, when inquiries are made respecting them, and they are taken as by favour from the mothers who relinquish all natural knowledge of them and claim to them for evermore.

The moon is at the full, and the night is fair with light clouds. The day has been otherwise than fair, for slush and mud, thickened with the droppings of heavy fog, lie black in the streets. The veiled lady who flutters up and down near the postern-gate of the Hospital for Foundling Children has need to be well shod to-night.

She flutters to and fro, avoiding the stand of hackney-coaches, and often pausing in the shadow of the western end of the great quadrangle wall, with her face turned towards the gate.   As above her there is the purity of the moonlit sky, and below her there are the defilements of the pavement, so may she, haply, be divided in her mind between two vistas of reflection or experience?   As her footprints crossing and recrossing one another have made a labyrinth in the mire, so may her track in life have involved itself in an intricate and unravellable tangle?

The postern-gate of the Hospital for Foundling Children opens, and a young woman comes out.   The lady stands aside, observes closely, sees that the gate is quietly closed again from within, and follows the young woman.

Two or three streets have been traversed in silence before she, following close behind the object of her attention, stretches out her hand and touches her.   Then the young woman stops and looks round, startled.

"You touched me last night, and, when I turned my head, you would not speak.   Why do you follow me like a silent ghost?"

"It was not," returned the lady, in a low voice, "that I would not speak, but that I could not when I tried."

"What do you want of me?   I have never done you any harm?"

"Never."

"Do I know you?"

"No."

"Then what can you want of me?"

"Here are two guineas in this paper.   Take my poor little present, and I will tell you."

Into the young woman's face, which is honest and comely, comes a flush as she replies: "There is neither grown person nor child in all the large establishment that I belong to, who hasn't a good word for Sally.   I am Sally.   Could I be so well thought of, if I was to be bought?"

"I do not mean to buy you; I mean only to reward you very slightly."

Sally firmly, but not urgently, closes and puts back the offering hand.   "If there is anything that I can do for you, ma'am, that I will not do for its own sake, you are much mistaken in me if you think that I will do it for money.   What is it you want?"

"You are one of the nurses or attendants at the Hospital, I saw you leave to-night and last night."

"Yes, I am. I am Sally."

"There is a pleasant patience in your face which makes me believe that very young children would take readily to you."

"God bless 'em! So they do."

The lady lifts her veil, and shows a face no older than the nurse's. A face far more refined and capable than hers, but wild and worn with sorrow.

"I am the miserable mother of a baby lately received under your care. I have a prayer to make to you."

Instinctively respecting the confidence which has drawn aside the veil, Sally—whose ways are all ways of simplicity and spontaneity—replaces it, and begins to cry.

"You will listen to my prayer?" the lady urges. "You will not be deaf to the agonised entreaty of such a broken suppliant as I am?"

"Oh, dear, dear, dear!" cries Sally. "What shall I say, or can I say! Don't talk of prayers. Prayers are to be put up to the Good Father of All, and not to nurses and such. And there! I am only to hold my place for half a year longer, till another young woman can be trained up to it. I am going to be married. I shouldn't have been out last night, and I shouldn't have been out to-night, but that my Dick (he is the young man I am going to be married to) lies ill, and I help his mother and sister to watch him. Don't take on so, don't take on so!"

"O good Sally, dear Sally," moans the lady, catching at her dress entreatingly. "As you are hopeful and I am hopeless; as a fair way in life is before you, which can never, never, be before me; as you can aspire to become a respected wife, and as you can aspire to become a proud mother; as you are a living loving woman, and must die; for God's sake hear my distracted petition!"

"Deary, deary, deary ME!" cries Sally, her desperation culminating in the pronoun, "what am I ever to do? And there! See how you turn my own words back upon me. I tell you I am going to be married, on purpose to make it clearer to you that I am going to leave, and therefore couldn't help you if I would, Poor Thing, and you make it seem to my

own self as if I was cruel in going to be married and *not* helping
you. It ain't kind. Now, is it kind, Poor Thing?"

"Sally! Hear me, my dear. My entreaty is for no help in
the future. It applies to what is past. It is only to be told in
two words."

"There ! This is worse and worse," cries Sally, "supposing
that I understand what two words you mean."

"You do understand. What are the names they have
given my poor baby? I ask no more than that. I have read
of the customs of the place. He has been christened in the
chapel, and registered by some surname in the book. He was
received last Monday evening. What have they called him?"

Down upon her knees in the foul mud of the by-way into
which they have strayed—an empty street without a thoroughfare, giving on the dark gardens of the Hospital—the lady would
drop in her passionate entreaty, but that Sally prevents her.

"Don't! Don't! You make me feel as if I was setting
myself up to be good. Let me look in your pretty face again.
Put your two hands in mine. Now, promise. You will never
ask me anything more than the two words?"

"Never! Never!"

"You will never put them to a bad use, if I say them?"

"Never! Never!"

"Walter Wilding."

The lady lays her face upon the nurse's breast, draws her
close in her embrace with both arms, murmurs a blessing and
the words, "Kiss him for me!" and is gone.

Day of the month and year, the first Sunday in October,
one thousand eight hundred and forty-seven. London Time by
the great clock of Saint Paul's, half-past one in the afternoon.
The clock of the Hospital for Foundling Children is well up
with the Cathedral to-day. Service in the chapel is over, and
the Foundling children are at dinner.

There are numerous lookers-on at the dinner, as the custom
is. There are two or three governors, whole families from the
congregation, smaller groups of both sexes, individual stragglers
of various degrees. The bright autumnal sun strikes freshly
into the wards ; and the heavy-framed windows through which
it shines, and the panelled walls on which it strikes, are such

windows and such walls as pervade Hogarth's pictures. The girls' refectory (including that of the younger children) is the principal attraction. Neat attendants silently glide about the orderly and silent tables ; the lookers-on move or stop as the fancy takes them ; comments in whispers on face such a number from such a window are not unfrequent ; many of the faces are of a character to fix attention. Some of the visitors from the outside public are accustomed visitors. They have established a speaking acquaintance with the occupants of particular seats at the tables, and halt at those points to bend down and say a word or two. It is no disparagement to their kindness that those points are generally points where personal attractions are. The monotony of the long spacious rooms and the double lines of faces, is agreeably relieved by these incidents, although so slight.

A veiled lady, who has no companion, goes among the company. It would seem that curiosity and opportunity have never brought her there before. She has the air of being a little troubled by the sight, and, as she goes the length of the tables, it is with a hestitating step and an uneasy manner. At length she comes to the refectory of the boys. They are so much less popular than the girls that it is bare of visitors when she looks in at the doorway.

But just within the doorway, chances to stand, inspecting, an elderly female attendant : some order of matron or house-keeper. To whom the lady addresses natural questions : As, how many boys ? At what age are they usually put out in life ? Do they often take a fancy to the sea ? So, lower and lower in tone until the lady puts the question : "Which is Walter Wilding ?"

Attendant's head shaken. Against the rules.

"You know which is Walter Wilding ?"

So keenly does the attendant feel the closeness with which the lady's eyes examine her face, that she keeps her own eyes fast upon the floor, lest by wandering in the right direction they should betray her.

"I know which is Walter Wilding, but it is not my place, ma'am, to tell names to visitors."

"But you can show me without telling me."

The lady's hand moves quietly to the attendant's hand. Pause and silence.

"I am going to pass round the tables," says the lady's interlocutor, without seeming to address her. "Follow me with your eyes. The boy that I stop and speak to, will not matter to you. But the boy that I touch, will be Walter Wilding. Say nothing more to me, and move a little away."

Quickly acting on the hint, the lady passes on into the room, and looks about her. After a few moments, the attendant, in a staid official way, walks down outside the line of tables commencing on her left hand. She goes the whole length of the line, turns, and comes back on the inside. Very slightly glancing in the lady's direction, she stops, bends forward, and speaks. The boy whom she addresses, lifts his head and replies. Good humouredly and easily, as she listens to what he says, she lays her hand upon the shoulder of the next boy on his right. That the action may be well noted, she keeps her hand on the shoulder while speaking in return, and pats it twice or thrice before moving away. She completes her tour of the tables, touching no one else, and passes out by a door at the opposite end of the long room.

Dinner is done, and the lady, too, walks down outside the line of tables commencing on her left hand, goes the whole length of the line, turns, and comes back on the inside. Other people have strolled in, fortunately for her, and stand sprinkled about. She lifts her veil, and, stopping at the touched boy, asks how old he is?

"I am twelve, ma'am," he answers, with his bright eyes fixed on hers.

"Are you well and happy?"

"Yes, ma'am."

"May you take these sweetmeats from my hand?"

"If you please to give them to me."

In stooping low for the purpose, the lady touches the boy's face with her forehead and with her hair. Then, lowering her veil again, she passes on, and passes out without looking back.

ACT I.

In a court-yard in the City of London, which was No Thoroughfare either for vehicles or foot-passengers ; a court-yard diverging
from a steep, a slippery, and a winding street connecting Tower-
street with the Middlesex shore of the Thames ; stood the place
of business of Wilding and Co. Wine Merchants. Probably,
as a jocose acknowledgment of the obstructive character of this
main approach, the point nearest to its base at which one could
take the river (if so inodorously minded) bore the appellation
Break-Neck-Stairs. The court-yard itself had likewise been
descriptively entitled in old time, Cripple Corner.

Years before the year one thousand eight hundred and sixty-
one, people had left off taking boat at Break-Neck-Stairs, and
watermen had ceased to ply there. The slimy little causeway
had dropped into the river by a slow process of suicide, and
two or three stumps of piles and a rusty iron mooring-ring were
all that remained of the departed Break-Neck glories. Sometimes, indeed, a laden coal barge would bump itself into the
place, and certain laborious heavers, seemingly mud-engendered,
would arise, deliver the cargo in the neighbourhood, shove off,
and vanish ; but at most times the only commerce of Break-
Neck-Stairs arose out of the conveyance of casks and bottles,
both full and empty, both to and from the cellars of Wilding
and Co. Wine Merchants. Even that commerce was but occasional, and through three-fourths of its rising tides the dirty
indecorous drab of a river would come solitarily oozing and
lapping at the rusty ring, as if it had heard of the Doge and the

Adriatic, and wanted to be married to the great conserver of its filthiness, the Right Honourable the Lord Mayor.

Some two hundred and fifty yards on the right, up the opposite hill (approaching it from the low ground of Break-Neck-Stairs) was Cripple Corner. There was a pump in Cripple Corner, there was a tree in Cripple Corner. All Cripple Corner belonged to Wilding and Co. Wine Merchants. Their cellars burrowed under it, their mansion towered over it. It really had been a mansion in the days when merchants inhabited the City, and had a ceremonious shelter to the doorway without visible support, like the sounding-board over an old pulpit. It had also a number of long narrow strips of window, so disposed in its grave brick front as to render it symmetrically ugly. It had also on its roof, a cupola with a bell in it.

"When a man at five-and-twenty can put his hat on, and can say 'this hat covers the owner of this property and of the business which is transacted *on* this property,' I consider, Mr. Bintrey, that, without being boastful, he may be allowed to be deeply thankful. I don't know how it may appear to you, but so it appears to me."

Thus Mr. Walter Wilding to his man of law, in his own counting-house; taking his hat down from its peg to suit the action to the word, and hanging it up again when he had done so, not to overstep the modesty of nature.

An innocent, open-speaking, unused-looking man, Mr. Walter Wilding, with a remarkably pink and white complexion, and a figure much too bulky for so young a man, though of a good stature. With crispy curling brown hair, and amiable bright blue eyes. An extremely communicative man: a man with whom loquacity was the irrestrainable outpouring of contentment and gratitude. Mr. Bintrey, on the other hand, a cautious man with twinkling beads of eyes in a large overhanging bald head, who inwardly but intensely enjoyed the comicality of openness of speech, or hand, or heart.

"Yes," said Mr. Bintrey. "Yes. Ha, ha!"

A decanter, two wine-glasses, and a plate of biscuits, stood on the desk.

"You like this forty-five year old port wine?" said Mr. Wilding.

"Like it?" repeated Mr. Bintrey. "Rather, sir!"

"It's from the best corner of our best forty-five year old bin," said Mr. Wilding.

"Thank you, sir," said Mr. Bintrey. "It's most excellent."

He laughed again, as he held up his glass and ogled it, at the highly ludicrous idea of giving away such wine.

"And now," said Wilding, with a childish enjoyment in the discussion of affairs, "I think we have got everything straight, Mr. Bintrey."

"Everything straight," said Bintrey.

"A partner secured——"

"Partner secured," said Bintrey.

"A housekeeper advertised for——"

"Housekeeper advertised for," said Bintrey, "'apply personally at Cripple Corner, Great Tower-street, from ten to twelve'—to-morrow, by-the-by."

"My late dear mother's affairs wound up——"

"Wound up," said Bintrey.

"And all charges paid."

"And all charges paid," said Bintrey, with a chuckle: probably occasioned by the droll circumstance that they had been paid without a haggle.

"The mention of my late dear mother," Mr. Wilding continued, his eyes filling with tears and his pocket-handkerchief drying them, "unmans me still, Mr. Bintrey. You know how I loved her; you (her lawyer) know how she loved me. The utmost love of mother and child was cherished between us, and we never experienced one moment's division or unhappiness from the time when she took me under her care. Thirteen years in all ! Thirteen years under my late dear mother's care, Mr. Bintrey, and eight of them her confidentially acknowledged son ! You know the story, Mr. Bintrey, who but you, sir !" Mr. Wilding sobbed and dried his eyes, without attempt at concealment, during these remarks.

Mr. Bintrey enjoyed his comical port, and said, after rolling it in his mouth : "I know the story."

"My late dear mother, Mr. Bintrey," pursued the wine-merchant, "had been deeply deceived, and had cruelly suffered. But on that subject my late dear mother's lips were for ever sealed. By whom deceived, or under what circumstances, Heaven only knows. My late dear mother never betrayed her betrayer."

"She had made up her mind," said Mr. Bintrey, again turning his wine on his palate, "and she could hold her peace." An amused twinkle in his eyes pretty plainly added—"A devilish deal better than *you* ever will !"

" ' Honour,' " said Mr. Wilding, sobbing as he quoted from the Commandments, " 'thy father and thy mother, that thy days may be long in the land.' When I was in the Foundling, Mr. Bintrey, I was at such a loss how to do it, that I apprehended my days would be short in the land. But I afterwards came to honour my mother deeply, profoundly. And I honour and revere her memory. For seven happy years, Mr. Bintrey," pursued Wilding, still with the same innocent catching in his breath, and the same unabashed tears, "did my excellent mother article me to my predecessors in this business, Pebbleson Nephew. Her affectionate forethought likewise apprenticed me to the Vintners' Company, and made me in time a Free Vintner, and —and—everything else that the best of mothers could desire. When I came of age, she bestowed her inherited share in this business upon me ; it was her money that afterwards bought out Pebbleson Nephew, and painted in Wilding and Co. ; it was she who left me everything she possessed, but the mourning ring you wear. And yet, Mr. Bintrey," with a fresh burst of honest affection, "she is no more. It is a little over half a year since she came into the Corner to read on that door-post with her own eyes, WILDING AND Co. WINE MERCHANTS. And yet she is no more ! "

"Sad. But the common lot, Mr. Wilding," observed Bintrey. "At some time or other we must all be no more." He placed the forty-five year old port wine in the universal condition, with a relishing sigh.

"So now, Mr. Bintrey," pursued Wilding, putting away his pocket-handkerchief, and smoothing his eyelids with his fingers, "now that I can no longer show my love and honour for the dear parent to whom my heart was mysteriously turned by Nature when she first spoke to me, a strange lady, I sitting at our Sunday dinner-table in the Foundling, I can at least show that I am not ashamed of having been a Foundling, and that I, who never knew a father of my own, wish to be a father to all in my employment. Therefore," continued Wilding, becoming enthusiastic in his loquacity, "therefore, I want a thoroughly good housekeeper to undertake this dwelling-house of Wilding and Co. Wine Merchants, Cripple Corner, so that I may restore in it some of the old relations betwixt employer and employed! So that I may live in it on the spot where my money is made! So that I may daily sit at the head of the table at which the people in my employment eat together, and may eat of the same roast and boiled, and drink of the same beer! So that the people in my employment may lodge under the same roof with me! So that we may one and all——I beg your pardon, Mr. Bintrey, but that old singing in my head has suddenly come on, and I shall feel obliged if you will lead me to the pump."

Alarmed by the excessive pinkness of his client, Mr. Bintrey lost not a moment in leading him forth into the court-yard. It was easily done, for the counting-house in which they talked together opened on to it, at one side of the dwelling-house. There, the attorney pumped with a will, obedient to a sign from the client, and the client laved his head and face with both hands, and took a hearty drink. After these remedies, he declared himself much better.

"Don't let your good feelings excite you," said Bintrey, as they returned to the counting-house, and Mr. Wilding dried himself on a jack-towel behind an inner door

"No, no. I won't," he returned, looking out of the towel. "I won't. I have not been confused, have I?"

"Not at all. Perfectly clear."

"Where did I leave off, Mr. Bintrey?"

"Well, you left off—but I wouldn't excite myself, if I was you, by taking it up again just yet."

"I'll take care. I'll take care. The singing in my head came on at where, Mr. Bintrey?"

"At roast, and boiled, and beer," answered the lawyer, prompting—"lodging under the same roof—and one and all——"

"Ah! And one and all singing in the head together——"

"Do you know I really *would not* let my good feelings excite me, if I was you," hinted the lawyer again, anxiously. "Try some more pump."

"No occasion, no occasion. All right, Mr. Bintrey. And one and all forming a kind of family! You see, Mr. Bintrey, I was not used in my childhood to that sort of individual existence which most individuals have led, more or less, in their childhood. After that time I became absorbed in my late dear mother. Having lost her, I find that I am more fit for being one of a body than one by myself one. To be that, and at the same time to do my duty to those dependent on me, and attach them to me, has a patriarchal and pleasant air about it. I don't know how it may appear to you, Mr. Bintrey, but so it appears to me."

"It is not I who am all-important in the case, but you," returned Bintrey. "Consequently, how it may appear to me, is of very small importance."

"It appears to *me*," said Mr. Wilding, in a glow, "hopeful, useful, de-lightful!"

"Do you know," hinted the lawyer again, "I really would not ex——"

"I am not going to. Then there's Handel."

"There's who?" asked Bintrey.

"Handel, Mozart, Haydn, Kent, Purcell, Doctor Arne, Greene, Mendelssohn. I know the choruses to those anthems by heart. Foundling Chapel Collection. Why shouldn't we learn them together!"

"Who learn them together?" asked the lawyer, rather shortly.

"Employer and employed."

"Aye, aye!" returned Bintrey, mollified; as if he had half expected the answer to be, Lawyer and client. "That's another thing."

"Not another thing, Mr. Bintrey! The same thing. A part of the bond among us. We will form a Choir in some quiet church near the Corner here, and, having sung together of a Sunday with a relish, we will come home and take an early dinner together with a relish. The object that I have at heart now, is to get this system well in action without delay, so that my new partner may find it founded when he enters on his partnership."

"All good be with it!" exclaimed Bintrey, rising. "May it prosper! Is Joey Ladle to take a share in Handel, Mozart, Haydn, Kent, Purcell, Doctor Arne, Greene, and Mendelssohn?"

"I hope so."

"I wish them all well out of it," returned Bintrey, with much heartiness. "Good-bye, sir."

They shook hands and parted. Then (first knocking with
his knuckles for leave) entered to Mr. Wilding, from a door of
communication between his private counting-house and that in
which his clerks sat, the Head Cellarman of the cellars of
Wilding and Co. Wine Merchants, and erst Head Cellarman of
the cellars of Pebbleson Nephew The Joey Ladle in question.
A slow and ponderous man, of the drayman order of human
architecture, dressed in a corrugated suit and bibbed apron,
apparently a composite of door-mat and rhinoceros-hide.

"Respecting this same boarding and lodging, Young Master
Wilding," said he.

"Yes, Joey?"

"Speaking for myself, Young Master Wilding—and I never
did speak and I never do speak for no one else—*I* don't want
no boarding nor yet no lodging. But if you wish to board me
and to lodge me, take me. I can peck as well as most men.
Where I peck, ain't so high a object with me as What I peck.
Nor even so high a object with me as How Much I peck. Is
all to live in the house, Young Master Wilding? The two
other cellarmen, the three porters, the two 'prentices, and the
odd men?"

"Yes. I hope we shall all be an united family, Joey."

"Ah!" said Joey. "I hope they may be."

"They? Rather say we, Joey."

Joey Ladle shook his head. "Don't look to me to make
we on it, Young Master Wilding, not at my time of life and
under the circumstances which has formed my disposition. I
have said to Pebbleson Nephew many a time, when they have
said to me, 'Put a livelier face upon it, Joey'—I have said to
them, 'Gentlemen, it is all wery well for you that has been
accustomed to take your wine into your systems by the convivial channel of your throttles, to put a lively face upon it;
but,' I says, 'I have been accustomed to take *my* wine in
at the pores of the skin, and, took that away, it acts different.
It acts depressing. It's one thing, gentlemen,' I says to
Pebbleson Nephew, 'to charge your glasses in a dining-room
with a Hip Hurrah and a Jolly Companions Every One, and
it's another thing to be charged yourself, through the pores, in
a low dark cellar and a mouldy atmosphere. It makes all the
difference betwixt bubbles and wapours,' I tells Pebbleson

Nephew. And so it do. I've been a cellarman my life through, with my mind fully given to the business. What's the consequence? I'm as muddled a man as lives—you won't find a muddleder man than me—nor yet you won't find my equal in molloncolly. Sing of Filling the bumper fair, Every drop you sprinkle, O'er the brow of care, Smooths away a wrinkle? Yes. P'raps so. But try filling yourself through the pores, underground, when you don't want to it!"

"I am sorry to hear this, Joey. I had even thought that you might join a singing-class in the house."

"Me, sir? No, no, Young Master Wilding, you won't catch Joey Ladle muddling the Armony. A pecking-machine, sir, is all that I am capable of proving myself, out of my cellars; but that you're welcome to, if you think it's worth your while to keep such a thing on your premises."

"I do, Joey."

"Say no more, sir. The Business's word is my law. And you're a going to take Young Master George Vendale partner into the old Business?"

"I am, Joey."

"More changes, you see! But don't change the name of the Firm again. Don't do it, Young Master Wilding. It was bad luck enough to make it Yourself and Co. Better by far have left it Pebbleson Nephew that good luck always stuck to. You should never change luck when it's good, sir."

"At all events, I have no intention of changing the name of the House again, Joey."

"Glad to hear it, and wish you good day, Young Master Wilding. But you had better by half," muttered Joey Ladle, inaudibly, as he closed the door and shook his head, "have let the name alone from the first. You had better by half have followed the luck instead of crossing it."

ENTER THE HOUSEKEEPER.

The wine-merchant sat in his dining-room next morning, to receive the personal applicants for the vacant post in his establishment. It was an old-fashioned wainscoted room; the panels ornamented with festoons of flowers carved in wood; with an oaken floor, a well-worn Turkey carpet, and dark mahogany furniture, all of which had seen service and polish under Pebbleson Nephew. The great sideboard had assisted at many business-dinners given by Pebbleson Nephew to their connexion, on the principle of throwing sprats overboard to catch whales ; and Pebbleson Nephew's comprehensive three-sided plate-warmer, made to fit the whole front of the large fireplace, kept watch beneath it over a sarcophagus-shaped cellaret that had in its time held many a dozen of Pebbleson Nephew's wine. But the little rubicund old bachelor with a pigtail, whose portrait was over the sideboard (and who could easily be identified as decidedly Pebbleson and decidedly not Nephew), had retired into another sarcophagus, and the plate-warmer had grown as cold as he. So, the golden and black griffins that supported the candelabra, with black balls in their mouths at the end of gilded chains, looked as if in their old age they had lost all heart for playing at ball, and were dolefully exhibiting their chains in the missionary line of inquiry, whether they had not earned emancipation by this time, and were not griffins and brothers?

Such a Columbus of a morning was the summer morning, that it discovered Cripple Corner. The light and warmth pierced in at the open windows, and irradiated the picture of a lady hanging over the chimney-piece, the only other decoration of the walls.

"My mother at five-and-twenty," said Mr. Wilding to himself, as his eyes enthusiastically followed the light to the portrait's face, "I hang up here, in order that visitors may admire my mother in the bloom of her youth and beauty. My mother at fifty I hang in the seclusion of my own chamber, as a remembrance sacred to me. Oh! It's you, Jarvis!"

These latter words he addressed to a clerk who had tapped at the door, and now looked in.

"Yes, sir. I merely wish to mention that it's gone ten, sir, and that there are several females in the Counting-House."

"Dear me!" said the wine-merchant, deepening in the pink of his complexion and whitening in the white, "are there several? So many as several? I had better begin before there are more. I'll see them one by one, Jarvis, in the order of their arrival."

Hastily entrenching himself in his easy-chair at the table

behind a great inkstand, having first placed a chair on the other side of the table opposite his own seat, Mr. Wilding entered on his task with considerable trepidation.

He ran the gauntlet that must be run on any such occasion. There were the usual species of profoundly unsympathetic women, and the usual species of much too sympathetic women. There were the buccaneering widows who came to seize him, and who griped umbrellas under their arms, as if each umbrella were he, and each griper had got him. There were towering maiden ladies who had seen better days, and who came armed with clerical testimonials to their theology, as if he were Saint Peter with his keys. There were gentle maiden ladies who came to marry him. There were professional housekeepers, like non-commissioned officers, who put him through his domestic exercise, instead of submitting themselves to catechism. There were languid invalids to whom salary was not so much an object as the comforts of a private hospital. There were sensitive creatures who burst into tears on being addressed, and had to be restored with glasses of cold water. There were some respondents who came two together, a highly promising one and a wholly unpromising one: of whom the promising one answered all questions charmingly, until it would at last appear that she was not a candidate at all, but only the friend of the un-promising one, who had glowered in absolute silence and apparent injury.

At last, when the good wine-merchant's simple heart was failing him, there entered an applicant quite different from all the rest. A woman, perhaps fifty, but looking younger, with a face remarkable for placid cheerfulness, and a manner no less remarkable for its quiet expression of equability of temper. Nothing in her dress could have been changed to her advantage. Nothing in the noiseless self-possession of her manner could have been changed to her advantage. Nothing could have been in better unison with both, than her voice when she answered the question : " What name shall I have the pleasure of noting down ? " with the words, " My name is Sarah Goldstraw. Mrs. Goldstraw. My husband has been dead many years, and we had no family."

Half a dozen questions had scarcely extracted as much to the purpose from any one else. The voice dwelt so agreeably on Mr. Wilding's ear as he made his note, that he was rather long about it. When he looked up again, Mrs. Goldstraw's glance had naturally gone round the room, and now returned to him from the chimney-piece. Its expression was one of frank readiness to be questioned, and to answer straight.

"You will excuse my asking you a few questions?" said the modest wine-merchant.

"Oh, surely, sir. Or I should have no business here."

"Have you filled the station of housekeeper before?"

"Only once. I have lived with the same widow lady for twelve years. Ever since I lost my husband. She was an invalid, and is lately dead : which is the occasion of my now wearing black."

"I do not doubt that she has left you the best credentials?" said Mr. Wilding.

"I hope I may say, the very best. I thought it would save trouble, sir, if I wrote down the name and address of her representatives, and brought it with me." Laying a card on the table.

"You singularly remind me, Mrs. Goldstraw," said Wilding, taking the card beside him, "of a manner and tone of voice that I was once acquainted with. Not of an individual—I feel sure of that, though I cannot recal what it is I have in my mind—but of a general bearing. I ought to add, it was a kind and pleasant one."

She smiled, as she rejoined : "At least, I am very glad of that, sir."

"Yes," said the wine-merchant, thoughtfully repeating his last phrase, with a momentary glance at his future housekeeper, "it was a kind and pleasant one. But that is the most I can make of it. Memory is sometimes like a half-forgotten dream. I don't know how it may appear to you, Mrs. Goldstraw, but so it appears to me."

Probably it appeared to Mrs. Goldstraw in a similar light, for she quietly assented to the proposition. Mr. Wilding then offered to put himself at once in communication with the gentlemen named upon the card : a firm of proctors in Doctors' Commons. To this, Mrs. Goldstraw thankfully assented. Doctors' Commons not being far off, Mr. Wilding suggested the feasibility of Mrs. Goldstraw's looking in again, say in three hours' time. Mrs. Goldstraw readily undertook to do so. In fine, the result of Mr. Wilding's inquiries being eminently satisfactory, Mrs. Goldstraw was that afternoon engaged (on her own perfectly fair terms) to come to-morrow and set up her rest as housekeeper in Cripple Corner.

THE HOUSEKEEPER SPEAKS.

On the next day Mrs. Goldstraw arrived, to enter on her domestic duties.

Having settled herself in her own room, without troubling the servants, and without wasting time, the new housekeeper announced herself as waiting to be favoured with any instructions which her master might wish to give her. The wine-merchant received Mrs. Goldstraw in the dining-room, in which he had seen her on the previous day; and, the usual preliminary civilities having passed on either side, the two sat down to take counsel together on the affairs of the house.

"About the meals, sir?" said Mrs. Goldstraw. "Have I a large, or a small, number to provide for?"

"If I can carry out a certain old-fashioned plan of mine," replied Mr. Wilding, "you will have a large number to provide for. I am a lonely single man, Mrs. Goldstraw; and I hope to live with all the persons in my employment as if they were members of my family. Until that time comes, you will only have me, and the new partner whom I expect immediately, to provide for. What my partner's habits may be, I cannot yet say. But I may describe myself as a man of regular hours, with an invariable appetite that you may depend upon to an ounce."

"About breakfast, sir?" asked Mrs. Goldstraw. "Is there anything particular——?"

She hesitated, and left the sentence unfinished. Her eyes turned slowly away from her master, and looked towards the chimney-piece. If she had been a less excellent and experienced housekeeper, Mr. Wilding might have fancied that her attention was beginning to wander at the very outset of the interview.

"Eight o'clock is my breakfast-hour," he resumed. "It is one of my virtues to be never tired of broiled bacon, and it is one of my vices to be habitually suspicious of the freshness of eggs." Mrs. Goldstraw looked back at him, still a little divided between her master's chimney-piece and her master. "I take tea," Mr. Wilding went on; "and I am perhaps rather nervous and fidgety about drinking it, within a certain time after it is made. If my tea stands too long——"

He hesitated, on his side, and left the sentence unfinished. If he had not been engaged in discussing a subject of such paramount interest to himself as his breakfast, Mrs. Goldstraw might have fancied that *his* attention was beginning to wander at the very outset of the interview.

"If your tea stands too long, sir——?" said the housekeeper, politely taking up her master's lost thread.

"If my tea stands too long," repeated the wine-merchant, mechanically, his mind getting further and further away from his breakfast, and his eyes fixing themselves more and more inquiringly on his housekeeper's face. "If my tea—— Dear, dear me, Mrs. Goldstraw! what *is* the manner and tone of voice that you remind me of? It strikes me even more strongly to-day, than it did when I saw you yesterday. What can it be?"

"What can it be?" repeated Mrs. Goldstraw.

She said the words, evidently thinking while she spoke them of something else. The wine-merchant, still looking at her inquiringly, observed that her eyes wandered towards the chimney-piece once more. They fixed on the portrait of his mother, which hung there, and looked at it with that slight contraction of the brow which accompanies a scarcely conscious effort of memory. Mr. Wilding remarked:

"My late dear mother, when she was five-and-twenty."

Mrs. Goldstraw thanked him with a movement of the head for being at the pains to explain the picture, and said, with a cleared brow, that it was the portrait of a very beautiful lady.

Mr. Wilding, falling back into his former perplexity, tried once more to recover that lost recollection, associated so closely, and yet so undiscoverably, with his new housekeeper's voice and manner.

"Excuse my asking you a question which has nothing to do with me or my breakfast," he said. "May I inquire if you have ever occupied any other situation than the situation of housekeeper?"

"Oh yes, sir. I began life as one of the nurses at the Foundling."

" Why, that's it !" cried the wine merchant, pushing back his chair. " By Heaven ! Their manner is the manner you remind me of ! "

In an astonished look at him, Mrs. Goldstraw changed colour, checked herself, turned her eyes upon the ground, and sat still and silent.

" What is the matter ?" asked Mr. Wilding.

" Do I understand that you were in the Foundling, sir ?"

" Certainly. I am not ashamed to own it."

" Under the name you now bear ?"

" Under the name of Walter Wilding."

" And the lady—— ? " Mrs. Goldstraw stopped short, with a look at the portrait which was now unmistakably a look of alarm.

" You mean my mother," interrupted Mr. Wilding.

" Your—mother," repeated the housekeeper, a little constrainedly, " removed you from the Foundling ? At what age, sir ?"

" At between eleven and twelve years old. It's quite a romantic adventure, Mrs. Goldstraw."

He told the story of the lady having spoken to him, while he sat at dinner with the other boys in the Foundling, and of all that had followed, in his innocently communicative way. " My poor mother could never have discovered me," he added, " if she had not met with one of the matrons who pitied her. The matron consented to touch the boy whose name was ' Walter Wilding ' as she went round the dinner-tables—and so my mother discovered me again, after having parted from me as an infant at the Foundling doors."

At those words Mrs. Goldstraw's hand, resting on the table, dropped helplessly into her lap. She sat, looking at her new master, with a face that had turned deadly pale, and with eyes that expressed an unutterable dismay.

" What does this mean ?" asked the wine-merchant. " Stop !" he cried. " Is there something else in the past time which I ought to associate with you ? I remember my mother telling me of another person at the Foundling, to whose kindness she owed a debt of gratitude. When she first parted with

me, as an infant, one of the nurses informed her of the name
that had been given to me in the institution. You were that
nurse ? "

"God forgive me, sir—I was that nurse ! "

"God forgive you ? "

" We had better get back, sir (if I may make so bold as to
say so), to my duties in the house," said Mrs. Goldstraw.
" Your breakfast-hour is eight. Do you lunch, or dine, in the
middle of the day ? "

The excessive pinkness which Mr. Bintrey had noticed in
his client's face began to appear there once more. Mr. Wilding
put his hand to his head, and mastered some momentary
confusion in that quarter, before he spoke again.

" Mrs. Goldstraw," he said "you are concealing something
from me ! "

The housekeeper obstinately repeated, " Please to favour
me, sir, by saying whether you lunch, or dine, in the middle of
the day ? "

" I don't know what I do in the middle of the day. I can't
enter into my household affairs, Mrs. Goldstraw, till I know
why you regret an act of kindness to my mother, which she
always spoke of gratefully to the end of her life. You are not
doing me a service by your silence. You are agitating me, you
are alarming me, you are bringing on the singing in my head."

His hand went up to his head again, and the pink in his
face deepened by a shade or two.

"It's hard, sir, on just entering your service," said the
housekeeper, "to say what may cost me the loss of your good
will. Please to remember, end how it may, that I only speak
because you have insisted on my speaking, and because I see
that I am alarming you by my silence. When I told the poor
lady, whose portrait you have got there, the name by which
her infant was christened in the Foundling, I allowed myself
to forget my duty, and dreadful consequences, I am afraid, have
followed from it. I'll tell you the truth, as plainly as I can.
A few months from the time when I had informed the lady of
her baby's name, there came to our institution in the country
another lady (a stranger), whose object was to adopt one of our
children. She brought the needful permission with her, and
after looking at a great many of the children, without being

able to make up her mind, she took a sudden fancy to one of
the babies—a boy—under my care. Try, pray try, to compose
yourself, sir ! It's no use disguising it any longer. The child
the stranger took away was the child of that lady whose portrait
hangs there !"

Mr. Wilding started to his feet. "Impossible !" he cried
out, vehemently. "What are you talking about ? What
absurd story are you telling me now ? There's her portrait !
Haven't I told you so already ? The portrait of my mother !"

"When that unhappy lady removed you from the Foundling,
in after years," said Mrs. Goldstraw, gently, "she was the
victim, and you were the victim, sir, of a dreadful mistake."

He dropped back into his chair. "The room goes round
with me," he said. "My head ! my head !" The housekeeper
rose in alarm, and opened the windows. Before she could get
to the door to call for help, a sudden burst of tears relieved the
oppression which had at first almost appeared to threaten his
life. He signed entreatingly to Mrs. Goldstraw not to leave
him. She waited until the paroxysm of weeping had worn
itself out. He raised his head as he recovered himself, and
looked at her with the angry unreasoning suspicion of a weak
man.

"Mistake ?" he said, wildly repeating her last word. "How
do I know you are not mistaken yourself ?"

"There is no hope that I am mistaken, sir. I will tell you
why, when you are better fit to hear it."

"Now ! now !"

The tone in which he spoke warned Mrs. Goldstraw that it
would be cruel kindness to let him comfort himself a moment
longer with the vain hope that she might be wrong. A few
words more would end it—and those few words she determined
to speak.

"I have told you," she said, "that the child of the lady
whose portrait hangs there, was adopted in its infancy, and
taken away by a stranger. I am as certain of what I say as
that I am now sitting here, obliged to distress you, sir, sorely
against my will. Please to carry your mind on, now, to about
three months after that time. I was then at the Foundling, in
London, waiting to take some children to our institution in the
country. There was a question that day about naming an

WILDING IS ENLIGHTENED.

infant—a boy—who had just been received. We generally
named them out of the Directory. On this occasion, one of the
gentlemen who managed the Hospital happened to be looking
over the Register. He noticed that the name of the baby who
had been adopted ('Walter Wilding') was scratched out—for
the reason, of course, that the child had been removed for good
from our care. 'Here's a name to let,' he said. 'Give it to
the new foundling who has been received to-day.' The name was
given, and the child was christened. You, sir, were that child."

The wine-merchant's head dropped on his breast. "I was
that child!" he said to himself, trying helplessly to fix the
idea in his mind. "I was that child!"

"Not very long after you had been received into the
Institution, sir," pursued Mrs. Goldstraw, "I left my situation
there, to be married. If you will remember that, and if you
can give your mind to it, you will see for yourself how the
mistake happened. Between eleven and twelve years passed
before the lady, whom you have believed to be your mother,
returned to the Foundling, to find her son, and to remove him
to her own home. The lady only knew that her infant had
been called 'Walter Wilding.' The matron who took pity on
her, could but point out the only 'Walter Wilding' known
in the Institution. I, who might have set the matter right, was
far away from the Foundling and all that belonged to it.
There was nothing—there was really nothing that could prevent
this terrible mistake from taking place. I feel for you—I do
indeed, sir! You must think—and with reason—that it was
in an evil hour that I came here (innocently enough, I'm sure),
to apply for your housekeeper's place. I feel as if I was to
blame—I feel as if I ought to have had more self-command.
If I had only been able to keep my face from showing you,
what that portrait and what your own words put into my mind
—you need never, to your dying day, have known what you
know now."

Mr. Wilding looked up suddenly. The inbred hones'y of
the man rose in protest against the housekeeper's last words.
His mind seemed to steady itself, for the moment, under the
shock that had fallen on it.

"Do you mean to say that you would have concealed this
from me if you could?" he exclaimed.

"I hope I should always tell the truth, sir, if I was asked,"
said Mrs. Goldstraw. "And I know it is better for *me* that I
should not have a secret of this sort weighing on my mind.
But is it better for *you?* What use can it serve now——?"

"What use? Why, good Lord! if your story is true——"

"Should I have told it, sir, as I am now situated, if it had
not been true?"

"I beg your pardon," said the wine-merchant. "You must
make allowance for me. This dreadful discovery is something
I can't realise even yet. We loved each other so dearly—I
felt so fondly that I was her son. She died, Mrs. Goldstraw,
in my arms—she died blessing me as only a mother *could* have
blessed me. And now, after all these years, to be told she was
not my mother! O me, O me! I don't know what I am
saying!" he cried, as the impulse of self-control under which
he had spoken a moment since, flickered, and died out. "It
was not this dreadful grief—it was something else that I had it
in my mind to speak of. Yes, yes. You surprised me—you
wounded me just now. You talked as if you would have
hidden this from me, if you could. Don't talk in that way
again. It would have been a crime to have hidden it. You
mean well, I know. I don't want to distress you—you are a
kind-hearted woman. But you don't remember what my position
is. She left me all that I possess, in the firm persuasion that I
was her son. I am not her son. I have taken the place, I have
innocently got the inheritance of another man. He must be
found! How do I know he is not at this moment in misery,
without bread to eat? He must be found! My only hope of
bearing up against the shock that has fallen on me, is the hope
of doing something which *she* would have approved. You must
know more, Mrs. Goldstraw, than you have told me yet. Who
was the stranger who adopted the child? You must have heard
the lady's name?"

"I never heard it, sir. I have never seen her, or heard of
her, since."

"Did she say nothing when she took the child away?
Search your memory. She must have said something."

"Only one thing, sir, that I can remember. It was a
miserably bad season, that year; and many of the children were
suffering from it. When she took the baby away, the lady

said to me, laughing, 'Don't be alarmed about his health. He will be brought up in a better climate than this—I am going to take him to Switzerland.'"

"To Switzerland? What part of Switzerland?"

"She didn't say, sir."

"Only that faint clue!" said Mr. Wilding. "And a quarter of a century has passed since the child was taken away! What am I to do?"

"I hope you won't take offence at my freedom, sir," said Mrs. Goldstraw; "but why should you distress yourself about what is to be done? He may not be alive now, for anything you know. And, if he is alive, it's not likely he can be in any distress. The lady who adopted him was a bred and born lady —it was easy to see that. And she must have satisfied them at the Foundling that she could provide for the child, or they would never have let her take him away. If I was in your place, sir—please to excuse my saying so—I should comfort myself with remembering that I had loved that poor lady whose portrait you have got there—truly loved her as my mother, and that she had truly loved me as her son. All she gave to you, she gave for the sake of that love. It never altered while she lived; and it won't alter, I'm sure, as long as *you* live. How can you have a better right, sir, to keep what you have got than that?"

Mr. Wilding's immovable honesty saw the fallacy in his housekeeper's point of view at a glance.

"You don't understand me," he said. "It's *because* I loved her that I feel it a duty—a sacred duty—to do justice to her son. If he is a living man, I must find him: for my own sake, as well as for his. I shall break down under this dreadful trial, unless I employ myself—actively, instantly employ myself —in doing what my conscience tells me ought to be done. I must speak to my lawyer; I must set my lawyer at work before I sleep to-night." He approached a tube in the wall of the room, and called down through it to the office below. "Leave me for a little, Mrs. Goldstraw," he resumed; "I shall be more composed, I shall be better able to speak to you later in the day. We shall get on well—I hope we shall get on well together—in spite of what has happened. It isn't your fault; I know it isn't your fault. There! there! shake hands; and—

and do the best you can in the house—I can't talk about it now."

The door opened as Mrs. Goldstraw advanced towards it; and Mr. Jarvis appeared.

"Send for Mr. Bintrey," said the wine-merchant.   "Say I want to see him directly."

The clerk unconsciously suspended the execution of the order, by announcing " Mr. Vendale," and showing in the new partner in the firm of Wilding and Co.

" Pray excuse me for one moment, George Vendale," said Wilding.   " I have a word to say to Jarvis.   Send for Mr. Bintrey," he repeated—" send at once."

Mr. Jarvis laid a letter on the table before he left the room.

" From our correspondents at Neuchâtel, I think, sir.   The letter has got the Swiss postmark."

NEW CHARACTERS ON THE SCENE.

The words, " The Swiss Postmark," following so soon upon the housekeeper's reference to Switzerland, wrought Mr. Wilding's agitation to such a remarkable height, that his new partner could not decently make a pretence of letting it pass unnoticed.

" Wilding," he asked hurriedly, and yet stopping short and glancing around as if for some visible cause of his state of mind : " what is the matter?"

" My good George Vendale," returned the wine-merchant, giving his hand with an appealing look, rather as if he wanted help to get over some obstacle, than as if he gave it in welcome or salutation: "my good George Vendale, so much is the matter, that I shall never be myself again. It is impossible that I can ever be myself again. For, in fact, I am not myself."

The new partner, a brown-cheeked handsome fellow, of about his own age, with a quick determined eye and an impulsive manner, retorted with natural astonishment : " Not yourself?"

" Not what I supposed myself to be," said Wilding.

" What, in the name of wonder, *did* you suppose yourself to be that you are not?" was the rejoinder, delivered with a cheerful frankness, inviting confidence from a more reticent man. " I may ask without impertinence, now that we are partners."

"There again!" cried Wilding, leaning back in his chair, with a lost look at the other. "Partners! I had no right to come into this business. It was never meant for me. My mother never meant it should be mine. I mean, his mother meant it should be his—if I mean anything—or if I am anybody."

"Come, come," urged his partner, after a moment's pause, and taking possession of him with that calm confidence which inspires a strong nature when it honestly desires to aid a weak one. "Whatever has gone wrong, has gone wrong through no fault of yours, I am very sure. I was not in this counting-house with you under the old *régime*, for three years, to doubt you, Wilding. We were not younger men than we are, together, for that. Let me begin our partnership by being a serviceable partner, and setting right whatever is wrong. Has that letter anything to do with it?"

"Hah!" said Wilding, with his hand to his temple. "There again! My head! I was forgetting the coincidence. The Swiss postmark."

"At a second glance I see that the letter is unopened, so it is not very likely to have much to do with the matter," said Vendale, with comforting composure. "Is it for you, or for us?"

"For us," said Wilding.

"Suppose I open it and read it aloud, to get it out of our way?"

"Thank you, thank you."

"The letter is only from our champagne-making friends, the House at Neuchâtel. 'Dear Sir. We are in receipt of yours of the 28th ult., informing us that you have taken your Mr. Vendale into partnership, whereon we beg you to receive the assurance of our felicitations. Permit us to embrace the occasion of specially commending to you, M. Jules Obenreizer.' Impossible!"

Wilding looked up in quick apprehension, and cried, "Eh?"

"Impossible sort of name," returned his partner, slightly—"Obenreizer. '—Of specially commending to you M. Jules Obenreizer, of Soho-square, London (north side), henceforth fully accredited as our agent, and who has already had the honour of making the acquaintance of your Mr. Vendale, in his (said M. Obenreizer's) native country, Switzerland.' To be sure : pooh pooh, what have I been thinking of ! I remember now ; ' when travelling with his niece.' "

" With his——? " Vendale had so slurred the last word, that Wilding had not heard it.

" When travelling with his Niece. Obenreizer's Niece," said Vendale, in a somewhat superfluously lucid manner. " Niece of Obenreizer. (I met them in my first Swiss tour, travelled a little with them, and lost them for two years ; met them again, my Swiss tour before last, and have lost them ever since.) Obenreizer. Niece of Obenreizer. To be sure ! Possible sort of name, after all ! ' M. Obenreizer is in-possession of our absolute confidence, and we do not doubt you will esteem his merits.' Duly signed by the House, ' Defresnier et Cie.' Very well. I undertake to see M. Obenreizer presently, and clear him out of the way. That clears the Swiss postmark out of the way. So now, my dear Wilding, tell me what I can clear out of *your* way, and I'll find a way to clear it."

More than ready and grateful to be thus taken charge of, the honest wine-merchant wrung his partner's hand, and, beginning his tale by pathetically declaring himself an Impostor, told it.

" It was on this matter, no doubt, that you were sending for Bintrey, when I came in ? " said his partner, after reflecting.

" It was."

" He has experience and a shrewd head ; I shall be anxious to know his opinion. It is bold and hazardous in me to give you mine before I know his, but I am not good at holding back. Plainly, then, I do not see these circumstances as you see them. I do not see your position as you see it. As to your being an Impostor, my dear Wilding, that is simply absurd, because no man can be that without being a consenting party to an imposition. Clearly you never were so. As to your enrichment by the lady who believed you to be her son, and whom you were forced to believe, on her own showing, to be your mother, consider whether that did not arise out of the personal relations between you. You gradually became much attached to her ; she gradually became much attached to you. It was on you, personally you, as I see the case, that she conferred these worldly advantages ; it was from her, personally her, that you took them."

"She supposed me," objected Wilding, shaking his head, "to have a natural claim upon her, which I had not."

"I must admit that," replied his partner, "to be true. But if she had made the discovery that you have made, six months before she died, do you think it would have cancelled the years you were together, and the tenderness that each of you had conceived for the other, each on increasing knowledge of the other?"

"What I think," said Wilding, simply but stoutly holding to the bare fact, "can no more change the truth than it can bring down the sky. The truth is that I stand possessed of what was meant for another man."

"He may be dead," said Vendale.

"He may be alive," said Wilding. "And if he is alive, have I not—innocently, I grant you innocently—robbed him of enough? Have I not robbed him of all the happy time that I enjoyed in his stead? Have I not robbed him of the exquisite delight that filled my soul when that dear lady," stretching his hand towards the picture, "told me she was my mother? Have I not robbed him of all the care she lavished on me? Have I not even robbed him of all the devotion and duty that I so proudly gave to her? Therefore it is that I ask myself, George Vendale, and I ask you, where is he? What has become of him?"

"Who can tell!"

"I must try to find out who can tell. I must institute inquiries. I must never desist from prosecuting inquiries. I will live upon the interest of my share—I ought to say his share—in this business, and will lay up the rest for him. When I find him, I may perhaps throw myself upon his generosity; but I will yield up all to him. I will, I swear. As I loved and honoured her," said Wilding, reverently kissing his hand towards the picture, and then covering his eyes with it. "As I loved and honoured her, and have a world of reasons to be grateful to her!" And so broke down again.

His partner rose from the chair he had occupied, and stood beside him with a hand softly laid upon his shoulder. "Walter, I knew you before to-day to be an upright man, with a pure conscience and a fine heart. It is very fortunate for me that I have the privilege to travel on in life so near to so trustworthy

a man. I am thankful for it. Use me as your right hand, and
rely upon me to the death. Don't think the worse of me if I
protest to you that my uppermost feeling at present is a confused, you may call it an unreasonable, one. I feel far more
pity for the lady and for you, because you did not stand in
your supposed relations, than I can feel for the unknown man
(if he ever became a man), because he was unconsciously displaced. You have done well in sending for Mr. Bintrey.
What I think will be a part of his advice, I know is the whole of
mine. Do not move a step in this serious matter precipitately.
The secret must be kept among us with great strictness, for to
part with it lightly would be to invite fraudulent claims, to
encourage a host of knaves, to let loose a flood of perjury and
plotting. I have no more to say now, Walter, than to remind
you that you sold me a share in your business, expressly to save
yourself from more work than your present health is fit for, and
that I bought it expressly to do work, and mean to do it."

With these words, and a parting grip of his partner's
shoulder that gave them the best emphasis they could have had,
George Vendale betook himself presently to the counting-house,
and presently afterwards to the address of M. Jules Obenreizer.

As he turned into Soho-square, and directed his steps
towards its north side, a deepened colour shot across his sun-
browned faced, which Wilding, if he had been a better observer,
or had been less occupied with his own trouble, might have
noticed when his partner read aloud a certain passage in their
Swiss correspondent's letter, which he had not read so distinctly
as the rest.

A curious colony of mountaineers has long been enclosed
within that small flat London district of Soho. Swiss watch-
makers, Swiss silver-chasers, Swiss jewellers, Swiss importers of
Swiss musical boxes and Swiss toys of various kinds, draw
close together there. Swiss professors of music, painting, and
languages ; Swiss artificers in steady work ; Swiss couriers, and
other Swiss servants chronically out of place ; industrious Swiss
laundresses and clear-starchers ; mysteriously existing Swiss of
both sexes ; Swiss, creditable and Swiss discreditable ; Swiss
to be trusted by all means, and Swiss to be trusted by no
means ; these diverse Swiss particles are attracted to a centre in
the district of Soho. Shabby Swiss eating-houses, coffee-houses,

and lodging-houses, Swiss drinks and dishes, Swiss service for Sundays, and Swiss schools for week-days, are all to be found there. Even the native-born English taverns drive a sort of broken-English trade ; announcing in their windows Swiss whets and drams, and sheltering in their bars Swiss skirmishes of love and animosity on most nights in the year.

When the new partner in Wilding and Co. rang the bell of a door bearing the blunt inscription OBENREIZER on a brass plate—the inner door of a substantial house, whose ground story was devoted to the sale of Swiss clocks—he passed at once into domestic Switzerland. A white-tiled stove for winter-time filled the fireplace of the room into which he was shown, the room's bare floor was laid together in a neat pattern of several ordinary woods, the room had a prevalent air of surface bareness and much scrubbing ; and the little square of flowery carpet by the sofa, and the velvet chimney-board with its capacious clock and vases of artificial flowers, contended with that tone, as if, in bringing out the whole effect, a Parisian had adapted a dairy to domestic purposes.

Mimic water was dropping off a mill-wheel under the clock. The visitor had not stood before it, following it with his eyes, a minute, when M. Obenreizer, at his elbow, startled him by saying, in very good English, very slightly clipped : "How do you do? So glad !"

"I beg your pardon. I didn't hear you come in."

"Not at all ! Sit, please."

Releasing his visitor's two arms, which he had lightly pinioned at the elbows by way of embrace, M. Obenreizer also sat, remarking, with a smile : "You are well? So glad !" and touching his elbows again.

"I don't know," said Vendale, after exchange of salutations, "whether you may yet have heard of me from your house at Neuchâtel ?"

"Ah, yes !"

"In connection with Wilding and Co. ?"

"Ah, surely !"

"Is it not odd that I should come to you, in London here, as one of the Firm of Wilding and Co., to pay the Firm's respects ?"

"Not at all ! What did I always observe when we were on

the mountains? We call them vast; but the world is so little.
So little is the world, that one cannot keep away from persons.
There are so few persons in the world, that they continually
cross and re-cross. So very little is the world, that one cannot
get rid of a person. Not," touching his elbows again, with an
ingratiatory smile, "that one would desire to get rid of you."

"I hope not, M. Obenreizer."

"Please call me, in your country, Mr. I call myself so,
for I love your country. If I *could* be English! But I am
born. And you? Though descended from so fine a family,
you have had the condescension to come into trade? Stop
though. Wines? Is it trade in England or profession? Not
fine art?"

"Mr. Obenreizer," returned Vendale, somewhat out of
countenance, "I was but a silly young fellow, just of age,
when I first had the pleasure of travelling with you, and when
you and I and Mademoiselle your niece—who is well?"

"Thank you. Who is well."

"—Shared some slight glacier dangers together. If, with a
boy's vanity, I rather vaunted my family, I hope I did so as a
kind of introduction of myself. It was very weak, and in very
bad taste; but perhaps you know our English proverb, 'Live
and learn.'"

"You make too much of it," returned the Swiss. "And
what the devil! After all, yours *was* a fine family."

George Vendale's laugh betrayed a little vexation as he
rejoined : "Well! I was strongly attached to my parents, and
when we first travelled together, Mr. Obenreizer, I was in the
first flush of coming into what my father and mother left me.
So I hope it may have been, after all, more youthful openness
of speech and heart than boastfulness."

"All openness of speech and heart! No boastfulness!"
cried Obenreizer. "You tax yourself too heavily. You tax
yourself, my faith! as if you was your Government taxing you!
Besides, it commenced with me. I remember, that evening in
the boat upon the lake, floating among the reflections of the
mountains and valleys, the crags and pine woods, which were
my earliest remembrance, I drew a word-picture of my sordid
childhood. Of our poor hut, by the waterfall which my mother
showed to travellers; of the cow-shed where I slept with the

cow; of my idiot half-brother always sitting at the door, or limping down the Pass to beg; of my half-sister always spinning, and resting her enormous goitre on a great stone; of my being a famished naked little wretch of two or three years, when they were men and women with hard hands to beat me, I, the only child of my father's second marriage—if it even was a marriage. What more natural than for you to compare notes with me, and say, 'We are as one by age; at that same time I sat upon my mother's lap in my father's carriage, rolling through the rich English streets, all luxury surrounding me, all squalid poverty kept far from me. Such is *my* earliest remembrance as opposed to yours!'"

Mr. Obenreizer was a black-haired young man of a dark complexion, through whose swarthy skin no red glow ever shone. When colour would have come into another cheek, a hardly discernible beat would come into his, as if the machinery for bringing up the ardent blood were there, but the machinery were dry. He was robustly made, well proportioned, and had handsome features. Many would have perceived that some surface change in him would have set them more at their ease with him, without being able to define what change. If his lips could have been made much thicker, and his neck much thinner, they would have found their want supplied.

But the great Obenreizer peculiarity was, that a certain nameless film would come over his eyes—apparently by the action of his own will—which would impenetrably veil, not only from those tellers of tales, but from his face at large, every expression save one of attention. It by no means followed that his attention should be wholly given to the person with whom he spoke, or even wholly bestowed on present sounds and objects. Rather, it was a comprehensive watchfulness of everything he had in his own mind, and everything that he knew to be, or suspected to be, in the minds of other men.

At this stage of the conversation, Mr. Obenreizer's film came over him.

"The object of my present visit," said Vendale, "is, I need hardly say, to assure you of the friendliness of Wilding and Co., and of the goodness of your credit with us, and of our desire to be of service to you. We hope shortly to offer you our hospitality. Things are not quite in train with us yet, for

my partner, Mr. Wilding, is reorganising the domestic part of
our establishment, and is interrupted by some private affairs.
You don't know Mr. Wilding, I believe?"

Mr. Obenreizer did not.

"You must come together soon. He will be glad to have
made your acquaintance, and I think I may predict that you
will be glad to have made his. You have not been long
established in London, I suppose, Mr. Obenreizer?"

"It is only now that I have undertaken this agency."

"Mademoiselle your niece—is—not married?"

"Not married."

George Vendale glanced about him, as if for any tokens of her.

"She has been in London?"

"She *is* in London."

"When, and where, might I have the honour of recalling
myself to her remembrance?"

Mr. Obenreizer, discarding his film and touching his visitor's
elbows as before, said lightly: "Come up-stairs."

Fluttered enough by the suddenness with which the interview he had sought was coming upon him after all, George
Vendale followed up-stairs. In a room over the chamber he
had just quitted—a room also Swiss-appointed—a young lady
sat near one of three windows, working at an embroidery-frame;
and an older lady sat with her face turned close to another
white-tiled stove (though it was summer, and the stove was not
lighted), cleaning gloves. The young lady wore an unusual
quantity of fair bright hair, very prettily braided about a rather
rounder white forehead than the average English type, and so
her face might have been a shade—or say a light—rounder than
the average English face, and her figure slightly rounder than
the figure of the average English girl at nineteen. A remarkable
indication of freedom and grace of limb, in her quiet attitude,
and a wonderful purity and freshness of colour in her dimpled
face and bright grey eyes, seemed fraught with mountain air.
Switzerland, too, though the general fashion of her dress was
English, peeped out of the fanciful bodice she wore, and lurked
in the curious clocked red stocking, and in its little silver-buckled
shoe. As to the elder lady, sitting with her feet apart upon the
lower brass ledge of the stove, supporting a lap-full of gloves
while she cleaned one stretched on her left hand, she was a true

Swiss impersonation of another kind; from the breadth of her cushion-like back, and the ponderosity of her respectable legs (if the word be admissible), to the black velvet band tied tightly round her throat for the repression of a rising tendency to *goître;* or, higher still, to her great copper-coloured gold ear-rings; or, higher still, to her head-dress of black gauze stretched on wire.

"Miss Marguerite," said Obenreizer to the young lady, "do you recollect this gentleman?"

"I think," she answered, rising from her seat, surprised and a little confused: "it is Mr. Vendale?"

"I think it is," said Obenreizer, dryly. "Permit me, Mr. Vendale. Madame Dor."

The elder lady by the stove, with the glove stretched on her left hand, like a glover's sign, half got up, half looked over her broad shoulder, and wholly plumped down again and rubbed away.

"Madame Dor," said Obenreizer, smiling, "is so kind as to keep me free from stain or tear. Madame Dor humours my weakness for being always neat, and devotes her time to removing every one of my specks and spots."

Madame Dor, with the stretched glove in the air, and her eyes closely scrutinising its palm, discovered a tough spot in Mr. Obenreizer at that instant, and rubbed hard at him. George Vendale took his seat by the embroidery-frame (having first taken the fair right hand that his entrance had checked), and glanced at the gold cross that dipped into the bodice, with something of the devotion of a pilgrim who had reached his shrine at last. Obenreizer stood in the middle of the room with his thumbs in his waistcoat-pockets, and became filmy.

"He was saying down-stairs, Miss Obenreizer," observed Vendale, "that the world is so small a place, that people cannot escape one another. I have found it much too large for me since I saw you last."

"Have you travelled so far, then?" she inquired.

"Not so far, for I have only gone back to Switzerland each year; but I could have wished—and indeed I have wished very often—that the little world did not afford such opportunities for long escapes as it does. If it had been less, I might have found my fellow-travellers sooner, you know."

The pretty Marguerite coloured, and very slightly glanced in the direction of Madame Dor.

"You find us at length, Mr. Vendale. Perhaps you may lose us again."

"I trust not. The curious coincidence that has enabled me to find you, encourages me to hope not."

"What is that coincidence, sir, if you please?" A dainty little native touch in this turn of speech, and in its tone, made it perfectly captivating, thought George Vendale, when again he noticed an instantaneous glance towards Madame Dor. A caution seemed to be conveyed in it, rapid flash though it was; so he quietly took heed of Madame Dor from that time forth.

"It is that I happen to have become a partner in a House of business in London, to which Mr. Obenreizer happens this very day to be expressly recommended: and that, too, by another house of business in Switzerland, in which (as it turns out) we both have a commercial interest. He has not told you?"

"Ah!" cried Obenreizer, striking in, filmless. "No. I had not told Miss Marguerite. The world is so small and so monotonous that a surprise is worth having in such a little jog-trot place. It is as he tells you, Miss Marguerite. He, of so fine a family, and so proudly bred, has condescended to trade. To trade! Like us poor peasants who have risen from ditches!"

A cloud crept over the fair brow, and she cast down her eyes.

"Why, it is good for trade!" pursued Obenreizer, enthusiastically. "It ennobles trade! It is the misfortune of trade, it is its vulgarity, that any low people—for example, we poor peasants—may take to it, and climb by it. See you, my dear Vendale!" He spoke with great energy. "The father of Miss Marguerite, my eldest half-brother, more than two times your age or mine, if living now, wandered without shoes, almost without rags, from that wretched Pass—wandered—wandered— got to be fed with the mules and dogs at an Inn in the main valley far away—got to be Boy there—got to be Ostler—got to be Waiter—got to be Cook—got to be Landlord. As Landlord, he took me (could he take the idiot beggar his brother, or the spinning monstrosity his sister?) to put as pupil to the famous watchmaker, his neighbour and friend. His wife dies when

Miss Marguerite is born. What is his will, and what are his
words, to me, when *he* dies, she being between girl and woman?
' All for Marguerite, except so much by the year for you. You are
young, but I make her your ward, for you were of the obscurest
and the poorest peasantry, and so was I, and so was her mother ;
we were abject peasants all, and you will remember it.' The
thing is equally true of most of my countrymen, now in trade
in this your London quarter of Soho. Peasants once ; low-born
drudging Swiss peasants. Then how good and great for trade : "
here, from having been warm, he became playfully jubilant,
and touched the young wine-merchant's elbows again with his
light embrace : " to be exalted by gentlemen ! "

"I do not think so," said Marguerite, with a flushed cheek,
and a look away from the visitor, that was almost defiant.   "I
think it is as much exalted by us peasants."

" Fie, fie, Miss Marguerite," said Obenreizer.   " You speak
in proud England."

" I speak in proud earnest," she answered, quietly resuming
her work, "and I am not English, but a Swiss peasant's
daughter."

There was a dismissal of the subject in her words, which
Vendale could not contend against.   He only said in an earnest
manner, " I most heartily agree with you, Miss Obenreizer, and
I have already said so, as Mr. Obenreizer will bear witness,"
which he by no means did, " in this house."

Now, Vendale's eyes were quick eyes, and sharply watching
Madame Dor by times, noted something in the broad back view
of that lady. There was considerable pantomimic expression
in her glove-cleaning. It had been very softly done when he
spoke with Marguerite, or it had altogether stopped, like the
action of a listener. When Obenreizer's peasant-speech came to
an end, she rubbed most vigorously, as if applauding it. And
once or twice, as the glove (which she always held before her, a
little above her face) turned in the air, or as this finger went
down, or that went up, he even fancied that it made some tele-
graphic communication to Obenreizer : whose back was certainly
never turned upon it, though he did not seem at all to heed it.

Vendale observed, too, that in Marguerite's dismissal of the
subject twice forced upon him to his misrepresentation, there
was an indignant treatment of her guardian which she tried to

check : as though she would have flamed out against him, but for the influence of fear. He also observed—though this was not much—that he never advanced within the distance of her at which he first placed himself : as though there were limits fixed between them. Neither had he ever spoken of her without the prefix " Miss," though whenever he uttered it, it was with the faintest trace of an air of mockery. And now it occurred to Vendale for the first time that something curious in the man which he had never before been able to define, was definable as a certain subtle essence of mockery that eluded touch or analysis. He felt convinced that Marguerite was in some sort a prisoner as to her free will—though she held her own against those two combined, by the force of her character, which was nevertheless inadequate to her release. To feel convinced of this, was not to feel less disposed to love her than he had always been. In a word, he was desperately in love with her, and thoroughly determined to pursue the opportunity which had opened at last.

For the present, he merely touched upon the pleasure that Wilding and Co. would soon have in entreating Miss Obenreizer to honour their establishment with her presence—a curious old place, though a bachelor house withal—and so did not protract his visit beyond such a visit's ordinary length. Going down stairs, conducted by his host, he found the Obenreizer counting-house at the back of the entrance-hall, and several shabby men in outlandish garments, hanging about, whom Obenreizer put aside that he might pass, with a few words in *patois*.

" Countrymen," he explained, as he attended Vendale to the door. " Poor compatriots. Grateful and attached, like dogs ! Good-bye. To meet again. So glad ! "

Two more light touches on his elbows dismissed him into the street.

Sweet Marguerite at her frame, and Madame Dor's broad back at her telegraph, floated before him to Cripple Corner. On his arrival there, Wilding was closeted with Bintrey. The cellar doors happening to be open, Vendale lighted a candle in a cleft stick, and went down for a cellarous stroll. Graceful Marguerite floated before him faithfully, but Madame Dor's broad back remained outside.

The vaults were very spacious, and very old. There had

been a stone crypt down there, when bygones were not bygones; some said, part of a monkish refectory ; some said, of a chapel ; some said, of a Pagan temple. It was all one now. Let who would, make what he liked of a crumbled pillar and a broken arch or so. Old Time had made what *he* liked of it, and was quite indifferent to contradiction.

The close air, the musty smell, and the thunderous rumbling in the streets above, as being out of the routine of ordinary life, went well enough with the picture of pretty Marguerite holding her own against those two. So Vendale went on until, at a turning in the vaults, he saw a light like the light he carried.

"Oh ! You are here, are you, Joey ?"

"Oughtn't it rather to go, 'Oh ! *You're* here, are you, Master George ?' For it's my business to be here. But it ain't yourn."

"Don't grumble, Joey."

"Oh ! *I* don't grumble," returned the Cellarman. "If anything grumbles, it's what I've took in through the pores ; it ain't me. Have a care as something in *you* don't begin a-grumbling, Master George. Stop here long enough for the wapours to work, and they'll be at it."

His present occupation consisted of poking his head into the bins, making measurements and mental calculations, and entering them in a rhinoceros-hide-looking note-book, like a piece of himself.

"They'll be at it," he resumed, laying the wooden rod that he measured with, across two casks, entering his last calculation, and straightening his back, "trust 'em ! And so you've regularly come into the business, Master George ?"

"Regularly. I hope you don't object, Joey ?"

"*I* don't, bless you. But Wapours objects that you're too young. You're both on you too young."

"We shall get over that objection day by day, Joey."

"Aye, Master George ; but I shall day by day get over the objection that I'm too old, and so I shan't be capable of seeing much improvement in you."

The retort so tickled Joey Ladle that he grunted forth a laugh and delivered it again, grunting forth another laugh after the second edition of "improvement in you."

"But what's no laughing matter, Master George," he resumed, straightening his back once more, "is, that Young Master Wilding has gone and changed the luck. Mark my words. He has changed the luck, and he'll find it out. *I* ain't been down here all my life for nothing! *I* know, by what I notices down here, when it's a-going to rain, when it's a-going to hold up, when it's a-going to blow, when it's a-going to be calm. *I* know, by what I notices down here, when the luck's changed, quite as well."

"Has this growth on the roof anything to do with your divination?" asked Vendale, holding his light towards a gloomy ragged growth of dark fungus, pendent from the arches with a very disagreeable and repellent effect. "We are famous for this growth in this vault, aren't we?"

"We are, Master George," replied Joey Ladle, moving a step or two away, "and if you'll be advised by me, you'll let it alone."

Taking up the rod just now laid across the two casks, and faintly moving the languid fungus with it, Vendale asked, "Aye, indeed? Why so?"

"Why, not so much because it rises from the casks of wine, and may leave you to judge what sort of stuff a Cellarman takes into himself when he walks in the same all the days of his life, nor yet so much because at a stage of its growth it's maggots, and you'll fetch 'em down upon you," returned Joey Ladle, still keeping away, "as for another reason, Master George."

"What other reason?"

"(I wouldn't keep on touchin' it, if I was you, sir.) I'll tell you if you'll come out of the place. First, take a look at its colour, Master George."

"I am doing so."

"Done, sir. Now, come out of the place."

He moved away with his light, and Vendale followed with his. When Vendale came up with him, and they were going back together, Vendale, eyeing him as they walked through the arches, said: "Well, Joey? The colour."

"Is it like clotted blood, Master George?"

"Like enough, perhaps."

"More than enough, I think," muttered Joey Ladle, shaking his head solemnly.

" Well, say it is like ; say it is exactly like.   What then ?"

" Master George, they do say——"

" Who ? "

" How should I know who ? " rejoined the Cellarman, apparently much exasperated by the unreasonable nature of the question.   "Them !   Them as says pretty well everything, you know.   How should I know who They are, if you don't ?"

" True.   Go on."

"They do say that the man that gets by any accident a piece of that dark growth right upon his breast, will, for sure and certain, die by Murder."

As Vendale laughingly stopped to meet the Cellarman's eyes, which he had fastened on his light while dreamily saying those words, he suddenly became conscious of being struck upon his own breast by a heavy hand.   Instantly following with his eyes the action of the hand that struck him—which was his companion's—he saw that it had beaten off his breast a web or clot of the fungus, even then floating to the ground.

For a moment he turned upon the cellarman almost as scared a look as the cellarman turned upon him.   But in another moment they had reached the daylight at the foot of the cellar-steps, and before he cheerfully sprang up them, he blew out his candle and the superstition together.

EXIT WILDING.

On the morning of the next day, Wilding went out alone, after leaving a message with his clerk.   " If Mr. Vendale should ask for me," he said, " or if Mr. Bintrey should call, tell them I am gone to the Foundling."   All that his partner had said to him, all that his lawyer, following on the same side, could urge, had left him persisting unshaken in his own point of view.   To find the lost man, whose place he had usurped, was now the paramount interest of his life, and to inquire at the Foundling was plainly to take the first step in the direction of discovery.   To the Foundling, accordingly, the wine-merchant now went.

The once-familiar aspect of the building was altered to him, as the look of the portrait over the chimney-piece was altered to him. His one dearest association with the place which had sheltered his childhood had been broken away from it for ever. A strange reluctance possessed him, when he stated his business at the door. His heart ached as he sat alone in the waiting-room while the Treasurer of the institution was being sent for to see him. When the interview began, it was only by a painful effort that he could compose himself sufficiently to mention the nature of his errand.

The Treasurer listened with a face which promised all needful attention, and promised nothing more.

"We are obliged to be cautious," he said, when it came to his turn to speak, "about all inquiries which are made by strangers."

"You can hardly consider me a stranger," answered Wilding, simply. "I was one of your poor lost children here, in the bygone time."

The Treasurer politely rejoined that this circumstance inspired him with a special interest in his visitor. But he pressed, nevertheless, for that visitor's motive in making his inquiry. Without further preface, Wilding told him his motive, suppressing nothing.

The Treasurer rose, and led the way into the room in which the registers of the institution were kept. "All the information which our books can give is heartily at your service," he said. "After the time that has elapsed, I am afraid it is the only information we have to offer you."

The books were consulted, and the entry was found, expressed as follows:

"3rd March, 1836. Adopted, and removed from the Foundling Hospital, a male infant, named Walter Wilding. Name and condition of the person adopting the child—Mrs. Jane Ann Miller, widow. Address—Lime-Tree Lodge, Groombridge Wells. References—the Reverend John Harker, Groombridge Wells; and Messrs. Giles, Jeremie, and Giles, bankers, Lombard-street."

"Is that all?" asked the wine-merchant. "Had you no after-communication with Mrs. Miller?"

"None—or some reference to it must have appeared in this book."

"May I take a copy of the entry?"

"Certainly! You are a little agitated. Let me make the copy for you."

"My only chance, I suppose," said Wilding, looking sadly at the copy, "is to inquire at Mrs. Miller's residence, and to try if her references can help me?"

"That is the only chance I see at present," answered the Treasurer. "I heartily wish I could have been of some further assistance to you."

With those farewell words to comfort him, Wilding set forth on the journey of investigation which began from the Foundling doors. The first stage to make for, was plainly the house of business of the bankers in Lombard-street. Two of the partners in the firm were inaccessible to chance-visitors when he asked for them. The third, after raising certain inevitable difficulties, consented to let a clerk examine the Ledger marked with the initial letter "M." The account of Mrs. Miller, widow, of Groombridge Wells, was found. Two long lines, in faded ink, were drawn across it; and at the bottom of the page there appeared this note: "Account closed, September 30th, 1837."

So the first stage of the journey was reached—and so it ended in No Thoroughfare! After sending a note to Cripple Corner to inform his partner that his absence might be prolonged for some hours, Wilding took his place in the train, and started for the second stage on the journey—Mrs. Miller's residence at Groombridge Wells.

Mothers and children travelled with him; mothers and children met each other at the station; mothers and children were in the shops when he entered them to inquire for Lime-Tree Lodge. Everywhere, the nearest and dearest of human relations showed itself happily in the happy light of day. Everywhere, he was reminded of the treasured delusion from which he had been awakened so cruelly—of the lost memory which had passed from him like a reflection from a glass.

Inquiring here, inquiring there, he could hear of no such place as Lime-Tree Lodge. Passing a house-agent's office, he went in wearily, and put the question for the last time. The house-agent pointed across the street to a dreary mansion of many windows, which might have been a manufactory, but which was an hotel. "That's where Lime-Tree Lodge stood, sir," said the man, "ten years ago."

The second stage reached, and No Thoroughfare again !

But one chance was left. The clerical reference, Mr. Harker, still remained to be found. Customers coming in at the moment to occupy the house-agent's attention, Wilding went down the street, and, entering a bookseller's shop, asked if he could be informed of the Reverend John Harker's present address.

The bookseller looked unaffectedly shocked and astonished, and made no answer.

Wilding repeated his question.

The bookseller took up from his counter a prim little volume in a binding of sober grey. He handed it to his visitor, open at the title-page. Wilding read :

"The martyrdom of the Reverend John Harker in New Zealand. Related by a former member of his flock."

Wilding put the book down on the counter. "I beg your pardon," he said, thinking a little, perhaps, of his own present martyrdom while he spoke. The silent bookseller acknowledged the apology by a bow. Wilding went out.

Third and last stage, and No Thoroughfare for the third and last time.

There was nothing more to be done ; there was absolutely no choice but to go back to London, defeated at all points. From time to time on the return journey, the wine-merchant looked at his copy of the entry in the Foundling Register. There is one among the many forms of despair—perhaps the most pitiable of all—which persists in disguising itself as Hope. Wilding checked himself in the act of throwing the useless morsel of paper out of the carriage window. "It may lead to something yet," he thought. "While I live, I won't part with it. When I die, my executors shall find it sealed up with my will."

Now, the mention of his will set the good wine-merchant on a new track of thought, without diverting his mind from its engrossing subject. He must make his will immediately.

The application of the phrase, No Thoroughfare to the case had originated with Mr. Bintrey. In their first long conference following the discovery, that sagacious personage had a hundred times repeated, with an obstructive shake of the head, "No Thoroughfare, Sir, No Thoroughfare. My belief is that there is no way out of this at this time of day, and my advice is, make yourself comfortable where you are."

In the course of the protracted consultation, a magnum of the forty-five-year-old port wine had been produced for the wetting of Mr. Bintrey's legal whistle; but the more clearly he saw his way through the wine, the more emphatically he did not see his way through the case; repeating as often as he set his glass down empty, "Mr. Wilding, No Thoroughfare. Rest and be thankful."

It is certain that the honest wine-merchant's anxiety to make a will, originated in profound conscientiousness; though it is possible (and quite consistent with his rectitude) that he may unconsciously have derived some feeling of relief from the prospect of delegating his own difficulty to two other men who were to come after him. Be that as it may, he pursued his new track of thought with great ardour, and lost no time in begging George Vendale and Mr. Bintrey to meet him in Cripple Corner and share his confidence.

"Being all three assembled with closed doors," said Mr. Bintrey, addressing the new partner on the occasion, "I wish to observe, before our friend (and my client) entrusts us with his further views, that I have endorsed what I understand from him to have been your advice, Mr. Vendale, and what would be the advice of every sensible man. I have told him that he positively must keep his secret. I have spoken with Mrs. Goldstraw, both in his presence and in his absence ; and if anybody is to be trusted (which is a very large IF), I think she is to be trusted to that extent. I · have pointed out to our friend (and my client), that to set on foot random inquiries would not only be to raise the Devil, in the likeness of all the swindlers in the kingdom, but would also be to waste the estate. Now, you see, Mr. Vendale, our friend (and my client) does not desire to waste the estate, but, on the contrary, desires to husband it for what he considers—but I can't say I do—the rightful owner, if such rightful owner should ever be found. I am very much mistaken if he ever will be, but never mind that. Mr. Wilding and I are, at least, agreed that the estate is not to be wasted. Now, I have yielded to Mr. Wilding's desire to keep an advertisement at intervals flowing through the newspapers, cautiously inviting any person who may know anything about that adopted infant, taken from the Foundling Hospital, to come to my office; and I have pledged myself that such advertisement shall regularly appear. I have gathered from our friend (and my client) that I meet you here to-day to take his instructions, not to give him advice. I am prepared to receive his instructions, and to respect his wishes; but you will please observe that this does not imply my approval of either as a matter of professional opinion."

Thus Mr. Bintrey; talking quite as much *at* Wilding as *to* Vendale. And yet, in spite of his care for his client, he was so amused by his client's Quixotic conduct, as to eye him from time to time with twinkling eyes, in the light of a highly comical curiosity.

"Nothing," observed Wilding, "can be clearer. I only wish my head were as clear as yours, Mr. Bintrey."

"If you feel that singing in it, coming on," hinted the lawyer, with an alarmed glance, "put it off.—I mean the interview."

"Not at all, I thank you," said Wilding. "What was I going to——"

"Don't excite yourself, Mr. Wilding," urged the lawyer.

"No; I *wasn't* going to," said the wine-merchant. "Mr. Bintrey and George Vendale, would you have any hesitation or objection to become my joint trustees and executors, or can you at once consent?"

"*I* consent," replied George Vendale, readily.

"*I* consent," said Bintrey, not so readily.

"Thank you both. Mr. Bintrey, my instructions for my last will and testament are short and plain. Perhaps you will now have the goodness to take them down. I leave the whole of my real and personal estate, without any exception or reservation whatsoever, to you two, my joint trustees and executors, in trust to pay over the whole to the true Walter Wilding, if he shall be found and identified within two years after the day of my death. Failing that, in trust to you two to pay over the whole as a benefaction and legacy to the Foundling Hospital."

"Those are all your instructions, are they, Mr. Wilding?" demanded Bintrey, after a blank silence, during which nobody had looked at anybody.

"The whole."

"And as to those instructions, you have absolutely made up your mind, Mr. Wilding?"

"Absolutely, decidedly, finally."

"It only remains," said the lawyer, with one shrug of his shoulders, "to get them into technical and binding form, and to execute and attest. Now, does that press? Is there any hurry about it? You are not going to die yet, sir."

"Mr. Bintrey," answered Wilding, gravely "when I am going to die is within other knowledge than yours or mine. I shall be glad to have this matter off my mind, if you please."

"We are lawyer and client again," rejoined Bintrey, who, for the nonce, had become almost sympathetic. "If this day week—here, at the same hour—will suit Mr. Vendale and yourself, I will enter in my Diary that I attend you accordingly."

The appointment was made, and in due sequence kept. The will was formally signed, sealed, delivered, and witnessed, and was carried off by Mr. Bintrey for safe storage among the papers of his clients, ranged in their respective iron boxes, with their respective owners' names outside, on iron tiers in his consulting-room, as if that legal sanctuary were a condensed Family Vault of Clients.

With more heart than he had lately had for former subjects of interest, Wilding then set about completing his patriarchal establishment, being much assisted not only by Mrs. Goldstraw but by Vendale too: who, perhaps, had in his mind the giving of an Obenreizer dinner as soon as possible. Anyhow, the establishment being reported in sound working order, the Obenreizers, Guardian and Ward, were asked to dinner, and Madame Dor was included in the invitation. If Vendale had been over head and ears in love before—a phrase not to be taken as implying the faintest doubt about it—this dinner plunged him down in love ten thousand fathoms deep. Yet, for the life of him, he could not get one word alone with charming Marguerite. So surely as a blessed moment seemed to come, Obenreizer, in his filmy state, would stand at Vendale's elbow, or the broad back of Madame Dor would appear before his eyes. That speechless matron was never seen in a front view, from the moment of her arrival to that of her departure —except at dinner. And from the instant of her retirement

to the drawing-room, **after a** hearty **participation in that meal,
she** turned her face to the wall again.

Yet, through four or five delightful though distracting **hours,
Marguerite was to** be seen, Marguerite was to be heard, Marguerite
was to be occasionally touched. When they made the round **of**
the **old** dark cellars, Vendale **led her by** the hand ; **when she
sang to** him in the lighted **room at** night, Vendale, standing by
her, held her relinquished gloves, and would **have** bartered
against them every drop of the forty-five year old, though it had
**been forty-five times forty-five years old, and its nett price
forty-five times forty-five pounds per dozen. And still, when
she was gone, and a great gap of an extinguisher was clapped on**
Cripple **Corner, he tormented himself by wondering. Did she**
think **that he admired her ! Did she think that he adored her !
Did she suspect that she had won him, heart and soul ! Did
she care to think at all about it ! And so, Did she and Didn't
she, up and down the gamut, and above the line and below the**
line, dear, **dear ! Poor restless heart of** humanity **! To think
that the men who** were mummies **thousands of years ago, did
the same, and ever found the secret how to be quiet after it !**

"**What do you think, George," Wilding asked him next
day, "of Mr. Obenreizer ? (I won't ask you what you think of
Miss Obenreizer.)"**

"**I don't know," said Vendale, "and I never did know,
what to think of him."**

"**He is well informed and clever," said** Wilding.

"**Certainly clever.**"

"**A good musician." (He had played very well, and sung
very well, overnight.)**

"**Unquestionably a good musician.**"

"**And talks well.**"

"**Yes," said George Vendale, ruminating, "and talks well.
Do you know, Wilding, it oddly** occurs **to me, as I think about
him, that he doesn't keep** silence well**!**"

"**How do you mean ? He is not obtrusively** talkative.**"

"**No, and I don't mean** that. **But when he is silent, you
can hardly help vaguely, though perhaps most unjustly, mis-**
trusting him. **Take people whom you know and like. Take
any one you know and like.**"

"**Soon done, my good fellow," said** Wilding. "**I take you.**"

"I didn't bargain for that, or foresee it," returned Vendale, laughing. "However, take me. Reflect for a moment. Is your approving knowledge of my interesting face, mainly founded (however various the momentary expressions it may include) on my face when I am silent?"

"I think it is," said Wilding.

"I think so too. Now, you see, when Obenreizer speaks— in other words, when he is allowed to explain himself away—he comes out right enough ; but when he has not the opportunity of explaining himself away, he comes out rather wrong. There- fore it is, that I say he does not keep silence well. And passing hastily in review such faces as I know, and don't trust, I am inclined to think, now I give my mind to it, that none of them keep silence well."

This proposition in Physiognomy being new to Wilding, he was at first slow to admit it, until asking himself the question whether Mrs. Goldstraw kept silence well, and remembering that her face in repose decidedly invited trustfulness, he was as glad as men usually are to believe what they desire to believe.

But, as he was very slow to regain his spirits or his health, his partner, as another means of setting him up—and perhaps also with contingent Obenreizer views—reminded him of those musical schemes of his in connection with his family, and how a singing-class was to be formed in the house, and a Choir in a neighbouring church. The class was established speedily, and two or three of the people having already some musical know- ledge, and singing tolerably, the Choir soon followed. The latter was led and chiefly taught, by Wilding himself : who had hopes of converting his dependents into so many Foundlings, in respect of their capacity to sing sacred choruses.

Now, the Obenreizers being skilled musicians it was easily brought to pass that they should be asked to join these musical unions. Guardian and Ward consenting, or Guardian con- senting for both, it was necessarily brought to pass that Vendale's life became a life of absolute thraldom and enchantment. For, in the mouldy Christopher-Wren church on Sundays, with its dearly beloved brethren assembled and met together, five-and- twenty strong, was not that Her voice that shot like light into the darkest places, thrilling the walls and pillars as though they were pieces of his heart ! What time, too, Madame Dor in a corner of the high pew, turning her back upon everybody and everything, could not fail to be Ritualistically right at some moment of the service; like the man whom the doctors recommended to get drunk once a month, and who, that he might not overlook it, got drunk every day.

But, even those seraphic Sundays were surpassed by the Wednesday concerts established for the patriarchal family. At those concerts she would sit down to the piano and sing them, in her own tongue, songs of her own land, songs calling from the mountain-tops to Vendale, "Rise above the grovelling level country; come far away from the crowd; pursue me as I mount higher, higher, higher, melting into the azure distance; rise to my supremest height of all, and love me here!" Then would the pretty bodice, the clocked stocking, and the silver-buckled shoe be, like the broad forehead and the bright eyes, fraught with the spring of a very chamois, until the strain was over.

Not even over Vendale himself did these songs of hers cast a more potent spell than over Joey Ladle in his different way. Steadily refusing to muddle the harmony by taking any share in it, and evincing the supremest contempt for scales and such like rudiments of music—which, indeed, seldom captivate mere listeners—Joey did at first give up the whole business for a bad job, and the whole of the performers for a set of howling Dervishes. But, descrying traces of unmuddled harmony in a part-song one day, he gave his two under-cellarmen faint hopes of getting on towards something in course of time. An anthem of Handel's led to further encouragement from him : though he objected that that great musician must have been down in some of them foreign cellars pretty much, for to go and say the same thing so many times over; which, took it in how you might, he considered a certain sign of your having took it in somehow. On a third occasion, the public appearance of Mr. Jarvis with a flute, and of an odd man with a violin, and the performance of a duet by the two, did so astonish him that, solely of his own impulse and motion, he became inspired with the words, "Ann Koar!" repeatedly pronouncing them as if calling in a familiar manner for some lady who had distinguished herself in the orchestra. But this was his final testimony to the merits of his mates, for, the instrumental duet being performed at the first Wednesday concert, and being presently followed by the voice of Marguerite Obenreizer, he sat with his mouth wide open, entranced, until she had finished; when, rising in his place with much solemnity, and prefacing what he was about to say with a bow that specially included Mr. Wilding in it, he delivered himself of the gratifying sentiment: "Arter that, ye may all on ye get to bed!" And ever afterwards declined to ren ler homage in any other words to the musical powers of the family.

Thus began a separate personal acquaintance between Marguerite Obenreizer and Joey Ladle. She laughed so heartily at his compliment, and yet was so abashed by it, that Joey made bold to say to her, after the concert was over, he hoped he wasn't so muddled in his head as to have took a liberty? She made him a gracious reply, and Joey ducked in return.

"You'll change the luck time about, Miss," said Joey, ducking again. "It's such as you in the place that can bring round the luck of the place."

"Can I? Round the luck?" she answered, in her pretty English, and with a pretty wonder. "I fear I do not undei stand. I am so stupid."

"Young Master Wilding, Miss," Joey explained confidentially, though not much to her enlightenment, "changed the luck, afore he took in young Master George. So I say, and so they'll find. Lord! Only come into the place and sing over the luck a few times, Miss, and it won't be able to help itself!"

With this, and with a whole brood of ducks, Joey backed out of the presence. But Joey being a privileged person, and even an involuntary conquest being pleasant to youth and beauty, Marguerite merrily looked out for him next time.

"Where is my Mr. Joey, please?" she asked of Vendale.

So Joey was produced and shaken hands with, and that became an Institution.

Another Institution arose in this wise. Joey was a little hard of hearing. He himself said it was "Wapours," and perhaps it might have been; but whatever the cause of the effect, there the effect was, upon him. On this first occasion he had been seen to sidle along the wall, with his left hand to his left ear, until he had sidled himself into a seat pretty near the singer, in which place and position he had remained, until

addressing to his friends the amateurs the compliment before
mentioned.   It was observed on the following Wednesday that
Joey's action as a Pecking Machine was impaired at dinner,
and it was rumoured about the table that this was explainable
by his high-strung expectations of Miss Obenreizer's singing, and
his fears of not getting a place where he could hear every note
and syllable.   The rumour reaching Wilding's ears, he in his
good nature called Joey to the front at night before Marguerite
began.   Thus the Institution came into being that on suc-
ceeding nights, Marguerite, running her hands over the keys
before singing, always said to Vendale, "Where is my Mr. Joey,
please?" and that Vendale always brought him forth, and
stationed him near by.   That he should then, when all eyes
were upon him, express in his face the utmost contempt for the
exertions of his friends and confidence in Marguerite alone,
whom he would stand contemplating, not unlike the rhinoceros
out of the spelling-book, tamed and on his hind legs, was a part
of the Institution.   Also that when he remained after the
singing in his most ecstatic state, some bold spirit from the
back should say, "What do you think of it, Joey?" and he
should be goaded to reply, as having that instant conceived the
retort, "Arter that ye may all on ye get to bed!"   These were
other parts of the Institution.

But, the simple pleasures and small jests of Cripple Corner
were not destined to have a long life.   Underlying them from
the first was a serious matter, which every member of the
patriarchal family knew of, but which, by tacit agreement, all
forbore to speak of.   Mr. Wilding's health was in a bad way.

He might have overcome the shock he had sustained in the
one great affection of his life, or he might have overcome his
consciousness of being in the enjoyment of another man's
property; but the two together were too much for him.   A
man haunted by twin ghosts, he became deeply depressed.
The inseparable spectres sat at the board with him, ate from his
platter, drank from his cup, and stood by his bedside at night.
When he recalled his supposed mother's love, he felt as though
he had stolen it.   When he rallied a little under the respect and
attachment of his dependents, he felt as though he were even
fraudulent in making them happy, for that should have been
the unknown man's duty and gratification.

Gradually, under the pressure of his brooding mind, his body stooped, his step lost its elasticity, his eyes were seldom lifted from the ground. He knew he could not help the deplorable mistake that had been made, but he knew he could not mend it; for the days and weeks went by, and no one claimed his name or his possessions. And now there began to creep over him, a cloudy consciousness of often-recurring confusion in his head. He would unaccountably lose, sometimes whole hours, sometimes a whole day and night. Once, his remembrance stopped as he sat at the head of the dinner-table, and was blank until daybreak. Another time, it stopped as he was beating time to their singing, and went on again when he and his partner were walking in the courtyard by the light of the moon, half the night later. He asked Vendale (always full of consideration, work, and help) how this was? Vendale only replied, "You have not been quite well; that's all." He looked for explanation into the faces of his people. But they would put it off with, "Glad to see you looking so much better, sir;" or "Hope you're doing nicely now, sir;" in which was no information at all.

At length, when the partnership was but five months old, Walter Wilding took to his bed, and his housekeeper became his nurse.

"Lying here, perhaps you will not mind my calling you Sally, Mrs. Goldstraw?" said the poor wine-merchant.

"It sounds more natural to me, sir, than any other name, and I like it better."

"Thank you, Sally. I think, Sally, I must of late have been subject to fits. Is that so, Sally? Don't mind telling me now."

"It has happened, sir."

"Ah! That is the explanation!" he quietly remarked. "Mr. Obenreizer, Sally, talks of the world being so small that it is not strange how often the same people come together, and come together, at various places, and in various stages of life. But it does seem strange, Sally, that I should, as I may say, come round to the Foundling to die."

He extended his hand to her, and she gently took it.

"You are not going to die, dear Mr. Wilding."

"So Mr. Bintrey said, but I think he was wrong. The old.

child-feeling is coming back upon me, Sally.   The old hush and
rest, as I used to fall asleep."

After an interval he said, in a placid voice, " Please kiss me,
Nurse," and, it was evident, believed himself to be lying in the
old Dormitory.

As she had been used to bend over the fatherless and
motherless children, Sally bent over the fatherless and motherless
man, and put her lips to his forehead, murmuring :

"God bless you ! "

"God bless you ! " he replied, in the same tone.

After another interval, he opened his eyes in his own
character, and said : " Don't move me, Sally, because of what I
am going to say ; I lie quite easily.   I think my time is come.
I don't know how it may appear to you, Sally, but——"

Insensibility fell upon him for a few minutes ; he emerged
from it once more.

" —I don't know how it may appear to you, Sally, but so it
appears to me."

When he had thus conscientiously finished his favourite
sentence, his time came, and he died.

ACT II.

THE summer and the autumn had passed. Christmas and the New Year were at hand.

As executors honestly bent on performing their duty towards the dead, Vendale and Bintrey had held more than one anxious consultation on the subject of Wilding's will. The lawyer had declared, from the first, that it was simply impossible to take any useful action in the matter at all. The only obvious inquiries to make, in relation to the lost man, had been made already by Wilding himself; with this result, that time and death together had not left a trace of him discoverable. To advertise for the claimant to the property, it would be necessary to mention particulars—a course of proceeding which would invite half the impostors in England to present themselves in the character of the true Walter Wilding. "If we find a chance of tracing the lost man, we will take it. If we don't, let us meet for another consultation on the first anniversary of Wilding's death." So Bintrey advised. And so, with the most earnest desire to fulfil his dead friend's wishes, Vendale was fain to let the matter rest for the present.

Turning from his interest in the past to his interest in the future, Vendale still found himself confronting a doubtful prospect. Months on months had passed since his first visit to Soho-square—and through all that time, the one language in which he had told Marguerite that he loved her was the language of the eyes, assisted, at convenient opportunities, by the language of the hand.

What was the obstacle in his way? The one immovable

M

obstacle which had been in his way from the first. No matter how fairly the opportunities looked, Vendale's efforts to speak with Marguerite alone, ended invariably in one and the same result. Under the most accidental circumstances, in the most innocent manner possible, Obenreizer was always in the way.

With the last days of the old year came an unexpected chance of spending an evening with Marguerite, which Vendale resolved should be a chance of speaking privately to her as well. A cordial note from Obenreizer invited him, on New Year's Day, to a little family dinner in Soho-square. "We shall be on'y four," the note said. "We shall be only two," Vendale determined, " before the evening is out ! "

New Year's Day, among the English, is associated with the giving and receiving of dinners, and with nothing more. New Year's Day, among the foreigners, is the grand opportunity of the year for the giving and receiving of presents. It is occasionally possible to acclimatise a foreign custom. In this instance Vendale felt no hesitation about making the attempt. His one difficulty was to decide what his New Year's gift to Marguerite should be. The defensive pride of the peasant's daughter—morbidly sensitive to the inequality between her social position and his—would be secretly roused against him if he ventured on a rich offering. A gift, which a poor man's purse might purchase, was the one gift that could be trusted to find its way to her heart, for the giver's sake. Stoutly resisting temptation, in the form of diamonds and rubies, Vendale bought a brooch of the filagree-work of Genoa—the simplest and most unpretending ornament that he could find in the jeweller's shop.

He slipped his gift into Marguerite's hand as she held it out to welcome him on the day of the dinner.

"This is your first New Year's Day in England," he said. "Will you let me help to make it like a New Year's Day at home ? "

She thanked him, a little constrainedly, as she looked at the jeweller's box, uncertain what it might contain. Opening the box, and discovering the studiously simple form under which Vendale's little keepsake offered itself to her, she penetrated his motive on the spot. Her face turned on him brightly, with a look which said, " I own you have pleased and flattered me." Never had she been so charming, in Vendale's eyes, as she was at that moment. Her winter dress—a petticoat of dark silk, with a bodice of black velvet rising to her neck, and enclosing it softly in a little circle of swansdown— heightened, by all the force of contrast, the dazzling fairness of her hair and her complexion. It was only when she turned aside from him to the glass, and, taking out the brooch that she wore, put his New Year's gift in its place, that Vendale's attention wandered far enough away from her to discover the presence of other persons in the room. He now became conscious that the hands of Obenreizer were affectionately in possession of his elbows. He now heard the voice of Obenreizer thanking him for his attention to Marguerite, with the faintest possible ring of mockery in its tone. ("Such a simple present, dear sir ! and showing such nice tact !") He now discovered, for the first time, that there was one other guest, and but one, besides himself, whom Obenreizer presented as a compatriot and friend. The friend's face was mouldy, and the friend's figure was fat. His age was suggestive of the autumnal period of human life. In the course of the evening he developed two extraordinary capacities. One was a capacity for silence ; the other was a capactity for emptying bottles.

Madame Dor was not in the room. Neither was there any visible place reserved for her when they sat down to table. Obenreizer explained that it was " the good Dor's simple habit to dine always in the middle of the day. She would make her excuses later in the evening." Vendale wondered whether the good Dor had, on this occasion, varied her domestic employment from cleaning Obenreizer's gloves to cooking Obenreizer's dinner. This at least was certain—the dishes served were, one and all, as achievements in cookery, high above the reach of the rude elementary art of England. The dinner was unobtrusively perfect. As for the wine, the eyes of the speechless friend rolled over it, as in solemn ecstasy. Sometimes he said " Good!" when a bottle came in full ; and sometimes he said " Ah !" when a bottle went out empty—and there his contributions to the gaiety of the evening ended.

Silence is occasionally infectious. Oppressed by private anxieties of their own, Marguerite and Vendale appeared to feel the influence of the speechless friend. The whole responsibility of keeping the talk going rested on Obenreizer's shoulders, and manfully did Obenreizer sustain it. He opened his heart in the character of an enlightened foreigner, and sang the praises of England. When other topics ran dry, he returned to this inexhaustible source, and always set the stream running again as copiously as ever. Obenreizer would have given an arm, an eye, or a leg to have been born an Englishman. Out of England there was no such institution as a home, no such thing as a fireside, no such object as a beautiful woman. His dear Miss Marguerite would excuse him, if he accounted for *her* attractions on the theory that English blood must have mixed at some former time with their obscure and unknown ancestry. Survey this English nation, and behold a tall, clean, plump, and solid people ! Look at their cities ! What magnificence in their public buildings ! What admirable order and propriety in their streets ! Admire their laws, combining the eternal principle of justice with the other eternal principle of pounds, shillings, and pence ; and applying the product to all civil injuries, from an injury to a man's honour, to an injury to a man's nose ! You have ruined my daughter—pounds, shillings, and pence ! You have knocked me down with a blow in my face—pounds, shillings, and pence ! Where was the material prosperity of such a country as *that* to stop ? Obenreizer, projecting himself into the future, failed to see the end of it. Obenreizer's enthusiasm entreated permission to exhale itself, English fashion, in a toast. Here is our modest little dinner over, here is our frugal dessert on the table, and here is the admirer of England conforming to national customs, and making a speech ! A toast to your white cliffs of Albion, Mr. Vendale ! to your national virtues, your charming climate, and your fascinating women ! to your Hearths, to your Homes, to your Habeas Corpus, and to all your other institutions ! In one word—to England ! Heep-heep-heep ! hooray !

Obenreizer's voice had barely chanted the last note of the English cheer, the speechless friend had barely drained the last drop out of his glass, when the festive proceedings were interrupted by a modest tap at the door. A woman-servant came in, and approached her master with a little note in her hand. Obenreizer opened the note with a frown ; and, after reading it with an expression of genuine annoyance, passed it on to his compatriot and friend. Vendale's spirits rose as he watched these proceedings. Had he found an ally in the annoying little note? Was the long-looked-for chance actually coming at last?

"I am afraid there is no help for it?" said Obenreizer, addressing his fellow-countryman. "I am afraid we must go."

The speechless friend handed back the letter, shrugged his heavy shoulders, and poured himself out a last glass of wine. His fat fingers lingered fondly round the neck of the bottle. They pressed it with a little amatory squeeze at parting. His globular eyes looked dimly, as through an intervening haze, at Vendale and Marguerite. His heavy articulation laboured, and brought forth a whole sentence at a birth. "I think," he said, "I should have liked a little more wine." His breath failed him after that effort; he gasped, and walked to the door.

Obenreizer addressed himself to Vendale with an appearance of the deepest distress.

"I am so shocked, so confused, so distressed," he began. "A misfortune has happened to one of my compatriots. He is alone, he is ignorant of your language—I and my good friend, here, have no choice but to go and help him. What can I say in my excuse? How can I describe my affliction at depriving myself in this way of the honour of your company?"

He paused, evidently expecting to see Vendale take up his hat and retire. Discerning his opportunity at last, Vendale determined to do nothing of the kind. He met Obenreizer dexterously, with Obenreizer's own weapons.

"Pray don't distress yourself," he said. "I'll wait here with the greatest pleasure till you come back."

Marguerite blushed deeply, and turned away to her embroidery-frame in a corner by the window. The film showed itself in Obenreizer's eyes, and the smile came something sourly to Obenreizer's lips. To have told Vendale that there was no reasonable prospect of his coming back in good time would have been to risk offending a man whose favourable opinion was of solid commercial importance to him. Accepting his defeat with the best possible grace, he declared himself to be equally honoured and delighted by Vendale's proposal. "So frank, so friendly, so English!" He bustled about, apparently looking for something he wanted, disappeared for a moment through

the folding-doors communicating with the next room, came back
with his hat and coat, and protesting that he would return at
the earliest possible moment, embraced Vendale's elbows, and
vanished from the scene in company with the speechless
friend.

Vendale turned to the corner by the window, in which
Marguerite had placed herself with her work. There, as if she
had dropped from the ceiling, or come up through the floor—
there, in the old attitude, with her face to the stove—sat an
Obstacle that had not been foreseen, in the person of Madame
Dor! She half got up, half looked over her broad shoulder at
Vendale, and plumped down again. Was she at work? Yes.
Cleaning Obenreizer's gloves, as before? No; darning Oben-
reizer's stockings.

The case was now desperate. Two serious considerations
presented themselves to Vendale. Was it possible to put
Madame Dor into the stove? The stove wouldn't hold her.
Was it possible to treat Madame Dor, not as a living woman
but as an article of furniture? Could the mind be brought to
contemplate this respectable matron purely in the light of a
chest of drawers, with a black gauze head-dress accidentally
left on the top of it? Yes, the mind could be brought to do
that. With a comparatively trifling effort, Vendale's mind did
it. As he took his place on the old-fashioned window-seat,
close by Marguerite and her embroidery, a slight movement
appeared in the chest of drawers, but no remark issued from it.
Let it be remembered that solid furniture is not easy to move,
and that it has this advantage in consequence—there is no fear
of upsetting it.

Unusually silent and unusually constrained—with the bright
colour fast fading from her face, with a feverish energy possessing her fingers—the pretty Marguerite bent over her embroidery, and worked as if her life depended on it. Hardly
less agitated himself, Vendale felt the importance of leading her
very gently to the avowal which he was eager to make—to the
other sweeter avowal still, which he was longing to hear. A
woman's love is never to be taken by storm; it yields insensibly
to a system of gradual approach. It ventures by the roundabout
way, and listens to the low voice. Vendale led her memory
back to their past meetings when they were travelling together

in Switzerland. They revived the impressions, they recalled the events, of the happy bygone time. Little by little, Marguerite's constraint vanished. She smiled, she was interested, she looked at Vendale, she grew idle with her needle, she made false stitches in her work. Their voices sank lower and lower; their faces bent nearer and nearer to each other as they spoke. And Madame Dor? Madame Dor behaved like an angel. She never looked round; she never said a word; she went on with Obenreizer's stockings. Pulling each stocking up tight over her left arm, and holding that arm aloft from time to time, to catch the light on her work, there were moments, delicate and indescribable moments, when Madame Dor appeared to be sitting upside down, and contemplating one of her own respectable legs elevated in the air. As the minutes wore on, these elevations followed each other at longer and longer intervals. Now and again, the black gauze head-dress nodded, dropped forward, recovered itself. A little heap of stockings slid softly from Madame Dor's lap, and remained unnoticed on the floor. A prodigious ball of worsted followed the stockings, and rolled lazily under the table. The black gauze head-dress nodded, dropped forward, recovered itself, nodded again, dropped forward again, and recovered itself no more. A composite sound, partly as of the purring of an immense cat, partly as of the planing of a soft board, rose over the hushed voices of the lovers, and hummed at regular intervals through the room. Nature and Madame Dor had combined together in Vendale's interests. The best of women was asleep.

Marguerite rose to stop—not the snoring—let us say, the audible repose of Madame Dor. Vendale laid his hand on her arm, and pressed her back gently into her chair.

"Don't disturb her," he whispered. "I have been waiting to tell you a secret. Let me tell it now."

Marguerite resumed her seat. She tried to resume her needle. It was useless; her eyes failed her; her hand failed her; she could find nothing.

"We have been talking," said Vendale, "of the happy time when we first met, and first travelled together. I have a confession to make. I have been concealing something. When we spoke of my first visit to Switzerland, I told you of all the

impressions I had brought back with me to England—except
one. Can you guess what that one is?"

Her eyes looked steadfastly at the embroidery, and her face
turned a little away from him. Signs of disturbance began to
appear in her neat velvet bodice, round the region of the
brooch. She made no reply. Vendale pressed the question
without mercy.

"Can you guess what the one Swiss impression is, which I
have not told you yet?"

Her face turned back towards him, and a faint smile
trembled on her lips.

"An impression of the mountains, perhaps?" she said,
slily.

"No; a much more precious impression than that."

"Of the lakes?"

"No. The lakes have not grown dearer and dearer in
remembrance to me every day. The lakes are not associated
with my happiness in the present, and my hopes in the future.
Marguerite! all that makes life worth having hangs, for me, on
a word from your lips. Marguerite! I love you!"

Her head dropped, as he took her hand. He drew her to
him, and looked at her. The tears escaped from her downcast
eyes, and fell slowly over her cheeks.

"Oh, Mr. Vendale," she said, sadly, "it would have been
kinder to have kept your secret. Have you forgotten the
distance between us? It can never, never, be!"

"There can be but one distance between us, Marguerite—a
distance of your making. My love, my darling, there is no
higher rank in goodness, there is no higher rank in beauty, than
yours! Come! whisper the one little word which tells me you
will be my wife!"

She sighed bitterly. "Think of your family," she mur-
murmed; "and think of mine!"

Vendale drew her a little nearer to him.

"If you dwell on such an obstacle as that," he said, "I
shall think but one thought—I shall think I have offended
you."

She started, and looked up. "Oh, no!" she exclaimed,
innocently. The instant the words passed her lips, she saw
the construction that might be placed on them. Her confession

VENDALE AND MARGUERITE.

had escaped her in spite of herself. A lovely flush of colour overspread her face. She made a momentary effort to disengage herself from her lover's embrace. She looked up at him entreatingly. She tried to speak. The words died on her lips in the kiss that Vendale pressed on them. " Let me go, Mr. Vendale!" she said, faintly.

"Call me George."

She laid her head on his bosom. All her heart went out to him at last. "George!" she whispered.

"Say you love me!"

Her arms twined themselves gently round his neck. Her lips, timidly touching his cheek, murmured the delicious words —"I love you!"

In the moment of silence that followed, the sound of the opening and closing of the house-door came clear to them through the wintry stillness of the street.

Marguerite started to her feet.

"Let me go!" she said. "He has come back!"

She hurried from the room, and touched Madame Dor's shoulder in passing. Madame Dor woke up with a loud snort, looked first over one shoulder and then over the other, peered down into her lap, and discovered neither stockings, worsted, nor darning-needle in it. At the same moment, footsteps became audible ascending the stairs. "Mon Dieu!" said Madame Dor, addressing herself to the stove, and trembling violently. Vendale picked up the stockings and the ball, and huddled them all back in a heap over her shoulder. "Mon Dieu!" said Madame Dor, for the second time, as the avalanche of worsted poured into her capacious lap.

The door opened, and Obenreizer came in. His first glance round the room showed him that Marguerite was absent.

"What!" he exclaimed, "my niece is away? My niece is not here to entertain you in my absence? This is unpardonable. I shall bring her back instantly."

Vendale stopped him.

"I beg you will not disturb Miss Obenreizer," he said. "You have returned, I see, without your friend?"

"My friend remains, and consoles our afflicted compatriot. A heart-rending scene, Mr. Vendale! The household gods at the pawnbroker's—the family immersed in tears. We all embraced in silence. My admirable friend alone possessed his composure. He sent out, on the spot, for a bottle of wine."

"Can I say a word to you in private, Mr. Obenreizer?"

"Assuredly." He turned to Madame Dor. "My good creature, you are sinking for want of repose. Mr. Vendale will excuse you."

Madame Dor rose, and set forth sideways on her journey from the stove to bed. She dropped a stocking. Vendale picked it up for her, and opened one of the folding-doors. She advanced a step, and dropped three more stockings. Vendale, stooping to recover them as before, Obenreizer interfered with profuse apologies, and with a warning look at Madame Dor. Madame Dor acknowledged the look by dropping the whole of the stockings in a heap, and then shuffling away panic-stricken from the scene of disaster. Obenreizer swept up the complete collection fiercely in both hands. "Go!" he cried, giving his prodigious handful a preparatory swing in the air. Madame Dor said, "Mon Dieu," and vanished into the next room, pursued by a shower of stockings.

"What must you think, Mr. Vendale," said Obenreizer, closing the door, "of this deplorable intrusion of domestic details? For myself, I blush at it. We are beginning the New Year as badly as possible; everything has gone wrong to-night. Be seated, pray—and say, what may I offer you? Shall we pay our best respects to another of your noble English institutions? It is my study to be, what you call, jolly. I propose a grog."

Vendale declined the grog with all needful respect for that noble institution.

"I wish to speak to you on a subject in which I am deeply interested," he said. "You must have observed, Mr. Obenreizer, that I have, from the first, felt no ordinary admiration for your charming niece?"

"You are very good. In my niece's name, I thank you."

"Perhaps you may have noticed, latterly, that my admiration for Miss Obenreizer has grown into a tenderer and deeper feeling—— ?"

"Shall we say friendship, Mr. Vendale?"

"Say love—and we shall be nearer to the truth."

Obenreizer started out of his chair. The faintly discernible beat, which was his nearest approach to a change of colour, showed itself suddenly in his cheeks.

"You are Miss Obenreizer's guardian," pursued Vendale. "I ask you to confer upon me the greatest of all favours—I ask you to give me her hand in marriage."

Obenreizer dropped back into his chair. "Mr. Vendale," he said, "you petrify me."

"I will wait," rejoined Vendale, "until you have recovered yourself."

"One word before I recover myself. You have said nothing about this to my niece?"

"I have opened my whole heart to your niece. And I have reason to hope——"

"What!" interposed Obenreizer. "You have made a proposal to my niece, without first asking for my authority to pay your addresses to her?" He struck his hand on the table, and lost his hold over himself for the first time in Vendale's experience of him. "Sir!" he exclaimed, indignantly, "what sort of conduct is this? As a man of honour, speaking to a man of honour, how can you justify it?"

"I can only justify it as one of our English institutions," said Vendale, quietly. "You admire our English institutions. I can't honestly tell you, Mr. Obenreizer, that I regret what I have done. I can only assure you that I have not acted in the matter with any intentional disrespect towards yourself. This said, may I ask you to tell me plainly what objection you see to favouring my suit?"

"I see this immense objection," answered Obenreizer, "that my niece and you are not on a social equality together. My niece is the daughter of a poor peasant; and you are the son of a gentleman. You do us an honour," he added, lowering himself again gradually to his customary polite level, "which deserves, and has, our most grateful acknowledgments. But the inequality is too glaring; the sacrifice is too great. You English are a proud people, Mr. Vendale. I have observed enough of this country to see that such a marriage as you propose would be a scandal here. Not a hand would be held out to your peasant-wife; and all your best friends would desert you."

"One moment," said Vendale, interposing on his side. "I may claim, without any great arrogance, to know more of my

country-people in general, and of my own friends in particular,
than you do. In the estimation of everybody whose opinion is
worth having, my wife herself would be the one sufficient
justification of my marriage. If I did not feel certain—observe,
I say certain—that I am offering her a position which she can
accept without so much as the shadow of a humiliation—I
would never (cost me what it might) have asked her to be my
wife. Is there any other obstacle that you see? Have you
any personal objection to me?"

Obenreizer spread out both his hands in courteous protest.
"Personal objection!" he exclaimed. "Dear sir, the bare
question is painful to me."

"We are both men of business," pursued Vendale, "and
you naturally expect me to satisfy you that I have the means of
supporting a wife. I can explain my pecuniary position in two
words. I inherit from my parents a fortune of twenty thousand
pounds. In half of that sum I have only a life-interest, to
which, if I die, leaving a widow, my widow succeeds. If I die,
leaving children, the money itself is divided among them, as
they come of age. The other half of my fortune is at my own
disposal, and is invested in the wine-business. I see my way
to greatly improving that business. As it stands at present, I
cannot state my return from my capital embarked at more than
twelve hundred a year. Add the yearly value of my life-interest
—and the total reaches a present annual income of fifteen hundred
pounds. I have the fairest prospect of soon making it more. In
the mean time, do you object to me on pecuniary grounds?"

Driven back to his last entrenchment, Obenreizer rose, and
took a turn backwards and forwards in the room. For the
moment, he was plainly at a loss what to say or do next.

"Before I answer that last question," he said, after a little
close consideration with himself, "I beg leave to revert for a
moment to Miss Marguerite. You said something just now
which seemed to imply that she returns the sentiment with
which you are pleased to regard her?"

"I have the inestimable happiness," said Vendale, "of
knowing that she loves me."

Obenreizer stood silent for a moment, with the film over his
eyes, and the faintly perceptible beat becoming visible again in
his cheeks.

"If you will excuse me for a few minutes," he said, with ceremonious politeness, "I should like to have the opportunity of speaking to my niece." With those words, he bowed, and quitted the room.

Left by himself, Vendale's thoughts (as a necessary result of the interview, thus far) turned instinctively to the consideration of Obenreizer's motives. He had put obstacles in the way of the courtship; he was now putting obstacles in the way of the marriage—a marriage offering advantages which even his ingenuity could not dispute. On the face of it, his conduct was incomprehensible. What did it mean?

Seeking, under the surface, for the answer to that question —and remembering that Obenreizer was a man of about his own age; also, that Marguerite was, strictly speaking, his half-niece only—Vendale asked himself, with a lover's ready jealousy, whether he had a rival to fear, as well as a guardian to conciliate. The thought just crossed his mind, and no more. The sense of Marguerite's kiss still lingering on his cheek reminded him gently that even the jealousy of a moment was now a treason to *her*.

On reflection, it seemed most likely that a personal motive of another kind might suggest the true explanation of Obenreizer's conduct. Marguerite's grace and beauty were precious ornaments in that little household. They gave it a special social attraction and a special social importance. They armed Obenreizer with a certain influence in reserve, which he could always depend upon to make his house attractive, and which he might always bring more or less to bear on the forwarding of his own private ends. Was he the sort of man to resign such advantages as were here implied, without obtaining the fullest possible compensation for the loss? A connexion by marriage with Vendale offered him solid advantages, beyond all doubt. But there were hundreds of men in London with far greater power and far wider influence than Vendale possessed. Was it possible that this man's ambition secretly looked higher than the highest prospects that could be offered to him by the alliance now proposed for his niece? As the question passed through Vendale's mind, the man himself reappeared—to answer it, or not to answer it, as the event might prove.

A marked change was visible in Obenreizer when he resumed

his place. His manner was less assured, and there were plain traces about his mouth of recent agitation which had not been successfully composed. Had he said something, referring either to Vendale or to himself, which had roused Marguerite's spirit, and which had placed him, for the first time, face to face with a resolute assertion of his niece's will? It might or might not be. This only was certain—he looked like a man who had met with a repulse.

"I have spoken to my niece," he began. "I find, Mr. Vendale, that even your influence has not entirely blinded her to the social objections to your proposal."

"May I ask," returned Vendale, "if that is the only result of your interview with Miss Obenreizer?"

A momentary flash leapt out through the Obenreizer film.

"You are master of the situation," he answered, in a tone of sardonic submission. "If you insist on my admitting it, I do admit it in those words. My niece's will and mine used to be one, Mr. Vendale. You have come between us, and her will is now yours. In my country, we know when we are beaten, and we submit with our best grace. I submit, with my best grace, on certain conditions. Let us revert to the state-ment of your pecuniary position. I have an objection to you, my dear sir—a most amazing, a most audacious objection, from a man in my position to a man in yours."

"What is it?"

"You have honoured me by making a proposal for my niece's hand. For the present (with best thanks and respects), I beg to decline it."

"Why?"

"Because you are not rich enough."

The objection, as the speaker had foreseen, took Vendale completely by surprise. For the moment he was speechless.

"Your income is fifteen hundred a year," pursued Obenreizer. "In my miserable country I should fall on my knees before your income, and say, 'What a princely fortune!' In wealthy England, I sit as I am, and say, 'A modest independence, dear sir; nothing more. Enough, perhaps, for a wife in your own rank of life, who has no social prejudices to conquer. Not more than half enough for a wife who is a meanly born foreigner, and who has all your social prejudices against her.' Sir! if my niece is ever to marry you, she will have what you call uphill work of it in taking her place at starting. Yes, yes; this is not your view, but it remains, immovably remains, my view for all that. For my niece's sake, I claim that this uphill work shall be made as smooth as possible. Whatever material advantages she can have to help her, ought, in common justice, to be hers. Now, tell me, Mr. Vendale, on your fifteen hundred a year can your wife have a house in a fashionable quarter, a footman to open her door, a butler to wait at her table, and a carriage and horses to drive about in? I see the answer in your face—your face says, No. Very good. Tell me one more thing, and I have done. Take the mass of your educated, accomplished, and lovely country women, is it, or is it not, the fact that a lady who has a house in a fashionable quarter, a footman to open her door, a butler to wait at her table, and a carriage and horses to drive about in, is a lady who has gained four steps, in female estimation, at starting? Yes? or No?"

"Come to the point," said Vendale. "You view this question as a question of terms. What are your terms?"

"The lowest terms, dear sir, on which you can provide your wife with those four steps at starting. Double your present income—the most rigid economy cannot do it in England on less. You said just now that you expected greatly to increase the value of your business. To work—and increase it! I am a good devil after all! On the day when you satisfy me, by plain proofs, that your income has risen to three thousand a year, ask me for my niece's hand, and it is yours."

"May I inquire if you have mentioned this arrangement to Miss Obenreizer?"

"Certainly. She has a last little morsel of regard still left for me, Mr. Vendale, which is not yours yet; and she accepts my terms. In other words, she submits to be guided by her guardian's regard for her welfare, and by her guardian's superior knowledge of the world." He threw himself back in his chair, in firm reliance on his position, and in full possession of his excellent temper.

Any open assertion of his own interests, in the situation in which Vendale was now placed, seemed to be (for the present at least) hopeless. He found himself literally left with no ground to stand on. Whether Obenreizer's objections were the genuine product of Obenreizer's own view of the case, or whether he was simply delaying the marriage in the hope of ultimately breaking it off altogether—in either of these events, any present resistance on Vendale's part would be equally useless. There was no help for it but to yield, making the best terms that he could on his own side.

"I protest against the conditions you impose on me," he began.

"Naturally," said Obenreizer; "I dare say I should protest, myself, in your place."

"Say, however," pursued Vendale, "that I accept your terms. In that case, I must be permitted to make two stipulations on my part. In the first place, I shall expect to be allowed to see your niece."

"Aha! to see my niece? and to make her in as great a hurry to be married as you are yourself? Suppose I say, No? you would see her perhaps without my permission?"

"Decidedly!"

"How delightfully frank! How exquisitely English! You shall see her, Mr. Vendale, on certain days, which we will appoint together. What next?"

"Your objection to my income," proceeded Vendale, "has taken me completely by surprise. I wish to be assured against any repetition of that surprise. Your present views of my qualification for marriage require me to have an income of three thousand a year. Can I be certain, in the future, as your experience of England enlarges, that your estimate will rise no higher?"

"In plain English," said Obenreizer, "you doubt my word?"

"Do you purpose to take *my* word for it when I inform you that I have doubled my income?" asked Vendale. "If my memory does not deceive me, you stipulated, a minute since, for plain proofs?"

"Well played, Mr. Vendale! You combine the foreign quickness with the English solidity. Accept my best congratulations. Accept, also, my written guarantee."

He rose; seated himself at a writing-desk at a side-table, wrote a few lines, and presented them to Vendale with a low bow. The engagement was perfectly explicit, and was signed and dated with scrupulous care.

"Are you satisfied with your guarantee?"

"I am satisfied."

"Charmed to hear it, I am sure. We have had our little skirmish—we have really been wonderfully clever on both sides. For the present our affairs are settled. I bear no malice. You bear no malice. Come, Mr. Vendale, a good English shake hands."

Vendale gave his hand, a little bewildered by Obenreizer's sudden transitions from one humour to another.

"When may I expect to see Miss Obenreizer again?" he asked, as he rose to go.

"Honour me with a visit to-morrow," said Obenreizer, "and we will settle it then. Do have a grog before you go! No? Well! well! we will reserve the grog till you have your three thousand a year, and are ready to be married. Aha! When will that be?"

"I made an estimate, some months since, of the capacities of my business," said Vendale. "If that estimate is correct, I shall double my present income——"

"And be married!" added Obenreizer.

"And be married," repeated Vendale, "within a year from this time. Good night."

VENDALE MAKES MISCHIEF.

When Vendale entered his office the next morning, the dull commercial routine at Cripple Corner met him with a new face. Marguerite had an interest in it now! The whole machinery which Wilding's death had set in motion, to realise the value of the business—the balancing of ledgers, the estimating of debts, the taking of stock, and the rest of it—was now transformed into machinery which indicated the chances for and against a speedy marriage. After looking over results, as presented by his accountant, and checking additions and subtractions, as rendered by the clerks, Vendale turned his attention to the stock-taking department next, and sent a message to the cellars, desiring to see the report.

The Cellarman's appearance, the moment he put his head in at the door of his master's private room, suggested that something very extraordinary must have happened that morning. There was an approach to alacrity in Joey Ladle's movements!

N

There was something which actually simulated cheerfulness in Joey Ladle's face !

"What's the matter?" asked Vendale. "Anything wrong?"

"I should wish to mention one thing," answered Joey. "Young Mr. Vendale, I have never set myself up for a prophet."

"Who ever said you did?"

"No prophet, as far as I've heard tell of that profession," proceeded Joey, "ever lived principally underground. No prophet, whatever else he might take in at the pores, ever took in wine from morning to night, for a number of years together. When I said to young Master Wilding, respecting his changing the name of the firm, that one of these days he might find he'd changed the luck of the firm—did I put myself forward as a prophet? No, I didn't. Has what I said to him come true? Yes, it has. In the time of Pebbleson Nephew, Young Mr. Vendale, no such thing was ever known as a mistake made in a consignment delivered at these doors. There's a mistake been made now. Please to remark that it happened before Miss Margaret came here. For which reason it don't go against what I've said respecting Miss Margaret singing round the luck. Read that, sir," concluded Joey, pointing attention to a special passage in the report, with a forefinger which appeared to be in process of taking in through the pores nothing more remarkable than dirt. "It's foreign to my nature to crow over the house I serve, but I feel it a kind of a solemn duty to ask you to read that."

Vendale read as follows :—"Note, respecting the Swiss champagne. An irregularity has been discovered in the last consignment received from the firm of Defresnier and Co." Vendale stopped, and referred to a memorandum-book by his side. "That was in Mr. Wilding's time," he said. "The vintage was a particularly good one, and he took the whole of it. The Swiss champagne has done very well, hasn't it?"

"I don't say it's done badly," answered the Cellarman. "It may have got sick in our customers' bins, or it may have bust in our customers' hands. But I don't say it's done badly with *us*."

Vendale resumed the reading of the note : "We find the number of the cases to be quite correct by the books. But six of them, which present a slight difference from the rest in the brand, have been opened, and have been found to contain a red wine instead of champagne. The similarity in the brands, we suppose, caused a mistake to be made in sending the consignment from Neuchâtel. The error has not been found to extend beyond six cases."

"Is that all!" exclaimed Vendale, tossing the note away from him.

Joey Ladle's eye followed the flying morsel of paper drearily.

"I'm glad to see you take it easy, sir," he said. "Whatever happens, it will be always a comfort to you to remember that you took it easy at first. Sometimes one mistake leads to another. A man drops a bit of orange-peel on the pavement by mistake, and another man treads on it by mistake, and there's a job at the hospital, and a party crippled for life. I'm glad you take it easy, sir. In Pebbleson Nephew's time we shouldn't have taken it easy till we had seen the end of it. Without desiring to crow over the house, Young Mr. Vendale, I wish you well through it. No offence, sir," said the Cellarman, opening the door to go out, and looking in again ominously before he shut it. "I'm muddled and molloncolly, I grant you. But I'm an old servant of Pebbleson Nephew, and I wish you well through them six cases of red wine."

Left by himself, Vendale laughed, and took up his pen. "I may as well send a line to Defresnier and Company," he thought, "before I forget it." He wrote at once in these terms:

"Dear Sirs. We are taking stock, and a trifling mistake has been discovered in the last consignment of champagne sent by your house to ours. Six of the cases contain red wine—which we hereby return to you. The matter can easily be set right, either by your sending us six cases of the champagne, if they can be produced, or, if not, by your crediting us with the value of six cases on the amount last paid (five hundred pounds) by our firm to yours. Your faithful servants,

"WILDING AND Co."

This letter despatched to the post, the subject dropped at once out of Vendale's mind. He had other and far more interesting matters to think of. Later in the day he paid the visit to Obenreizer which had been agreed on between them. Certain evenings in the week were set apart which he was privileged to spend with Marguerite—always, however, in the

presence of a third person. On this stipulation Obenreizer
politely but positively insisted. The one concession he made
was to give Vendale his choice of who the third person should
be. Confiding in past experience, his choice fell unhesitatingly
upon the excellent woman who mended Obenreizer's stockings.
On hearing of the responsibility entrusted to her, Madame Dor's
intellectual nature burst suddenly into a new stage of develop-
ment. She waited till Obenreizer's eye was off her—and then
she looked at Vendale and dimly winked.

The time passed—the happy evenings with Marguerite came
and went. It was the tenth morning since Vendale had written
to the Swiss firm, when the answer appeared on his desk, with
the other letters of the day :

"Dear Sirs. We beg to offer our excuses for the little mistake which
has happened. At the same time, we regret to add that the statement
of our error, with which you have favoured us, has led to a very
unexpected discovery. The affair is a most serious one for you and
for us. The particulars are as follows :

"Having no more champagne of the vintage last sent to you, we made
arrangements to credit your firm with the value of the six cases, as
suggested by yourself. On taking this step, certain forms observed in
our mode of doing business necessitated a reference to our bankers'
book, as well as to our ledger. The result is a moral certainty that no
such remittance as you mention can have reached our house, and a
literal certainty that no such remittance has been paid to our account at
the bank.

"It is needless, at this stage of the proceedings, to trouble you with
details. The money has unquestionably been stolen in the course of its
transit from you to us. Certain peculiarities which we observe, relating
to the manner in which the fraud has been perpetrated, lead us to conclude that the thief may have calculated on being able to pay the
missing sum to our bankers, before an inevitable discovery followed the
annual striking of our balance. This would not have happened, in the
usual course, for another three months. During that period, but for
your letter, we might have remained perfectly unconscious of the
robbery that has been committed.

"We mention this last circumstance, as it may help to show you that
we have to do, in this case, with no ordinary thief. Thus far we have
not even a suspicion of who that thief is. But we believe you will
assist us in making some advance towards discovery, by examining the
receipt (forged, of course) which has no doubt purported to come to you
from our house. Be pleased to look and see whether it is a receipt
entirely in manuscript, or whether it is a numbered and printed form
which merely requires the filling in of the amount. The settlement of
this apparently trivial question is, we assure you, a matter of vital
importance. Anxiously awaiting your reply, we remain, with high
esteem and consideration,

"DEFRESNIER & CIE."

Vendale laid the letter on his desk, and waited a moment to steady his mind under the shock that had fallen on it. At the time of all others when it was most important to him to increase the value of his business, that business was threatened with a loss of five hundred pounds. He thought of Marguerite, as he took the key from his pocket and opened the iron chamber in the wall in which the books and papers of the firm were kept.

He was still in the chamber, searching for the forged receipt, when he was startled by a voice speaking close behind him.

"A thousand pardons," said the voice; "I am afraid I disturb you."

He turned, and found himself face to face with Marguerite's guardian.

"I have called," pursued Obenreizer, " to know if I can be of any use. Business of my own takes me away for some days to Manchester and Liverpool. Can I combine any business of yours with it? I am entirely at your disposal, in the character of commercial traveller for the firm of Wilding and Co."

"Excuse me for one moment," said Vendale; "I will speak to you directly." He turned round again, and continued his search among the papers. "You come at a time when friendly offers are more than usually precious to me," he resumed. "I have had very bad news this morning from Neuchâtel."

"Bad news!" exclaimed Obenreizer. "From Defresnier and Company?"

"Yes. A remittance we sent to them has been stolen. I am threatened with a loss of five hundred pounds. What's that?"

Turning sharply, and looking into the room for the second time, Vendale discovered his envelope-case overthrown on the floor, and Obenreizer on his knees picking up the contents.

"All my awkwardness!" said Obenreizer. "This dreadful news of yours startled me; I stepped back——" He became too deeply interested in collecting the scattered envelopes to finish the sentence.

"Don't trouble yourself," said Vendale. "The clerk will pick the things up."

"This dreadful news!" repeated Obenreizer, persisting in collecting the envelopes. "This dreadful news!"

"If you will read the letter," said Vendale, "you will find I have exaggerated nothing. There it is, open on my desk."

He resumed his search, and in a moment more discovered the forged receipt. It was on the numbered and printed form, described by the Swiss firm. Vendale made a memorandum of the number and the date. Having replaced the receipt and locked up the iron chamber, he had leisure to notice Obenreizer, reading the letter in the recess of a window at the far end of the room.

"Come to the fire," said Vendale. "You look perished with the cold out there. I will ring for some more coals."

Obenreizer rose, and came slowly back to the desk. "Marguerite will be as sorry to hear of this as I am," he said, kindly. "What do you mean to do?"

"I am in the hands of Defresnier and Company," answered Vendale. "In my total ignorance of the circumstances, I can only do what they recommend. The receipt which I have just found, turns out to be the numbered and printed form. They seem to attach some special importance to its discovery. You have had experience, when you were in the Swiss house, of their way of doing business. Can you guess what object they have in view?"

Obenreizer offered a suggestion.

"Suppose I examine the receipt?" he said.

"Are you ill?" asked Vendale, startled by the change in his face, which now showed itself plainly for the first time. "Pray go to the fire. You seem to be shivering—I hope you are not going to be ill?"

"Not I!" said Obenreizer. "Perhaps I have caught cold. Your English climate might have spared an admirer of your English institutions. Let me look at the receipt."

Vendale opened the iron chamber. Obenreizer took a chair, and drew it close to the fire. He held both hands over the flames. "Let me look at the receipt," he repeated, eagerly, as Vendale reappeared with the paper in his hand. At the same moment a porter entered the room with a fresh supply of coals. Vendale told him to make a good fire. The man obeyed the order with a disastrous alacrity. As he stepped forward and raised the scuttle, his foot caught in a fold of the rug, and he discharged his entire cargo of coals into the grate. The result was an instant smothering of the flame, and the production of a stream of yellow smoke, without a visible morsel of fire to account for it.

"Imbecile!" whispered Obenreizer to himself, with a look at the man which the man remembered for many a long day afterwards.

"Will you come into the clerks' room?" asked Vendale. "They have a stove there."

"No, no. No matter."

Vendale handed him the receipt. Obenreizer's interest in examining it appeared to have been quenched as suddenly and as effectually as the fire itself. He just glanced over the document, and said, "No; I don't understand it! I am sorry to be of no use."

"I will write to Neuchâtel by to-night's post," said Vendale, putting away the receipt for the second time. "We must wait, and see what comes of it."

"By to-night's post," repeated Obenreizer. "Let me see. You will get the answer in eight or nine days' time. I shall be back before that. If I can be of any service, as commercial traveller, perhaps you will let me know between this and then. You will send me written instructions? My best thanks. I shall be most anxious for your answer from Neuchâtel. Who knows? It may be a mistake, my dear friend, after all. Courage! courage! courage!" He had entered the room with no appearance of being pressed for time. He now snatched up his hat, and took his leave with the air of a man who had not another moment to lose.

Left by himself, Vendale took a turn thoughtfully in the room.

His previous impression of Obenreizer was shaken by what he had heard and seen at the interview which had just taken place. He was disposed, for the first time, to doubt whether, in this case, he had not been a little hasty and hard in his judgment on another man. Obenreizer's surprise and regret, on hearing the news from Neuchâtel, bore the plainest marks of being honestly felt—not politely assumed for the occasion. With troubles of his own to encounter, suffering, to all appearance, from the first insidious attack of a serious illness, he

had looked and spoken like a man who really deplored the
disaster that had fallen on his friend. Hitherto, Vendale had
tried vainly to alter his first opinion of Marguerite's guardian,
for Marguerite's sake. All the generous instincts in his nature
now combined together and shook the evidence which had
seemed unanswerable up to this time. "Who knows?" he
thought, "I may have read that man's face wrongly, after all."

The time passed—the happy evenings with Marguerite came
and went. It was again the tenth morning since Vendale had
written to the Swiss firm; and again the answer appeared on
his desk with the other letters of the day.

"Dear Sir. My senior partner, M. Defresnier, has been called away,
by urgent business, to Milan. In his absence (and with his full con-
currence and authority), I now write you again on the subject of the
missing five hundred pounds.

"Your discovery that the forged receipt is executed upon one of our
numbered and printed forms has caused inexpressible surprise and
distress to my partner and to myself. At the time when your remittance
was stolen, but three keys were in existence opening the strong box
in which our receipt-forms are invariably kept. My partner had one
key; I had the other. The third was in the possession of a gentleman
who, at that period, occupied a position of trust in our house. We
should as soon have thought of suspecting one of ourselves as of
suspecting this person. Suspicion now points at him, nevertheless. I
cannot prevail on myself to inform you who the person is, so long as
there is the shadow of a chance that he may come innocently out of the
inquiry which must now be instituted. Forgive my silence; the motive
of it is good.

"The form our investigation must now take is simple enough. The
handwriting on your receipt must be compared, by competent persons
whom we have at our disposal, with certain specimens of handwriting
in our possession. I cannot send you the specimens, for business
reasons, which, when you hear them, you are sure to approve. I must
beg you to send me the receipt to Neuchâtel—and, in making this
request, I must accompany it by a word of necessary warning.

"If the person, at whom suspicion now points, really proves to be
the person who has committed this forgery and theft, I have reason to
fear that circumstances may have already put him on his guard. The
only evidence against him is the evidence in your hands, and he will
move heaven and earth to obtain and destroy it. I strongly urge you
not to trust the receipt to the post. Send it to me, without loss of time,
by a private hand, and choose nobody for your messenger but a person
long established in your own employment, accustomed to travelling,
capable of speaking French; a man of courage, a man of honesty, and,
above all things, a man who can be trusted to let no stranger scrape
acquaintance with him on the route. Tell no one—absolutely no one—
but your messenger of the turn this matter has now taken. The safe

transit of the receipt may depend on your interpreting *literally* the advice which I give you at the end of this letter.

"I have only to add that every possible saving of time is now of the last importance. More than one of our receipt-forms is missing—and it is impossible to say what new frauds may not be committed, if we fail to lay our hands on the thief.

"Your faithful servant,

"ROLLAND,

"(Signing for Defresnier and Cie)."

Who was the suspected man? In Vendale's position, it seemed useless to inquire.

Who was to be sent to Neuchâtel with the receipt? Men of courage and men of honesty were to be had at Cripple Corner for the asking. But where was the man who was accustomed to foreign travelling, who could speak the French language, and who could be really relied on to let no stranger scrape acquaintance with him on his route? There was but one man at hand who combined all those requisites in his own person, and that man was Vendale himself.

It was a sacrifice to leave his business; it was a greater sacrifice to leave Marguerite. But a matter of five hundred pounds was involved in the pending inquiry; and a literal interpretation of M. Rolland's advice was insisted on in terms which there was no trifling with. The more Vendale thought of it, the more plainly the necessity faced him, and said, "Go!"

As he locked up the letter with the receipt, the association of ideas reminded him of Obenreizer. A guess at the identity of the suspected man looked more possible now. Obenreizer might know.

The thought had barely passed through his mind, when the door opened, and Obenreizer entered the room.

"They told me at Soho-square you were expected back last night," said Vendale, greeting him. "Have you done well in the country? Are you better?"

A thousand thanks. Obenreizer had done admirably well; Obenreizer was infinitely better. And now, what news? Any letter from Neuchâtel?

"A very strange letter," answered Vendale. "The matter has taken a new turn, and the letter insists—without excepting anybody—on my keeping our next proceedings a profound secret."

"Without excepting anybody?" repeated Obenreizer. As he said the words, he walked away again, thoughtfully, to the window at the other end of the room, looked out for a moment, and suddenly came back to Vendale. "Surely they must have forgotten?" he resumed, "or they would have excepted *me*?"

"It is Monsieur Rolland who writes," said Vendale. "And, as you say, he must certainly have forgotten. That view of the matter quite escaped me. I was just wishing I had you to consult, when you came into the room. And here I am tied by a formal prohibition, which cannot possibly have been intended to include you. How very annoying!"

Obenreizer's filmy eyes fixed on Vendale attentively.

"Perhaps it is more than annoying!" he said. "I came this morning not only to hear the news, but to offer myself as messenger, negotiator—what you will. Would you believe it? I have letters which oblige me to go to Switzerland immediately. Messages, documents, anything—I could have taken them all to Defresnier and Rolland for you."

"You are the very man I wanted," returned Vendale. "I had decided, most unwillingly, on going to Neuchâtel myself, not five minutes since, because I could find no one here capable of taking my place. Let me look at the letter again."

He opened the strong room to get at the letter. Obenreizer, after first glancing round him to make sure that they were alone, followed a step or two and waited, measuring Vendale with his eye. Vendale was the tallest man, and unmistakably the strongest man also of the two. Obenreizer turned away, and warmed himself at the fire.

Meanwhile, Vendale read the last paragraph in the letter for the third time. There was the plain warning—there was the closing sentence, which insisted on a literal interpretation of it. The hand, which was leading Vendale in the dark, led him on that condition only. A large sum was at stake: a terrible suspicion remained to be verified. If he acted on his own responsibility, and if anything happened to defeat the object in view, who would be blamed? As a man of business, Vendale had but one course to follow. He locked the letter up again.

"It is most annoying," he said to Obenreizer—"it is a piece of forgetfulness on Monsieur Rolland's part which puts me to serious inconvenience, and places me in an absurdly false position towards you. What am I to do? I am acting in a very serious matter, and acting entirely in the dark. I have no choice but to be guided, not by the spirit, but by the letter of my instructions. You understand me, I am sure? You know, if I had not been fettered in this way, how gladly I should have accepted your services?"

"Say no more!" returned Obenreizer. "In your place I should have done the same. My good friend, I take no offence. I thank you for your compliment. We shall be travelling companions, at any rate," added Obenreizer. "You go, as I go, at once?"

"At once. I must speak to Marguerite first, of course!"

"Surely! surely! Speak to her this evening. Come, and pick me up on the way to the station. We go together by the mail train to-night?"

"By the mail train to-night."

It was later than Vendale had anticipated when he drove up to the house in Soho-square. Business difficulties, occasioned by his sudden departure, had presented themselves by dozens. A cruelly large share of the time which he had hoped to devote to Marguerite had been claimed by duties at his office which it was impossible to neglect.

To his surprise and delight, she was alone in the drawing-room when he entered it.

"We have only a few minutes, George," she said. "But Madame Dor has been good to me—and we can have those few minutes alone." She threw her arms round his neck, and whispered eagerly, "Have you done anything to offend Mr. Obenreizer?"

"I!" exclaimed Vendale, in amazement.

"Hush!" she said, "I want to whisper it. You know the little photograph I have got of you. This afternoon it happened to be on the chimney-piece. He took it up and looked at it— and I saw his face in the glass. I know you have offended him! He is merciless; he is revengeful; he is as secret as the grave. Don't go with him, George—don't go with him!"

"My own love," returned Vendale, "you are letting your fancy frighten you! Obenreizer and I were never better friends than we are at this moment."

Before a word more could be said, the sudden movement of
some ponderous body shook the floor of the next room. The
shock was followed by the appearance of Madame Dor. "Obenreizer!" exclaimed this excellent person in a whisper, and
plumped down instantly in her regular place by the stove.

Obenreizer came in with a courier's bag strapped over his
shoulder.

"Are you ready?" he asked, addressing Vendale. "Can I
take anything for you? You have no travelling-bag. I have
got one. Here is the compartment for papers, open at your
service."

"Thank you," said Vendale. "I have only one paper of
importance with me; and that paper I am bound to take charge
of myself. Here it is," he added, touching the breast-pocket of
his coat, "and here it must remain till we get to Neuchâtel."

As he said those words, Marguerite's hand caught his, and
pressed it significantly. She was looking towards Obenreizer.
Before Vendale could look, in his turn, Obenreizer had wheeled
round, and was taking leave of Madame Dor.

"Adieu, my charming niece!" he said, turning to Marguerite
next. "En route, my friend, for Neuchâtel!" He tapped
Vendale lightly over the breast-pocket of his coat, and led the
way to the door.

Vendale's last look was for Marguerite. Marguerite's last
words to him were, "Don't go!"

ACT III.

It was about the middle of the month of February when Vendale and Obenreizer set forth on their expedition. The winter being a hard one, the time was bad for travellers. So bad was it that these two travellers, coming to Strasbourg, found its great inns almost empty. And even the few people they did encounter in that city, who had started from England or from Paris on business journeys towards the interior of Switzerland, were turning back.

Many of the railroads in Switzerland that tourists pass easily enough now, were almost or quite impracticable then. Some were not begun; more were not completed. On such as were open, there were still large gaps of old road where communication in the winter season was often stopped ; on others, there were weak points where the new work was not safe, either under conditions of severe frost, or of rapid thaw. The running of trains on this last class was not to be counted on in the worst time of the year, was contingent upon weather, or was wholly abandoned through the months considered the most dangerous.

At Strasbourg there were more travellers' stories afloat, respecting the difficulties of the way further on, than there were travellers to relate them. Many of these tales were as wild as usual ; but the more modestly marvellous did derive some colour from the circumstance that people were indisputably turning back. However, as the road to Basle was open, Vendale's resolution to push on was in no wise disturbed. Obenreizer's resolution was necessarily Vendale's, seeing that he stood at bay thus desperately :—He must be ruined, or must

destroy the evidence that Vendale carried about him, even if he
destroyed Vendale with it.

The state of mind of each of these two fellow-travellers
towards the other was this. Obenreizer, encircled by impending
ruin through Vendale's quickness of action, and seeing the
circle narrowed every hour by Vendale's energy, hated him with
the animosity of a fierce cunning lower animal. He had always
had instinctive movements in his breast against him ; perhaps,
because of that old sore of gentleman and peasant ; perhaps,
because of the openness of his nature ; perhaps, because of his
better looks ; perhaps, because of his success with Marguerite ;
perhaps, on all those grounds, the two last not the least. And
now he saw in him, besides, the hunter who was tracking him
down. Vendale, on the other hand, always contending gene-
rously against his first vague mistrust, now felt bound to contend
against it more than ever : reminding himself, "He is Marguerite's guardian. We are on perfectly friendly terms ; he is
my companion of his own proposal, and can have no interested
motive in sharing this undesirable journey." To which pleas
in behalf of Obenreizer, chance added one consideration more,
when they came to Basle, after a journey of more than twice
the average duration.

They had had a late dinner, and were alone in an inn room
there, overhanging the Rhine : at that place rapid and deep,
swollen and loud. Vendale lounged upon a couch, and Obenreizer walked to and fro : now, stopping at the window, looking
at the crooked reflections of the town lights in the dark water
(and peradventure thinking, "If I could fling him into it !") ;
now, resuming his walk with his eyes upon the floor.

"Where shall I rob him, if I can ? Where shall I murder
him, if I must ?" So, as he paced the room, ran the river, ran
the river, ran the river.

The burden seemed to him at last, to be growing so plain
that he stopped ; thinking it as well to suggest another burden
to his companion.

"The Rhine sounds to-night," he said with a smile, "like
the old waterfall at home. That waterfall which my mother
showed to travellers (I told you of it once). The sound of it
changed with the weather, as does the sound of all falling
waters and flowing waters. When I was pupil of the watch-

maker, I remembered it as sometimes saying to me for whole days, 'Who are you, my little wretch? Who are you, my little wretch?' I remembered it as saying, other times, when its sound was hollow, and storm was coming up the Pass: 'Boom, boom, boom. Beat him, beat him, beat him.' Like my mother enraged—if she was my mother."

"If she was?" said Vendale, gradually changing his attitude to a sitting one. "If she was? Why do you say 'if'?"

"What do I know?" replied the other negligently, throwing up his hands and letting them fall as they would. "What would you have? I am so obscurely born, that how can I say? I was very young, and all the rest of the family were men and women, and my so-called parents were old. Anything is possible of a case like that?"

"Did you ever doubt—— ?"

"I told you once, I doubt the marriage of those two," he replied, throwing up his hands again, as if he were throwing the unprofitable subject away. "But here I am in Creation. *I* come of no fine family. What does it matter?"

"At least you are Swiss," said Vendale, after following him with his eyes to and fro.

"How do I know?" he retorted abruptly, and stopping to look back over his shoulder. "I say to you, at least you are English. How do you know?"

"By what I have been told from infancy."

"Ah! I know of myself that way."

"And," added Vendale, pursuing the thought that he could not drive back, "by my earliest recollections."

"I also. I know of myself that way—if that way satisfies."

"Does it not satisfy you?"

"It must. There is nothing like 'it must' in this little world. It must. Two short words those, but stronger than long proof or reasoning."

"You and poor Wilding were born in the same year. You were nearly of an age," said Vendale, again thoughtfully looking after him as he resumed his pacing up and down.

"Yes. Very nearly."

Could Obenreizer be the missing man? In the unknown associations of things, was there a subtler meaning than he himself thought, in that theory so often on his lips about the smallness of the world? Had the Swiss letter presenting him, followed so close on Mrs. Goldstraw's revelation concerning the infant who had been taken away to Switzerland, because he was that infant grown a man? In a world where so many depths lie unsounded, it might be. The chances, or the laws—call them either—that had wrought out the revival of Vendale's own acquaintance with Obenreizer, and had ripened it into intimacy, and had brought them here together this present winter night, were hardly less curious; while read by such a light, they were seen to cohere towards the furtherance of a continuous and an intelligible purpose.

Vendale's awakened thoughts ran high while his eyes musingly followed Obenreizer pacing up and down the room, the river ever running to the tune : " Where shall I rob him, if I can? Where shall I murder him, if I must?" The secret of his dead friend was in no hazard from Vendale's lips ; but just as his friend had died of its weight, so did he in his lighter succession feel the burden of the trust, and the obligation to follow any clue, however obscure. He rapidly asked himself, would he like this man to be the real Wilding? No. Argue down his mistrust as he might, he was unwilling to put such a substitute in the place of his late guileless, outspoken, childlike partner. He rapidly asked himself, would he like this man to be rich? No. He had more power than enough over Marguerite as it was, and wealth might invest him with more. Would he like this man to be Marguerite's Guardian, and yet proved to stand in no degree of relationship towards her, however disconnected and distant? No. But these were not considerations to come between him and fidelity to the dead. Let him see to it that they passed him with no other notice than the knowledge that they *had* passed him, and left him bent on the discharge of a solemn duty. And he did see to it, so soon that he followed his companion with ungrudging eyes, while he still paced the room ; that companion, whom he supposed to be moodily reflecting on his own birth, and not on another man's— least of all what man's—violent Death.

The road in advance from Basle to Neuchâtel was better than had been represented. The latest weather had done it good. Drivers, both of horses and mules, had come in that evening after dark, and had reported nothing more difficult to be overcome than trials of patience, harness, wheels, axles, and whip-cord. A bargain was soon struck for a carriage and horses, to take them on in the morning, and to start before daylight.

"Do you lock your door at night when travelling?" asked Obenreizer, standing warming his hands by the wood fire in Vendale's chamber, before going to his own.

"Not I. I sleep too soundly."

"You are so sound a sleeper?" he retorted, with an admiring look. "What a blessing!"

"Anything but a blessing to the rest of the house," rejoined Vendale, "if I had to be knocked up in the morning from the outside of my bedroom door."

"I, too," said Obenreizer, "leave open my room. But let me advise you, as a Swiss who knows: always, when you travel in my country, put your papers—and, of course, your money—under your pillow. Always the same place."

"You are not complimentary to your countrymen," laughed Vendale.

"My countrymen," said Obenreizer, with that light touch of his friend's elbows by way of Good Night and benediction, "I suppose, are like the majority of men. And the majority of men will take what they can get. Adieu! At four in the morning."

"Adieu! At four."

Left to himself, Vendale raked the logs together, sprinkled over them the white wood-ashes lying on the hearth, and sat down to compose his thoughts. But they still ran high on their latest theme, and the running of the river tended to agitate rather than to quiet them. As he sat thinking, what little disposition he had had to sleep, departed. He felt it hopeless to lie down yet, and sat dressed by the fire. Marguerite, Wilding, Obenreizer, the business he was then upon, and a thousand hopes and doubts that had nothing to do with it, occupied his mind at once. Everything seemed to have power over him, but slumber. The departed disposition to sleep kept far away.

He had sat for a long time thinking, on the hearth, when his candle burned down, and its light went out. It was of little moment; there was light enough in the fire. He changed his attitude, and, leaning his arm on the chair-back, and his chin upon that hand, sat thinking still.

But he sat between the fire and the bed, and, as the fire
flickered in the play of air from the fast-flowing river, his
enlarged shadow fluttered on the white wall by the bedside.
His attitude gave it an air, half of mourning, and half of
bending over the bed imploring. His eyes were observant
of it, when he became troubled by the disagreeable fancy that
it was like Wilding's shadow, and not his own.

A slight change of place would cause it to disappear. He
made the change, and the apparition of his disturbed fancy
vanished. He now sat in the shade of a little nook beside the
fire, and the door of the room was before him.

It had a long cumbrous iron latch. He saw the latch slowly
and softly rise. The door opened a very little, and came to
again : as though only the air had moved it. But he saw that
the latch was out of the hasp.

The door opened again very slowly, until it opened wide
enough to admit some one. It afterwards remained still for
a while, as though cautiously held open on the other side. The
figure of a man then entered, with its face turned towards the
bed, and stood quiet just within the door. Until it said, in a
low half-whisper, at the same time taking one step forward :
" Vendale ! "

" What now ? " he answered, springing from his seat ; "who
is it ? "

It was Obenreizer, and he uttered a cry of surprise as
Vendale came upon him from that unexpected direction.
"Not in bed?" he said, catching him by both shoulders with
an instinctive tendency to a struggle, " Then something *is*
wrong ! "

" What do you mean ? " said Vendale, releasing himself.

" First tell me ; you are not ill ? "

" Ill ?   No."

" I have had a bad dream about you.   How is it that I see
you up and dressed ? "

" My good fellow, I may as well ask you how is it that I
see *you* up and undressed ? "

" I have told you why.   I have had a bad dream about
you.   I tried to rest after it, but it was impossible.   I could
not make up my mind to stay where I was, without knowing
you were safe ; and yet I could not make up my mind to come

in here. I have been minutes hesitating at the door. It is so easy to laugh at a dream that you have not dreamed. Where is your candle ? "

" Burnt out."

" I have a whole one in my room. Shall I fetch it ? "

" Do so."

His room was very near, and he was absent for but a few seconds. Coming back with the candle in his hand, he kneeled down on the hearth and lighted it. As he blew with his breath a charred billet into flame for the purpose, Vendale, looking down at him, saw that his lips were white and not easy of control.

" Yes ! " said Obenreizer, setting the lighted candle on the table, " it was a bad dream. Only look at me ! "

' His feet were bare ; his red-flannel shirt was thrown back at the throat, and its sleeves were rolled above the elbows ; his only other garment, a pair of under pantaloons or drawers, reaching to the ankles, fitted him close and tight. A certain lithe and savage appearance was on his figure, and his eyes were very bright.

" If there had been a wrestle with a robber, as I dreamed," said Obenreizer, " you see, I was stripped for it."

" And armed, too," said Vendale, glancing at his girdle.

" A traveller's dagger, that I always carry on the road," he answered carelessly, half drawing it from its sheath with his left hand, and putting it back again. " Do you carry no such thing ? "

" Nothing of the kind."

" No pistols ? " said Obenreizer, glancing at the table, and from it to the untouched pillow.

" Nothing of the sort."

" You Englishmen are so confident ! You wish to sleep ? "

" I have wished to sleep this long time, but I can't do it."

" I neither, after the bad dream. My fire has gone the way of your candle. May I come and sit by yours ? Two o'clock ! It will so soon be four, that it is not worth the trouble to go to bed again."

" I shall not take the trouble to go to bed at all, now," said Vendale ; " sit here and keep me company, and welcome."

Going back to his room to arrange his dress, Obenreizer

soon returned in a loose cloak and slippers, and they sat down on opposite sides of the hearth. In the interval, Vendale had replenished the fire from the wood-basket in his room, and Obenreizer had put upon the table a flask and cup from his.

"Common cabaret brandy, I am afraid," he said, pouring out; "bought upon the road, and not like yours from Cripple Corner. But yours is exhausted; so much the worse. A cold night, a cold time of night, a cold country, and a cold house. This may be better than nothing; try it."

Vendale took the cup, and did so.

"How do you find it?"

"It has a coarse after-flavour," said Vendale, giving back the cup with a slight shudder, "and I don't like it."

"You are right," said Obenreizer, tasting, and smacking his lips; "it *has* a coarse after-flavour, and *I* don't like it. Booh! it burns, though!" He had flung what remained in the cup, upon the fire.

Each of them leaned an elbow on the table, reclining his head upon his hand, and sat looking at the flaring logs. Obenreizer remained watchful and still; but Vendale, after certain nervous twitches and starts, in one of which he rose to his feet and looked wildly about him, fell into the strangest confusion of dreams. He carried his papers in a leather case or pocket-book, in an inner breast-pocket of his buttoned travelling coat; and whatever he dreamed of, in the lethargy that got possession of him, something importunate in these papers called him out of that dream, though he could not wake from it. He was belated on the steppes of Russia (some shadowy person gave that name to the place) with Marguerite; and yet the sensation of a hand at his breast, softly feeling the outline of the pocket-book as he lay asleep before the fire, was present to him. He was shipwrecked in an open boat at sea, and having lost his clothes, had no other covering than an old sail; and yet a creeping hand, tracing outside all the other pockets of the dress he actually wore, for papers, and finding none answer its touch, warned him to rouse himself. He was in the ancient vault at Cripple Corner, to which was transferred the very bed substantial and present in that very room at Basle; and Wilding (not dead, as he had supposed, and yet he did not wonder much) shook him, and whispered, "Look at that man!

Don't you see he has risen, and is turning the pillow? Why should he turn the pillow, if not to seek those papers that are in your breast? Awake!" And yet he slept, and wandered off into other dreams.

Watchful and still, with his elbow on the table and his head upon that hand, his companion at length said: "Vendale! We are called. Past Four!" Then, opening his eyes, he saw, turned sideways on him, the filmy face of Obenreizer.

"You have been in a heavy sleep," he said. "The fatigue of constant travelling and the cold!"

"I am broad awake now," cried Vendale, springing up, but with an unsteady footing. "Haven't you slept at all?"

"I may have dozed, but I seem to have been patiently looking at the fire. Whether or no, we must wash, and breakfast, and turn out. Past four, Vendale; past four!"

It was said in a tone to rouse him, for already he was half asleep again. In his preparation for the day, too, and at his breakfast, he was often virtually asleep while in mechanical action. It was not until the cold dark day was closing in, that he had any distincter impressions of the ride than jingling bells, bitter weather, slipping horses, frowning hill-sides, bleak woods, and a stoppage at some wayside house of entertainment, where they had passed through a cowhouse to reach the travellers' room above. He had been conscious of little more, except of Obenreizer sitting thoughtful at his side all day, and eyeing him much.

But when he shook off his stupor, Obenreizer was not at his side. The carriage was stopping to bait at another wayside house; and a line of long narrow carts, laden with casks of wine, and drawn by horses with a quantity of blue collar and head-gear, were baiting too. These came from the direction in which the travellers were going, and Obenreizer (not thoughtful now, but cheerful and alert) was talking with the foremost driver. As Vendale stretched his limbs, circulated his blood, and cleared off the lees of his lethargy, with a sharp run to and fro in the bracing air, the line of carts moved on: the drivers all saluting Obenreizer as they passed him.

"Who are those?" asked Vendale.

"They are our carriers—Defresnier and Company's," replied Obenreizer. "Those are our casks of wine." He was singing to himself, and lighting a cigar.

"I have been drearily dull company to-day," said Vendale, "I don't know what has been the matter with me."

"You had no sleep last night; and a kind of brain-congestion frequently comes, at first, of such cold," said Obenreizer. "I have seen it often. After all, we shall have our journey for nothing, it seems."

"How for nothing?"

"The House is at Milan. You know, we are a Wine House at Neuchâtel, and a Silk House at Milan? Well, Silk happening to press of a sudden, more than Wine, Defresnier was summoned to Milan. Rolland, the other partner, has been taken ill since his departure, and the doctors will allow him to see no one. A letter awaits you at Neuchâtel to tell you so. I have it from our chief carrier whom you saw me talking with. He was surprised to see me, and said he had that word for you if he met you. What do you do? Go back?"

"Go on," said Vendale.

"On?"

"On? Yes. Across the Alps, and down to Milan."

Obenreizer stopped in his smoking to look at Vendale, and then smoked heavily, looked up the road, looked down the road, looked down at the stones in the road at his feet.

"I have a very serious matter in charge," said Vendale; "more of these missing forms may be turned to as bad account, or worse; I am urged to lose no time in helping the House to take the thief; and nothing shall turn me back."

"No?" cried Obenreizer, taking out his cigar to smile, and giving his hand to his fellow-traveller. "Then nothing shall turn *me* back. Ho, driver! Despatch. Quick there! Let us push on!"

They travelled through the night. There had been snow, and there was a partial thaw, and they mostly travelled at a foot-pace, and always with many stoppages to breathe the splashed and floundering horses. After an hour's broad daylight, they drew rein at the inn-door at Neuchâtel, having been some eight-and-twenty hours in conquering some eighty English miles.

When they had hurriedly refreshed and changed, they went together to the house of business of Defresnier and Company. There they found the letter which the wine-carrier had described, enclosing the tests and comparisons of hand-writing essential to

the discovery of the Forger.   Vendale's determination to press
forward, without resting, being already taken, the only question
to delay them was by what Pass could they cross the Alps?
Respecting the state of the two Passes of the St. Gotthard and
the Simplon, the guides and mule-drivers differed greatly; and
both Passes were still far enough off, to prevent the travellers
from having the benefit of any recent experience of either.
Besides which, they well knew that a fall of snow might
altogether change the described conditions in a single hour, even
if they were correctly stated.   But, on the whole, the Simplon
appearing to be the hopefuller route, Vendale decided to take it.
Obenreizer bore little or no part in the discussion, and scarcely
spoke.

To Geneva, to Lausanne, along the level margin of the lake
to Vevay, so into the winding valley between the spurs of the
mountains, and into the valley of the Rhone.   The sound of
the carriage-wheels, as they rattled on, through the day,
through the night, became as the wheels of a great clock,
recording the hours.   No change of weather varied the journey,
after it had hardened into a sullen frost.   In a sombre-yellow
sky, they saw the Alpine ranges; and they saw enough of snow
on nearer and much lower hill-tops and hill-sides, to sully, by
contrast, the purity of lake, torrent, and waterfall, and make
the villages look discoloured and dirty.   But no snow fell, nor
was there any snow-drift on the road.   The stalking along the
valley of more or less of white mist, changing on their hair and
dress into icicles, was the only variety between them and the
gloomy sky.   And still by day, and still by night, the wheels.
And still they rolled, in the hearing of one of them, to the
burden, altered from the burden of the Rhine: "The time is
gone for robbing him alive, and I must murder him."

They came, at length, to the poor little town of Brieg, at
the foot of the Simplon.   They came there after dark, but yet
could see how dwarfed men's work and men became with the
immense mountains towering over them.   Here they must lie
for the night; and here was warmth of fire, and lamp, and
dinner, and wine, and after-conference resounding, with guides
and drivers.   No human creature had come across the Pass for
four days.   The snow above the snow-line was too soft for
wheeled carriage, and not hard enough for sledge.   There was

snow in the sky.   There had been snow in the sky for days
past, and the marvel was that it had not fallen, and the certainty
was that it must fall.   No vehicle could cross.   The journey
might be tried on mules, or it might be tried on foot ; but the
best guides must be paid danger-price in either case, and that,
too, whether they succeeded in taking the two travellers across,
or turned for safety and brought them back.

In this discussion, Obenreizer bore no part whatever.   He
sat silently smoking by the fire until the room was cleared and
Vendale referred to him.

"Bah ! I am weary of these poor devils and their trade,"
he said, in reply.   "Always the same story.   It is the story of
their trade to-day, as it was the story of their trade when I was
a ragged boy.   What do you and I want ?   We want a knapsack each, and a mountain-staff each.   We want no guide ; we
should guide him ; he would not guide us.   We leave our
portmanteaus here, and we cross together.   We have been on
the mountains together before now, and I am mountain-born,
and I know this Pass—Pass !—rather High Road !—by heart.
We will leave these poor devils, in pity, to trade with others ;
but they must not delay us to make a pretence of earning
money.   Which is all they mean."

Vendale, glad to be quit of the dispute, and to cut the
knot : active, adventurous, bent on getting forward, and therefore very susceptible to the last hint : readily assented.
Within two hours, they had purchased what they wanted for
the expedition, had packed their knapsacks, and lay down to
sleep.

At break of day, they found half the town collected in the
narrow street to see them depart.   The people talked together
in groups ; the guides and drivers whispered apart, and looked
up at the sky ; no one wished them a good journey.

As they began the ascent, a gleam of sun shone from the
otherwise unaltered sky, and for a moment turned the tin
spires of the town to silver.

" A good omen ! " said Vendale (though it died out while he
spoke).   " Perhaps our example will open the Pass on this side."

"No ; we shall not be followed," returned Obenreizer,
looking up at the sky and back at the valley.   " We shall be
alone up yonder."

ON THE MOUNTAIN.

The road was fair enough for stout walkers, and the air grew lighter and easier to breathe as the two ascended. But the settled gloom remained as it had remained for days back. Nature seemed to have come to a pause. The sense of hearing, no less than the sense of sight, was troubled by having to wait so long for the change, whatever it might be, that impended. The silence was as palpable and heavy as the lowering clouds— or rather cloud, for there seemed to be but one in all the sky, and that one covering the whole of it.

Although the light was thus dismally shrouded, the prospect was not obscured. Down in the valley of the Rhône behind them, the stream could be traced through all its many windings, oppressively sombre and solemn in its one leaden hue, a colourless waste. Far and high above them, glaciers and suspended avalanches overhung the spots where they must pass by-and-by; deep and dark below them on their right, were awful precipice and roaring torrent; tremendous mountains arose in every vista. The gigantic landscape, uncheered by a touch of changing light or a solitary ray of sun, was yet terribly distinct in its ferocity. The hearts of two lonely men might shrink a little, if they had to win their way for miles and hours among a legion of silent and motionless men—mere men like themselves—all looking at them with fixed and frowning front. But how much more, when the legion is of Nature's mightiest works, and the frown may turn to fury in an instant!

As they ascended, the road became gradually more rugged and difficult. But the spirits of Vendale rose as they mounted higher, leaving so much more of the road behind them conquered. Obenreizer spoke little, and held on with a determined purpose. Both, in respect of agility and endurance, were well qualified for the expedition. Whatever the born mountaineer read in the weather-tokens, that was illegible to the other, he kept to himself.

"Shall we get across to-day?" asked Vendale.

"No," replied the other. "You see how much deeper the snow lies here than it lay half a league lower. The higher we mount, the deeper the snow will lie. Walking is half wading even now. And the days are so short! If we get as high as the fifth Refuge, and lie to-night at the Hospice, we shall do well."

"Is there no danger of the weather rising in the night," asked Vendale, anxiously, "and snowing us up?"

"There is danger enough about us," said Obenreizer, with a cautious glance onward and upward, "to render silence our best policy. You have heard of the Bridge of the Ganther?"

"I have crossed it once."

"In the summer?"

"Yes; in the travelling season."

"Yes; but it is another thing at this season;" with a sneer, as though he were out of temper. "This is not a time of year, or a state of things, on an Alpine Pass, that you gentlemen holiday-travellers know much about."

"You are my Guide," said Vendale, good humouredly. "I trust to you."

"I am your Guide," said Obenreizer, "and I will guide you to your journey's end. There is the Bridge before us."

They had made a turn into a desolate and dismal ravine, where the snow lay deep below them, deep above them, deep on every side. While speaking, Obenreizer stood pointing at the Bridge, and observing Vendale's face with a very singular expression on his own.

"If I, as Guide, had sent you over there, in advance, and encouraged you to give a shout or two, you might have brought down upon yourself tons and tons and tons of snow, that would not only have struck you dead, but buried you deep, at a blow."

"No doubt," said Vendale.

"No doubt. But that is not what I have to do, as Guide. So pass silently. Or, going as we go, our indiscretion might else crush and bury me. Let us go on!"

There was a great accumulation of snow on the Bridge; and such enormous accumulations of snow overhung them from projecting masses of rock, that they might have been making their way through a stormy sky of white clouds. Using his staff skilfully, sounding as he went, and looking upward, with bent shoulders, as it were to resist the mere idea of a fall from above, Obenreizer softly led. Vendale closely followed. They were yet in the midst of their dangerous way, when there came a mighty rush, followed by a sound as of thunder. Obenreizer clapped his hand on Vendale's mouth and pointed to the track behind them. Its aspect had been wholly changed in a moment. An avalanche had swept over it, and plunged into the torrent at the bottom of the gulf below.

Their appearance at the solitary Inn not far beyond this terrible Bridge, elicited many expressions of astonishment from the people shut up in the house. "We stay but to rest," said Obenreizer, shaking the snow from his dress at the fire. "This gentleman has very pressing occasion to get across;—tell them, Vendale."

"Assuredly, I have very pressing occasion. I must cross."

"You hear, all of you. My friend has very pressing occasion to get across, and we want no advice and no help. I am as good a guide, my fellow-countrymen, as any of you. Now, give us to eat and drink."

In exactly the same way, and in nearly the same words, when it was coming on dark and they had struggled through the greatly increased difficulties of the road, and had at last reached their destination for the night, Obenreizer said to the astonished people of the Hospice, gathering about them at the fire, while they were yet in the act of getting their wet shoes off, and shaking the snow from their clothes:

"It is well to understand one another, friends all. This gentleman——"

—"Has," said Vendale, readily taking him up with a smile, "very pressing occasion to get across. Must cross."

"You hear?—has very pressing occasion to get across, must cross. We want no advice and no help. I am mountain-born, and act as Guide. Do not worry us by talking about it, but let us have supper, and wine, and bed."

All through the intense cold of the night, the same awful stillness. Again at sunrise, no sunny tinge to gild or redden the snow. The same interminable waste of deathly white; the same immovable air; the same monotonous gloom in the sky.

"Travellers!" a friendly voice called to them from the door,

after they were afoot, knapsack on back and staff in hand, as
yesterday : "recollect! There are five places of shelter, near
together, on the dangerous road before you ; and there is the
wooden cross, and there is the next Hospice. Do not stray from
the track. If the *Tourmente* comes on, take shelter instantly!"

"The trade of these poor devils!" said Obenreizer to his
friend, with a contemptuous backward wave of his hand towards
the voice. "How they stick to their trade! You Englishmen
say we Swiss are mercenary. Truly, it does look like it."

They had divided between the two knapsacks, such refresh-
ments as they had been able to obtain that morning, and as they
deemed it prudent to take. Obenreizer carried the wine as his
share of the burden; Vendale, the bread and meat and cheese,
and the flask of brandy.

They had for some time laboured upward and onward
through the snow—which was now above their knees in the
track, and of unknown depth elsewhere—and they were still
labouring upward and onward through the most frightful part
of that tremendous desolation, when snow began to fall. At
first, but a few flakes descended slowly and steadily. After a
little while the fall grew much denser, and suddenly it began
without apparent cause to whirl itself into spiral shapes. Instantly ensuing upon this last change, an icy blast came roaring
at them, and every sound and force imprisoned until now was let
loose.

One of the dismal galleries through which the road is
carried at that perilous point, a cave eked out by arches of
great strength, was near at hand. They struggled into it, and
the storm raged wildly. The noise of the wind, the noise
of the water, the thundering down of displaced masses of rock
and snow, the awful voices with which not only that gorge but
every gorge in the whole monstrous range seemed to be suddenly
endowed, the darkness as of night, the violent revolving of the
snow which beat and broke it into spray and blinded them, the
madness of everything around insatiate for destruction, the rapid
substitution of furious violence for unnatural calm, and hosts
of appalling sounds for silence : these were things, on the edge
of a deep abyss, to chill the blood, though the fierce wind, made
actually solid by ice and snow, had failed to chill it.

Obenreizer, walking to and fro in the gallery without ceasing, signed to Vendale to help him unbuckle his knapsack. They could see each other, but could not have heard each other speak. Vendale complying, Obenreizer produced his bottle of wine, and poured some out, motioning Vendale to take that for warmth's sake, and not brandy. Vendale again complying, Obenreizer seemed to drink after him, and the two walked backwards and forwards side by side; both well knowing that to rest or sleep would be to die.

The snow came driving heavily into the gallery by the upper end at which they would pass out of it, if they ever passed out; for greater dangers lay on the road behind them than before. The snow soon began to choke the arch. An hour more, and it lay so high as to block out half of the returning daylight. But it froze hard now, as it fell, and could be clambered through or over. The violence of the mountain storm was gradually yielding to a steady snowfall. The wind still raged at intervals, but not incessantly; and when it paused, the snow fell in heavy flakes.

They might have been two hours in their frightful prison, when Obenreizer, now crunching into the mound, now creeping over it with his head bowed down and his body touching the top of the arch, made his way out. Vendale followed close upon him, but followed without clear motive or calculation. For the lethargy of Basle was creeping over him again, and mastering his senses.

How far he had followed out of the gallery, or with what obstacles he had since contended, he knew not. He became roused to the knowledge that Obenreizer had set upon him, and that they were struggling desperately in the snow. He became roused to the remembrance of what his assailant carried in a girdle. He felt for it, drew it, struck at him, struggled again, struck at him again, cast him off, and stood face to face with him.

"I promised to guide you to your journey's end," said Obenreizer, "and I have kept my promise. The journey of your life ends here. Nothing can prolong it. You are sleeping as you stand."

"You are a villain. What have you done to me?"

"You are a fool. I have drugged you. You are doubly a fool, for I drugged you once before upon the journey, to try you. You are trebly a fool, for I am the thief and forger, and in a few moments I shall take those proofs against the thief and forger from your insensible body."

The entrapped man tried to throw off the lethargy, but its fatal hold upon him was so sure that, even while he heard those words, he stupidly wondered which of them had been wounded, and whose blood it was that he saw sprinkled on the snow.

"What have I done to you," he asked, heavily and thickly, "that you should be—so base—a murderer?"

"Done to me? You would have destroyed me, but that you have come to your journey's end. Your cursed activity interposed between me, and the time I had counted on in which I might have replaced the money. Done to me? You have come in my way—not once, not twice, but again and again and again. Did I try to shake you off in the beginning, or no? You were not to be shaken off. Therefore you die here."

Vendale tried to think coherently, tried to speak coherently, tried to pick up the iron-shod staff he had let fall; failing to touch it, tried to stagger on without its aid. All in vain, all in vain! He stumbled, and fell heavily forward on the brink of the deep chasm.

Stupefied, dozing, unable to stand upon his feet, a veil before his eyes, his sense of hearing deadened, he made such a vigorous rally that, supporting himself on his hands, he saw his enemy standing calmly over him, and heard him speak.

"You call me murderer," said Obenreizer, with a grim laugh. "The name matters very little. But at least I have set my life against yours, for I am surrounded by dangers, and may never make my way out of this place. The *Tourmente* is rising again. The snow is now on the whirl. I must have the papers now. Every moment has my life in it."

"Stop!" cried Vendale, in a terrible voice, staggering up with a last flash of fire breaking out of him, and clutching the thievish hands at his breast, in both of his. "Stop! Stand away from me! God bless my Marguerite! Happily she will never know how I died. Stand off from me, and let me look at your murderous face. Let it remind me—of something—left to say."

The sight of him fighting so hard for his senses, and the doubt whether he might not for the instant be possessed by the

strength of a dozen men, kept his opponent still. Wildly glaring
at him, Vendale faltered out the broken words :

"It shall not be—the trust—of the dead—betrayed by me
—reputed parents—misinherited fortune—see to it !"

As his head dropped on his breast, and he stumbled on the
brink of the chasm as before, the thievish hands went once
more, quick and busy, to his breast. He made a convulsive
attempt to cry "No !" desperately rolled himself over into the
gulf; and sank away from his enemy's touch, like a phantom in
a dreadful dream.

The mountain storm raged again, and passed again. The
awful mountain-voices died away, the moon rose, and the soft
and silent snow fell.

Two men and two large dogs came out at the door of the
Hospice. The men looked carefully around them, and up at
the sky. The dogs rolled in the snow, and took it into their
mouths, and cast it up with their paws.

One of the men said to the other : "We may venture now.
We may find them in one of the five Refuges." Each fastened
on his back, a basket ; each took in his hand, a strong spiked
pole; each girded under his arms, a looped end of a stout rope,
so that they were tied together.

Suddenly the dogs desisted from their gambols in the snow,
stood looking down the ascent, put their noses up, put their
noses down, became greatly excited, and broke into a deep loud
bay together.

The two men looked in the faces of the two dogs. The two
dogs looked, with at least equal intelligence, in the faces of the
two men.

"Au secours, then ! Help ! To the rescue!" cried the two men.
The two dogs, with a glad, deep, generous bark, bounded away.

"Two more mad ones !" said the men, stricken motionless,
and looking away into the moonlight. "Is it possible in such
weather ! And one of them a woman !"

Each of the dogs had the corner of a woman's dress in its
mouth, and drew her along. She fondled their heads as she
came up, and she came up through the snow with an accustomed
tread. Not so the large man with her, who was spent and
winded.

"Dear guides, dear friends of travellers! I am of your country. We seek two gentlemen crossing the Pass, who should have reached the Hospice this evening."

"They have reached it, ma'amselle."

"Thank Heaven! O thank Heaven!"

"But, unhappily, they have gone on again. We are setting forth to seek them even now. We had to wait until the *Tourmente* passed. It has been fearful up here."

"Dear guides, dear friends of travellers! Let me go with you. Let me go with you, for the love of God! One of those gentlemen is to be my husband. I love him, oh, so dearly. O so dearly! You see I am not faint, you see I am not tired. I am born a peasant girl. I will show you that I know well how to fasten myself to your ropes. I will do it with my own hands. I will swear to be brave and good. But let me go with you, let me go with you! If any mischance should have befallen him, my love would find him, when nothing else could. On my knees, dear friends of travellers! By the love your dear mothers had for your fathers!"

The good rough fellows were moved. "After all," they murmured to one another, "she speaks but the truth. She knows the ways of the mountains. See how marvellously she has come here! But as to Monsieur there, ma'amselle?"

"Dear Mr. Joey," said Marguerite, addressing him in his own tongue, "you will remain at the house, and wait for me; will you not?"

"If I know'd which o' you two recommended it," growled Joey Ladle, eyeing the two men with great indignation, "I'd fight you for sixpence, and give you half-a-crown towards your expenses. No, miss. I'll stick by you as long as there's any sticking left in me, and I'll die for you when I can't do better."

The state of the moon rendering it highly important that no time should be lost, and the dogs showing signs of great uneasiness, the two men quickly took their resolution. The rope that yoked them together was exchanged for a longer one; the party were secured, Marguerite second, and the Cellarman last; and they set out for the Refuges. The actual distance of those places was nothing; the whole five and the next Hospice to boot, being within two miles; but the ghastly way was whitened out and sheeted over.

They made no miss in reaching the Gallery where the two had taken shelter. The second storm of wind and snow had so wildly swept over it since, that their tracks were gone. But the dogs went to and fro with their noses down, and were confident. The party stopping, however, at the further arch, where the second storm had been especially furious, and where the drift was deep, the dogs became troubled, and went about and about, in quest of a lost purpose.

The great abyss being known to lie on the right, they wandered too much to the left, and had to regain the way with infinite labour through a deep field of snow. The leader of the line had stopped it, and was taking note of the landmarks, when one of the dogs fell to tearing up the snow a little before them. Advancing and stooping to look at it, thinking that some one might be overwhelmed there, they saw that it was stained, and that the stain was red.

The other dog was now seen to look over the brink of the gulf, with his fore legs straightened out, lest he should fall into it, and to tremble in every limb. Then the dog who had found the stained snow joined him, and then they ran to and fro, distressed and whining. Finally, they both stopped on the brink together, and setting up their heads, howled dolefully.

"There is some one lying below," said Marguerite.

"I think so," said the foremost man. "Stand well inward, the two last, and let us look over."

The last man kindled two torches from his basket, and handed them forward. The leader taking one, and Marguerite the other, they looked down : now shading the torches, now moving them to the right or left, now raising them, now depressing them, as moonlight far below contended with black shadows. A piercing cry from Marguerite broke a long silence.

"My God! On a projecting point, where a wall of ice stretches forward over the torrent, I see a human form !"

"Where, ma'amselle, where ?"

"See, there ! On the shelf of ice below the dogs : "

The leader, with a sickened aspect, drew inward, and they were all silent. But they were not all inactive, for Marguerite, with swift and skilful fingers, had detached both herself and him from the rope in a few seconds.

"Show me the baskets. These two are the only ropes ?"

"The only ropes here, ma'amselle; but at the Hospice——

"If he is alive—I know it is my lover—he will be dead before you can return. Dear Guides! Blessed friends of travellers! Look at me! Watch my hands. If they falter or go wrong, make me your prisoner by force. If they are steady and go right, help me to save him!"

She girded herself with a cord under the breast and arms, she formed it into a kind of jacket, she drew it into knots, she laid its end side by side with the end of the other cord, she twisted and twined the two together, she knotted them together, she set her foot upon the knots, she strained them, she held them for the two men to strain at.

"She is inspired," they said to one another.

"By the Almighty's mercy!" she exclaimed. "You both know that I am by far the lightest here. Give me the brandy and the wine, and lower me down to him. Then go for assistance and a stronger rope. You see that when it is lowered to me—look at this about me now—I can make it fast and safe to his body. Alive or dead, I will bring him up, or die with him. I love him passionately. Can I say more?"

They turned to her companion, but he was lying senseless on the snow.

"Lower me down to him," she said, taking two little kegs they had brought, and hanging them about her, "or I will dash myself to pieces! I am a peasant, and I know no giddiness or fear; and this is nothing to me, and I passionately love him. Lower me down!"

"Ma'amselle, ma'amselle, he must be dying or dead."

"Dying or dead, my husband's head shall lie upon my breast, or I will dash myself to pieces."

They yielded, overborne. With such precautions as their skill and the circumstances admitted, they let her slip from the summit, guiding herself down the precipitous icy wall with her hand, and they lowered down, and lowered down, and lowered down, until the cry came up: "Enough!"

"Is it really he, and is he dead?" they called down, looking over.

The cry came up: "He is insensible; but his heart beats. It beats against mine."

"How does he lie?"

The cry came up : "Upon a ledge of ice. It has thawed beneath him, and it will thaw beneath me. Hasten. If we die, I am content.

One of the two men hurried off with the dogs at such topmost speed as he could make; the other set up the lighted torches in the snow, and applied himself to recovering the Englishman. Much snow-chafing and some brandy got him on his legs, but delirious and quite unconscious where he was.

The watch remained upon the brink, and his cry went down continually : "Courage ! They will soon be here. How goes it ?" And the cry came up : "His heart still beats against mine. I warm him in my arms. I have cast off the rope, for the ice melts under us, and the rope would separate me from him ; but I am not afraid."

The moon went down behind the mountain tops, and all the abyss lay in darkness. The cry went down : How goes it ?" The cry came up : "We are sinking lower, but his heart still beats against mine."

At length, the eager barking of the dogs, and a flare of light upon the snow, proclaimed that help was coming on. Twenty or thirty men, lamps, torches, litters, ropes, blankets, wood to kindle a great fire, restoratives and stimulants, came in fast. The dogs ran from one man to another, and from this thing to that, and ran to the edge of the abyss, dumbly entreating Speed, speed, speed !

The cry went down : "Thanks to God, all is ready. How goes it ?"

The cry came up : "We are sinking still, and we are deadly cold. His heart no longer beats against mine. Let no one come down to add to our weight. Lower the rope only."

The fire was kindled high, a great glare of torches lighted the sides of the precipice, lamps were lowered, a strong rope was lowered. She could be seen passing it round him, and making it secure.

The cry came up into a deathly silence : "Raise ! Softly !" They could see her diminished figure shrink, as he was swung into the air.

They gave no shout when some of them laid him on a litter, and others lowered another strong rope. The cry again came up into a deathly silence : "Raise ! Softly !" But when they caught her at the brink, then they shouted, then they wept, then they gave thanks to Heaven, then they kissed her feet, then they kissed her dress, then the dogs caressed her, licked her icy hands, and with their honest faces warmed her frozen bosom !

She broke from them all, and sank over him on his litter, with both her loving hands upon the heart that stood still.

ACT IV.

THE pleasant scene was Neuchâtel ; the pleasant month was April ; the pleasant place was a notary's office ; the pleasant person in it was the notary : a rosy, hearty, handsome old man, chief notary of Neuchâtel, known far and wide in the canton as Maître Voigt. Professionally and personally, the notary was a popular citizen. His innumerable kindnesses and his innumerable oddities had for years made him one of the recognised public characters of the pleasant Swiss town. His long brown frock-coat and his black skull-cap were among the institutions of the place ; and he carried a snuff-box which, in point of size, was popularly believed to be without a parallel in Europe.

There was another person in the notary's office, not so pleasant as the notary. This was Obenreizer.

An oddly pastoral kind of office it was, and one that would never have answered in England. It stood in a neat back yard, fenced off from a pretty flower-garden. Goats browsed in the doorway, and a cow was within half-a-dozen feet of keeping company with the clerk. Maître Voigt's room was a bright and varnished little room, with panelled walls, like a toy-chamber. According to the seasons of the year, roses, sunflowers, hollyhocks, peeped in at the windows. Maître Voigt's bees hummed through the office all the summer, in at this window and out at that, taking it frequently in their day's work, as if honey were to be made from Maître Voigt's sweet disposition. A large musical box on the chimney-piece, often trilled away at the Overture to Fra Diavolo, or a Selection from William Tell, with a chirruping liveliness that had to be stopped by force on the entrance of a client, and irrepressibly broke out again the moment his back was turned.

"Courage, courage, my good fellow!" said Maître Voigt, patting Obenreizer on the knee, in a fatherly and comforting way. "You will begin a new life to-morrow morning in my office here."

Obenreizer—dressed in mourning, and subdued in manner—lifted his hand, with a white handkerchief in it, to the region of his heart. "The gratitude is here," he said. "But the words to express it are not here."

"Ta-ta-ta! Don't talk to me about gratitude!" said Maître Voigt. "I hate to see a man oppressed. I see you oppressed, and I hold out my hand to you by instinct. Besides, I am not too old yet, to remember my young days. Your father sent me my first client. (It was on a question of half an acre of vineyard that seldom bore any grapes.) Do I owe nothing to your father's son? I owe him a debt of friendly obligation, and I pay it to you. That's rather neatly expressed, I think," added Maître Voigt, in high good humour with himself. "Permit me to reward my own merit with a pinch of snuff!"

Obenreizer dropped his eyes to the ground, as though he were not even worthy to see the notary take snuff.

"Do me one last favour, sir," he said, when he raised his eyes. "Do not act on impulse. Thus far, you have only a general knowledge of my position. Hear the case for and against me, in its details, before you take me into your office. Let my claim on your benevolence be recognised by your sound reason as well as by your excellent heart. In *that* case, I may hold up my head against the bitterest of my enemies, and build myself a new reputation on the ruins of the character I have lost."

"As you will," said Maître Voigt. "You speak well, my son. You will be a fine lawyer one of these days."

"The details are not many," pursued Obenreizer. "My troubles begin with the accidental death of my late travelling companion, my lost dear friend, Mr. Vendale."

"Mr. Vendale," repeated the notary. "Just so. I have heard and read of the name, several times within these two months. The name of the unfortunate English gentleman who was killed on the Simplon. When you got that scar upon your cheek and neck."

"—From my own knife," said Obenreizer, touching what must have been an ugly gash at the time of its infliction.

"From your own knife," assented the notary, "and in trying to save him. Good, good, good. That was very good. Vendale. Yes. I have several times, lately, thought it droll that I should once have had a client of that name."

"But the world, sir," returned Obenreizer, "is *so* small!" Nevertheless he made a mental note that the notary had once had a client of that name.

"As I was saying, sir, the death of that dear travelling comrade begins my troubles. What follows? I save myself. I go down to Milan. I am received with coldness by Defresnier and Company. Shortly afterwards, I am discharged by Defresnier and Company. Why? They give no reason why. I ask, do they assail my honour? No answer. I ask, what is the imputation against me? No answer. I ask, where are their proofs against me? No answer. I ask, what am I to think? The reply is, 'M. Obenreizer is free to think what he will. What M. Obenreizer thinks, is of no importance to Defresnier and Company.' And that is all."

"Perfectly. That is all," assented the notary, taking a large pinch of snuff.

"But is that enough, sir?"

"That is not enough," said Maître Voigt. "The House of Defresnier are my fellow-townsmen—much respected, much esteemed—but the House of Defresnier must not silently destroy a man's character. You can rebut assertion. But how can you rebut silence?"

"Your sense of justice, my dear patron," answered Obenreizer, "states in a word the cruelty of the case. Does it stop there? No. For, what follows upon that?"

"True, my poor boy," said the notary, with a comforting nod or two; "your ward rebels upon that."

"Rebels is too soft a word," retorted Obenreizer. "My ward revolts from me with horror. My ward defies me. My ward withdraws herself from my authority, and takes shelter (Madame Dor with her) in the house of that English lawyer, Mr. Bintrey, who replies to your summons to her to submit herself to my authority, that she will not do so."

"—And who afterwards writes," said the notary, moving

his large snuff-box to look among the papers underneath it for the letter, " that he is coming to confer with me."

" Indeed ? " replied Obenreizer, rather checked.   " Well, sir.   Have I no legal rights ? "

" Assuredly, my poor boy," returned the notary.   " All but felons have their legal rights."

" And who calls me felon ? " said Obenreizer, fiercely.

" No one.   Be calm under your wrongs.   If the House of Defresnier would call you felon, indeed, we should know how to deal with them."

While saying these words, he had handed Bintrey's very short letter to Obenreizer, who now read it and gave it back.

" In saying," observed Obenreizer with recovered composure, " that he is coming to confer with you, this English lawyer means that he is coming to deny my authority over my ward."

" You think so ? "

" I am sure of it.   I know him.   He is obstinate and contentious.   You will tell me, my dear sir, whether my authority is unassailable, until my ward is of age ? "

" Absolutely unassailable."

" I will enforce it.   I will make her submit herself to it. For," said Obenreizer, changing his angry tone to one of grateful submission, " I owe it to you, sir ; to you, who have so confidingly taken an injured man under your protection, and into your employment."

" Make your mind easy," said Maître Voigt.   " No more of this now, and no thanks !   Be here to-morrow morning, before the other clerk comes—between seven and eight.   You will find me in this room ; and I will myself initiate you in your work.   Go away ! go away !   I have letters to write.   I won't hear a word more."

Dismissed with this generous abruptness, and satisfied with the favourable impression he had left on the old man's mind, Obenreizer was at leisure to revert to the mental note he had made that Maître Voigt once had a client whose name was Vendale.

" I ought to know England well enough by this time ; " so his meditations ran, as he sat on a bench in the yard ; " and it is not a name I ever encountered there, except—" he looked involuntarily over his shoulder—" as *his* name.   Is the world so small that I cannot get away from him, even now when he is dead ? He confessed at the last that he had betrayed the trust of the dead, and misinherited a fortune. And I was to see to it. And I was to stand off, that my face might remind him of it. Why *my* face, unless it concerned *me ?* I am sure of his words, for they have been in my ears ever since. Can there be anything bearing on them, in the keeping of this old idiot? Anything to repair my fortunes, and blacken his memory? He dwelt upon my earliest remembrances, that night at Basle. Why, unless he had a purpose in it?"

Maître Voigt's two largest he-goats were butting at him to butt him out of the place, as if for that disrespectful mention of their master. So he got up and left the place. But he walked alone for a long time on the border of the lake, with his head drooped in deep thought.

Between seven and eight next morning, he presented himself at the office. He found the notary ready for him, at work on some papers which had come in on the previous evening. In a few clear words, Maître Voigt explained the routine of the office, and the duties Obenreizer would be expected to perform. It still wanted five minutes to eight, when the preliminary instructions were declared to be complete.

"I will show you over the house and the offices," said Maître Voigt, "but I must put away these papers first. They come from the municipal authorities, and they must be taken special care of."

Obenreizer saw his chance, here, of finding out the repository in which his employer's private papers were kept.

"Can't I save you the trouble, sir?" he asked. "Can't I put those documents away under your directions?"

Maître Voigt laughed softly to himself; closed the portfolio in which the papers had been sent to him; handed it to Obenreizer.

"Suppose you try," he said. "All my papers of importance are kept yonder."

He pointed to a heavy oaken door, thickly studded with nails, at the lower end of the room. Approaching the door, with the portfolio, Obenreizer discovered, to his astonishment, that there were no means whatever of opening it from the outside. There was no handle, no bolt, no key, and (climax of passive obstruction !) no keyhole.

"There is a second door to this room?" said Obenreizer, appealing to the notary.

"No," said Maître Voigt.   "Guess again."

"There is a window?"

"Nothing of the sort.   The window has been bricked up. The only way in, is the way by that door.   Do you give it up?" cried Maître Voigt in high triumph.   "Listen my good fellow, and tell me if you hear nothing inside?"

Obenreizer listened for a moment, and started back from the door.

"I know!" he exclaimed.   "I heard of this when I was apprenticed here at the watchmaker's.   Perrin Brothers have finished their famous clock-lock at last—and you have got it?"

"Bravo!" said Maître Voigt. "The clock-lock it is!   There, my son!   There you have one more of what the good people of this town call, 'Daddy Voigt's follies.'   With all my heart! Let those laugh who win.   No thief can steal *my* keys.   No burglar can pick *my* lock.   No power on earth, short of a battering-ram or a barrel of gunpowder, can move that door, till my little sentinel inside—my worthy friend who goes 'Tick, Tick,' as I tell him—says, 'Open!'   The big door obeys the little Tick, Tick, and the little Tick, Tick, obeys *me*.   That!" cried Daddy Voigt, snapping his fingers, "for all the thieves in Christendom!"

"May I see it in action?" asked Obenreizer.   "Pardon my curiosity, dear sir!   You know that I was once a tolerable worker in the clock trade."

"Certainly you shall see it in action," said Maître Voigt. "What is the time now?   One minute to eight.   Watch, and in one minute you will see the door open of itself."

In one minute, smoothly and slowly and silently, as if invisible hands had set it free, the heavy door opened inward, and disclosed a dark chamber beyond.   On three sides, shelves filled the walls, from floor to ceiling.   Arranged on the shelves, were rows upon rows of boxes made in the pretty inlaid wood-work of Switzerland, and bearing inscribed on their fronts (for the most part in fanciful coloured letters) the names of the notary's clients.

Maître Voigt lighted a taper, and led the way into the room.

"You shall see the clock," he said, proudly.   "I possess the

greatest curiosity in Europe.   It is only a privileged few whose
eyes can look at it.   I give the privilege to your good father's
son—you shall be one of the favoured few who enter the room
with me.   See! here it is, on the right-hand wall at the side of
the door."

"An ordinary clock," exclaimed Obenreizer.   "No! Not
an ordinary clock.   It has only one hand."

"Aha!" said Maître Voigt.   "Not an ordinary clock, my
friend.   No, no.   That one hand goes round the dial.   As I
put it, so it regulates the hour at which the door shall open.
See!   The hand points to eight.   At eight the door opened, as
you saw for yourself."

"Does it open more than once in the four-and-twenty hours?"
asked Obenreizer.

"More than once?" repeated the notary, with great scorn.
"You don't know, my good friend, Tick, Tick!   He will open
the door as often as I ask him.   All he wants, is his directions,
and he gets them here.   Look below the dial.   Here is a half-
circle of steel let into the wall, and here is a hand (called
the regulator) that travels round it, just as *my* hand chooses.
Notice, if you please, that there are figures to guide me on the
half-circle of steel.   Figure I. means: Open once in the four-
and-twenty hours.   Figure II. means: Open twice; and so on
to the end.   I set the regulator every morning, after I have
read my letters, and when I know what my day's work is to be.
Would you like to see me set it now?   What is to day?
Wednesday.   Good!   This is the day of our rifle-club; there
is little business to do; I grant a half-holiday.   No work here
to-day, after three o'clock.   Let us first put away this portfolio
of municipal papers.   There!   No need to trouble Tick-Tick to
open the door until eight to-morrow.   Good!   I leave the
dial hand at eight; I put back the regulator to 'I.'; I close
the door; and closed the door remains, past all opening by anybody, till to-morrow morning at eight."

Obenreizer's quickness instantly saw the means by which
he might make the clock-lock betray its master's confidence,
and place its master's papers at his disposal.

"Stop, sir!" he cried, at the moment when the notary was
closing the door.   "Don't I see something moving among the
boxes—on the floor there?"

(Maître Voigt turned his back for a moment to look. In that moment, Obenreizer's ready hand put the regulator on, from the figure 'I.' to the figure 'II.' Unless the notary looked again at the half-circle of steel, the door would open at eight that evening, as well as at eight next morning, and nobody but Obenreizer would know it.)

"There is nothing!" said Maître Voigt. "Your troubles have shaken your nerves, my son. Some shadow thrown by my taper; or some poor little beetle, who lives among the old lawyer's secrets, running away from the light. Hark! I hear your fellow-clerk in the office. To work! to work! and build to-day the first step that leads to your new fortunes!"

He good humouredly pushed Obenreizer out before him; extinguished the taper, with a last fond glance at his clock which passed harmlessly over the regulator beneath; and closed the oaken door.

At three the office was shut up. The notary and everybody in the notary's employment, with one exception, went to see the rifle-shooting. Obenreizer had pleaded that he was not in spirits for a public festival. Nobody knew what had become of him. It was believed that he had slipped away for a solitary walk.

The house and offices had been closed but a few minutes, when the door of a shining wardrobe, in the notary's shining room, opened, and Obenreizer stepped out. He walked to a window, unclosed the shutters, satisfied himself that he could escape unseen by way of the garden, turned back into the room, and took his place in the notary's easy chair. He was locked up in the house, and there were five hours to wait before eight o'clock came.

He wore his way through the five hours: sometimes reading the books and newspapers that lay on the table: sometimes thinking: sometimes walking to and fro. Sunset came on. He closed the window-shutters before he kindled a light. The candle lighted, and the time drawing nearer and nearer, he sat, watch in hand, with his eyes on the oaken door.

At eight, smoothly and softly and silently the door opened.

One after another, he read the names on the outer rows of boxes. No such name as Vendale! He removed the outer row, and looked at the row behind. These were older boxes, and shabbier boxes. The four first that he examined, were inscribed

OBENREIZER PUTS ON THE REGULATOR.

with French and German names. The fifth bore a name which was almost illegible. He brought it out into the room, and examined. it closely. There, covered thickly with time-stains and dust, was the name : "Vendale."

The key hung to the box by a string. He unlocked the box, took out four loose papers that were in it, spread them open on the table, and began to read them. He had not so occupied a minute, when his face fell from its expression of eagerness and avidity, to one of haggard astonishment and disappointment. But, after a little consideration, he copied the papers. He then replaced the papers, replaced the box, closed the door, extinguished the candle, and stole away.

As his murderous and thievish footfall passed out of the garden, the steps of the notary and some one accompanying him stopped at the front door of the house. The lamps were lighted in the little street, and the notary had his door-key in his hand.

"Pray do not pass my house, Mr. Bintrey," he said. "Do me the honour to come in. It is one of our town half-holidays —our Tir—but my people will be back directly. It is droll that you should ask your way to the Hotel of me. Let us eat and drink before you go there."

"Thank you ; not to-night," said Bintrey. "Shall I come to you at ten to-morrow ? "

"I shall be enchanted, sir, to take so early an opportunity of redressing the wrongs of my injured client," returned the good notary.

"Yes," retorted Bintrey ; "your injured client is all very well—but—a word in your ear."

He whispered to the notary, and walked off. When the notary's housekeeper came home, she found him standing at his door motionless, with the key still in his hand, and the door unopened.

OBENREIZER'S VICTORY.

The scene shifts again—to the foot of the Simplon, on the Swiss side.

In one of the dreary rooms of the dreary little inn at Brieg, Mr. Bintrey and Maître Voigt sat together at a professional council of two. Mr. Bintrey was searching in his despatch-box.

Maître Voigt was looking towards a closed door, painted brown to imitate mahogany, and communicating with an inner room.

"Isn't it time he was here?" asked the notary, shifting his position, and glancing at a second door at the other end of the room, painted yellow to imitate deal.

"He *is* here," answered Bintrey, after listening for a moment.

The yellow door was opened by a waiter, and Obenreizer walked in.

After greeting Maître Voigt with a cordiality which appeared to cause the notary no little embarrassment, Obenreizer bowed with grave and distant politeness to Bintrey. "For what reason have I been brought from Neuchâtel to the foot of the mountain?" he inquired, taking the seat which the English lawyer had indicated to him.

"You shall be quite satisfied on that head before our interview is over," returned Bintrey. "For the present, permit me to suggest proceeding at once to business. There has been a correspondence, Mr. Obenreizer, between you and your niece. I am here to represent your niece."

"In other words, you, a lawyer, are here to represent an infraction of the law."

"Admirably put!" said Bintrey. "If all the people I have to deal with were only like you, what an easy profession mine would be! I am here to represent an infraction of the law—that is your point of view. I am here to make a compromise between you and your niece—that is my point of view."

"There must be two parties to a compromise," rejoined Obenreizer. "I decline, in this case, to be one of them. The law gives me authority to control my niece's actions, until she comes of age. She is not yet of age; and I claim my authority."

At this point Maître Voigt attempted to speak. Bintrey silenced him with a compassionate indulgence of tone and manner, as if he was silencing a favourite child.

"No, my worthy friend, not a word. Don't excite yourself unnecessarily; leave it to me." He turned, and addressed himself again to Obenreizer. "I can think of nothing comparable to you, Mr. Obenreizer, but granite—and even that wears out in course of time. In the interests of peace and quietness—for the sake of your own dignity—relax a little. If you will only delegate your authority to another person whom I know of, that person may be trusted never to lose sight of your niece, night or day !"

"You are wasting your time and mine," returned Obenreizer. "If my niece is not rendered up to my authority within one week from this day, I invoke the law. If you resist the law, I take her by force."

He rose to his feet as he said the last word. Maître Voigt looked round again towards the brown door which led into the inner room.

"Have some pity on the poor girl," pleaded Bintrey. "Remember how lately she lost her lover by a dreadful death ! Will nothing move you ?"

"Nothing."

Bintrey, in his turn, rose to his feet, and looked at Maître Voigt. Maître Voigt's hand, resting on the table, began to tremble. Maître Voigt's eyes remained fixed, as if by irresistible fascination, on the brown door. Obenreizer, suspiciously observing him, looked that way too.

"There is somebody listening in there !" he exclaimed, with a sharp backward glance at Bintrey.

"There are two people listening," answered Bintrey.

"Who are they ?"

"You shall see."

With that answer, he raised his voice and spoke the next words—the two common words which are on everybody's lips, at every hour of the day : "Come in !"

The brown door opened. Supported on Marguerite's arm—his sunburnt colour gone, his right arm bandaged and slung over his breast—Vendale stood before the murderer, a man risen from the dead.

In the moment of silence that followed, the singing of a caged bird in the courtyard outside was the one sound stirring in the room. Maître Voigt touched Bintrey, and pointed to Obenreizer. "Look at him !" said the notary, in a whisper.

The shock had paralysed every movement in the villain's body, but the movement of the blood. His face was like the face of a corpse. The one vestige of colour left in it was a livid purple streak which marked the course of the scar, where his victim had wounded him on the cheek and neck.　Speechless, breathless, motionless alike in eye and limb, it seemed as if, at the sight of Vendale, the death to which he had doomed Vendale had struck him where he stood.

"Somebody ought to speak to him," said Maître Voigt. "Shall I?"

Even at that moment, Bintrey persisted in silencing the notary, and in keeping the lead in the proceedings to himself. Checking Maître Voigt by a gesture, he dismissed Marguerite and Vendale in these words:—"The object of your appearance here is answered," he said.　"If you will withdraw for the present, it may help Mr. Obenreizer to recover himself."

It did help him.　As the two passed through the door, and closed it behind them, he drew a deep breath of relief.　He looked round him for the chair from which he had risen, and dropped into it.

"Give him time!" pleaded Maître Voigt.

"No," said Bintrey.　"I don't know what use he may make of it, if I do."　He turned once more to Obenreizer, and went on.　"I owe it to myself," he said—"I don't admit, mind, that I owe it to *you*—to account for my appearance in these proceedings, and to state what has been done under my advice, and on my sole responsibility.　Can you listen to me?"

"I can listen to you."

"Recal the time when you started for Switzerland with Mr. Vendale," Bintrey began.　"You had not left England four-and-twenty hours, before your niece committed an act of imprudence which not even your penetration could foresee.　She followed her promised husband on his journey, without asking anybody's advice or permission, and without any better companion to protect her than a Cellarman in Mr. Vendale's employment."

"Why did she follow me on the journey? and how came the Cellarman to be the person who accompanied her?"

"She followed you on the journey," answered Bintrey, "because she suspected there had been some serious collision between you and Mr. Vendale, which had been kept secret from her; and because she rightly believed you to be capable of serving your interests, or of satisfying your enmity, at the price of a crime.　As for the Cellarman, he was one, among the other people in Mr. Vendale's establishment, to whom she had applied (the moment your back was turned) to know if anything had happened between their master and you. The Cellarman alone had something to tell her. A senseless superstition, and a common accident which had happened to his master, in his master's cellar, had connected Mr. Vendale in this man's mind with the idea of danger by murder. Your niece surprised him into a confession, which aggravated tenfold the terrors that possessed her. Aroused to a sense of the mischief he had done, the man, of his own accord, made the one atonement in his power. 'If my master is in danger, miss,' he said, 'it's my duty to follow him, too; and it's more than my duty to take care of *you*.' The two set forth together—and, for once, a superstition has had its use. It decided your niece on taking the journey; and it led the way to saving a man's life. Do you understand me, so far?"

"I understand you, so far."

"My first knowledge of the crime that you had committed," pursued Bintrey, "came to me in the form of a letter from your niece. All you need know is that her love and her courage recovered the body of your victim, and aided the after-efforts which brought him back to life. While he lay helpless at Brieg, under her care, she wrote to me to come out to him. Before starting, I informed Madame Dor that I knew Miss Obenreizer to be safe, and knew where she was. Madame Dor informed me, in return, that a letter had come for your niece, which she knew to be in your handwriting. I took possession of it, and arranged for the forwarding of any other letters which might follow. Arrived at Brieg, I found Mr. Vendale out of danger, and at once devoted myself to hastening the day of reckoning with you. Defresnier and Company turned you off. on suspicion ; acting on information privately supplied by me. Having stripped you of your false character, the next thing to do was to strip you of your authority over your niece. To reach this end, I not only had no scruple in digging the pitfall under your feet in the dark—I felt a certain professional pleasure in fighting you with your own weapons. By my advice, the truth has been carefully concealed from you, up to this day. By my advice, the trap into which you have walked was set for you (you know why, now, as well as I do) in this place. There

was but one certain way of shaking the devilish self-control
which has hitherto made you a formidable man. That way has
been tried, and (look at me as you may) that way has succeeded.
The last thing that remains to be done," concluded Bintrey,
producing two little slips of manuscript from his despatch-box,
" is to set your niece free. You have attempted murder, and
you have committed forgery and theft. We have the evidence
ready against you in both cases. If you are convicted as a
felon, you know as well as I do what becomes of your authority
over your niece. Personally, I should have preferred taking
that way out of it. But considerations are pressed on me which
I am not able to resist, and this interview must end, as I have
told you already, in a compromise. Sign those lines, resigning
all authority over Miss Obenreizer, and pledging yourself never
to be seen in England or in Switzerland again ; and I will sign
an indemnity which secures you against further proceedings on
our part."

Obenreizer took the pen, in silence, and signed his niece's
release. On receiving the indemnity in return, he rose, but
made no movement to leave the room. He stood looking at
Maître Voigt with a strange smile gathering at his lips, and a
strange light flashing in his filmy eyes.

" What are you waiting for ?" asked Bintrey.

Obenreizer pointed to the brown door. " Call them back,"
he answered. " I have something to say in their presence
before I go."

" Say it in my presence," retorted Bintrey. " I decline to
call them back."

Obenreizer turned to Maître Voigt. " Do you remember
telling me that you once had an English client named Vendale ?"
he asked.

" Well," answered the notary. " And what of that ?"

" Maître Voigt, your clock-lock has betrayed you."

" What do you mean ?"

" I have read the letters and certificates in your client's box.
I have taken copies of them. I have got the copies here. Is
there, or is there not, a reason for calling them back ?"

For a moment the notary looked to and fro, between Obenreizer and Bintrey, in helpless astonishment. Recovering
himself, he drew his brother-lawyer aside, and hurriedly spoke

a few words close at his ear. The face of Bintrey—after first faithfully reflecting the astonishment on the face of Maître Voigt—suddenly altered its expression. He sprang, with the activity of a young man, to the door of the inner room, entered it, remained inside for a minute, and returned followed by Marguerite and Vendale. "Now, Mr. Obenreizer," said Bintrey, "the last move in the game is yours. Play it."

"Before I resign my position as that young lady's guardian," said Obenreizer, "I have a secret to reveal in which she is interested. In making my disclosure, I am not claiming her attention for a narrative which she, or any other person present, is expected to take on trust. I am possessed of written proofs, copies of originals, the authenticity of which Maître Voigt himself can attest. Bear that in mind, and permit me to refer you, at starting, to a date long past—the month of February, in the year one thousand eight hundred and thirty-six."

"Mark the date, Mr. Vendale," said Bintrey.

"My first proof," said Obenreizer, taking a paper from his pocket-book. "Copy of a letter, written by an English lady (married) to her sister, a widow. The name of the person writing the letter I shall keep suppressed until I have done. The name of the person to whom the letter is written I am willing to reveal. It is addressed to 'Mrs. Jane Ann Miller, of Groombridge Wells, England.'"

Vendale started, and opened his lips to speak. Bintrey instantly stopped him, as he had stopped Maître Voigt. "No," said the pertinacious lawyer. "Leave it to me."

Obenreizer went on :

"It is needless to trouble you with the first half of the letter," he said. "I can give the substance of it in two words. The writer's position at the time is this. She has been long living in Switzerland with her husband—obliged to live there for the sake of her husband's health. They are about to move to a new residence on the Lake of Neuchâtel in a week, and they will be ready to receive Mrs. Miller as visitor in a fortnight from that time. This said, the writer next enters into an important domestic detail. She has been childless for years—she and her husband have now no hope of children ; they are lonely ; they want an interest in life ; they have decided on adopting a child. Here the important part of the

letter begins; and here, therefore, I read it to you word for
word."

He folded back the first page of the letter and read as follows:

"   *   *   *   Will you help us, my dear sister, to realise our new project ?
As English people, we wish to adopt an English child. This may be
done, I believe, at the Foundling : my husband's lawyers in London
will tell you how. I leave the choice to you, with only these conditions
attached to it—that the child is to be an infant under a year old, and is
to be a boy. Will you pardon the trouble I am giving you, for my
sake ; and will you bring our adopted child to us, with your own children,
when you come to Neuchâtel ?

"I must add a word as to my husband's wishes in this matter. He
is resolved to spare the child whom we make our own, any future
mortification and loss of self-respect which might be caused by a
discovery of his true origin. He will bear my husband's name, and he
will be brought up in the belief that he is really our son. His inheritance of what we have to leave will be secured to him—not only
according to the laws of England in such cases, but according to the
laws of Switzerland also; for we have lived so long in this country, that
there is a doubt whether we may not considered as 'domiciled' in
Switzerland. The one precaution left to take is to prevent any after-
discovery at the Foundling. Now, our name is a very uncommon one ;
and if we appear on the Register of the Institution, as the persons
adopting the child, there is just a chance that something might result
from it. Your name, my dear, is the name of thousands of other
people ; and if you will consent to appear on the Register, there need be
no fear of any discoveries in that quarter. We are moving, by the
doctor's orders, to a part of Switzerland in which our circumstances are
quite unknown; and you, as I understand, are about to engage a new nurse
for the journey when you come to see us. Under these circumstances,
the child may appear as my child, brought back to me under my sister's
care.   The only servant we take with us from our old home is my own
maid, who can be safely trusted. As for the lawyers in England and in
Switzerland, it is their profession to keep secrets—and we may feel quite
easy in that direction. So there you have our harmless little con-
spiracy ! Write by return of post, my love, and tell me you will join
it."   *   *   *   *   *   *   *   *

"Do you still conceal the name of the writer of that letter?"
asked Vendale.

"I keep the name of the writer till the last," answered
Obenreizer, "and I proceed to my second proof—a mere slip of
paper, this time, as you see. Memorandum given to the Swiss
lawyer, who drew the documents referred to in the letter I have
just read, expressed as follows :—'Adopted from the Foundling
Hospital of England, 3rd March, 1836, a male infant, called, in
the Institution, Walter Wilding. Person appearing on the
register, as adopting the child, Mrs. Jane Anne Miller, widow,

acting in this matter for her married sister, domiciled in Switzerland.' Patience!" resumed Obenreizer, as Vendale, breaking loose from Bintrey, started to his feet. "I shall not keep the name concealed much longer. Two more little slips of paper, and I have done. Third proof! Certificate of Doctor Ganz, still living in practice at Neuchâtel, dated July, 1838. The doctor certifies (you shall read it for yourselves directly), first, that he attended the adopted child in its infant maladies; second, that, three months before the date of the certificate, the gentleman adopting the child as his son died; third, that *on* the date of the certificate, his widow and her maid, taking the adopted child with them, left Neuchâtel on their return to England. One more link now added to this, and my chain of evidence is complete. The maid remained with her mistress till her mistress's death, only a few years since. The maid can swear to the identity of the adopted infant, from his childhood to his youth —from his youth to his manhood, as he is now. There is her address in England—and there, Mr. Vendale, is the fourth, and final proof!"

"Why do you address yourself to *me?*" said Vendale, as Obenreizer threw the written address on the table.

Obenreizer turned on him, in a sudden frenzy of triumph.

"*Because you are the man!* If my niece marries you, she marries a bastard, brought up by public charity. If my niece marries you, she marries an impostor, without name or lineage, disguised in the character of a gentleman of rank and family."

"Bravo!" cried Bintrey. "Admirably put, Mr. Obenreizer! It only wants one word more to complete it. She marries —thanks entirely to your exertions—a man who inherits a handsome fortune, and a man whose origin will make him prouder than ever of his peasant-wife. George Vendale, as brother-executors, let us congratulate each other! Our dear dead friend's last wish on earth is accomplished. We have found the lost Walter Wilding. As Mr. Obenreizer said just now— you are the man!"

The words passed by Vendale unheeded. For the moment he was conscious of but one sensation; he heard but one voice. Marguerite's hand was clasping his. Marguerite's voice was whispering to him: "I never loved you, George, as I love you now!"

THE CURTAIN FALLS.

May-Day. There is merry-making in Cripple Corner, the chimneys smoke, the patriarchal dining-hall is hung with garlands, and Mrs. Goldstraw, the respected housekeeper, is very busy. For, on this bright morning the young master of Cripple Corner is married to its young mistress, far away: to wit, in the little town of Brieg, in Switzerland, lying at the foot of the Simplon Pass where she saved his life.

The bells ring gaily in the little town of Brieg, and flags are stretched across the street, and rifle shots are heard, and sounding music from brass instruments. Streamer-decorated casks of wine have been rolled out under a gay awning in the public way before the Inn, and there will be free feasting and revelry. What with bells and banners, draperies hanging from windows, explosion of gunpowder, and reverberation of brass music, the little town of Brieg is all in a flutter, like the hearts of its simple people.

It was a stormy night last night, and the mountains are covered with snow. But the sun is bright to-day, the sweet air is fresh, the tin spires of the little town of Brieg are burnished silver, and the Alps are ranges of far-off white cloud in a deep blue sky.

The primitive people of the little town of Brieg have built a greenwood arch across the street, under which the newly married pair shall pass in triumph from the church. It is inscribed, on that side, "HONOUR AND LOVE TO MARGUERITE VENDALE!" for the people are proud of her to enthusiasm. This greeting of the bride under her new name is affectionately meant as a surprise, and therefore the arrangement has been made that she, unconscious why, shall be taken to the Church by a tortuous back way. A scheme not difficult to carry into execution in the crooked little town of Brieg.

So, all things are in readiness, and they are to go and come on foot. Assembled in the Inn's best chamber, festively adorned, are the bride and bridegroom, the Neuchâtel notary, the London lawyer, Madame Dor, and a certain large mysterious Englishman, popularly known as Monsieur Zhoé-Ladelle. And behold Madame Dor, arrayed in a spotless pair of gloves of her own, with no hand in the air, but both hands clasped round the neck of the bride; to embrace whom Madame Dor has turned her broad back on the company, consistent to the last.

"Forgive me, my beautiful," pleads Madame Dor, "for that I ever was his she-cat!"

"She-cat, Madame Dor?"

"Engaged to sit watching my so charming mouse," are the explanatory words of Madame Dor, delivered with a penitential sob.

"Why, you were our best friend! George, dearest, tell Madame Dor. Was she not our best friend?"

"Undoubtedly, darling. What should we have done without her?"

"You are both so generous," cries Madame Dor, accepting consolation, and immediately relapsing. "But I commenced as a she-cat."

"Ah! But like the cat in the fairy-story, good Madame Dor," says Vendale, saluting her cheek, "you were a true woman. And, being a true woman, the sympathy of your heart was with true love."

"I don't wish to deprive Madame Dor of her share in the embraces that are going on," Mr. Bintrey puts in, watch in hand, "and I don't presume to offer any objection to your having got yourselves mixed together, in the corner there, like the three Graces. I merely remark that I think it's time we were moving. What are *your* sentiments on that subject, Mr. Ladle?"

"Clear, sir," replies Joey, with a gracious grin. "I'm clearer altogether, sir, for having lived so many weeks upon the surface. I never was half so long upon the surface afore, and it's done me a power of good. At Cripple Corner, I was too much below it. Atop of the Simpleton, I was a deal too high above it. I've found the medium here, sir. And if ever I take it in convivial, in all the rest of my days, I mean to do it this day, to the toast of 'Bless 'em both.'"

"I, too!" says Bintrey. "And now, Monsieur Voigt, let you and me be two men of Marseilles, and allons, marchons, arm-in-arm!"

They go down to the door, where others are waiting for them, and they go quietly to the church, and the happy marriage takes place. While the ceremony is yet in progress, the notary is called out. When it is finished, he has returned, is standing behind Vendale, and touches him on the shoulder.

"Go to the side door, one moment, Monsieur Vendale. Alone. Leave Madame to me."

At the side door of the church, are the same two men from the Hospice. They are snow-stained and travel-worn. They wish him joy, and then each lays his broad hand upon Vendale's breast, and one says in a low voice, while the other steadfastly regards him :

"It is here, Monsieur. Your litter. The very same."

"My litter is here ? Why ?"

"Hush ! For the sake of Madame. Your companion of that day——"

"What of him ?"

The man looks at his comrade, and his comrade takes him up. Each keeps his hand laid earnestly on Vendale's breast.

"He had been living at the first Refuge, monsieur, for some days. The weather was now good, now bad."

"Yes ?"

"He arrived at our Hospice the day before yesterday, and, having refreshed himself with sleep on the floor before the fire, wrapped in his cloak, was resolute to go on, before dark, to the next Hospice. He had a great fear of that part of the way, and thought it would be worse to-morrow."

"Yes ?"

"He went on alone. He had passed the gallery, when an avalanche—like that which fell behind you near the Bridge of the Ganther——"

"Killed him ?"

"We dug him out, suffocated and broken all to pieces ! But, monsieur, as to Madame. We have brought him here on the litter, to be buried. We must ascend the street outside. Madame must not see. It would be an accursed thing to bring the litter through the arch across the street, until Madame has passed through. As you descend, we who accompany the litter will set it down on the stones of the street the second to the right, and will stand before it. But do not let Madame turn her head towards the street the second to the right. There is no time to lose. Madame will be alarmed by your absence. Adieu !"

Vendale returns to his bride, and draws her hand through his unmaimed arm. A pretty procession awaits them at the main door of the church. They take their station in it, and descend the street amidst the ringing of the bells, the firing of the guns, the waving of the flags, the playing of the music, the shouts, the smiles, and tears, of the excited town. Heads are uncovered as she passes, hands are kissed to her, all the people bless her. " Heaven's benediction on the dear girl ! See where she goes in her youth and beauty ; she who so nobly saved his life ! "

Near the corner of the street the second to the right, he speaks to her, and calls her attention to the windows on the opposite side. The corner well passed, he says : " Do not look round, my darling, for a reason that I have," and turns his head. Then, looking back along the street, he sees the litter and its bearers passing up alone under the arch, as he and she and their marriage train go down towards the shining valley.

THE PERILS OF CERTAIN ENGLISH PRISONERS.

THE PERILS OF CERTAIN ENGLISH PRISONERS.

CHAPTER I.

THE ISLAND OF SILVER-STORE.

It was in the year of our Lord one thousand seven hundred and forty-four, that I, Gill Davis to command, His Mark, having then the honor to be a private in the Royal Marines, stood a-leaning over the bulwarks of the armed sloop Christopher Columbus, in the South American waters off the Mosquito shore.

My lady remarks to me, before I go any further, that there is no such christian-name as Gill, and that her confident opinion is, that the name given to me in the baptism wherein I was made, &c., was Gilbert. She is certain to be right, but I never heard of it. I was a foundling child, picked up somewhere or another, and I always understood my christian-name to be Gill. It is true that I was called Gills when employed at Snorridge Bottom betwixt Chatham and Maidstone, to frighten birds; but that had nothing to do with the Baptism wherein I was made, &c., and wherein a number of things were promised for me by somebody, who let me alone ever afterwards as to performing any of them, and who, I consider, must have been the Beadle. Such name of Gills was entirely owing to my cheeks, or gills, which at that time of my life were of a raspy description.

My lady stops me again, before I go any further, by laughing exactly in her old way and waving the feather of her pen at me. That action on her part, calls to my mind as I look at her hand with the rings on it——Well! I won't! To be sure it will come in, in its own place. But it's always strange to me, noticing the quiet hand, and noticing it (as I have done, you know, so many times) a-fondling children and grandchildren asleep, to think that when blood and honor were up—there! I won't! not at present!—Scratch it out.

She won't scratch it out, and quite honorable; because we have made an understanding that everything is to be taken down, and that nothing that is once taken down shall be scratched out. I have the great misfortune not to be able to read and write, and I am speaking my true and faithful account of those Adventures, and my lady is writing it, word for word.

I say, there I was, a-leaning over the bulwarks of the sloop Christopher Columbus in the South American waters off the Mosquito shore: a subject of his Gracious Majesty King George of England, and a private in the Royal Marines.

In those climates, you don't want to do much. I was doing nothing. I was thinking of the shepherd (my father, I wonder?) on the hill-sides by Snorridge Bottom, with a long staff, and with a rough white coat in all weathers all the year round, who used to let me lie in a corner of his hut by night, and who used to let me go about with him and his sheep by day when I could get nothing else to do, and who used to give me so little of his victuals and so much of his staff, that I ran away from him— which was what he wanted all along, I expect—to be knocked about the world in preference to Snorridge Bottom. I had been knocked about the world for nine-and-twenty years in all, when I stood looking along those bright blue South American waters. Looking after the shepherd, I may say. Watching him in a half-waking dream, with my eyes half-shut, as he, and his flock of sheep, and his two dogs, seemed to move away from the ship's side, far away over the blue water, and go right down into the sky.

"It's rising out of the water, steady," a voice said close to me. I had been thinking on so, that it like woke me with a start, though it was no stranger voice than the voice of Harry Charker, my own comrade.

"What's rising out of the water, steady?" I asked my comrade.

"What?" says he. "The Island."

"O! The Island!" says I, turning my eyes towards it. "True. I forgot the Island."

"Forgot the port you're going to?   That's odd, an't it?"

"It is odd," says I.

"And odd," he said, slowly considering with himself, "an't even. Is it, Gill?"

He had always a remark just like that to make, and seldom another. As soon as he had brought a thing round to what it was not, he was satisfied. He was one of the best of men, and, in a certain sort of a way, one with the least to say for himself. I qualify it, because, besides being able to read and write like a Quarter-master, he had always one most excellent idea in his mind. That was, Duty. Upon my soul, I don't believe, though I admire learning beyond everything, that he could have got a better idea out of all the books in the world, if he had learnt them every word, and been the cleverest of scholars.

My comrade and I had been quartered in Jamaica, and from there we had been drafted off to the British settlement of Belize, lying away West and North of the Mosquito coast. At Belize there had been great alarm of one cruel gang of pirates (there were always more pirates than enough in those Caribbean Seas), and as they got the better of our English cruisers by running into out-of-the-way creeks and shallows, and taking the land when they were hotly pressed, the governor of Belize had received orders from home to keep a sharp look-out for them along shore. Now, there was an armed sloop came once a-year from Port Royal, Jamaica, to the Island, laden with all manner of necessaries, to eat and to drink, and to wear, and to use in various ways; and it was aboard of that sloop which had touched at Belize, that I was a-standing, leaning over the bulwarks.

The Island was occupied by a very small English colony. It had been given the name of Silver-Store. The reason of its being so called, was, that the English colony owned and worked a silver mine over on the mainland, in Honduras, and used this island as a safe and convenient place to store their silver in, until it was annually fetched away by the sloop. It was brought down from the mine to the coast on the backs of mules, attended by friendly Indians and guarded by white men ; from thence, it was conveyed over to Silver-Store, when the weather was fair, in the canoes of that country ; from Silver Store, it was carried to Jamaica by the armed sloop once a-year, as I have already mentioned ; from Jamaica it went, of course, all over the world.

How I came to be aboard the armed sloop, is easily told. Four-and-twenty marines under command of a lieutenant—that officer's name was Linderwood—had been told off at Belize, to proceed to Silver-Store, in aid of boats and seamen stationed there for the chace of the Pirates. The island was considered a good post of observation against the pirates, both by land and sea ; neither the pirate ship nor yet her boats had been seen by any of us, but they had been so much heard of, that the rein-forcement was sent. Of that party, I was one. It included a corporal and a serjeant. Charker was corporal, and the ser-jeant's name was Drooce. He was the most tyrannical non-commissioned officer in His Majesty's service.

The night came on, soon after I had had the foregoing words with Charker. All the wonderful bright colors went out of the sea and sky, in a few minutes, and all the stars in the Heavens seemed to shine out together, and to look down at themselves in the sea, over one another's shoulders, millions deep. Next morning, we cast anchor off the Island. There was a snug harbor within a little reef ; there was a sandy beach ; there were cocoa-nut trees with high straight stems, quite bare, and foliage at the top like plumes of magnificent green feathers ; there were all the objects that are usually seen in those parts, and I am not going to describe them, having something else to tell about.

Great rejoicings, to be sure, were made on our arrival. All the flags in the place were hoisted, all the guns in the place were fired, and all the people in the place came down to look at us. One of those Sambo fellows—they call those natives Sambos, when they are half-negro and half-Indian—had come off out-side the reef, to pilot us in, and remained on board after we had let go our anchor. He was called Christian George King, and was fonder of all hands than anybody else was. Now, I con-fess, for myself, that on that first day, if I had been captain of the Christopher Columbus, instead of private in the Royal Marines, I should have kicked Christian George King—who was no more a Christian, than he was a King, or a George—over the side, without exactly knowing why, except that it was the right thing to do.

But, I must likewise confess, that I was not in a particularly pleasant humor, when I stood under arms that morning, aboard the Christopher Columbus in the harbor of the Island of Silver-Store. I had had a hard life, and the life of the English on the Island seemed too easy and too gay, to please me. "Here you are," I thought to myself, "good scholars and good livers; able to read what you like, able to write what you like, able to eat and drink what you like, and spend what you like, and do what you like; and much *you* care for a poor, ignorant Private in the Royal Marines! Yet it's hard, too, I think, that you should have all the half-pence, and I all the kicks; you all the smooth, and I all the rough; you all the oil, and I all the vinegar." It was as envious a thing to think as might be, let alone its being nonsensical; but, I thought it. I took it so much amiss, that, when a very beautiful young English lady came aboard, I grunted to myself, "Ah! *you* have got a lover, I'll be bound!" As if there was any new offence to me in that, if she had!

She was sister to the captain of our sloop, who had been in a poor way for some time, and who was so ill then that he was obliged to be carried ashore. She was the child of a military officer, and had come out there with her sister, who was married to one of the owners of the silver-mine, and who had three children with her. It was easy to see that she was the light and spirit of the Island. After I had got a good look at her, I grunted to myself again, in an even worse state of mind than before, "I'll be damned, if I don't hate him, whoever he is!"

My officer, Lieutenant Linderwood, was as ill as the captain of the sloop, and was carried ashore, too. They were both young men of about my age, who had been delicate in the West India climate. I even took *that*, in bad part. I thought I was much fitter for the work than they were, and that if all of us had our deserts, I should be both of them rolled into one. (It may be imagined what sort of an officer of marines I should have made, without the power of reading a written order. And as to any knowledge how to command the sloop—Lord! I should have sunk her in a quarter of an hour!)

However, such were my reflections; and when we men were ashore and dismissed, I strolled about the place along with Charker, making my observations in a similar spirit.

It was a pretty place: in all its arrangements partly South American and partly English, and very agreeable to look at on that account, being like a bit of home that had got chipped off and had floated away to that spot, accommodating itself to circumstances as it drifted along. The huts of the Sambos, to the number of five-and-twenty, perhaps, were down by the beach to the left of the anchorage. On the right was a sort of barrack, with a South American Flag and the Union Jack, flying from the same staff, where the little English colony could all come together, if they saw occasion. It was a walled square of building, with a sort of pleasure-ground inside, and inside that again a sunken block like a powder magazine, with a little square trench round it, and steps down to the door. Charker and I were looking in at the gate, which was not guarded; and I had said to Charker, in reference to the bit like a powder magazine, "that's where they keep the silver, you see;" and Charker had said to me, after thinking it over, "And silver an't gold. Is it, Gill?" when the beautiful young English lady I had been so bilious about, looked out of a door, or a window— at all events looked out, from under a bright awning. She no sooner saw us two in uniform, than she came out so quickly that she was still putting on her broad Mexican hat of plaited straw when we saluted.

"Would you like to come in," she said, "and see the place? It is rather a curious place."

We thanked the young lady, and said we didn't wish to be troublesome; but, she said it could be no trouble to an English soldier's daughter, to show English soldiers how their countrymen and countrywomen fared, so far away from England; and consequently we saluted again, and went in. Then, as we stood in the shade, she showed us (being as affable as beautiful), how the different families lived in their separate houses, and how there was a general house for stores, and a general reading-room, and a general room for music and dancing, and a room for Church; and how there were other houses on the rising-ground called the Signal Hill, where they lived in the hotter weather.

"Your officer has been carried up there," she said, "and my brother, too, for the better air. At present, our few residents are dispersed over both spots : deducting, that is to say, such of our number as are always going to, or coming from, or staying at, the Mine."

("*He* is among one of those parties," I thought, "and I wish somebody would knock his head off.")

"Some of our married ladies live here," she said, "during at least half the year, as lonely as widows, with their children."

"Many children here, ma'am ? "

"Seventeen. There are thirteen married ladies, and there are eight like me."

There were not eight like her—there was not one like her—in the world. She meant, single.

"Which, with about thirty Englishmen of various degrees," said the young lady, "form the little colony now on the Island. I don't count the sailors, for they don't belong to us. Nor the soldiers," she gave us a gracious smile when she spoke of the soldiers, "for the same reason."

"Nor the Sambos, ma'am," said I.

"No."

"Under your favor, and with your leave, ma'am," said I, "are they trustworthy ? "

"Perfectly ! We are all very kind to them, and they are very grateful to us."

"Indeed, ma'am ? Now—Christian George King ?——"

"Very much attached to us all. Would die for us."

She was, as in my uneducated way I have observed very beautiful women almost always to be, so composed, that her composure gave great weight to what she said, and I believed it.

Then, she pointed out to us the building like a powder magazine, and explained to us in what manner the silver was brought from the mine, and was brought over from the main-land, and was stored there. The Christopher Columbus would have a rich lading, she said, for there had been a great yield that year, a much richer yield than usual, and there was a chest of jewels besides the silver.

When we had looked about us, and were getting sheepish, through fearing we were troublesome, she turned us over to a young woman, English born but West India bred, who served her as her maid. This young woman was the widow of a non-commissioned officer in a regiment of the line. She had got married and widowed at St. Vincent, with only a few months between the two events. She was a little saucy woman, with a bright pair of eyes, rather a neat little foot and figure, and rather a neat little turned-up nose. The sort of young woman, I considered at the time, who appeared to invite you to give her a kiss, and who would have slapped your face if you accepted the invitation.

I couldn't make out her name at first; for, when she gave it in answer to my inquiry, it sounded like Beltot, which didn't sound right. But, when we came better acquainted—which was while Charker and I were drinking sugar-cane sangaree, which she made in a most excellent manner—I found that her Christian name was Isabella, which they shortened into Bell, and that the name of the deceased non-commissioned officer was Tott. Being the kind of neat little woman it was natural to make a toy of,—I never saw a woman so like a toy in my life—she had got the plaything name of Belltott. In short, she had no other name on the island. Even Mr. Commissioner Pordage (and *he* was a grave one!) formally addressed her as Mrs. Belltott. But, I shall come to Mr. Commissioner Pordage presently.

The name of the captain of the sloop was Captain Maryon, and therefore it was no news to hear from Mrs. Belltott, that his sister, the beautiful unmarried young English lady, was Miss Maryon. The novelty was, that her Christian name was Marion too. Marion Maryon. Many a time I have run off those two names in my thoughts, like a bit of verse. O many, and many, and many, a time!

We saw out all the drink that was produced, like good men and true, and then took our leaves, and went down to the beach. The weather was beautiful; the wind steady, low, and gentle; the island, a picture; the sea, a picture; the sky, a picture. In that country there are two rainy seasons in the year. One sets in at about our English Midsummer; the other, about a fortnight after our English Michaelmas. It was

the beginning of August at that time; the first of these rainy
seasons was well over; and everything was in its most beautiful
growth, and had its loveliest look upon it.

"They enjoy themselves here," I says to Charker, turning
surly again.   "This is better than private-soldiering."

We had come down to the beach, to be friendly with the
boat's-crew who were camped and hutted there; and we were
approaching towards their quarters over the sand, when
Christian George King comes up from the landing-place at a
wolf's-trot, crying, " Yup, So-Jeer ! "—which was that Sambo
Pilot's barbarous way of saying, Hallo, Soldier ! I have stated
myself to be a man of no learning, and, if I entertain prejudices,
I hope allowance may be made.   I will now confess to one.
It may be a right one or it may be a wrong one; but, I never
did like Natives, except in the form of oysters.

So, when Christian George King, who was individually unpleasant to me besides, comes a trotting along the sand,
clucking " Yup, So-Jeer !" I had a thundering good mind to
let fly at him with my right.   I certainly should have done it,
but that it would have exposed me to reprimand.

" Yup, So Jeer !" says he.   " Bad job."

" What do you mean ?" says I.

" Yup, So-Jeer !" says he, " Ship Leakee."

" Ship leaky ?" says I.

" Iss," says he, with a nod that looked as if it was jerked
out of him by a most violent hiccup—which is the way with
those savages.

I cast my eyes at Charker, and we both heard the pumps
going aboard the sloop, and saw the signal run up, " Come on
board; hands wanted from the shore." In no time some of the
sloop's liberty-men were already running down to the water's
edge, and the party of seamen, under orders against the Pirates,
were putting off to the Columbus in two boats.

" Oh Christian George King sar berry sorry !" says that
Sambo vagabond, then.   " Christian George King cry, English
fashion !" His English fashion of crying was to screw his
black knuckles into his eyes, howl like a dog, and roll himself
on his back on the sand.   It was trying not to kick him, but I
gave Charker the word, " Double quick, Harry !" and we got
down to the water's edge, and got on board the sloop.

By some means or other, she had sprung such a leak, that no pumping would keep her free; and what between the two fears that she would go down in the harbor, and that, even if she did not, all the supplies she had brought for the colony would be destroyed by the sea-water as it rose in her, there was great confusion. In the midst of it, Captain Maryon was heard hailing from the beach. He had been carried down in his hammock, and looked very bad; but, he insisted on being stood there on his feet; and I saw him, myself, come off in the boat, sitting upright in the stern-sheets, as if nothing was wrong with him.

A quick sort of council was held, and Captain Maryon soon resolved that we must all fall to work to get the cargo out, and, that when that was done, the guns and heavy matters must be got out, and that the sloop must be hauled ashore, and careened, and the leak stopped. We were all mustered (the Pirate-Chace party volunteering), and told off into parties, with so many hours of spell and so many hours of relief, and we all went at it with a will. Christian George King was entered one of the party in which I worked, at his own request, and he went at it with as good a will as any of the rest. He went at it with so much heartiness, to say the truth, that he rose in my good opinion, almost as fast as the water rose in the ship. Which was fast enough, and faster.

Mr. Commissioner Pordage kept in a red and black japanned box, like a family lump-sugar box, some document or other which some Sambo chief or other had got drunk and spilt some ink over (as well as I could understand the matter), and by that means had given up lawful possession of the Island. Through having hold of this box, Mr. Pordage got his title of Commissioner. He was styled Consul, too, and spoke of himself as "Government."

He was a stiff-jointed, high-nosed old gentleman, without an ounce of fat on him, of a very angry temper and a very yellow complexion. Mrs. Commissioner Pordage, making allowance for difference of sex, was much the same. Mr. Kitten, a small, youngish, bald, botanical and mineralogical gentleman, also connected with the mine—but everybody there was that, more or less—was sometimes called by Mr. Commissioner Pordage, his Vice-commissioner, and sometimes his Deputy-consul. Or sometimes he spoke of Mr. Kitten, merely as being "under Government."

The beach was beginning to be a lively scene with the preparations for careening the sloop, and, with cargo, and spars, and rigging, and water-casks, dotted about it, and with temporary quarters for the men rising up there out of such sails and odds and ends as could be best set on one side to make them, when Mr. Commissioner Pordage comes down in a high fluster, and asks for Captain Maryon. The Captain, ill as he was, was slung in his hammock betwixt two trees, that he might direct; and he raised his head, and answered for himself.

"Captain Maryon," cries Mr. Commissioner Pordage, "this is not official. This is not regular."

"Sir," says the Captain, "it hath been arranged with the clerk and supercargo, that you should be communicated with, and requested to render any little assistance that may lie in your power. I am quite certain that hath been duly done."

"Captain Maryon," replies Mr. Commissioner Pordage, "there hath been no written correspondence. No documents have passed, no memoranda have been made, no minutes have been made, no entries and counter-entries appear in the official muniments. This is indecent. I call upon you, sir, to desist, until all is regular, or Government will take this up."

"Sir," said Captain Maryon, chafing a little, as he looked out of his hammock; "between the chances of Government taking this up, and my ship taking herself down, I much prefer to trust myself to the former."

"You do, sir?" cries Mr. Commissioner Pordage.

"I do, sir," says Captain Maryon, lying down again.

"Then, Mr. Kitten," says the Commissioner, "send up instantly for my Diplomatic coat." .

He was dressed in a linen suit at that moment; but, Mr. Kitten started off himself and brought down the Diplomatic coat, which was a blue cloth one, gold-laced, and with a crown on the button.

"Now, Mr. Kitten," says Pordage, "I instruct you, as Vice-commissioner, and Deputy-consul of this place, to demand of Captain Maryon, of the sloop Christopher Columbus, whether he drives me to the act of putting this coat on?"

"Mr. Pordage," says Captain Maryon, looking out of his

hammock again, "as I can hear what you say, I can answer it without troubling the gentleman. I should be sorry that you should be at the pains of putting on too hot a coat on my account; but, otherwise, you may put it on hind-side before, or inside-out, or with your legs in the sleeves, or your head in the skirts, for any objection that I have to offer to your thoroughly pleasing yourself."

"Very good, Captain Maryon," says Pordage, in a tremendous passion. "Very good, sir. Be the consequences on your own head! Mr. Kitten, as it has come to this, help me on with it."

When he had given that order, he walked off in the coat, and all our names were taken, and I was afterwards told that Mr. Kitten wrote from his dictation more than a bushel of large paper on the subject, which cost more before it was done with, than ever could be calculated, and which only got done with after all, by being lost.

Our work went on merrily, nevertheless, and the Christopher Columbus, hauled up, lay helpless on her side like a great fish out of water. While she was in that state, there was a feast, or a ball, or an entertainment, or more properly all three together, given us in honor of the ship, and the ship's company, and the other visitors. At that assembly, I believe, I saw all the inhabitants then upon the Island, without any exception. I took no particular notice of more than a few, but I found it very agreeable in that little corner of the world to see the children, who were of all ages, and mostly very pretty—as they mostly are. There was one handsome elderly lady, with very dark eyes and grey hair, that I inquired about. I was told that her name was Mrs. Venning; and her married daughter, a fair slight thing, was pointed out to me by the name of Fanny Fisher. Quite a child she looked, with a little copy of herself holding to her dress; and her husband, just come back from the mine, exceeding proud of her. They were a good-looking set of people on the whole, but I didn't like them. I was out of sorts; in conversation with Charker, I found fault with all of them. I said of Mrs. Venning, she was proud; of Mrs. Fisher, she was a delicate little baby-fool. What did I think of this one? Why, he was a fine gentleman. What did I say to that one? Why, she was a fine lady. What could you

PORDAGE THREATENS TO PUT ON HIS COAT.

expect them to be (I asked Charker), nursed in that climate, with the tropical night shining for them, musical instruments playing to them, great trees bending over them, soft lamps lighting them, fire-flies sparkling in among them, bright flowers and birds brought into existence to please their eyes, delicious drinks to be had for the pouring out, delicious fruits to be got for the picking, and every one dancing and murmuring happily in the scented air, with the sea breaking low on the reef for a pleasant chorus.

"Fine gentlemen and fine ladies, Harry?" I says to Charker. "Yes, I think so! Dolls! Dolls! Not the sort of stuff for wear, that comes of poor private soldiering in the Royal Marines!"

However, I could not gainsay that they were very hos pitable people, and that they treated us uncommonly well Every man of us was at the entertainment, and Mrs. Belltott had more partners than she could dance with: though she danced all night, too. As to Jack (whether of the Christopher Columbus, or of the Pirate pursuit party, it made no difference), he danced with his brother Jack, danced with himself, danced with the moon, the stars, the trees, the prospect, anything. I didn't greatly take to the chief-officer of that party, with his bright eyes, brown face, and easy figure. I didn't much like his way when he first happened to come where we were, with Miss Maryon on his arm. "Oh, Captain Carton," she says, "here are two friends of mine!" He says, "Indeed? These two Marines?"—meaning Charker and self. "Yes," says she, "I showed these two friends of mine when they first came, all the wonders of Silver-Store." He gave us a laughing look, and says he, "You are in luck, men. I would be disrated and go before the mast to-morrow, to be shown the way upward again by such a guide. You are in luck, men." When we had saluted, and he and the young lady had waltzed away, I said, "You are a pretty fellow, too, to talk of luck. You may go to the Devil!"

Mr. Commissioner Pordage and Mrs. Commissioner, showed among the company on that occasion like the King and Queen of a much Greater Britain than Great Britain. Only two other circumstances in that jovial night made much separate impression on me. One was this. A man in our draft of marines, named Tom Packer, a wild unsteady young fellow, but the son of a respectable shipwright in Portsmouth Yard, and a good scholar who had been well brought up, comes to me after a spell of dancing, and takes me aside by the elbow, and says, swearing angrily :

"Gill Davis, I hope I may not be the death of Serjeant Drooce one day ! "

Now, I knew Drooce always had borne particularly hard on this man, and I knew this man to be of a very hot temper : so, I said :

"Tut, nonsense ! don't talk so to me !   If there's a man in the corps who scorns the name of an assassin, that man and Tom Packer are one."

Tom wipes his head, being in a mortal sweat, and says he :

"I hope so, but I can't answer for myself when he lords it over me, as he has just now done, before a woman.   I tell you what, Gill ! Mark my words ! It will go hard with Serjeant Drooce, if ever we are in an engagement together, and he has to look to me to save him.   Let him say a prayer then, if he knows one, for it's all over with him, and he is on his Death-bed.   Mark my words ! "

I did mark his words, and very soon afterwards, too, as will shortly be taken down.

The other circumstance that I noticed at that ball, was, the gaiety and attachment of Christian George King. The innocent spirits that Sambo Pilot was in, and the impossibility he found himself under of showing all the little colony, but especially the ladies and children, how fond he was of them, how devoted to them, and how faithful to them for life and death, for present, future, and everlasting, made a great impression on me. If ever a man, Sambo or no Sambo, was trustful and trusted, to what may be called quite an infantine and sweetly beautiful extent, surely, I thought that morning when I did at last lie down to rest, it was that Sambo Pilot, Christian George King.

This may account for my dreaming of him. He stuck in my sleep, cornerwise, and I couldn't get him out. He was always flitting about me, dancing round me, and peeping in over my hammock, though I woke and dozed off again fifty times. At last, when I opened my eyes, there he really was, looking in at the open side of the little dark hut ; which was made of leaves, and had Charker's hammock slung in it as well as mine.

"So-Jeer!" says he, in a sort of a low croak. "Yup!"

"Hallo!" says I, starting up. "What? You *are* there, are you?"

"Iss," says he. "Christian George King got news."

"What news has he got?"

"Pirates out!"

I was on my feet in a second. So was Charker. We were both aware that Captain Carton, in command of the boats, constantly watched the main land for a secret signal, though, of course, it was not known to such as us what the signal was.

Christian George King had vanished before we touched the ground. But, the word was already passing from hut to hut to turn out quietly, and we knew that the nimble barbarian had got hold of the truth, or something near it.

In a space among the trees behind the encampment of us visitors, naval and military, was a snugly-screened spot, where we kept the stores that were in use, and did our cookery. The word was passed to assemble here. It was very quickly given, and was given (so far as we were concerned) by Serjeant Drooce, who was as good in a soldier point of view, as he was bad in a tyrannical one. We were ordered to drop into this space, quietly, behind the trees, one by one. As we assembled here, the seamen assembled too. Within ten minutes, as I should estimate, we were all here, except the usual guard upon the beach. The beach (we could see it through the wood) looked as it always had done in the hottest time of the day. The guard were in the shadow of the sloop's hull, and nothing was moving but the sea, and that moved very faintly. Work had always been knocked off at that hour, until the sun grew less fierce, and the sea-breeze rose; so that its being holiday with us, made no difference, just then, in the look of the place. But, I may mention that it was a holiday, and the first we had had since our hard work began. Last night's ball had been given, on the leak's being repaired, and the careening done. The worst of the work was over, and to-morrow we were to begin to get the sloop afloat again.

We marines were now drawn up here, under arms. The chace-party were drawn up separate. The men of the Columbus were drawn up separate. The officers stepped out into the midst of the three parties, and spoke so as all might hear.

Captain Carton was the officer in command, and he had a spy-glass in his hand. His coxswain stood by him with another spy-glass, and with a slate on which he seemed to have been taking down signals.

"Now, men!" says Captain Carton; "I have to let you know, for your satisfaction: Firstly, that there are ten pirate-boats, strongly-manned and armed, lying hidden up a creek yonder on the coast, under the overhanging branches of the dense trees. Secondly, that they will certainly come out this night when the moon rises, on a pillaging and murdering expedition, of which some part of the main land is the object. Thirdly—don't cheer, men!—that we will give chace, and, if we can get at them, rid the world of them, please God!"

Nobody spoke, that I heard, and nobody moved, that I saw. Yet there was a kind of ring, as if every man answered and approved with the best blood that was inside of him.

"Sir," says Captain Maryon, "I beg to volunteer on this service, with my boats. My people volunteer, to the ship's boys."

"In His Majesty's name and service," the other answers, touching his hat, "I accept your aid with pleasure. Lieutenant Linderwood, how will you divide your men?"

I was ashamed—I give it out to be written down as large and plain as possible—I was heart and soul ashamed of my thoughts of those two sick officers, Captain Maryon and Lieutenant Linderwood, when I saw them, then and there. The spirit in those two gentlemen beat down their illness (and very ill I knew them to be) like Saint George beating down the Dragon. Pain and weakness, want of ease and want of rest, had no more place in their minds than fear itself. Meaning now to express for my lady to write down, exactly what I felt then and there, I felt this: "You two brave fellows that I have been so grudgeful of, I know that if you were dying you would put it off to get up and do your best, and then you would be so modest that in lying down again to die, you would hardly say, 'I did it!'"

It did me good. It really did me good.

But, to go back to where I broke off. Says Captain Carton to Lieutenant Linderwood, "Sir, how will you divide your men? There is not room for all; and a few men should, in any case, be left here."

There was some debate about it.   At last, it was resolved to leave eight Marines and four seamen on the Island, besides the sloop's two boys.   And because it was considered that the friendly Sambos would only want to be commanded in case of any danger (though none at all was apprehended there), the officers were in favour of leaving the two non-commissioned officers, Drooce and Charker.   It was a heavy disappointment to them, just as my being one of the left was a heavy disappointment to me—then, but not soon afterwards.   We men drew lots for it, and I drew "Island."   So did Tom Packer.   So, of course, did four more of our rank and file.

When this was settled, verbal instructions were given to all hands to keep the intended expedition secret, in order that the women and children might not be alarmed, or the expedition put in a difficulty by more volunteers.   The assembly was to be on that same spot, at sunset.   Every man was to keep up an appearance, meanwhile, of occupying himself in his usual way. That is to say, every man excepting four old trusty seamen, who were appointed, with an officer, to see to the arms and ammunition, and to muffle the rullocks of the boats, and to make everything as trim and swift and silent as it could be made.

The Sambo Pilot had been present all the while, in case of his being wanted, and had said to the officer in command, five hundred times over if he had said it once, that Christian George King would stay with the So-Jeers, and take care of the booffer ladies and the booffer childs—booffer being that native's expression for beautiful.   He was now asked a few questions concerning the putting off of the boats, and in particular whether there was any way of embarking at the back of the Island : which Captain Carton would have half liked to do, and then have dropped round in its shadow and slanted across to the main.   But, "No," says Christian George King. "No, no, no !   Told you so, ten time.   No, no, no !   All reef, all rock, all swim, all drown !"   Striking out as he said it, like a swimmer gone mad, and turning over on his back on dry land, and spluttering himself to death, in a manner that made him quite an exhibition.

The sun went down, after appearing to be a long time about it, and the assembly was called.   Every man answered to his name, of course, and was at his post.   It was not yet black dark, and the roll was only just gone through, when up comes Mr. Commissioner Pordage with his Diplomatic coat on.

"Captain Carton," says he, " Sir, what is this ? "

"This, Mr. Commissioner," (he was very short with him) " is an expedition against the Pirates.   It is a secret expedition, so please to keep it a secret."

" Sir," says Commissioner Pordage, "I trust there is going to be no unnecessary cruelty committed ? "

" Sir," returns the officer, " I trust not."

"That is not enough, sir," cries Commissioner Pordage, getting wroth.   "Captain Carton, I give you notice.   Government requires you to treat the enemy with great delicacy, consideration, clemency, and forbearance."

" Sir," says Captain Carton, "I am an English Officer, commanding English Men, and I hope I am not likely to disappoint the Government's just expectations.   But, I presume you know that these villains under their black flag have despoiled our countrymen of their property, burnt their homes, barbarously murdered them and their little children, and worse than murdered their wives and daughters ? "

"Perhaps I do, Captain Carton," answers Pordage, waving his hand, with dignity; "perhaps I do not. It is not customary, sir, for Government to commit itself."

"It matters very little, Mr. Pordage, whether or no. Believing that I hold my commission by the allowance of God, and not that I have received it direct from the Devil, I shall certainly use it, with all avoidance of unnecessary suffering and with all merciful swiftness of execution, to exterminate these people from the face of the earth.   Let me recommend you to go home, sir, and to keep out of the night-air."

Never another syllable did that officer say to the Commissioner, but turned away to his men.   The Commissioner buttoned his Diplomatic coat to the chin, said, " Mr. Kitten, attend me ! " gasped, half choked himself, and took himself off.

It now fell very dark, indeed.   I have seldom, if ever, seen it darker, nor yet so dark.   The moon was not due until one in the morning, and it was but a little after nine when our men lay down where they were mustered.   It was pretended that

they were to take a nap, but everybody knew that no nap was
to be got under the circumstances. Though all were very quiet,
there was a restlessness among the people; much what I have
seen among the people on a race-course, when the bell has rung
for the saddling for a great race with large stakes on it.

At ten, they put off; only one boat putting off at a time;
another following in five minutes; both then lying on their oars
until another followed. Ahead of all, paddling his own outlandish little canoe without a sound, went the Sambo pilot, to
take them safely outside the reef. No light was shown but
once, and that was in the commanding officer's own hand. I
lighted the dark lantern for him, and he took it from me when
he embarked. They had blue lights and such like with them,
but kept themselves as dark as Murder.

The expedition got away with wonderful quietness, and
Christian George King soon came back, dancing with joy.

"Yup, So-Jeer," says he to myself in a very objectionable kind
of convulsions, "Christian George King sar berry glad. Pirates
all be blown a-pieces. Yup! Yup!"

My reply to that cannibal was, "However glad you may be,
hold your noise, and don't dance jigs and slap your knees about
it, for I can't abear to see you do it."

I was on duty then; we twelve who were left, being divided
into four watches of three each, three hours' spell. I was
relieved at twelve. A little before that time, I had challenged,
and Miss Maryon and Mrs. Belltott had come in.

"Good Davis," says Miss Maryon, "what is the matter?
Where is my brother?"

I told her what was the matter, and where her brother was.

"O Heaven help him!" says she, clasping her hands and
looking up—she was close in front of me, and she looked most
lovely to be sure; "he is not sufficiently recovered, not strong
enough, for such strife!"

"If you had seen him, miss," I told her, "as I saw him
when he volunteered, you would have known that his spirit is
strong enough for any strife. It will bear his body, miss, to
wherever duty calls him. It will always bear him to an honorable life, or a brave death."

"Heaven bless you!" says she, touching my arm. "I know
it. Heaven bless you!"

Mrs. Belltott surprised me by trembling and saying nothing. They were still standing looking towards the sea and listening, after the relief had come round. It continuing very dark, I asked to be allowed to take them back. Miss Maryon thanked me, and she put her arm in mine, and I did take them back. I have now got to make a confession that will appear singular. After I had left them, I laid myself down on my face on the beach, and cried, for the first time since I had frightened birds as a boy at Snorridge Bottom, to think what a poor, ignorant, low-placed, private soldier I was.

It was only for half a minute or so. A man can't at all times be quite master of himself, and it was only for half a minute or so. Then I up and went to my hut, and turned into my hammock, and fell asleep with wet eyelashes, and a sore, sore heart. Just as I had often done when I was a child, and had been worse used than usual.

I slept (as a child under those circumstances might) very sound, and yet very sore at heart all through my sleep. I was awoke by the words, "He is a determined man." I had sprung out of my hammock, and had seized my firelock, and was standing on the ground, saying the words myself. "He is a determined man." But, the curiosity of my state was, that I seemed to be repeating them after somebody, and to have been wonderfully startled by hearing them.

As soon as I came to myself, I went out of the hut, and away to where the guard was. Charker challenged: "Who goes there?" "A friend." "Not Gill?" says he, as he shouldered his piece. "Gill," says I. "Why, what the deuce do you do, out of your hammock?" says he. "Too hot for sleep," says I; "is all right?" "Right!" says Charker, "yes, yes; all's right enough here; what should be wrong here? It's the boats that we want to know of. Except for fire-flies twinkling about, and the lonesome splashes of great creatures as they drop into the water, there's nothing going on here to ease a man's mind from the boats."

The moon was above the sea, and had risen, I should say, some half-an-hour. As Charker spoke, with his face towards the sea, I, looking landward, suddenly laid my right hand on his breast, and said, "Don't move. Don't turn. Don't raise your voice! You never saw a Maltese face here?"

"No.   What do you mean?" he asks, staring at me.

"Nor yet an English face, with one eye and a patch across the nose?"

"No.   What ails you?   What do you mean?"

I had seen both, looking at us round the stem of a cocoa-nut tree, where the moon struck them.   I had seen that Sambo Pilot, with one hand laid on the stem of the tree, drawing them back into the heavy shadow.   I had seen their naked cutlasses twinkle and shine, like bits of the moonshine in the water that had got blown ashore among the trees by the light wind.   I had seen it all, in a moment.   And I saw in a moment (as any man would), that the signalled move of the pirates on the main-land was a plot and a feint; that the leak had been made to disable the sloop; that the boats had been tempted away, to leave the Island unprotected; that the pirates had landed by some secreted way at the back; and that Christian George King was a double-dyed traitor, and a most infernal villain.

I considered, still all in one and the same moment, that Charker was a brave man, but not quick with his head; and that Serjeant Drooce, with a much better head, was close by. All I said to Charker was, "I am afraid we are betrayed.   Turn your back full to the moonlight on the sea, and cover the stem of the cocoa-nut tree which will then be right before you, at the height of a man's heart.   Are you right?"

"I am right," says Charker, turning instantly, and falling into the position with a nerve of iron; "and right an't left.   Is it, Gill?"

A few seconds brought me to Serjeant Drooce's hut.   He was fast asleep, and being a heavy sleeper, I had to lay my hand upon him to rouse him.   The instant I touched him he came rolling out of his hammock, and upon me like a tiger.   And a tiger he was, except that he knew what he was up to, in his utmost heat, as well as any man.

I had to struggle with him pretty hard to bring him to his senses, panting all the while (for he gave me a breather), "Serjeant, I am Gill Davis! Treachery! Pirates on the Island!"

The last words brought him round, and he took his hands off.   "I have seen two of them within this minute," said I. And so I told him what I had told Harry Charker.

His soldierly, though tyrannical, head was clear in an instant. He didn't waste one word, even of surprise. "Order the guard," says he, "to draw off quietly into the Fort." (They called the enclosure I have before mentioned, the Fort, though it was not much of that.) "Then get you to the Fort as quick as you can, rouse up every soul there, and fasten the gate. I will bring in all those who are up at the Signal Hill. If we are surrounded before we can join you, you must make a sally and cut us out if you can. The word among our men is, 'Women and children!'"

He burst away, like fire going before the wind over dry reeds. He roused up the seven men who were off duty, and had them bursting away with him, before they knew they were not asleep. I reported orders to Charker, and ran to the Fort, as I have never run at any other time in all my life: no, not even in a dream.

The gate was not fast, and had no good fastening: only a double wooden bar, a poor chain, and a bad lock. Those, I secured as well as they could be secured in a few seconds by one pair of hands, and so ran to that part of the building where Miss Maryon lived. I called to her loudly by her name until she answered. I then called loudly all the names I knew— Mrs. Macey (Miss Maryon's married sister), Mr. Macey, Mrs. Venning, Mr. and Mrs. Fisher, even Mr. and Mrs. Pordage. Then I called out, "All you gentlemen here, get up and defend the place! We are caught in a trap. Pirates have landed. We are attacked!"

At the terrible word "Pirates!"—for, those villains had done such deeds in those seas as never can be told in writing, and can scarcely be so much as thought of—cries and screams rose up from every part of the place. Quickly lights moved about from window to window, and the cries moved about with them, and men, women and children came flying down into the square. I remarked to myself, even then, what a number of things I seemed to see at once. I noticed Mrs. Macey coming towards me, carrying all her three children together. I noticed Mr. Pordage, in the greatest terror, in vain trying to get on his Diplomatic coat; and Mr. Kitten respectfully tying his pocket-handkerchief over Mrs. Pordage's nightcap. I noticed Mrs. Belltott run out screaming, and shrink upon the ground near me, and cover her face in her hands, and lie, all of a bundle, shivering. But, what I noticed with the greatest pleasure was, the determined eyes with which those men of the Mine that I had thought fine gentlemen, came round me with what arms they had: to the full as cool and resolute as I could be, for my life—aye, and for my soul, too, into the bargain!

The chief person being Mr. Macey, I told him how the three men of the guard would be at the gate directly, if they were not already there, and how Serjeant Drooce and the other seven were gone to bring in the outlying part of the people of Silver-Store. I next urged him, for the love of all who were dear to him, to trust no Sambo, and, above all, if he could get any good chance at Christian George King, not to lose it, but to put him out of the world. "I will follow your advice to the letter, Davis," says he; "what next?" My answer was, "I think, sir, I would recommend you next to order down such heavy furniture and lumber as can be moved, and make a barricade within the gate." "That's good again," says he; "will you see it done?" "I'll willingly help to do it," says I, "unless or until my superior, Serjeant Drooce, gives me other orders." He shook me by the hand, and having told off some of his companions to help me, bestirred himself to look to the arms and ammunition. A proper quick, brave, steady, ready gentleman!

One of their three little children was deaf and dumb. Miss Maryon had been from the first with all the children, soothing them, and dressing them (poor little things, they had been brought out of their beds), and making them believe that it was a game of play, so that some of them were now even laughing. I had been working hard with the others at the barricade, and had got up a pretty good breastwork within the gate. Drooce and the seven had come back, bringing in the people from the Signal Hill, and had worked along with us: but, I had not so much as spoken a word to Drooce, nor had Drooce so much as spoken a word to me, for we were both too busy. The breastwork was now finished, and I found Miss Maryon at my side, with a child in her arms. Her dark hair was fastened round her head with a band. She had a quantity of it, and it looked even richer and more precious, put up hastily out of her way, than I had seen it look when it was carefully arranged. She was very pale, but extraordinarily quiet and still.

"Dear good Davis," said she, "I have been waiting to speak one word to you."

I turned to her directly. If I had received a musket-ball in the heart, and she had stood there, I almost believe I should have turned to her before I dropped.

"This pretty little creature," said she, kissing the child in her arms, who was playing with her hair and trying to pull it down, "cannot hear what we say—can hear nothing. I trust you so much, and have such great confidence in you, that I want you to make me a promise."

"What is it, Miss?"

"That if we are defeated, and you are absolutely sure of my being taken, you will kill me."

"I shall not be alive to do it, Miss. I shall have died in your defence before it comes to that. They must step across my body, to lay a hand on you."

"But if you are alive, you brave soldier." How she looked at me! "And if you cannot save me from the Pirates, living, you will save me, dead. Tell me so."

Well! I told her I would do that, at the last, if all else failed. She took my hand—my rough, coarse hand—and put it to her lips. She put it to the child's lips, and the child kissed it. I believe I had the strength of half a dozen men in me, from that moment, until the fight was over.

All this time, Mr. Commissioner Pordage had been wanting to make a Proclamation to the Pirates, to lay down their arms and go away; and everybody had been hustling him about and tumbling over him, while he was calling for pen and ink to write it with. Mrs. Pordage, too, had some curious ideas about the British respectability of her nightcap (which had as many frills to it, growing in layers one inside another, as if it was a white vegetable of the artichoke sort), and she wouldn't take the nightcap off, and would be angry when it got crushed by the other ladies who were handing things about, and, in short, she gave as much trouble as her husband did. But, as we were now forming for the defence of the place, they were both poked out of the way with no ceremony. The children and ladies were got into the little trench which surrounded the silver-house (we were afraid of leaving them in any of the light buildings, lest they should be set on fire), and we made the best disposition we could.   There was a pretty good store, in point of amount, of tolerable swords and cutlasses.   Those were issued.   There were, also, perhaps a score or so of spare muskets. Those were brought out.   To my astonishment, little Mrs. Fisher that I had taken for a doll and a baby, was not only very active in that service, but volunteered to load the spare arms.

"For, I understand it well," says she, cheerfully, without a shake in her voice.

"I am a soldier's daughter and a sailor's sister, and I understand it too," says Miss Maryon, just in the same way.

Steady and busy behind where I stood, those two beautiful and delicate young women fell to handling the guns, hammering the flints, looking to the locks, and quietly directing others to pass up powder and bullets from hand to hand, as unflinching as the best of tried soldiers.

Serjeant Drooce had brought in word that the pirates were very strong in numbers—over a hundred, was his estimate—and that they were not, even then, all landed; for, he had seen them in a very good position on the further side of the Signal Hill, evidently waiting for the rest of their men to come up.   In the present pause, the first we had had since the alarm, he was telling this over again to Mr. Macey, when Mr. Macey suddenly cried out :

"The signal !   Nobody has thought of the signal !"

We knew of no signal, so we could not have thought of it. "What signal may you mean, sir?" says Serjeant Drooce, looking sharp at him.

"There is a pile of wood upon the Signal Hill.   If it could be lighted—which never has been done yet—it would be a signal of distress to the mainland."

Charker cries, directly : "Serjeant Drooce, dispatch me on that duty.   Give me the two men who were on guard with me to-night, and I'll light the fire, if it can be done."

"And if it can't, Corporal——" Mr. Macey strikes in.

"Look at these ladies and children, sir !" says Charker. "I'd sooner *light myself*, than not try any chance to save them."

We gave him a Hurrah !—it burst from us, come of it what might—and he got' his two men, and was let out at the gate, and crept away. I had no sooner come back to my place from being one of the party to handle the gate, than Miss Maryon said in a low voice behind me:

"Davis, will you look at this powder. This is not right?"

I turned my head. Christian George King again, and treachery again! Sea-water had been conveyed into the magazine, and every grain of powder was spoiled!

"Stay a moment," said Serjeant Drooce, when I had told him, without causing a movement in a muscle of his face: "look to your pouch, my lad. You Tom Packer, look to your pouch, confound you! Look to your pouches, all you Marines."

The same artful savage had got at them, somehow or another, and the cartridges were all unserviceable. "Hum!" says the Serjeant, "Look to your loading, men. You are right so far?"

Yes; we were right so far.

"Well, my lads, and gentlemen all," says the Serjeant, "this will be a hand-to-hand affair, and so much the better."

He treated himself to a pinch of snuff, and stood up, square, shouldered and broad-chested, in the light of the moon—which was now very bright—as cool as if he was waiting for a play to begin. He stood quiet, and we all stood quiet, for a matter of something like half-an-hour. I took notice from such whispered talk as there was, how little we that the silver did not belong to, thought about it, and how much the people that it did belong to, thought about it. At the end of the half-hour, it was reported from the gate that Charker and the two were falling back on us, pursued by about a dozen.

"Sally! Gate-party, under Gill Davis," says the Serjeant, "and bring 'em in! Like men, now!"

We were not long about it, and we brought them in. "Don't take me," says Charker, holding me round the neck, and stumbling down at my feet when the gate was fast, "don't take me near the ladies or the children, Gill. They had better not see Death, till it can't be helped. They'll see it soon enough."

"Harry!" I answered, holding up his head. "Comrade!"

He was cut to pieces. The signal had been secured by the first pirate party that landed; his hair was all singed off, and his face was blackened with the running pitch from a torch.

He made no complaint of pain, or of anything. "Good bye, old chap," was all he said, with a smile. "I've got my death. And Death an't life. Is it, Gill?"

Having helped to lay his poor body on one side, I went back to my post. Serjeant Drooce looked at me, with his eyebrows a little lifted. I nodded. "Close up here, men, and gentlemen all!" said the Serjeant. "A place too many, in the line."

The Pirates were so close upon us at this time, that the foremost of them were already before the gate. More and more came up with a great noise, and shouting loudly. When we believed from the sound that they were all there, we gave three English cheers. The poor little children joined, and were so fully convinced of our being at play, that they enjoyed the noise, and were heard clapping their hands in the silence that followed.

Our disposition was this, beginning with the rear. Mrs. Venning, holding her daughter's child in her arms, sat on the steps of the little square trench surrounding the silver-house, encouraging and directing those women and children as she might have done in the happiest and easiest time of her life. Then, there was an armed line, under Mr. Macey, across the width of the enclosure, facing that way and having their backs towards the gate, in order that they might watch the walls and prevent our being taken by surprise. Then, there was a space of eight or ten feet deep, in which the spare arms were, and in which Miss Maryon and Mrs. Fisher, their hands and dresses blackened with the spoilt gunpowder, worked on their knees, tying such things as knives, old bayonets, and spear-heads, to the muzzles of the useless muskets. Then, there was a second armed line, under Serjeant Drooce, also across the width of the enclosure, but facing to the gate. Then, came the breastwork we had made, with a zig-zag way through it for me and my little party to hold good in retreating, as long as we could, when we were driven from the gate. We all knew that it was impossible to hold the place long, and that our only hope was in the timely discovery of the plot by the boats, and in their coming back.

I and my men were now thrown forward to the gate. From a spy-hole, I could see the whole crowd of Pirates. There were Malays among them, Dutch, Maltese, Greeks, Sambos, Negroes, and Convict Englishmen from the West India Islands; among the last, him with the one eye and the patch across the nose.   There were some Portuguese, too, and a few Spaniards. The captain was a Portuguese; a little man with very large ear-rings under a very broad hat, and a great bright shawl twisted about his shoulders.   They were all strongly armed, but like a boarding party, with pikes, swords, cutlasses, and axes.   I noticed a good many pistols, but not a gun of any kind among them.   This gave me to understand that they had considered that a continued roll of musketry might perhaps have been heard on the mainland; also, that for the reason that fire would be seen from the mainland they would not set the Fort in flames and roast us alive; which was one of their favourite ways of carrying on.   I looked about for Christian George King, and if I had seen him I am much mistaken if he would not have received my one round of ball-cartridge in his head.   But, no Christian George King was visible.

A sort of a wild Portuguese demon, who seemed either fierce-mad or fierce-drunk—but, they all seemed one or the other—came forward with the black flag, and gave it a wave or two.   After that, the Portuguese captain called out in shrill English.   "I say you!   English fools!   Open the gate! Surrender!"

As we kept close and quiet, he said something to his men which I didn't understand, and when he had said it, the one-eyed English rascal with the patch (who had stepped out when he began), said it again in English.   It was only this.   "Boys of the black flag, this is to be quickly done.   Take all the prisoners you can.   If they don't yield, kill the children to make them.   Forward!"   Then, they all came on at the gate, and, in another half minute were smashing and splitting it in.

We struck at them through the gaps and shivers, and we dropped many of them, too; but, their very weight would have carried such a gate, if they had been unarmed.   I soon found Serjeant Drooce at my side, forming us six remaining marines in line—Tom Packer next to me—and ordering us to fall back three paces, and, as they broke in, to give them our one little volley at short distance.   "Then," says he "receive them behind your breastwork on the bayonet, and at least let every man of you pin one of the cursed cockchafers through the body."

We checked them by our fire, slight as it was, and we checked them at the breastwork. However, they broke over it like swarms of devils—they were, really and truly, more devils than men—and then it was hand to hand, indeed.

We clubbed our muskets and laid about us; even then, those two ladies—always behind me—were steady and ready with the arms. I had a lot of Maltese and Malays upon me, and, but for a broadsword that Miss Maryon's own hand put in mine, should have got my end from them. But, was that all? No. I saw a heap of banded dark hair and a white dress come thrice between me and them, under my own raised right arm, which each time might have destroyed the wearer of the white dress; and each time one of the lot went down, struck dead.

Drooce was armed with a broadsword, too, and did such things with it, that there was a cry, in half-a-dozen languages, of "Kill that serjeant!" as I knew, by the cry being raised in English, and taken up in other tongues. I had received a severe cut across the left arm a few moments before, and should have known nothing of it, except supposing that somebody had struck me a smart blow, if I had not felt weak, and seen myself covered with spouting blood, and, at the same instant of time, seen Miss Maryon tearing her dress, and binding it with Mrs. Fisher's help round the wound. They called to Tom Packer, who was scouring by, to stop and guard me for one minute, while I was bound, or I should bleed to death in trying to defend myself. Tom stopped directly, with a good sabre in his hand.

In that same moment—all things seem to happen in that same moment, at such a time—half-a-dozen had rushed howling at Serjeant Drooce. The Serjeant, stepping back against the wall, stopped one howl for ever with such a terrible blow, and waited for the rest to come on, with such a wonderfully unmoved face, that they stopped and looked at him.

"See him now!" cried Tom Packer. "Now, when I could cut him out! Gill! Did I tell you to mark my words?"

I implored Tom Packer in the Lord's name, as well as I could in my faintness, to go to the Serjeant's aid.

"I hate and detest him," said Tom, moodily wavering. "Still, he is a brave man." Then he calls out, "Serjeant Drooce, Serjeant Drooce! Tell me you have driven me too hard, and are sorry for it."

The Serjeant, without turning his eyes from his assailants, which would have been instant death to him, answers:

"No. I won't."

"Serjeant Drooce!" cries Tom, in a kind of an agony. "I have passed my word that I would never save you from Death, if I could, but would leave you to die. Tell me you have driven me too hard and are sorry for it, and that shall go for nothing."

One of the group laid the Serjeant's bald bare head open. The Serjeant laid him dead.

"I tell you," says the Serjeant, breathing a little short, and waiting for the next attack. "No. I won't. If you are not man enough to strike for a fellow-soldier because he wants help, and because of nothing else I'll go into the other world and look for a better man."

Tom swept upon them, and cut him out. Tom and he fought their way through another knot of them, and sent them flying, and came over to where I was beginning again to feel, with inexpressible joy, that I had got a sword in my hand.

They had hardly come to us, when I heard, above all the other noises, a tremendous cry of women's voices. I also saw Miss Maryon, with quite a new face, suddenly clap her two hands over Mrs. Fisher's eyes. I looked towards the silver-house, and saw Mrs. Venning—standing upright on the top of the steps of the trench, with her grey hair and her dark eyes—hide her daughter's child behind her, among the folds of her dress, strike a pirate with her other hand, and fall, shot by his pistol.

The cry rose again, and there was a terrible and confusing rush of the women into the midst of the struggle. In another moment something came tumbling down upon me that I thought was the wall. It was a heap of Sambos who had come over the wall; and of four men who clung to my legs like serpents, one who clung to my right leg was Christian George King.

"Yup, So-Jeer!" says he, "Christian George King sar berry glad So-Jeer a prisoner. Christian George King been waiting for So-Jeer sech long time. Yup, yup!"

What could I do, with five-and-twenty of them on me, but be tied hand and foot? So, I was tied hand and foot. It was all over now—boats not come back—all lost! When I was fast bound and was put up against the wall, the one-eyed English convict came up with the Portuguese Captain, to have a look at me.

"See!" says he, "Here's the determined man! If you had slept sounder, last night, you'd have slept your soundest last night, my determined man."

The Portuguese Captain laughed in a cool way, and, with the flat of his cutlass, hit me crosswise, as if I was the bough of a tree that he played with : first on the face, and then across the chest and the wounded arm. I looked him steady in the face without tumbling while he looked at me, I am happy to say ; but, when they went away, I fell, and lay there.

The sun was up, when I was roused and told to come down to the beach and be embarked. I was full of aches and pains, and could not at first remember ; but, I remembered quite soon enough. The killed were lying about all over the place, and the Pirates were burying their dead, and taking away their wounded on hastily-made litters, to the back of the Island. As for us prisoners, some of their boats had come round to the usual harbour, to carry us off. We looked a wretched few, I thought, when I got down there ; still, it was another sign that we had fought well, and made the enemy suffer.

The Portuguese Captain had all the women already embarked in the boat he himself commanded, which was just putting off when I got down. Miss Maryon sat on one side of him, and gave me a moment's look, as full of quiet courage, and pity, and confidence, as if it had been an hour long. On the other side of him was poor little Mrs. Fisher, weeping for her child and her mother. I was shoved into the same boat with Drooce and Packer, and the remainder of our party of marines : of whom we had lost two privates, besides Charker, my poor, brave comrade. We all made a melancholy passage, under the hot sun, over to the mainland. There, we landed in a solitary

place, and were mustered on the sea sand. Mr. and Mrs. Macey
and their children were amongst us, Mr. and Mrs. Pordage, Mr.
Kitten, Mr. Fisher, and Mrs. Belltott.   We mustered only
fourteen men, fifteen women, and seven children.   Those
were all that remained of the English who had lain down
to sleep last night, unsuspecting and happy, on the Island of
Silver-Store.

CHAPTER II.

THERE we all stood, huddled up on the beach under the burning sun, with the pirates closing us in on every side — as forlorn a company of helpless men, women, and children as ever was gathered together out of any nation in the world. I kept my thoughts to myself; but I did not in my heart believe that any one of our lives was worth five minutes' purchase.

The man on whose will our safety or our destruction depended was the Pirate Captain. All our eyes, by a kind of instinct, fixed themselves on him — excepting in the case of the poor children, who, too frightened to cry, stood hiding their faces against their mothers' gowns. The ruler who held all the ruffians about us in subjection, was, judging by appearances, the very last man I should have picked out as likely to fill a place of power among any body of men, good or bad, under heaven. By nation, he was a Portuguese; and, by name, he was generally spoken of among his men as The Don. He was a little, active, weazen, monkey-faced man, dressed in the brightest colours and the finest-made clothes I ever saw. His three-cornered hat was smartly cocked on one side. His coat-skirts were stiffened and stuck out, like the skirts of the dandies in the Mall in London. When the dance was given at the Island, I saw no such lace on any lady's dress there as I saw on his cravat and ruffles. Round his neck he wore a thick gold chain, with a diamond cross hanging from it. His lean, wiry, brown fingers were covered with rings. Over his shoulders, and falling down in front to below his waist, he wore a sort of sling of broad scarlet cloth, embroidered with beads and little feathers, and holding, at the lower part, four loaded pistols, two on a side, lying ready to either hand. His face was mere skin and bone, and one of his wrinkled cheeks had a blue scar running all across it, which drew up that part of his face, and showed his white shining teeth on that side of his mouth. An uglier, meaner, weaker, man-monkey to look at, I never saw; and yet there was not one of his crew, from his mate to his cabin-boy, who did not obey him as if he had been the greatest monarch in the world. As for the Sambos, including especially that evil-minded scoundrel, Christian George King, they never went near him without seeming to want to roll before him on the ground, for the sake of winning the honour of having one of his little dancing-master's feet set on their black bullock bodies.

There this fellow stood, while we were looking at him, with his hands in his pockets, smoking a cigar. His mate (the one-eyed Englishman), stood by him; a big, hulking fellow he was, who might have eaten the Captain up, pistols and all, and looked about for more afterwards. The Don himself seemed, to an ignorant man like me, to have a gift of speaking in any tongue he liked. I can testify that his English rattled out of his crooked lips as fast as if it was natural to them; making allowance, of course, for his foreign way of clipping his words.

"Now, Captain," says the big mate, running his eye over us as if we were a herd of cattle, "here they are. What's to be done with them?"

"Are they all off the Island?" says the Pirate Captain.

"All of them that are alive," says the mate.

"Good, and very good," says the captain. "Now, Giant-Georgy, some paper, a pen, and a horn of ink."

Those things were brought immediately.

"Something to write on," says the Pirate Captain. "What? Ha! why not a broad nigger back?"

He pointed with the end of his cigar to one of the Sambos. The man was pulled forward, and set down on his knees with his shoulders rounded. The Pirate Captain laid the paper on them, and took a dip of ink—then suddenly turned up his snub-nose with a look of disgust, and, removing the paper again, took from his pocket a fine cambric handkerchief edged with lace, smelt at the scent on it, and afterwards laid it delicately over the Sambo's shoulders.

"A table of black man's back, with the sun on it, close under my nose—ah, Giant-Georgy, pah ! pah !" says the Pirate Captain, putting the paper on the handkerchief, with another grimace expressive of great disgust.

He began to write immediately, waiting from time to time to consider a little with himself; and once stopping, apparently, to count our numbers as we stood before him. To think of that villain knowing how to write, and of my not being able to make so much as a decent pothook, if it had been to save my life !

When he had done, he signed to one of his men to take the scented handkerchief off the Sambo's back, and told the sailor he might keep it for his trouble. Then, holding the written paper open in his hand, he came forward a step or two closer to us, and said, with a grin, and a mock bow, which made my fingers itch with wanting to be at him :

"I have the honour of addressing myself to the ladies. According to my reckoning they are fifteen ladies in all. Does any one of them belong to the chief officer of the sloop ?"

There was a momentary silence.

"You don't answer me," says the Pirate Captain. "Now, I mean to be answered. Look here, women." He drew one of his four pistols out of his gay scarlet sling, and walked up to Tom Packer, who happened to be standing nearest to him of the men prisoners. "This is a pistol, and it is loaded. I put the barrel to the head of this man with my right hand, and I take out my watch with my left. I wait five minutes for an answer. If I don't get it in five minutes, I blow this man's brains out. I wait five minutes again, and if I don't get an answer, I blow the next man's brains out. And so I go on, if you are obstinate, and your nerves are strong, till not one of your soldiers or your sailors is left. On my word of honour, as a gentleman-buccanier, I promise you that. Ask my men if I ever broke my word."

He rested the barrel of the pistol against Tom Packer's head, and looked at his watch, as perfectly composed, in his cat-like cruelty, as if he was waiting for the boiling of an egg.

"If you think it best not to answer him, ladies," says Tom,

"never mind me. It's my trade to risk my life; and I shall lose it in a good cause."

"A brave man," said the Pirate Captain, lightly. "Well, ladies, are you going to sacrifice the brave man?"

"We are going to save him," said Miss Maryon, "as he has striven to save us. I belong to the captain of the sloop. I am his sister." She stopped, and whispered anxiously to Mrs. Macey, who was standing with her. "Don't acknowledge yourself, as I have done—you have children."

"Good!" said the Pirate Captain. "The answer is given, and the brains may stop in the brave man's head." He put his watch and pistol back, and took two or three quick puffs at his cigar to keep it alight—then handed the paper he had written on, and his penfull of ink, to Miss Maryon.

"Read that over," he said, "and sign it for yourself, and the women and children with you."

Saying those words, he turned round briskly on his heel, and began talking, in a whisper to Giant-Georgy, the big English mate. What he was talking about, of course, I could not hear; but I noticed that he motioned several times straight into the interior of the country.

"Davis," said Miss Maryon, "look at this."

She crossed before her sister, as she spoke, and held the paper which the Pirate Captain had given to her, under my eyes—my bound arms not allowing me to take it myself. Never to my dying day shall I forget the shame I felt, when I was obliged to acknowledge to Miss Maryon that I could not read a word of it!

"There are better men than me, ma'am," I said, with a sinking heart," who can read it, and advise you for the best."

"None better," she answered, quietly. "None, whose advice I would so willingly take. I have seen enough, to feel sure of that. Listen, Davis, while I read."

Her pale face turned paler still, as she fixed her eyes on the paper. Lowering her voice to a whisper, so that the women and children near might not hear, she read me these lines:

"To the Captains of English men-of-war, and to the commanders of vessels of other nations, cruising in the Caribbean Seas.

"The precious metal and the jewels laid up in the English Island of Silver-Store, are in the possession of the Buccaniers, at sea.

"The women and children of the Island of Silver-Store, to the number of Twenty-Two, are in the possession of the Buccaniers, on land.

"They will be taken up the country, with fourteen men prisoners (whose lives the Buccaniers have private reasons of their own for preserving), to a place of confinement, which is unapproachable by strangers. They will be kept there until a certain day, previously agreed on between the Buccaniers at sea, and the Buccaniers on land.

"If, by that time, no news from the party at sea, reaches the party on land, it will be taken for granted that the expedition which conveys away the silver and jewels has been met, engaged, and conquered by superior force; that the Treasure has been taken from its present owners; and that the Buccaniers guarding it, have been made prisoners, to be dealt with according to the law.

"The absence of the expected news at the appointed time, being interpreted in this way, it will be the next object of the Buccaniers on land to take reprisals for the loss and the injury inflicted on their companions at sea. The lives of the women and children of the Island of Silver-Store are absolutely at their mercy; and those lives will pay the forfeit, if the Treasure is taken away, and if the men in possession of it come to harm.

"This paper will be nailed to the lid of the largest chest taken from the Island. Any officer whom the chances of war may bring within reading distance of it, is warned to pause and consider, before his conduct signs the death-warrant of the women and children of an English colony.

"Signed, under the Black Flag,
"PEDRO MENDEZ,

"Commander of the Buccaniers, and Chief of the Guard over the English Prisoners."

"The statement above written, in so far as it regards the situation we are now placed in, may be depended on as the truth.

"Signed on behalf of the imprisoned women and children of the Island of Silver-Store."

"Beneath this last line," said Miss Maryon, pointing to it, "is a blank space, in which I am expected to sign my name."

"And in five minutes' time," added the Pirate Captain, who had stolen close up to us, "or the same consequences will follow which I had the pleasure of explaining to you a few minutes ago."

He again drew out his watch and pistol; but, this time, it was my head that he touched with the barrel.

"When Tom Packer spoke for himself, miss, a little while ago," I said, "please to consider that he spoke for me."

T

"Another brave man!" said the Pirate Captain, with his ape's grin. "Am I to fire my pistol this time, or am I to put it back again as I did before?"

Miss Maryon did not seem to hear him. Her kind eyes rested for a moment on my face, and then looked up to the bright Heaven above us.

"Whether I sign, or whether I do not sign," she said, "we are still in the hands of God, and the future which His wisdom has appointed will not the less surely come."

With those words she placed the paper on my breast, signed it, and handed it back to the Pirate Captain.

"This is our secret, Davis," she whispered. "Let us keep the dreadful knowledge of it to ourselves as long as we can."

I have another singular confession to make — I hardly expect anybody to believe me when I mention the circumstance —but it is not the less the plain truth that, even in the midst of that frightful situation, I felt, for a few moments, a sensation of happiness while Miss Maryon's hand was holding the paper on my breast, and while her lips were telling me that there was a secret between us which we were to keep together.

The Pirate Captain carried the signed paper at once to his mate.

"Go back to the Island," he says, "and nail that with your own hands on the lid of the largest chest. There is no occasion to hurry the business of shipping the Treasure, because there is nobody on the Island to make signals that may draw attention to it from the sea. I have provided for that; and I have provided for the chance of your being outmanœuvred afterwards, by English, or other cruisers. Here are your sailing orders" (he took them from his pocket while he spoke), "your directions for the disposal of the Treasure, and your appointment of the day and the place for communicating again with me and my prisoners. I have done my part—go you, now, and do yours."

Hearing the clearness with which he gave his orders; knowing what the devilish scheme was that he had invented for preventing the recovery of the Treasure, even if our ships happened to meet and capture the pirates at sea ; remembering what the look and the speech of him had been, when he put his pistol to my head and Tom Packer's; I began to understand how it was that this little, weak, weazen, wicked spider had got the first place and kept it among the villains about him.

The mate moved off, with his orders, towards the sea. Before he got there, the Pirate Captain beckoned another of the crew to come to him ; and spoke a few words in his own, or in some other foreign language. I guessed what they meant, when I saw thirty of the pirates told off together, and set in a circle all round us. The rest were marched away after the mate. In the same manner the Sambos were divided next. Ten, including Christian George King, were left with us ; and the others were sent down to the canoes. When this had been done, the Pirate Captain looked at his watch ; pointed to some trees, about a mile off, which fringed the land as it rose from the beach ; said to an American among the pirates round us, who seemed to hold the place of second mate, " In two hours from this time ; " and then walked away briskly, with one of his men after him, to some baggage piled up below us on the beach.

We were marched off at once to the shady place under the trees, and allowed to sit down there, in the cool, with our guard in a ring round us. Feeling certain from what I saw, and from what I knew to be contained in the written paper signed by Miss Maryon, that we were on the point of undertaking a long journey up the country, I anxiously examined my fellow prisoners to see how fit they looked for encountering bodily hardship and fatigue : to say nothing of mental suspense and terror, over and above.

With all possible respect for an official gentleman, I must admit that Mr. Commissioner Pordage struck me as being, beyond any comparison, the most helpless individual in our unfortunate company. What with the fright he had suffered, the danger he had gone through, and the bewilderment of finding himself torn clean away from his safe Government moorings, his poor unfortunate brains seemed to be as completely discomposed as his Diplomatic coat. He was perfectly harmless and quiet, but also perfectly light-headed — as anybody could discover who looked at his dazed eyes or listened to his maundering talk. I tried him with a word or two about our miserable situation ; thinking that, if any subject would get a trifle of sense out of him, it must surely be that.

"You will observe," said Mr. Pordage, looking at the torn cuffs of his Diplomatic coat instead of at me, "that I cannot take cognisance of our situation. No memorandum of it has been drawn up; no report in connexion with it has been presented to me. I cannot possibly recognise it until the necessary minutes and memorandums and reports have reached me through the proper channels. When our miserable situation presents itself to me, on paper, I shall bring it under the notice of Government; and Government, after a proper interval, will bring it back again under my notice; and then I shall have something to say about it. Not a minute before,—no, my man, not a minute before!"

Speaking of Mr. Pordage's wanderings of mind, reminds me that it is necessary to say a word next, about the much more serious case of Serjeant Drooce. The cut on his head, acted on by the heat of the climate, had driven him, to all appearance, stark mad. Besides the danger to himself, if he broke out before the Pirates, there was the danger to the women and children, of trusting him among them—a misfortune which, in our captive condition, it was impossible to avoid. Most providentially, however (as I found on inquiry), Tom Packer, who had saved his life, had a power of controlling him, which none of the rest of us possessed. Some shattered recollection of the manner in which he had been preserved from death, seemed to be still left in a corner of his memory. Whenever he showed symptoms of breaking out, Tom looked at him, and repeated with his hand and arm the action of cutting out right and left which had been the means of his saving the serjeant. On seeing that, Drooce always huddled himself up close to Tom, and fell silent. We,—that is, Packer and I—arranged it together that he was always to keep near Drooce, whatever happened, and however far we might be marched before we reached the place of our imprisonment.

The rest of us men—meaning Mr. Macey, Mr. Fisher, two

of my comrades of the Marines, and five of the sloop's crew—
were, making allowance for a little smarting in our wounds, in
tolerable health, and not half so much broken in spirit by troubles,
past, present, and to come, as some persons might be apt to
imagine. As for the seamen, especially, no stranger who looked
at their jolly brown faces would ever have imagined that they
were prisoners, and in peril of their lives. They sat together,
chewing their quids, and looking out good-humouredly at the
sea, like a gang of liberty-men resting themselves on shore.
"Take it easy, soldier," says one of the six, seeing me looking
at him. "And, if you can't do that, take it as easy as you can."
I thought, at the time, that many a wiser man might have given
me less sensible advice than this, though it was only offered by
a boatswain's mate.

A movement among the Pirates attracted my notice to the
beach below us, and I saw their Captain approaching our halting-
place, having changed his fine clothes for garments that were fit
to travel in.

His coming back to us had the effect of producing unmis-
takable signs of preparation for a long journey. Shortly after he
appeared, three Indians came up, leading three loaded mules; and
these were followed, in a few minutes, by two of the Sambos,
carrying between them a copper full of smoking meat and broth.
After having been shared among the Pirates, this mess was set
down before us, with some wooden bowls floating about in it, to
dip out the food with. Seeing that we hesitated before touching
it, the Pirate Captain recommended us not to be too mealy-
mouthed, as that was meat from our own stores on the Island,
and the last we were likely to taste for a long time to come. The
sailors, without any more ado about it, professed their readiness
to follow this advice, muttering among themselves that good
meat was a good thing, though the devil himself had cooked it.
The Pirate Captain then, observing that we were all ready to
accept the food, ordered the bonds that confined the hands of
us men to be loosened and cast off, so that we might help
ourselves. After we had served the women and children, we
fell to. It was a good meal—though I can't say that I myself
had much appetite for it. Jack, to use his own phrase, stowed
away a double allowance. The jolly faces of the seamen

lengthened a good deal, however, when they found there was nothing to drink afterwards but plain water. One of them, a fat man, named Short, went so far as to say that, in the turn things seemed to have taken, he should like to make his will before we started, as the stoppage of his grog and the stoppage of his life were two events that would occur uncommonly close together.

When we had done, we were all ordered to stand up. The Pirates approached me and the other men, to bind our arms again; but, the Captain stopped them.

"No," says he. "I want them to get on at a good pace; and they will do that best with their arms free. Now, prisoners," he continued, addressing us, "I don't mean to have any lagging on the road. I have fed you up with good meat, and you have no excuse for not stepping out briskly—women, children, and all. You men are without weapons and without food, and you know nothing of the country you are going to travel through. If you are mad enough, in this helpless condition, to attempt escaping on the march, you will be shot, as sure as you all stand there,—and if the bullet misses, you will starve to death in forests that have no path and no end."

Having addressed us in those words, he turned again to his men. I wondered then, as I had wondered once or twice already, what those private reasons might be, which he had mentioned in his written paper, for sparing the lives of us male prisoners. I hoped he would refer to them now—but I was disappointed.

"While the country allows it," he went on, addressing his crew, "march in a square, and keep the prisoners inside. Whether it is man, woman, or child, shoot any one of them who tries to escape, on peril of being shot yourselves if you miss. Put the Indians and mules in front, and the Sambos next to them. Draw up the prisoners all together. Tell off seven men to march before them, and seven more for each side; and leave the other nine for the rear-guard. A fourth mule for me, when I get tired, and another Indian to carry my guitar."

His guitar! To think of the murderous thief having a turn for strumming tunes, and wanting to cultivate it on such an expedition as ours! I could hardly believe my eyes when I saw the guitar brought forward in a neat green case, with the piratical skull and cross-bones and the Pirate Captain's initials painted on it in white.

"I can stand a good deal," whispers Tom Packer to me, looking hard at the guitar; "but con-found me, Davis, if it's not a trifle too much to be taken prisoner by such a fellow as that!"

The Pirate Captain lights another cigar.

"March!" says he, with a screech like a cat, and a flourish with his sword, of the sort that a stage-player would give at the head of a mock army.

We all moved off, leaving the clump of trees to the right, going, we knew not whither, to unknown sufferings and an unknown fate. The land that lay before us was wild and open, without fences or habitations. Here and there, cattle wandered about over it, and a few stray Indians. Beyond, in the distance, as far as we could see, rose a prospect of mountains and forests. Above us, was the pitiless sun, in a sky that was too brightly blue to look at. Behind us, was the calm murmuring ocean, with the dear island home which the women and children had lost, rising in the distance like a little green garden on the bosom of the sea. After half-an-hour's walking, we began to descend into the plain, and the last glimpse of the Island of Silver-Store disappeared from our view.

The order of march which we prisoners now maintained among ourselves, being the order which, with certain occasional variations, we observed for the next three days, I may as well give some description of it in this place, before I get occupied with other things, and forget it.

I myself, and the sailor I have mentioned under the name of Short, led the march. After us came Miss Maryon, and Mr. and Mrs. Macey. They were followed by two of my comrades of the Marines, with Mrs. Pordage, Mrs. Belltott, and two of the strongest of the ladies to look after them. Mr. Fisher, the ship's boy, and the three remaining men of the sloop's crew, with the rest of the women and children came next; Tom Packer, taking care of Serjeant Drooce, brought up the rear. So long as we got on quickly enough, the pirates showed no disposition to interfere with our order of march; but, if there were any signs of lagging—and God knows it was hard enough work for a man to walk under that burning sun! —the villains threatened the weakest of our company with the points of their swords. The younger among the children gave out, as might have been expected, poor things, very early on the march. Short and I set the example of taking two of them up, pick-a-back, which was followed directly by the rest of the men. Two of Mrs. Macey's three children fell to our share; the eldest, travelling behind us on his father's back. Short hoisted the next in age, a girl, on his broad shoulders. I see him now as if it was yesterday, with the perspiration pouring down his fat face and bushy whiskers, rolling along as if he was on the deck of a ship, and making a sling of his neck-hand-kerchief, with his clever sailor's fingers, to support the little girl on his back. "I expect you'll marry me, my darling, when you grow up," says he, in his oily, joking voice. And the poor child, in her innocence, laid her weary head down on his shoulder, and gravely and faithfully promised that she would.

A lighter weight fell to my share. I had the youngest of the children, the pretty little boy, already mentioned, who had been deaf and dumb from his birth. His mother's voice trembled sadly, as she thanked me for taking him up, and tenderly put his little dress right while she walked behind me. "He is very little and light of his age," says the poor lady, trying hard to speak steady. "He won't give you much trouble, Davis—he has always been a very patient child from the first." The boy's little frail arms clasped themselves round my neck while she was speaking; and something or other seemed to stop in my throat the cheerful answer that I wanted to make. I walked on with what must have looked, I am afraid, like a gruff silence; the poor child humming softly on my back, in his unchanging, dumb way, till he hummed himself to sleep. Often and often, since that time, in dreams, I have felt those small arms round my neck again, and have heard that dumb murmuring song in my ear, dying away fainter and fainter, till nothing was left but the light breath rising and falling regularly on my cheek, telling me that my little fellow-prisoner had forgotten his troubles in sleep.

We marched, as well as I could guess, somewhere about seven miles that day—a short spell enough, judging by distance, but a terrible long one judging by heat.   Our halting place was by the banks of a stream, across which, at a little distance, some wild pigs were swimming as we came up.   Beyond us, was the same view of forests and mountains that I have already mentioned; and all round us, was a perfect wilderness of flowers. The shrubs, the bushes, the ground, all blazed again with magnificent colours, under the evening sun.   When we were ordered to halt, wherever we set a child down, there that child had laps and laps full of flowers growing within reach of its hand.   We sat on flowers, eat on flowers, slept at night on flowers —any chance handful of which would have been worth a golden guinea among the gentlefolks in England.   It was a sight not easily described, to see niggers, savages, and Pirates, hideous, filthy, and ferocious in the last degree to look at, squatting about grimly upon a natural carpet of beauty, of the sort that is painted in pictures with pretty fairies dancing on it.

The mules were unloaded, and left to roll among the flowers to their hearts' content.   A neat tent was set up for the Pirate Captain, at the door of which, after eating a good meal, he laid himself down in a languishing attitude, with a nosegay in the bosom of his waistcoat, and his guitar on his knees, and jingled away at the strings, singing foreign songs, with a shrill voice and with his nose conceitedly turned up in the air.   I was obliged to caution Short and the sailors—or they would, to a dead certainty, have put all our lives in peril by openly laughing at him.

We had but a poor supper that night.   The Pirates now kept the provisions they had brought from the Island, for their own use; and we had to share the miserable starvation diet of the country, with the Indians and the Sambos.   This consisted of black beans fried, and of things they call Tortillas, meaning, in plain English, flat cakes made of crushed Indian corn, and baked on a clay griddle.   Not only was this food insipid, but the dirty manner in which the Indians prepared it, was disgusting.   However, complaint was useless : for we could see

for ourselves that no other provision had been brought for the
prisoners.   I heard some grumbling among our men, and some
little fretfulness among the children, which their mothers soon
quieted.   I myself was indifferent enough to the quality of the
food; for I had noticed a circumstance, just before it was brought
to us, which occupied my mind with more serious considerations.
One of the mules was unloaded near us, and I observed among
the baggage a large bundle of new axes, doubtless taken from
some ship.   After puzzling my brains for some time to know
what they could be wanted for, I came to the conclusion that
they were to be employed in cutting our way through, when we
came to the forests.   To think of the kind of travelling which
these preparations promised—if the view I took of them was
the right one—and then to look at the women and children,
exhausted by the first day's march, was sufficient to make any
man uneasy.   It weighed heavily enough on my mind, I know,
when I woke up among the flowers, from time to time, that
night.

Our sleeping arrangements, though we had not a single
civilised comfort, were, thanks to the flowers, simple and easy
enough.   For the first time in their lives, the women and children
laid down together, with the sky for a roof, and the kind earth
for a bed.   We men shook ourselves down, as well as we could,
all round them; and the Pirates, relieving guard regularly, ranged
themselves outside of all.   In that tropical climate, and at that
hot time, the night was only pleasantly cool.   The bubbling of
the stream, and, now and then, the course of the breeze through
the flowers, was all we heard.   During the hours of darkness, it
occurred to me—and I have no doubt the same idea struck my
comrades—that a body of determined men, making a dash for
it, might now have stood a fair chance of escaping.   We were
still near enough to the sea-shore to be certain of not losing our
way; and the plain was almost as smooth, for a good long run,
as a natural race-course.   However, the mere act of dwelling on
such a notion, was waste of time and thought, situated as we
were with regard to the women and children.   They were, so to
speak, the hostages who insured our submission to captivity, or
to any other hardship that might be inflicted on us; a result
which I have no doubt the Pirate Captain had foreseen, when

he made us all prisoners together on taking possession of the Island.

We were roused up at four in the morning, to travel on before the heat set in; our march under yesterday's broiling sun having been only undertaken for the purpose of getting us away from the sea-shore, and from possible help in that quarter, without loss of time. We forded the stream, wading through it waist-deep: except the children, who crossed on our shoulders. An hour before noon, we halted under two immense wild cotton-trees, about half a mile from a little brook, which probably ran into the stream we had passed in the morning. Late in the afternoon we were on foot again, and encamped for the night at three deserted huts, built of mud and poles. There were the remains of an enclosure here, intended, as I thought, for cattle; and there was an old well, from which our supply of water was got. The greater part of the women were very tired and sorrowful that night; but Miss Maryon did wonders in cheering them up.

On the third morning, we began to skirt the edge of a mountain, carrying our store of water with us from the well. We men prisoners had our full share of the burden. What with that, what with the way being all up-hill, and what with the necessity of helping on the weaker members of our company, that day's march was the hardest I remember to have ever got through. Towards evening, after resting again in the middle of the day, we stopped for the night on the verge of the forest. A dim, lowering, awful sight it was, to look up at the mighty wall of trees, stretching in front, and on either side of us without a limit and without a break. Through the night, though there was no wind blowing over our encampment, we heard deep, moaning, rushing sounds rolling about, at intervals, in the great inner wilderness of leaves; and, now and then, those among us who slept, were startled up by distant crashes in the depths of the forest—the death-knells of falling trees. We kept fires alight, in case of wild animals stealing out on us in the darkness; and the flaring red light, and the thick, winding smoke, alternately showed and hid the forest-prospect in a strangely treacherous and ghostly way. The children shuddered with fear; even the Pirate

Captain forgot, for the first time, to jingle his eternal guitar.

When we were mustered in the morning for the march, I fully expected to see the axes unpacked. To my surprise, they were not disturbed. The Indians drew their long chopping-knives (called machetes in the language of that country); made for a place among the trees where I could see no signs of a path; and began cutting at the bushes and shrubs, and at the wild vines and creepers, twirling down together in all sorts of fantastic forms from the lofty branches. After clearing a few dozen yards inwards they came out to us again, whooping and showing their wicked teeth, as they laid hold of the mules' halters to lead them on. The Pirate Captain, before we moved after, took out a pocket compass, set it, pondered over it for some time, shrugged his shoulders, and screeched out " March," as usual. We entered the forest, leaving behind us the last chance of escape, and the last hope of ever getting back to the regions of humanity and civilisation. By this time, we had walked inland, as nearly as I cou'd estimate, about thirty miles.

The order of our march was now, of necessity, somewhat changed. We all followed each other in a long line, shut in, however, as before, in front and in rear, by the Indians, the Sambos, and the pirates. Though none of us could see a vestige of any path, it was clear that our guides knew where they were going; for, we were never stopped by any obstacles, except the shrubs and wild-vines which they could cut through with their chopping-knives. Sometimes, we marched under great branches which met like arches high over our heads. Sometimes, the boughs were so low that we had to stoop to pass under them. Sometimes, we wound in and out among mighty trunks of trees, with their gnarled roots twisting up far above the ground, and with creepers in full flower twining down in hundreds from their lofty branches. The size of the leaves and the countless multitude of the trees, shut out the sun, and made a solemn dimness which it was awful and without hope to walk through. Hours would pass without our hearing a sound but the dreary rustle of our own feet over the leafy ground. At other times, whole troops of parrots, with feathers of all the colours of the rainbow, chattered and shrieked at us; and processions of monkeys, fifty or sixty at a time, followed our progress in the boughs overhead: passing through the thick leaves with a sound like the rush of a steady wind.   Every now and then, the children were startled by lizard-like creatures, three feet long, running up the trunks of the trees as we passed by them; more than once, swarms of locusts tormented us, startled out of their hiding-places by the monkeys in the boughs.   For five days we marched incessantly through this dismal forest-region, only catching a clear glimpse of the sky above us, on three occasions in all that time.   The distance we walked each day seemed to be regulated by the positions of springs and streams in the forest, which the Indians knew of.   Sometimes those springs and streams lay near together; and our day's work was short.   Sometimes they were far apart; and the march was long and weary.   On all occasions, two of the Indians, followed by two of the Sambos, disappeared as soon as we encamped for the night; and returned, in a longer or shorter time, bringing water with them.   Towards the latter part of the journey, weariness had so completely mastered the weakest among our company, that they ceased to take notice of anything.   They walked without looking to the right or to the left, and they eat their wretched food and lay down to sleep with a silent despair that was shocking.   Mr. Pordage left off maundering now, and Serjeant Drooce was so quiet and biddable, that Tom Packer had an easy time of it with him at last.   Those among us who still talked, began to get a habit of dropping our voices to a whisper. Shoit's jokes languished and dwindled; Miss Maryon's voice, still kind and tender as ever, began to lose its clearness; and the poor children, when they got weary and cried, shed tears silently, like old people.   It seemed as if the darkness and the hush of the endless forest had cast its shadow on our spirits, and had stolen drearily into our inmost hearts.

On the sixth day, we saw the blessed sunshine on the ground before us, once more.   Prisoners as we were, there was a feeling of freedom on stepping into the light again, and on looking up, without interruption, into the clear blue Heaven, from which no human creature can keep any other human creature, when the

time comes for rising to it.   A turn in the path brought us out
suddenly at an Indian village—a wretched place, made up of
two rows of huts built with poles, the crevices between them
stopped with mud, and the roofs thatched in the coarsest manner
with palm-leaves.   The savages squatted about, jumped to their
feet in terror as we came in view ; but, seeing the Indians at
the head of our party, took heart, and began chattering and
screeching, just like the parrots we had left in the forest.   Our
guides answered in their gibberish ; some lean, half-wild dogs
yelped and howled incessantly ; and the Pirates discharged their
muskets and loaded them again, to make sure that their powder
had not got damp on the march.   No want of muskets among
them now !   The noise and the light and the confusion, after
the silence, darkness, and discipline that we had been used to
for the last five days, so bewildered us all, that it was quite a
relief to sit down on the ground and let the guard about us shut
out our view on every side.

"Davis !   Are we at the end of the march ?" says Miss
Maryon, touching my arm.

The other women looked anxiously at me, as she put the
question.   I got on my feet, and saw the Pirate Captain communicating with the Indians of the village.   His hands were
making signs in the fussy foreign way, all the time he was
speaking.   Sometimes, they pointed away to where the forest
began again beyond us ; and sometimes they went up both
together to his mouth, as if he was wishful of getting a fresh
supply of the necessaries of life.

My eyes next turned towards the mules.   Nobody was
employed in unpacking the baggage ; nobody went near that
bundle of axes which had weighed on my mind so much already,
and the mystery of which still tormented me in secret.   I came
to the conclusion that we were not yet at the end of our journey ;
I communicated my opinion to Miss Maryon.   She got up herself,
with my help, and looked about her, and made the remark, very
justly, that all the huts in the village would not suffice to hold
us.   At the same time, I pointed out to her that the mule which
the Pirate Captain had ridden had been relieved of his saddle,
and was being led away, at that moment, to a patch of grass
behind one of the huts.

"That looks as if we were not going much farther on," says I.

"Thank Heaven if it be so, for the sake of the poor children!" says Miss Maryon. "Davis, suppose something happened which gave us a chance of escaping? Do you think we could ever find our way back to the sea?"

"Not a hope of getting back, miss. If the Pirates were to let us go this very instant, those pathless forests would keep us in prison for ever."

"Too true! Too true!" she said, and said no more.

In another half-hour we were roused up, and marched away from the village (as I had thought we should be) into the forest again. This time, though there was by no means so much cutting through the underwood needed as in our previous experience, we were accompanied by at least a dozen Indians, who seemed to me to be following us out of sheer idleness and curiosity. We had walked, as well as I could calculate, more than an hour, and I was trudging along with the little deaf-and-dumb boy on my back, as usual, thinking, not very hopefully, of our future prospects, when I was startled by a moan in my ear from the child. One of his arms was trembling round my neck, and the other pointed away towards my right hand. I looked in that direction—and there, as if it had started up out of the ground to dispute our passage through the forest, was a hideous monster carved in stone, twice my height at least. The thing loomed out of a ghostly white, against the dark curtain of trees all round it. Spots of rank moss stuck about over its great glaring stone-face; its stumpy hands were tucked up into its breast; its legs and feet were four times the size of any human limbs; its body and the flat space of spare stone which rose above its head, were all covered with mysterious devices— little grinning men's faces, heads of crocodiles and apes, twisting knots and twirling knobs, strangely shaped leaves, winding lattice-work; legs, arms, fingers, toes, skulls, bones, and such like. The monstrous statue leaned over on one side, and was only kept from falling to the ground by the roots of a great tree which had wound themselves all round the lower half of it. Altogether, it was as horrible and ghastly an object to come upon suddenly, in the unknown depths of a great forest, as the mind (or, at all events, my mind) can conceive. When I say that the first meeting with the statue struck me speechless, nobody can wonder that the children actually screamed with terror at the sight of it.

"It's only a great big doll, my darling," says Short, at his wit's end how to quiet the little girl on his back. "We'll get a nice soft bit of wood soon, and show these nasty savages how to make a better one."

While he was speaking, Miss Maryon was close behind me, soothing the deaf-and-dumb boy by signs which I could not understand.

"I have heard of these things, Davis," she says. "They are idols, made by a lost race of people, who lived, no one can say how many hundred or how many thousand years ago. That hideous thing was carved and worshipped while the great tree that now supports it was yet a seed in the ground. We must get the children used to these stone monsters. I believe we are coming to many more of them. I believe we are close to the remains of one of those mysterious ruined cities which have long been supposed to exist in this part of the world."

Before I could answer, the word of command from the rear drove us on again. In passing the idol, some of the Pirates fired their muskets at it. The echoes from the reports rang back on us with a sharp rattling sound. We pushed on a few paces, when the Indians a-head suddenly stopped, flourished their chopping-knives, and all screamed out together "El Palacio!" The Englishmen among the Pirates took up the cry, and, running forward through the trees on either side of us, roared out, "The Palace!" Other voices joined theirs in other tongues; and, for a minute or two, there was a general confusion of everybody,—the first that had occurred since we were marched away, prisoners, from the sea-shore.

I tightened my hold of the child on my back; took Miss Maryon closer to me, to save her from being roughly jostled by the men about us; and marched up as near to the front as the press and the trees would let me. Looking over the heads of the Indians, and between the trunks, I beheld a sight which I shall never forget: no, not to my dying day.

A wilderness of ruins spread out before me, overrun by a forest of trees. In every direction, look where I would, a frightful confusion of idols, pillars, blocks of stone, heavy walls, and flights of steps, met my eye; some, whole and upright; others, broken and scattered on the ground; and all, whatever their condition, overgrown and clasped about by roots, branches, and curling vines, that writhed round them like so many great snakes. Every here and there, strange buildings stood up, with walls on the tops of which three men might have marched abreast—buildings with their roofs burst off or tumbled in, and with the trees springing up from inside, and waving their restless shadows mournfully over the ruins. High in the midst of this desolation, towered a broad platform of rocky earth, scraped away on three sides, so as to make it unapproachable except by scaling ladders. On the fourth side, the flat of the platform was reached by a flight of stone steps, of such mighty size and strength that they might have been made for the use of a race of giants. They led to a huge building girded all round with a row of thick pillars, long enough and broad enough to cover the whole flat space of ground; solid enough, as to the walls, to stand for ever; but broken in, at most places, as to the roof; and overshadowed by the trees that sprang up from inside, like the smaller houses already mentioned, below it. This was the dismal ruin which was called the Palace; and this was the Prison in the Woods which was to be the place of our captivity.

The screeching voice of the Pirate Captain restored order in our ranks, and sent the Indians forward with their chopping-knives to the steps of the Palace. We were directed to follow them across the ruins, and in and out among the trees. Out of every ugly crevice and crack in the great stairs, there sprouted up flowers, long grasses, and beautiful large-leaved plants and bushes. When we had toiled to the top of the flight, we could look back from the height over the dark waving top of the forest behind us. More than a glimpse of the magnificent sight, however, was not allowed: we were ordered still to follow the Indians. They had already disappeared in the inside of the Palace; and we went in after them.

We found ourselves, first, under a square portico, supported upon immense flat slabs of stone, which were carved all over, at top and bottom, with death's-heads set in the midst of circles of sculptured flowers. I guessed the length of the portico to be, at the very least, three hundred feet. In the inside wall of it, appeared four high gaping doorways; three of them were entirely choked up by fallen stones: so jammed together, and so girt about by roots and climbing plants, that no force short of a blast of gunpowder, could possibly have dislodged them. The fourth entrance had, at some former time, been kept just clear enough to allow of the passing of one man at once through the gap that had been made in the fallen stones. Through this, the only passage left into the Palace, or out of it, we followed the Indians into a great hall, nearly one half of which was still covered by the remains of the roof. In the unsheltered half: surrounded by broken stones and with a carved human head, five times the size of life, leaning against it . rose the straight, naked trunk of a beautiful tree, that shot up high above the ruins, and dropped its enormous branches from the very top of it, bending down towards us, in curves like plumes of immense green feathers. In this hall, which was big enough to hold double our number, we were ordered to make a halt, while the Pirate Captain, accompanied by three of his crew, followed the Indians through a doorway, leading off to the left hand, as we stood with our backs to the portico. In front of us, towards the right, was another doorway, through which we could see some of the Indians, cutting away with their knives, right and left, at the overspreading underwood. Even the noise of the hacking, and the hum and murmur of the people outside, who were unloading the mules, seemed to be sounds too faint and trifling to break the awful stillness of the ruins. To my ears, at least, the unearthly silence was deepened rather than broken by the few feeble sounds which tried to disturb it. The wailings of the poor children were stifled within them. The whispers of the women, and the heavy breathing of the overlaboured men, sank and sank gradually till they were heard no more. Looking back now, at the whole course of our troubles, I think I can safely say that nothing— not even the first discovery of the treachery on the Island— tried our courage and endurance like that interval of speechless waiting in the Palace, with the hush of the ruined city, and the dimness of the endless forest, all about us.

When we next saw the Pirate Captain, he appeared at the doorway to the right, just as the Pirates began to crowd in from the portico, with the baggage they had taken from the mules.

"There is the way for the Buccaniers," squeaks the Pirate Captain, addressing the American mate, and pointing to the doorway on the left. "Three big rooms, that will hold you all, and that have more of the roof left on them than any of the others. The prisoners," he continues, turning to us, and pointing to the doorway behind him, "will file in, that way, and will find two rooms for them, with the ceilings on the floor, and the trees in their places. I myself, because my soul is big, shall live alone in this grand hall. My bed shall be there in the sheltered corner; and I shall eat, and drink, and smoke, and sing, and enjoy myself, with one eye always on my prisoners, and the other eye always on my guard outside."

Having delivered this piece of eloquence, he pointed with his sword to the prisoners' doorway. We all passed through it quickly, glad to be out of the sight and hearing of him.

The two rooms set apart for us, communicated with each other. The inner one of the two had a second doorway, leading, as I supposed, further into the building, but so choked up by rubbish, as to be impassable, except by climbing, and that must have been skilful climbing too. Seeing that this accident cut off all easy means of approach to the room from the Pirates' side, we determined, supposing nobody meddled with us, to establish the women and children here; and to take the room nearest to the Pirate Captain and his guard for ourselves.

The first thing to be done was to clear away the rubbish in the women's room. The ceiling was, indeed, as the Pirate Captain had told us, all on the floor; and the growth of trees, shrubs, weeds, and flowers, springing up everywhere among the fragments of stone, was so prodigious in this part of the Palace, that, but for the walls with their barbarous sculptures all round, we should certainly have believed ourselves to be encamped in the forest, without a building near us. All the lighter parts of the rubbish in the women's room we disposed of, cleverly, by piling it in the doorway on the Pirates' side, so as to make any approach from that direction all but impossible, even by climbing. The heavy blocks of stone—and it took two men to lift some of them that were not the heaviest—we piled up in the middle of the floor. Having by this means cleared away plenty of space round the walls, we gathered up all the litter of young branches, bushes, and leaves which the Indians had chopped away; added to them as much as was required of the underwood still standing; and laid the whole smooth and even, to make beds. I noticed, while we were at this work, that the ship's boy—whose name was Robert—was particularly helpful and considerate with the children, when it became necessary to quiet them and to get them to lie down. He was a rough boy to look at, and not very sharp; but, he managed better, and was more naturally tender-hearted with the little ones than any of the rest of us. This may seem a small thing to mention; but Robert's attentive ways with the children, attached them to him; and that attachment, as will be hereafter shown, turned out to be of great benefit to us, at a very dangerous and very important time.

Our next piece of work was to clear our own room. It was close at the side of the Palace; and a break in the outward wall looked down over the sheer precipice on which the building stood. We stopped this up, breast high, in case of accidents, with the rubbish on the floor; we then made our beds, just as we had made the women's beds already.

A little later, we heard the Pirate Captain in the hall, which he kept to himself for his big soul and his little body, giving orders to the American mate about the guard. On mustering the Pirates, it turned out that two of them, who had been wounded in the fight on the Island, were unfit for duty. Twenty-eight, therefore, remained. These, the Pirate Captain divided into companies of seven, who were to mount guard, in turn, for a spell of six hours each company; the relief coming round, as a matter of course, four times in the twenty-four hours. Of the guard of seven, two were stationed under the portico;

one was placed as a look-out, on the top landing of the great
flight of steps; and two were appointed to patrol the ground
below, in front of the Palace. This left only two men to watch
the three remaining sides of the building. So far as any risks
of attack were concerned, the precipices at the back and sides of
the Palace were a sufficient defence for it, if a good watch was
kept on the weak side. But what the Pirate Captain dreaded
was the chance of our escaping; and he would not trust the
precipices to keep us, knowing we had sailors in our company,
and suspecting that they might hit on some substitute for ropes,
and lower themselves and their fellow-prisoners down from the
back or the sides of the Palace, in the dark. Accordingly, the
Pirate Captain settled it that two men out of each company
should do double duty, after nightfall : the choice of them to be
decided by casting dice. This gave four men to patrol round the
sides and the back of the building : a sufficient number to keep
a bright look-out. The Pirates murmured a little at the prospect
of double duty ; but, there was no remedy for it. The Indians,
having a superstitious horror of remaining in the ruined city
after dark, had bargained to be allowed to go back to their
village, every afternoon. And, as for the Sambos, the Pirate
Captain knew them better than the English had known them at
Silver-Store, and would have nothing to do with them in any
matter of importance.

The setting of the watch was completed without much
delay. If any of us had felt the slightest hope of escaping, up
to this time, the position of our prison and the number of
sentinels appointed to guard it, would have been more than
enough to extinguish that hope for ever.

An hour before sunset, the Indians—whose only business at
the Palace was to supply us with food from the village, and to
prepare the food for eating—made their last batch of Tortillas,
and then left the ruins in a body, at the usual trot of those
savages when they are travelling in a hurry.

When the sun had set, the darkness came down upon us, I
might almost say, with a rush. Bats whizzed about, and the low
warning hum of Mosquitos sounded close to our ears. Flying
beetles, with lights in their heads, each light as bright as the
light of a dozen glowworms, sparkled through the darkness, in a

wonderful manner, all night long. When one of them settled on the walls, he lighted up the hideous sculptures for a yard all round him, at the very least. Outside, in the forest, the dreadful stillness seemed to be drawing its breath, from time to time, when the night-wind swept lightly through the million-million leaves. Sometimes, the surge of monkeys travelling through the boughs, burst out with a sound like waves on a sandy shore; sometimes, the noise of falling branches and trunks rang out suddenly with a crash, as if the great ruins about us were splitting into pieces; sometimes, when the silence was at its deepest—when even the tread of the watch outside had ceased—the quick rustle of a lizard or a snake, sounded treacherously close at our ears. It was long before the children in the women's room were all quieted and hushed to sleep—longer still before we, their elders, could compose our spirits for the night. After all sounds died away among us, and when I thought that I was the only one still awake, I heard Miss Maryon's voice saying, softly, "God help and deliver us!" A man in our room, moving on his bed of leaves, repeated the words after her; and the ship's boy, Robert, half-asleep, half-awake, whispered to himself sleepily, "Amen!" After that, the silence returned upon us, and was broken no more. So the night passed — the first night in our Prison in the Woods.

With the morning, came the discovery of a new project of the Pirate Captain's, for which none of us had been prepared.

Soon after sunrise, the Pirate Captain looked into our room, and ordered all the men in it out into the large hall, where he lived with his big soul and his little body. After eyeing us narrowly, he directed three of the sailors, myself, and two of my comrades, to step apart from the rest. When we had obeyed, the bundle of axes which had troubled my mind so much, was brought into the hall; and four men of the guard, then on duty, armed with muskets and pistols, were marched in afterwards. Six of the axes were chosen and put into our hands, the Pirate Captain pointing warningly, as we took them, to the men with fire-arms in the front of us. He and his mate, both armed to the teeth, then led the way out to the steps; we followed; the other four Pirates came after us. We were formed, down the steps, in single file; the Pirate Captain at the head; I myself next to him; a Pirate next to me; and so on to the end, in such order as to keep a man with a loaded musket between each one or two of us prisoners. I looked behind me as we started, and saw two of the Sambos—that Christian George King was one of them—following us. We marched round the back of the Palace, and over the ruins beyond it, till we came to a track through the forest, the first I had seen. After a quarter of an hour's walking, I saw the sunlight, bright beyond the trees in front of us. In another minute or two, we stood under the clear sky, and beheld at our feet a broad river, running with a swift silent current, and overshadowed by the forest, rising as thick as ever on the bank that was opposite to us.

On the bank where we stood, the trees were young; some great tempest of past years having made havoc in this part of the forest, and torn away the old growth to make room for the new. The young trees grew up, mostly, straight and slender,— that is to say, slender for South America, the slightest of them being, certainly, as thick as my leg. After peeping and peering about at the timber, with the look of a man who owned it all, the Pirate Captain sat himself down cross-legged on the grass, and did us the honour to address us.

"Aha! you English, what do you think I have kept you alive for?" says he. "Because I am fond of you? Bah! Because I don't like to kill you? Bah! What for, then? Because I want the use of your arms to work for me. See those trees!" He waved his hand backwards and forwards, over the whole prospect. "Cut them all down—lop off the branches—smooth them into poles—shape them into beams— chop them into planks. Camarado!" he went on, turning to the mate, "I mean to roof in the Palace again, and to lay new floors over the rubbish of stones. I will make the big house good and dry to live in, in the rainy weather—I will barricade the steps of it for defence against an army,—I will make it my strong castle of retreat for me and my men, and our treasure, and our prisoners, and all that we have, when the English cruisers of the devil get too many for us along the coast.

To work, you six! Look at those four men of mine,—their muskets are loaded. Look at these two Sambos who will stop here to fetch help if they want it. Remember the women and children you have left at the Palace—and at your peril and at their peril, turn those axes in your hands from their proper work! You understand? You English fools?"

With those words he jumped to his feet, and ordered the niggers to remain and place themselves at the orders of our guard. Having given these last directions, and having taken his mate's opinion as to whether three of the Buccaniers would not be enough to watch the Palace in the day, when the six stoutest men of the prisoners were away from it, the Pirate Captain offered his little weazen arm to the American, and strutted back to his castle, on better terms with himself than ever.

As soon as he and the mate were gone, Christian George King tumbled himself down on the grass, and kicked up his ugly heels in convulsions of delight.

"Oh, golly, golly, golly!" says he. "You dam English do work, and Christian George King look on. Yup, Sojeer! whack at them tree!"

I paid no attention to the brute, being better occupied in noticing my next comrade, Short. I had remarked that all the while the Pirate Captain was speaking, he was looking hard at the river, as if the sight of a large sheet of water did his sailorly eyes good. When we began to use the axes, greatly to my astonishment, he buckled to at his work like a man who had his whole heart in it: chuckling to himself at every chop, and wagging his head as if he was in the forecastle again telling his best yarns.

"You seem to be in spirits, Short?" I says, setting to on a tree close by him.

"The river's put a notion in my head," says he. "Chop away, Gill, as hard as you can, or they may hear us talking."

"What notion has the river put in your head?" I asked that man, following his directions.

"You don't know where that river runs to, I suppose?" says Short. "No more don't I. But, did it say anything particular to you, Gill, when you first set eyes on it? It said to *me*, as plain as words could speak, 'I'm the road out of this. Come and try me!'—Steady! Don't stop to look at the water. Chop away, man, chop away."

"The road out of this?" says I. "A road without any coaches, Short. I don't see so much as the ruins of one old canoe lying about anywhere."

Short chuckles again, and buries his axe in his tree.

"What are we cutting down these here trees for?" says he.

"Roofs and floors for the Pirate Captain's castle," says I.

"*Rafts for ourselves!*" says he, with another tremendous chop at the tree, which brought it to the ground—the first that had fallen.

His words struck through me as if I had been shot. For the first time since our imprisonment I now saw, clear as daylight, a chance of escape. Only a chance, to be sure; but, still a chance.

Although the guard stood several paces away from us, and could by no possibility hear a word that we said, through the noise of the axes, Short was too cautious to talk any more.

"Wait till night," he said, lopping the branches off the tree. "Pass the word on in a whisper to the nearest of our men to work with a will; and say, with a wink of your eye, there's a good reason for it."

After we had been allowed to knock off for that day, the Pirates had no cause to complain of the work we had done; and they reported us to the Pirate Captain as obedient and industrious, so far. When we lay down at night, I took the next place on the leaves to Short. We waited till the rest were asleep, and till we heard the Pirate Captain snoring in the great hall, before we began to talk again about the river and the rafts. This is the amount of what Short whispered in my ear on that occasion:

He told me he had calculated that it would take two large rafts to bear all our company, and that timber enough to make such two rafts might be cut down by six men in ten days, or, at most, in a fortnight. As for the means of fastening the rafts— the lashings, he called them—the stout vines and creepers supplied them abundantly; and the timbers of both rafts might be connected together, in this way, firmly enough for river navigation, in about five hours. That was the very shortest time the job would take, done by the willing hands of men who knew that they were working for their lives, said Short.

These were the means of escape. How to turn them to account was the next question. Short could not answer it; and though I tried all that night, neither could I.

The difficulty was one which, I think, might have puzzled wiser heads than ours. How were six-and-thirty living souls (being the number of us prisoners, including the children) to be got out of the Palace safely, in the face of the guard that watched it? And, even if that was accomplished, when could we count on gaining five hours all to ourselves for the business of making the rafts? The compassing of either of these two designs, absolutely necessary as they both were to our escape, seemed to be nothing more or less than a rank impossibility. Towards morning, I got a wild notion into my head about letting ourselves down from the back of the Palace, in the dark, and taking our chance of being able to seize the sentinels at that part of the building, unawares, and gag them before they could give the alarm to the Pirates in front. But, Short, when I mentioned my plan to him, would not hear of it. He said that men by themselves—provided they had not got a madman, like Drooce, and a maundering old gentleman, like Mr. Pordage, among them —might, perhaps, run some such desperate risk as I proposed; but, that letting women and children, to say nothing of Drooce and Pordage, down a precipice in the dark, with make-shift ropes which might give way at a moment's notice, was out of the question. It was impossible, on further reflection, not to see that Short's view of the matter was the right one. I acknowledged as much, and then I put it to Short whether our wisest course would not be to let one or two of the sharpest of our fellow-prisoners into our secret, and see what they said. Short asked me which two I had in my mind when I made that proposal?

" Mr. Macey," says I, " because he is naturally quick, and has improved his gifts by learning, and Miss Maryon——"

" How can a woman help us?" says Short, breaking in on me.

" A woman with a clear head and a high courage and a

patient resolution—all of which Miss Maryon has got, above all the world—may do more to help us, in our present strait, than any man of our company," says I.

"Well," says Short, "I dare say you're right. Speak to anybody you please, Gill; but, whatever you do, man, stick to it at the trees. Let's get the timber down—that's the first thing to be done, anyhow."

Before we were mustered for work, I took an opportunity of privately mentioning to Miss Maryon and Mr. Macey what had passed between Short and me. They were both thunder-struck at the notion of the rafts. Miss Maryon, as I had expected, made lighter of the terrible difficulties in the way of carrying out our scheme than Mr. Macey did.

"We are left here to watch and think, all day," she whispered—and I could almost hear the quick beating of her heart. "While you are making the best of your time among the trees, we will make the best of ours in the Palace. I can say no more, now—I can hardly speak at all for thinking of what you have told me. Bless you, bless you, for making me hope once more ! Go now—we must not risk the consequences of being seen talking together. When you come back at night, look at me. If I close my eyes, it is a sign that nothing has been thought of yet. If I keep them open, take the first safe opportunity of speaking secretly to me or to Mr. Macey."

She turned away ; and I went back to my comrades. Half an hour afterwards, we were off for our second day's work among the trees.

When we came back, I looked at Miss Maryon. She closed her eyes. So, nothing had been thought of, yet.

Six more days we worked at cutting down the trees, always meriting the same good character for industry from our Pirate-guard. Six more evenings I looked at Miss Maryon ; and six times her closed eyes gave me the same disheartening answer. On the ninth day of our work, Short whispered to me, that if we plied our axes for three days longer, he considered we should have more than timber enough down, to make the rafts. He had thought of nothing, I had thought of nothing, Miss Maryon and Mr. Macey had thought of nothing. I was beginning to get low in spirits; but, Short was just as cool and easy as ever. "Chop away, Davis," was all he said.   "The river won't run dry yet awhile.   Chop away !"

We knocked off, earlier than usual that day, the Pirates having a feast in prospect, off a wild hog.   It was still broad daylight (out of the forest) when we came back, and when I looked once more in Miss Maryon's face.

I saw a flush in her cheeks; and her eyes met mine brightly.   My heart beat quicker at the glance of them; for I saw that the time had come, and that the difficulty was conquered.

We waited till the light was fading, and the Pirates were in the midst of their feast.   Then, she beckoned me into the inner room, and I sat down by her in the dimmest corner of it.

"You have thought of something, at last, Miss?"

"I have.   But the merit of the thought is not all mine. Chance—no !   Providence—suggested the design; and the instrument with which its merciful Wisdom has worked, is—a child."

She stopped, and looked all round her anxiously, before she went on.

"This afternoon," she says, "I was sitting against the trunk of that tree, thinking of what has been the subject of my thoughts ever since you spoke to me.   My sister's little girl was whiling away the tedious time, by asking Mr. Kitten to tell her the names of the different plants which are still left growing about the room.   You know he is a learned man in such matters ?"

I knew that; and have, I believe, formerly given that out, for my Lady to take in writing.

"I was too much occupied," she went on, "to pay attention to them, till they came close to the tree against which I was sitting.   Under it and about it, there grew a plant with very elegantly-shaped leaves, and with a kind of berry on it.   The child showed it to Mr. Kitten ; and saying, 'Those berries look good to eat,' stretched out her hand towards them.   Mr. Kitten stopped her.   'You must never touch that,' he said.   'Why not ?' the child asked.   'Because if you eat much of it, it would poison you.'   'And if I only eat a little ?' said the child, laughing. 'If you only eat a little,' said Mr. Kitten, 'it would throw you into a deep sleep—a sleep that none of us could wake you from, when it was time for breakfast—a sleep that would make your mama think you were dead.' Those words were hardly spoken, when the thought that I have now to tell you of, flashed across my mind. But, before I say anything more, answer me one question. Am I right in supposing that our attempt at escape must be made in the night?"

"At night, certainly," says I, "because we can be most sure, then, that the Pirates off guard are all in this building, and not likely to leave it."

"I understand. Now, Davis, hear what I have observed of the habits of the men who keep us imprisoned in this place. The first change of guard at night, is at nine o'clock. At that time, seven men come in from watching, and nine men (the extra night-guard) go out to replace them; each party being on duty, as you know, for six hours. I have observed, at the nine o'clock change of guard, that the seven men who come off duty, and the nine who go on, have a supply of baked cakes of Indian corn, reserved expressly for their use. They divide the food between them; the Pirate Captain (who is always astir at the change of guard) generally taking a cake for himself, when the rest of the men take theirs. This makes altogether, seventeen men who partake of food especially reserved for them, at nine o'clock. So far you understand me?"

"Clearly, Miss."

"The next thing I have noticed, is the manner in which that food is prepared. About two hours before sunset, the Pirate Captain walks out to smoke, after he has eaten the meal which he calls his dinner. In his absence from the hall, the Indians light their fire on the unsheltered side of it, and prepare the last batch of food before they leave us for the night. They knead up two separate masses of dough. The largest is the first which is separated into cakes and baked. That is taken for the use of us prisoners and of the men who are off duty all the night. The second and smaller piece of dough is then prepared for the nine o'clock change of guard. On that food—come nearer, Davis, I must say it in a whisper—on that food all our chances of escape now turn. If we can drug it unobserved, the Pirates who go off duty, the Pirates who go on duty, and the Captain, who is more to be feared than all the rest, will be as absolutely insensible to our leaving the Palace, as if they were every one of them dead men."

I was unable to speak—I was unable even to fetch my breath at those words.

"I have taken Mr. Kitten, as a matter of necessity, into our confidence," she said. "I have learnt from him a simple way of obtaining the juice of that plant which he forbade the child to eat. I have also made myself acquainted with the quantity which it is necessary to use for our purpose; and I have resolved that no hands but mine shall be charged with the work of kneading it into the dough."

"Not you, Miss,—not you. Let one of us—let me—run that risk."

"You have work enough and risk enough already," said Miss Maryon. "It is time that the women, for whom you have suffered and ventured so much, should take their share. Besides, the risk is not great, where the Indians only are concerned. They are idle and curious. I have seen, with my own eyes, that they are as easily tempted away from their occupation by any chance sight or chance noise as if they were children; and I have already arranged with Mr. Macey that he is to excite their curiosity by suddenly pulling down one of the loose stones in that doorway, when the right time comes. The Indians are certain to run in here to find out what is the matter. Mr. Macey will tell them that he has seen a snake,—they will hunt for the creature (as I have seen them hunt, over and over again, in this ruined place)—and while they are so engaged, the opportunity that I want, the two minutes to myself, which are all that I require, will be mine. Dread the Pirate Captain, Davis, for the slightest caprice of his may ruin all our hopes, — but never dread the Indians, and never doubt me."

Nobody, who had looked in her face at that moment— or at any moment that ever I knew of—could have doubted her.

"There is one thing more," she went on. "When is the attempt to be made?"

"In three days' time," I answered; "there will be timber enough down to make the rafts."

"In three days' time, then, let us decide the question of our freedom or our death." She spoke those words with a firmness that amazed me. "Rest now," she said. "Rest and hope."

The third day was the hottest we had yet experienced; we were kept longer at work than usual; and when we had done, we left on the bank enough, and more than enough, of timber and poles, to make both the rafts.

The Indians had gone when we got back to the Palace, and the Pirate Captain was still smoking on the flight of steps. As we crossed the hall, I looked on one side and saw the Tortillas set up in a pile, waiting for the men who came in and went out at nine o'clock.

At the door which opened between our room and the women's room, Miss Maryon was waiting for us.

"Is it done?" I asked in a whisper.

"It is done," she answered.

It was, then, by Mr. Macey's watch (which he had kept hidden about him throughout our imprisonment), seven o'clock. We had two hours to wait: hours of suspense, but hours of rest also for the overworked men who had been cutting the wood. Before I lay down, I looked into the inner room. The women were all sitting together; and I saw by the looks they cast on me that Miss Maryon had told them of what was coming with the night. The children were much as usual, playing quiet games among themselves. In the men's room, I noticed that Mr. Macey had posted himself along with Tom Packer, close to Serjeant Drooce, and that Mr. Fisher seemed to be taking great pains to make himself agreeable to Mr. Pordage. I was glad to see that the two gentlemen of the company, who were quick-witted and experienced in most things, were already taking in hand the two unreasonable men.

The evening brought no coolness with it. The heat was so oppressive that we all panted under it. The stillness of the forest was awful. We could almost hear the falling of the leaves.

Half-past seven, eight, half-past eight, a quarter to nine—

Nine. The tramp of feet came up the steps on one side, and the tramp of feet came into the hall, on the other. There was a confusion of voices,—then, the voice of the Pirate Captain, speaking in his own language,—then, the voice of the American mate, ordering out the guard,—then silence.

I crawled to the door of our room, and laid myself down behind it, where I could see a strip of the hall, being that part of it in which the way out was situated. Here, also, the Pirate Captain's tent had been set up, about twelve or fourteen feet from the door. Two torches were burning before it. By their light, I saw the guard on duty file out, each man munching his Tortilla, and each man grumbling over it. At the same time, in the part of the hall which I could not see, I heard the men off duty grumbling also. The Pirate Captain, who had entered his tent the minute before, came out of it, and calling to the American mate, at the far end of the hall, asked sharply in English, what that murmuring meant.

"The men complain of the Tortillas," the mate tells him. " They say, they are nastier than ever to-night."

"Bring me one, and let me taste it," said the Captain. I had often before heard people talk of their hearts being in their mouths, but I never really knew what the sensation was, till I heard that order given.

The Tortilla was brought to him. He nibbled a bit off it, spat the morsel out with disgust, and threw the rest of the cake away.

"Those Indian beasts have burnt the Tortillas," he said, " and their dirty hides shall suffer for it to-morrow morning." With those words, he whisked round on his heel, and went back into his tent.

Some of the men had crept up behind me, and, looking over my head, had seen what I saw. They passed the account of it in whispers to those who could not see; and they, in their turn, repeated it to the women. In five minutes everybody in the two rooms knew that the scheme had failed with the very man whose sleep it was most important to secure. I heard no stifled crying among the women or stifled cursing among the men. The despair of that time was too deep for tears, and too deep for words.

I myself could not take my eyes off the tent. In a little while he came out of it again, puffing and panting with the heat.   He lighted a cigar at one of the torches, and laid himself down on his cloak just inside the doorway leading into the portico, so that all the air from outside might blow over him. Little as he was, he was big enough to lie right across the narrow way out.

He smoked and he smoked, slowly and more slowly, for, what seemed to me to be, hours, but for what, by the watch, was little more than ten minutes after all. Then, the cigar dropped out of his mouth—his hand sought for it, and sank lazily by his side—his head turned over a little towards the door—and he fell off: not into the drugged sleep that there was safety in, but into his light, natural sleep, which a touch on his body might have disturbed.

"Now's the time to gag him," says Short, creeping up close to me, and taking off his jacket and shoes.

"Steady," says I. "Don't let's try that till we can try nothing else. There are men asleep near us who have not eaten the drugged cakes—the Pirate Captain is light and active—and if the gag slips on his mouth, we are all done for. I'll go to his head, Short, with my jacket ready in my hands. When I'm there, do you lead the way with your mates, and step gently into the portico, over his body. Every minute of your time is precious on account of making the rafts. Leave the rest of the men to get the women and children over; and leave me to gag him if he stirs while we are getting out."

"Shake hands on it, Davis," says Short, getting to his feet. "A team of horses wouldn't have dragged me out first, if you hadn't said that about the rafts."

"Wait a bit," says I, "till I speak to Mr. Kitten."

I crawled back into the room, taking care to keep out of the way of the stones in the middle of it, and asked Mr. Kitten how long it would be before the drugged cakes acted on the men outside who had eaten them? He said we ought to wait another quarter of an hour, to make quite sure. At the same time, Mr. Macey whispered in my ear to let him pass over the Pirate Captain's body, alone with the dangerous man of our company—Serjeant Drooce. "I know how to deal with mad people," says he. "I have persuaded the Serjeant that if he is quiet, and if he steps carefully, I can help him to escape from Tom Packer, whom he is beginning to look on as his keeper. He has been as stealthy and quiet as a cat ever since—and I will answer for him till we get to the river side."

What a relief it was to hear that ! I was turning round to get back to Short, when a hand touched me lightly.

"I have heard you talking," whispered Miss Maryon ; "and I will prepare all in my room for the risk we must now run. Robert, the ship's boy, whom the children are so fond of, shall help us to persuade them, once more, that we are going to play a game. If you can get one of the torches from the tent, and pass it in here, it may prevent some of us from stumbling. Don't be afraid of the women and children, Davis. They shall not endanger the brave men who are saving them."

I left her at once to get the torch. The Pirate Captain was still fast asleep as I stole on tiptoe, into the hall, and took it from the tent. When I returned, and gave it to Miss Maryon, her sister's little deaf and dumb boy saw me, and, slipping between us, caught tight hold of one of my hands. Having been used to riding on my shoulders for so many days, he had taken a fancy to me ; and, when I tried to put him away, he only clung the tighter, and began to murmur in his helpless dumb way. Slight as the noise was which the poor little fellow could make, we all dreaded it. His mother wrung her hands in despair when she heard him ; and Mr. Fisher whispered to me for Heaven's sake to quiet the child, and humour him at any cost. I immediately took him up in my arms, and went back to Short.

"Sling him on my back," says I, "as you slung the little girl on your own the first day of the march. I want both my hands, and the child won't be quiet away from me."

Short did as I asked him in two minutes. As soon as he had finished, Mr. Macey passed the word on to me, that the quarter of an hour was up ; that it was time to try the experiment with Drooce ; and that it was necessary for us all to humour him by feigning sleep. We obeyed. Looking out of the corner of my eye, I saw Mr. Macey take the mad Serjeant's arm, point round to us all, and then lead him out. Holding tight by Mr. Macey, Drooce stepped as lightly as a woman, with as bright and wicked a look of cunning as ever I saw in any human eyes. They crossed the hall—Mr. Macey pointed to the Pirate Captain, and whispered, "Hush!"—the Serjeant imitated the action and repeated the word—then the two stepped over his body (Drooce cautiously raising his feet the highest), and disappeared through the portico. We waited to hear if there was any noise or confusion. Not a sound.

I got up, and Short handed me his jacket for the gag. The child, having been startled from his sleep by the light of the torch, when I brought it in, had fallen off again, already, on my shoulder. "Now for it," says I, and stole out into the hall.

I stopped at the tent, went in, and took the first knife I could find there. With the weapon between my teeth, with the little innocent asleep on my shoulder, with the jacket held ready in both hands, I kneeled down on one knee at the Pirate Captain's head, and fixed my eyes steadily on his ugly sleeping face.

The sailors came out first, with their shoes in their hands. No sound of footsteps from any one of them. No movement in the ugly face as they passed over it.

The women and children were ready next. Robert, the ship's boy, lifted the children over : most of them holding their little hands over their mouths to keep from laughing—so well had Robert persuaded them that we were only playing a game. The women passed next, all as light as air ; after them, in obedience to a sign from me, my comrades of the Marines, holding their shoes in their hands, as the sailors had done before them. So far, not a word had been spoken, not a mistake had been made —so far, not a change of any sort had passed over the Pirate Captain's face.

There were left now in the hall, besides myself and the child on my back, only Mr. Fisher and Mr. Pordage. Mr. Pordage ! Up to that moment, in the risk and excitement of the time, I had not once thought of him.

I was forced to think of him now, though ; and with anything but a friendly feeling.

At the sight of the Pirate Captain, asleep across the way

out, the unfortunate, mischievous old simpleton tossed up his head, and folded his arms, and was on the point of breaking out loud into a spoken document of some kind, when Mr. Fisher wisely and quickly clapped a hand over his mouth.

"Government despatches outside," whispers Mr. Fisher, in in agony. "Secret service. Forty-nine reports from headquarters, all waiting for you half a mile off. I'll show you the way, sir. Don't wake that man there, who is asleep: he must know nothing about it—he represents the Public."

Mr. Pordage suddenly looked very knowing and hugely satisfied with himself. He followed Mr. Fisher to within a foot of the Pirate Captain's body—then stopped short.

"How many reports?" he asked, very anxiously.

"Forty-nine," said Mr. Fisher. "Come along, sir,—and step clean over the Public, whatever you do."

Mr. Pordage instantly stepped over, as jauntily as if he was going to dance. At the moment of his crossing, a hanging rag of his cursed, useless, unfortunate, limp Diplomatic coat touched the Pirate Captain's forehead, and woke him.

I drew back softly, with the child still asleep on my shoulder, into the black shadow of the wall behind me. At the instant when the Pirate Captain awoke, I had been looking at Mr. Pordage, and had consequently lost the chance of applying the gag to his mouth suddenly, at the right time.

On rousing up, he turned his face inwards, towards the prisoners' room. If he had turned it outwards, he must to a dead certainty have seen the tail of Mr. Pordage's coat, disappearing in the portico.

Though he was awake enough to move, he was not awake enough to have the full possession of his sharp senses. The drowsiness of his sleep still hung about him. He yawned, stretched himself, spat wearily, sat up, spat again, got on his legs, and stood up, within three feet of the shadow in which I was hiding behind him.

I forgot the knife in my teeth,—I declare solemnly, in the frightful suspense of that moment, I forgot it—and doubled my fist as if I was an unarmed man, with the purpose of stunning him by a blow on the head if he came any nearer. I suppose I waited, with my fist clenched, nearly a minute, while he waited,

THE DON WAKES UP.

yawning and spitting. At the end of that time, he made for
his tent, and I heard him (with what thankfulness no words
can tell!) roll himself down, with another yawn, on his bed
inside.

I waited—in the interest of us all—to make quite sure,
before I left, that he was asleep again. In what I reckoned as
about five minutes' time, I heard him snoring, and felt free to
take myself and my little sleeping comrade out of the prison,
at last.

The drugged guards in the portico were sitting together,
dead asleep, with their backs against the wall. The third man
was lying flat, on the landing of the steps. Their arms and
ammunition were gone : wisely taken by our men—to defend
us, if we were meddled with before we escaped, and to kill
food for us when we committed ourselves to the river.

At the bottom of the steps I was startled by seeing two
women standing together. They were Mrs. Macey and Miss
Maryon : the first, waiting to see her child safe; the second
(God bless her for it!) waiting to see *me* safe.

In a quarter of an hour we were by the river-side, and saw
the work bravely begun ; the sailors and the marines under
their orders, labouring at the rafts in the shallow water by the
bank ; Mr. Macey and Mr. Fisher rolling down fresh timber as
it was wanted; the women cutting the vines, creepers, and
withies for the lashings. We brought with us three more pair
of hands to help; and all worked with such a will, that, in four
hours and twenty minutes, by Mr. Macey's watch, the rafts,
though not finished as they ought to have been, were still
strong enough to float us away.

Short, another seaman, and the ship's boy, got aboard the
first raft, carrying with them poles and spare timber. Miss
Maryon, Mrs. Fisher and her husband, Mrs. Macey and her
husband and three children, Mr. and Mrs. Pordage, Mr. Kitten,
myself, and women and children besides, to make up eighteen,
were the passengers on the leading raft. The second raft, under
the guidance of the two other sailors, held Serjeant Drooce
(gagged, for he now threatened to be noisy again), Tom Packer,
the two marines, Mrs. Belltott, and the rest of the women and
children. We all got on board silently and quickly, with a

fine moonlight over our heads, and without accidents or delays of any kind.

It was a good half-hour before the time would come for the change of guard at the prison, when the lashings which tied us to the bank were cast off, and we floated away, a company of free people, on the current of an unknown river.

WE contrived to keep afloat all night, and, the stream running strong with us, to glide a long way down the river. But, we found the night to be a dangerous time for such navigation, on account of the eddies and rapids, and it was therefore settled next day that in future we would bring-to at sunset and encamp on the shore. As we knew of no boats that the Pirates possessed, up at the Prison in the Woods, we settled always to encamp on the opposite side of the stream, so as to have the breadth of the river between our sleep and them. Our opinion was, that if they were acquainted with any near way by land to the mouth of this river, they would come up it in force, and retake us or kill us, according as they could; but, that if that was not the case, and if the river ran by none of their secret stations, we might escape.

When I say we settled this or that, I do not mean that we planned anything with any confidence as to what might happen an hour hence. So much had happened in one night, and such great changes had been violently and suddenly made in the fortunes of many among us, that we had got better used to uncertainty, in a little while, than I daresay most people do in the course of their lives.

The difficulties we soon got into, through the off-settings and point-currents of the stream, made the likelihood of our being drowned, alone—to say nothing of our being retaken—as broad and plain as the sun at noon-day to all of us. But, we all worked hard at managing the rafts, under the direction of the seamen (of our own skill, I think we never could have prevented them from oversetting), and we also worked hard at making good the defects in their first hasty construction—which the water soon found out. While we humbly resigned ourselves to going down, if it was the will of Our Father that was in Heaven, we humbly made up our minds, that we would all do the best that was in us.

And so we held on, gliding with the stream. It drove us to this bank, and it drove us to that bank, and it turned us, and whirled us; but yet it carried us on. Sometimes much too slowly, sometimes much too fast, but yet it carried us on.

My little deaf and dumb boy slumbered a good deal now, and that was the case with all the children. They caused very little trouble to any one. They seemed, in my eyes, to get more like one another, not only in quiet manner, but in the face, too. The motion of the raft was usually so much the same, the scene was usually so much the same, the sound of the soft wash and ripple of the water was usually so much the same, that they were made drowsy, as they might have been by the constant playing of one tune. Even on the grown people, who worked hard and felt anxiety, the same things produced something of the same effect. Every day was so like the other, that I soon lost count of the days, myself, and had to ask Miss Maryon, for instance, whether this was the third or fourth? Miss Maryon had a pocket-book and pencil, and she kept the log; that is to say, she entered up a clear little journal of the time, and of the distances our seamen thought we had made, each night.

So, as I say, we kept afloat and glided on. All day long, and every day, the water, and the woods, and sky; all day long, and every day, the constant watching of both sides of the river, and far a-head at every bold turn and sweep it made, for any signs of Pirate-boats, or Pirate-dwellings. So, as I say, we kept afloat and glided on. The days melting themselves together to that degree, that I could hardly believe my ears when I asked " How many, now, Miss?" and she answered, " Seven."

To be sure, poor Mr. Pordage had, by about now, got his Diplomatic coat into such a state as never was seen. What with the mud of the river, what with the water of the river, what with the sun, and the dews, and the tearing boughs, and the thickets, it hung about him in discoloured shreds like a mop. The sun had touched him a bit. He had taken to always polishing one particular button, which just held on to his left wrist, and to always calling for stationery. I suppose that man called for pens, ink, and paper, tape, and sealing-wax, upwards of one thousand times in four and twenty hours. He had an idea that we should never get out of that river unless we were written out of it in a formal Memorandum; and the more we laboured at navigating the rafts, the more he ordered us not to touch them at our peril, and the more he sat and roared for stationery.

Mrs. Pordage, similarly, persisted in wearing her night-cap. I doubt if any one but ourselves who had seen the progress of that article of dress, could by this time have told what it was meant for. It had got so limp and ragged that she couldn't see out of her eyes for it. It was so dirty, that whether it was vegetable matter out of a swamp, or weeds out of the river, or an old porter's-knot from England, I don't think any new spectator could have said. Yet, this unfortunate old woman had a notion that it was not only vastly genteel, but that it was the correct thing as to propriety. And she really did carry herself over the other ladies who had no night-caps, and who were forced to tie up their hair how they could, in a superior manner that was perfectly amazing.

I don't know what she looked like, sitting in that blessed night-cap, on a log of wood, outside the hut or cabin upon our raft. She would have rather resembled a fortune-teller in one of the picture-books that used to be in the shop windows in my boyhood, except for her stateliness. But, Lord bless my heart, the dignity with which she sat and moped, with her head in that bundle of tatters, was like nothing else in the world! She was not on speaking terms with more than three of the ladies. Some of them had, what she called, "taken precedence" of her—in getting into, or out of, that miserable little shelter!—and others had not called to pay their respects, or something of that kind. So, there she sat, in her own state and ceremony, while her husband sat on the same log of wood, ordering us one and all to let the raft go to the bottom, and to bring him stationery.

What with this noise on the part of Mr. Commissioner Pordage, and what with the cries of Serjeant Drooce on the raft astern (which were sometimes more than Tom Packer could silence), we often made our slow way down the river, anything but quietly. Yet, that it was of great importance that no ears should be able to hear us from the woods on the banks, could not be doubted. We were looked for, to a certainty, and we might be retaken at any moment. It was an anxious time; it was, indeed, indeed, an anxious time.

On the seventh night of our voyage on the rafts, we made fast, as usual, on the opposite side of the river to that from which we had started, in as dark a place as we could pick out. Our little encampment was soon made, and supper was eaten, and the children fell asleep. The watch was set, and everything made orderly for the night. Such a starlight night, with such blue in the sky, and such black in the places of heavy shade on the banks of the great stream!

Those two ladies, Miss Maryon and Mrs. Fisher, had always kept near me since the night of the attack. Mr. Fisher, who was untiring in the work of our raft, had said to me:

"My dear little childless wife has grown so attached to you, Davis, and you are such a gentle fellow, as well as such a determined one;" our party had adopted that last expression from the one-eyed English pirate, and I repeat what Mr. Fisher said, only because he said it; "that it takes a load off my mind to leave her in your charge."

I said to him: "Your lady is in far better charge than mine, sir, having Miss Maryon to take care of her; but, you may rely upon it, that I will guard them both—faithful and true."

Says he: "I do rely upon it, Davis, and I heartily wish all the silver on our old Island was yours."

That seventh starlight night, as I have said, we made our camp, and got our supper, and set our watch, and the children fell asleep. It was solemn and beautiful in those wild and solitary parts, to see them, every night before they lay down, kneeling under the bright sky, saying their little prayers at women's laps. At that time we men all uncovered, and mostly kept at a distance. When the innocent creatures rose up, we

murmured "Amen!" all together. For, though we had not
heard what they said, we knew it must be good for us.

At that time, too, as was only natural, those poor mothers in
our company whose children had been killed, shed many tears.
I thought the sight seemed to console them while it made them
cry; but, whether I was right or wrong in that, they wept very
much. On this seventh night, Mrs. Fisher had cried for her
lost darling until she cried herself asleep. She was lying on
a little couch of leaves and such-like (I made the best little
couch I could, for them every night), and Miss Maryon had
covered her, and sat by her, holding her hand. The stars
looked down upon them. As for me, I guarded them.

"Davis!" says Miss Maryon. (I am not going to say what
a voice she had. I couldn't if I tried.)

"I am here, Miss."

"The river sounds as if it were swollen to-night."

"We all think, Miss, that we are coming near the sea."

"Do you believe, now, we shall escape?"

"I do now, Miss, really believe it." I had always said I
did; but, I had in my own mind been doubtful.

"How glad you will be, my good Davis, to see England
again!"

I have another confession to make that will appear singular.
When she said these words, something rose in my throat; and
the stars I looked away at, seemed to break into sparkles that
fell down my face and burnt it.

"England is not much to me, Miss, except as a name."

"Oh! So true an Englishman should not say that!—Are
you not well to-night, Davis?" Very kindly, and with a
quick change.

"Quite well, Miss."

"Are you sure? Your voice sounds altered in my hearing."

"No, Miss, I am a stronger man than ever. But England
is nothing to me."

Miss Maryon sat silent for so long a while, that I believed
she had done speaking to me for one time. However, she had
not; for by and by she said in a distinct, clear tone:

"No, good friend; you must not say, that England is

nothing to you. It is to be much to you, yet—everything to you. You have to take back to England the good name you have earned here, and the gratitude and attachment and respect you have won here; and you have to make some good English girl very happy and proud, by marrying her; and I shall one day see her, I hope, and make her happier and prouder still, by telling her what noble services her husband's were in South America, and what a noble friend he was to me there."

Though she spoke these kind words in a cheering manner, she spoke them compassionately. I said nothing. It will appear to be another strange confession, that I paced to and fro, within call, all that night, a most unhappy man reproaching myself all the night long. "You are as ignorant as any man alive; you are as obscure as any man alive; you are as poor as any man alive; you are no better than the mud under your foot." That was the way in which I went on against myself until the morning.

With the day, came the day's labour. What I should have done without the labour, I don't know. We were afloat again at the usual hour, and were again making our way down the river. It was broader, and clearer of obstructions than it had been, and it seemed to flow faster. This was one of Drooce's quiet days; Mr. Pordage, besides being sulky, had almost lost his voice; and we made good way, and with little noise.

There was always a seaman forward on the raft, keeping a bright look-out. Suddenly, in the full heat of the day, when the children were slumbering, and the very trees and reeds appeared to be slumbering, this man—it was Short—holds up his hand, and cries with great caution:

"Avast! Voices ahead!"

We held on against the stream as soon as we could bring her up, and the other raft followed suit. At first, Mr. Macey, Mr. Fisher, and myself, could hear nothing; though both the seamen aboard of us agreed that they could hear voices and oars. After a little pause, however, we united in thinking that we *could* hear the sound of voices, and the dip of oars. But, you can hear a long way in those countries, and there was a bend of the river before us, and nothing was to be seen except such waters and such banks as we were now in the eighth day (and might, for the matter of our feelings have been in the eightieth), of having seen with anxious eyes.

It was soon decided to put a man ashore who should creep through the wood, see what was coming, and warn the rafts. The rafts in the meantime to keep the middle of the stream. The man to be put ashore, and not to swim ashore, as the first thing could be more quickly done than the second. The raft conveying him, to get back into mid-stream, and to hold on along with the other, as well as it could, until signalled by the man. In case of danger, the man to shift for himself until it should be safe to take him aboard again. I volunteered to be the man.

We knew that the voices and oars must come up slowly against the stream; and our seamen knew, by the set of the stream, under which bank they would come. I was put ashore accordingly. The raft got off well, and I broke into the wood.

Steaming hot it was, and a tearing place to get through. So much the better for me, since it was something to contend against and do. I cut off the bend in the river, at a great saving of space, came to the water's edge again, and hid myself, and waited. I could now hear the dip of the oars very distinctly; the voices had ceased.

The sound came on in a regular tune, and as I lay hidden, I fancied the tune so played to be, " Chris'en—George—King ! Chris'en—George—King ! Chris'en—George—King !" over and over again, always the same, with the pauses always at the same places. I had likewise time to make up my mind that if these were the Pirates, I could and would (barring my being shot), swim off to my raft, in spite of my wound, the moment I had given the alarm, and hold my old post by Miss Maryon.

" Chris'en — George — King !   Chris'en — George—King ! Chris'en—George—King !" coming up, now, very near.

I took a look at the branches about me, to see where a shower of bullets would be most likely to do me least hurt; and I took a look back at the track I had made in forcing my way in ; and now I was wholly prepared and fully ready for them.

" Chris'en — George — King !   Chris'en — George — King ! Chris'en—George—King !"   Here they were !

Who were they? The barbarous Pirates, scum of all nations

headed by such men as the hideous little Portuguese monkey, and the one-eyed English convict with the gash across his face, that ought to have gashed his wicked head off? The worst men in the world picked out from the worst, to do the cruellest and most atrocious deeds that ever stained it? The howling, murdering, black-flag waving, mad, and drunken crowd of devils that had overcome us by numbers and by treachery? No. These were English men in English boats—good blue-jackets and red-coats—marines that I knew myself, and sailors that knew our seamen! At the helm of the first boat, Captain Carton, eager and steady. At the helm of the second boat, Captain Maryon, brave and bold. At the helm of the third boat, an old seaman, with determination carved into his watchful face, like the figure-head of a ship. Every man doubly and trebly armed from head to foot. Every man lying-to at his work, with a will that had all his heart and soul in it. Every man looking out for any trace of friend or enemy, and burning to be the first to do good, or avenge evil. Every man with his face on fire when he saw me, his countryman who had been taken prisoner, and hailed me with a cheer, as Captain Carton's boat ran in and took me on board.

I reported, "All escaped, sir! All well, all safe, all here!"

God bless me—and God bless them—what a cheer! It turned me weak, as I was passed on from hand to hand to the stern of the boat: every hand patting me or grasping me in some way or other, in the moment of my going by.

"Hold up, my brave fellow," says Captain Carton, clapping me on the shoulder like a friend, and giving me a flask. "Put your lips to that, and they'll be red again. Now, boys, give way!"

The banks flew by us, as if the mightiest stream that ever ran was with us; and so it was, I am sure, meaning the stream of those men's ardour and spirit. The banks flew by us, and we came in sight of the rafts—the banks flew by us, and we came alongside of the rafts—the banks stopped; and there was a tumult of laughing and crying and kissing and shaking of hands, and catching up of children and setting of them down again, and a wild hurry of thankfulness and joy that melted every one and softened all hearts.

I had taken notice, in Captain Carton's boat, that there was a curious and quite new sort of fitting on board. It was a kind of a little bower made of flowers, and it was set up behind the captain, and betwixt him and the rudder. Not only was this arbor, so to call it, neatly made of flowers, but it was ornamented in a singular way. Some of the men had taken the ribbons and buckles off their hats, and hung them among the flowers; others, had made festoons and streamers of their handkerchiefs, and hung them there ; others, had intermixed such trifles as bits of glass and shining fragments of lockets and tobacco-boxes, with the flowers; so that altogether it was a very bright and lively object in the sunshine. But, why there, or what for, I did not understand.

Now, as soon as the first bewilderment was over, Captain Carton gave the order to land for the present. But, this boat of his, with two hands left in her, immediately put off again when the men were out of her, and kept off, some yards from the shore. As she floated there, with the two hands gently backing water to keep her from going down the stream, this pretty little arbor attracted many eyes. None of the boat's crew, however, had anything to say about it, except that it was the captain's fancy.

The captain, with the women and children clustering round him, and the men of all ranks grouped outside them, and all listening, stood telling how the Expedition, deceived by its bad intelligence, had chased the light Pirate boats all that fatal night, and had still followed in their wake next day, and had never suspected until many hours too late that the great Pirate body had drawn off in the darkness when the chace began, and shot over to the Island. He stood telling how the Expedition, supposing the whole array of armed boats to be ahead of it, got tempted into shallows and went aground ; but, not without having its revenge upon the two decoy-boats, both of which it had come up with, overland, and sent to the bottom with all on board. He stood telling how the Expedition, fearing then that the case stood as it did, got afloat again, by great exertion, after the loss of four more tides, and returned to the Island, where they found the sloop scuttled and the treasure gone. He stood telling how my officer, Lieutenant Linderwood, was left upon the Island, with as strong a force as could be got together hurriedly from the mainland, and how the three boats we saw before us were manned and armed and had come away, exploring the coast and inlets, in search of any tidings of us. He stood telling all this, with his face to the river; and, as he stood telling it, the little arbor of flowers floated in the sunshine before all the faces there.

Leaning on Captain Carton's shoulder, between him and Miss Maryon, was Mrs. Fisher, her head drooping on her arm. She asked him, without raising it, when he had told so much, whether he had found her mother?

"Be comforted! She lies," said the Captain, gently, "under the cocoa-nut trees on the beach."

"And my child, Captain Carton, did you find my child, too? Does my darling rest with my mother?"

"No. Your pretty child sleeps," said the Captain, "under a shade of flowers."

His voice shook; but, there was something in it that struck all the hearers. At that moment, there sprang from the arbor in his boat, a little creature, clapping her hands and stretching out her arms, and crying, "Dear papa! Dear mamma! I am not killed. I am saved. I am coming to kiss you. Take me to them, take me to them, good, kind sailors!"

Nobody who saw that scene has ever forgotten it, I am sure, or ever will forget it. The child had kept quite still, where her brave grandmamma had put her (first whispering in her ear, "Whatever happens to me, do not stir, my dear!"), and had remained quiet until the fort was deserted; she had then crept out of the trench, and gone into her mother's house; and there, alone on the solitary Island, in her mother's room, and asleep on her mother's bed, the Captain had found her. Nothing could induce her to be parted from him after he took her up in his arms, and he had brought her away with him, and the men had made the bower for her. To see those men now, was a sight. The joy of the women was beautiful; the joy of those women who had lost their own children, was quite sacred and divine; but the ecstasies of Captain Carton's boat's crew, when their pet was restored to her parents, were wonderful for the tenderness they showed in the midst of roughness.

As the Captain stood with the child in his arms, and the child's own little arms now clinging round his neck, now round her father's, now round her mother's, now round some one who pressed up to kiss her, the boat's crew shook hands with one another, waved their hats over their heads, laughed, sang, cried, danced— and all among themselves, without wanting to interfere with any-body—in a manner never to be represented. At last, I saw the coxswain and another, two very hard-faced men with grizzled heads who had been the heartiest of the hearty all along, close with one another, get each of them the other's head under his arm, and pummel away at it with his fist as hard as he could, in his excess of joy.

When we had well rested and refreshed ourselves—and very glad we were to have some of the heartening things to eat and drink that had come up in the boats—we recommenced our voyage down the river: rafts, and boats, and all. I said to myself, it was a very different kind of voyage now, from what it had been ; and I fell into my proper place and station among my fellow-soldiers.

But, when we halted for the night, I found that Miss Maryon had spoken to Captain Carton concerning me. For, the Captain came straight up to me, and says he, "My brave fellow, you have been Miss Maryon's body-guard all along, and you shall remain so. Nobody shall supersede you in the distinction and pleasure of protecting that young lady." I thanked his honor in the fittest words I could find, and that night I was placed on my old post of watching the place where she slept. More than once in the night, I saw Captain Carton come out into the air, and stroll about there, to see that all was well. I have now this other singular confession to make, that I saw him with a heavy heart. Yes; I saw him with a heavy, heavy heart.

In the day-time, I had the like post in Captain Carton's boat. I had a special station of my own, behind Miss Maryon, and no hands but hers ever touched my wound. (It has been healed these many long years ; but, no other hands have ever touched it.) Mr. Pordage was kept tolerably quiet now, with pen and ink, and began to pick up his senses a little. Seated in the second boat, he made documents with Mr. Kitten, pretty well all day ; and he generally handed in a Protest about something whenever we stopped. The Captain, however, made so very light of these papers that it grew into a saying among the men, when one of them wanted a match for his pipe, " Hand us over a Protest, Jack!" As to Mrs. Pordage, she still wore the nightcap, and she now had cut all the ladies on account of her not having been formally and separately rescued by Captain Carton before anybody else. The end of Mr. Pordage, to bring to an end all I know about him, was, that he got great compliments at home for his conduct on these trying occasions, and that he died of yellow jaundice, a Governor and a K.C.B.

Serjeant Drooce had fallen from a high fever into a low one. Tom Packer—the only man who could have pulled the Serjeant through it—kept hospital a-board the old raft, and Mrs. Belltott, as brisk as ever again (but the spirit of that little woman, when things tried it, was not equal to appearances), was head-nurse under his directions. Before we got down to the Mosquito coast, the joke had been made by one of our men, that we should see her gazetted Mrs. Tom Packer, *vice* Belltott exchanged.

When we reached the coast, we got native boats as substitutes for the rafts : and we rowed along under the land ; and in that beautiful climate, and upon that beautiful water, the blooming days were like enchantment. Ah ! They were running away, faster than any sea or river, and there was no tide to bring them back. We were coming very near the settlement where the people of Silver-Store were to be left, and from which we Marines were under orders to return to Belize.

Captain Carton had, in the boat by him, a curious long-barrelled Spanish gun, and he had said to Miss Maryon one day that it was the best of guns, and had turned his head to me, and said :

" Gill Davis, load her fresh with a couple of slugs, against a chance of showing how good she is."

So, I had discharged the gun over the sea, and had loaded her, according to orders, and there it had lain at the Captain's feet, convenient to the Captain's hand.

The last day but one of our journey was an uncommonly hot day. We started very early ; but, there was no cool air on the sea as the day got on, and by noon the heat was really hard to bear, considering that there were women and children to bear it. Now, we happened to open, just at that time, a very pleasant little cove or bay, where there was a deep shade from a great growth of trees. Now, the Captain, therefore, made the signal to the other boats to follow him in and lie by a while.

The men who were off duty went ashore, and lay down, but were ordered, for caution's sake, not to stray, and to keep within view. The others rested on their oars and dozed. Awnings had been made of one thing and another, in all the boats, and the passengers found it cooler to be under them in the shade, when there was room enough, than to be in the thick woods. So, the passengers were all afloat, and mostly sleeping. I kept my post behind Miss Maryon, and she was on Captain Carton's right in the boat, and Mrs. Fisher sat on her right again. The Captain had Mrs. Fisher's daughter on his knee. He and the two ladies were talking about the Pirates, and were talking softly: partly, because people do talk softly under such indolent circumstances, and partly because the little girl had gone off asleep.

I think I have before given it out for my Lady to write down, that Captain Carton had a fine bright eye of his own. All at once, he darted me a side look, as much as to say, "Steady—don't take on—I see something!"—and gave the child into her mother's arms. That eye of his was so easy to understand, that I obeyed it by not so much as looking either to the right or to the left out of a corner of my own, or changing my attitude the least trifle. The Captain went on talking in the same mild and easy way ; but began—with his arms resting across his knees, and his head a little hanging forward, as if the heat were rather too much for him—began to play with the Spanish gun.

"They had laid their plans, you see," says the Captain, taking up the Spanish gun across his knees, and looking, lazily, at the inlaying on the stock, "with a great deal of art ; and the corrupt or blundering local authorities were so easily deceived;" he ran his left hand idly along the barrel, but I saw, with my breath held, that he covered the action of cocking the gun with his right—"so easily deceived, that they summoned us out to

come into the trap.   But my intention as to future opera-
tions——" In a flash the Spanish gun was at his bright eye,
and he fired.

All started up; innumerable echoes repeated the sound of
the discharge; a cloud of bright-coloured birds flew out of the
woods screaming; a handful of leaves were scattered in the
place where the shot had struck; a crackling of branches was
heard; and some lithe but heavy creature sprang into the air,
and fell forward, head down, over the muddy bank.

"What is it?" cries Captain Maryon from his boat.   All
silent then, but the echoes rolling away.

"It is a Traitor and a Spy," said Captain Carton, handing
me the gun to load again.   "And I think the other name of the
animal is Christian George King!"

Shot through the heart.   Some of the people ran round to
the spot, and drew him out, with the slime and wet trickling
down his face; but, his face itself would never stir any more to
the end of time.

"Leave him hanging to that tree," cried Captain Carton;
his boat's crew giving way, and he leaping ashore.   "But first
into this wood, every man in his place.   And boats!   Out of
gunshot!"

It was a quick change, well meant and well made, though it
ended in disappointment.   No Pirates were there; no one but
the Spy was found.   It was supposed that the Pirates, unable
to retake us, and expecting a great attack upon them, to be the
consequence of our escape, had made from the ruins in the
Forest, taken to their ship along with the Treasure, and left the
Spy to pick up what intelligence he could.   In the evening we
went away, and he was left hanging to the tree, all alone,
with the red sun making a kind of a dead sunset on his black
face.

Next day, we gained the settlement on the Mosquito coast
for which we were bound.   Having stayed there to refresh,
seven days, and having been much commended, and highly
spoken of, and finely entertained, we Marines stood under
orders to march from the Town-Gate (it was neither much of a
town nor much of a gate), at five in the morning.

My officer had joined us before then.   When we turned

out at the gate, all the people were there; in the front of them all those who had been our fellow-prisoners, and all tho seamen.

"Davis," says Lieutenant Linderwood.   "Stand out, my friend!"

I stood out from the ranks, and Miss Maryon and Captain Carton came up to me.

"Dear Davis," says Miss Maryon, while the tears fell fast down her face, "your grateful friends, in most unwillingly taking leave of you, ask the favour that, while you bear away with you their affectionate remembrance which nothing can ever impair, you will also take this purse of money—far more valuable to you, we all know, for the deep attachment and thankfulness with which it is offered, than for its own contents, though we hope those may prove useful to you, too, in after life."

I got out, in answer, that I thankfully accepted the attachment and affection, but not the money.   Captain Carton looked at me very attentively, and stepped back, and moved away. I made him my bow as he stepped back, to thank him for being so delicate.

"No, miss," said I, "I think it would break my heart to accept the money.   But, if you could condescend to give to a man so ignorant and common as myself, any little thing you have worn—such as a bit of ribbon——"

She took a ring from her finger, and put it in my hand. And she rested her hand in mine, while she said these words:

"The brave gentlemen of old—but not one of them was braver, or had a nobler nature than you—took such gifts from ladies, and did all their good actions for the givers' sakes.   If you will do yours for mine, I shall think with pride that I continue to have some share in the life of a gallant and generous man."

For the second time in my life, she kissed my hand.   I made so bold, for the first time, as to kiss hers; and I tied the ring at my breast, and I fell back to my place.

Then, the horse-litter went out at the gate, with Serjeant Drooce in it; and the horse-litter went out at the gate with Mrs. Belltott in it; and Lieutenant Linderwood gave the word of command, "Quick march!" and, cheered and cried for, we went out of the gate too, marching along the level plain towards the serene blue sky as if we were marching straight to Heaven.

When I have added here that the Pirate scheme was blown to shivers, by the Pirate-ship which had the Treasure on board being so vigorously attacked by one of His Majesty's cruisers, among the West India Keys, and being so swiftly boarded and carried, that nobody suspected anything about the scheme until three-fourths of the Pirates were killed, and the other fourth were in irons and the Treasure was recovered; I come to the last singular confession I have got to make.

It is this. I well knew what an immense and hopeless distance there was between me and Miss Maryon; I well knew that I was no fitter company for her than I was for the angels; I well knew that she was as high above my reach as the sky over my head; and yet I loved her. What put it in my low heart to be so daring, or whether such a thing ever happened before or since, as that a man so uninstructed and obscure as myself got his unhappy thoughts lifted up to such a height, while knowing very well how presumptuous and impossible to be realised they were, I am unable to say; still, the suffering to me was just as great as if I had been a gentleman. I suffered agony—agony. I suffered hard, and I suffered long. I thought of her last words to me, however, and I never disgraced them. If it had not been for those dear words, I think I should have lost myself in despair and recklessness.

The ring will be found lying on my heart, of course, and will be laid with me wherever I am laid. I am getting on in years now, though I am able and hearty. I was recommended for promotion, and everything was done to reward me that could be done; but, my total want of all learning stood in my way, and I found myself so completely out of the road to it, that I could not conquer any learning, though I tried. I was long in the service, and I respected it, and was respected in it, and the service is dear to me at this present hour.

At this present hour, when I give this out to my Lady to be written down, all my old pain has softened away, and I am as happy as a man can be, at this present fine old country-house of Admiral Sir George Carton, Baronet. It was my Lady

Carton who herself sought me out, over a great many miles of the wide world, and found me in Hospital wounded, and brought me here.   It is my Lady Carton who writes down my words. My Lady was Miss Maryon.   And now, that I conclude what I had to tell, I see my Lady's honored grey hair droop over her face, as she leans a little lower at her desk ; and I fervently thank her for being so tender as I see she is, towards the past pain and trouble of her poor, old, faithful, humble soldier.

THE END.

F. M. EVANS AND CO., LIMITED, PRINTERS, CRYSTAL PALACE, S.E.

University of Toronto
Library

DO NOT
REMOVE
THE
CARD
FROM
THIS
POCKET

Acme Library Card Pocket
Under Pat. "Ref. Index File"
Made by LIBRARY BUREAU